POST-APOCALYPTIC SURVIVAL : BOOK ONE

ENEMIES
IN THE YARD

BUFFORD CLAY

ISBN: 979-8-9921845-0-1

This is a work of fiction. Names, characters, places, and incidents are products of the author's imagination or are used fictitiously. Any resemblance to actual events, locales, or persons, living or dead, is entirely coincidental.

Cover by: Deranged Doctor Design

DEDICATION

I have some special thanks to give to some special people in my life that have helped me with not only this book, but life in general. I try to grow and improve as a person, husband, father, son, brother, uncle and friend, sometimes I need help. Life will bring us forks in the road, we may not always choose the right one, but we can learn from choosing the wrong one. These people don't give up on me, continuing to push me.

Thank you to my wife for dealing with my crazy thoughts and actions. My wife is always supportive of my ideas when I come up with something new, regardless of how crazy they may seem. I love you for the special amazing person you are, and for raising our daughter as you do.

Thank you to my daughter, you are a guiding light for so many others, always staying positive and letting your light shine. Your dedication to school and education was inspiring to me in beginning and completing this first book. I am so proud of you and look forward to seeing your continued growth.

Thank you to my mother, who allowed me to play free as a child, roaming the mountains as a cowboy, Indian, firefighter, policeman, hunter, explorer and any other idea I came up with. You allowed me to always dream big, opening my mind to the stories I created.

Thank you to the shysters, fakes and frauds, you scoundrels have showed me not to trust just anyone and keep my circle small, you have taught me to see the enemies in the yard.

PROLOGUE

In the aftermath of a catastrophic attack by a coalition of foreign powers, the country finds itself teetering on the brink of collapse. Once-familiar streets now lay in ruins, and a profound silence settled over the land, broken only by the echoes of despair and the cries of those who had lost everything.

As supplies dwindle and food becomes scarce, the struggle for survival will transform society. The very fabric of community unraveling, revealing the raw and desperate sides of human nature. Neighbors and families, once bound by camaraderie and trust, now eye each other with suspicion and fear, their bonds severed by the harsh realities of a new world.

In this new era of uncertainty and chaos, Kyle Blaine stands as a beacon of hope and defiance. From his mountain top homestead, a place he has meticulously prepared as a sanctuary, Kyle must shield his family from the encroaching dangers. His homestead, once a refuge of tranquility, now becomes a fortress amidst the growing storm of violence and betrayal.

As the world around him fractures, Kyle is faced with the daunting task of protecting his loved ones while navigating the treacherous landscape of shifting alliances and unrelenting threats. In a time when survival demands more than just courage, Kyle's determination will be tested like never before. With every passing day, he must confront the harsh truth: in a world where neighbors become enemies, only those who adapt and endure will prevail. Kyle wants to protect his family, but are they willing to protect him? Will he avoid having enemies in the yard as he struggles to push back the enemies from afar?

CHAPTER ONE

"The Abandoned Hotel – Shattered Innocence"
Two Weeks After the Attack

"Hold it!" A voice commanded Kyle sharply as the door between the kitchen and dining area swung open.

"I don't want any trouble. I was looking for supplies. Who are you?" Kyle replied, squinting against the beam of the flashlight directed at him. His headlamp made him easily visible, but from the distance it was not strong enough to have the same effect on the man shining his light at Kyle. They were separated by three tables between them and thirty feet of distance in the old restaurant dining room.

"Turn your light down, you're blinding me," Kyle insisted.

The man persisted in shining the light at Kyle, making it difficult for him to see.

"Put that gun on the floor and get on your knees," the voice ordered firmly.

"We ain't telling you again. Do it," another voice added, thick with an Appalachian Mountain accent.

Kyle slowly lowered his left hand from his shotgun to his belt. Retrieving his flashlight, he brought his hand back to his gun. With a press of his thumb, the small but powerful Streamlight Pro-Tac sent a five hundred lumen beam piercing through the room. Kyle held the light firmly, squeezing it between his fingers and the pump action foregrip handle of his shotgun.

"I said lower the light, and that's my only warning. I won't repeat myself. I've told you, I don't want any trouble," Kyle asserted emphatically to the man. "It's only been two weeks since the attack. My death toll keeps climbing; don't force me to add you to it." Kyle watched intently as the man slowly directed his light downward, allowing Kyle's eyes to adjust to the dimness of the dining room.

"You lower yours," the man countered.

To the right of the man holding the light was the service window between the kitchen and server station. Kyle noticed movement inside the kitchen through the opening. He saw as the figure raised a pistol, aiming in his direction. Without hesitation, Kyle squeezed the trigger on his KSG shotgun. The blast erupted in the darkness, sending double aught buck pellets on a deadly trajectory towards the man with the flashlight. The shot maintained a tight pattern at thirty feet, striking him squarely in the chest and hurling him violently backwards onto the kitchen floor. He was most likely dead when he hit the surface, his flashlight flying from his hand and hitting the exit door behind him. His gun thudded on the vinyl tile floor, bouncing twice before resting.

Once, this dining room echoed with the lively sounds of people talking and laughing as they enjoyed meals together. The kitchen bustled with orders shouted through the pickup window and servers hustled delivering food and refills to dining guests. Now, the room was filled with the thunderous and deafening echo of the shotgun blast reverberating against the cinder block walls. Kyle quickly worked the action on his shotgun, ejecting the spent cartridge and chambering a fresh round.

Kyle pulled back, seeking to gain cover behind a nearby section of the wall he stood near in the doorway. This happened quickly, preventing him from getting accurate aim on his shots. He fired another round towards t the service window. The second shot struck the order ticket wheel, shearing off half of the wheel's spindle. Kyle again pumped the action on the gun and fired his third round that pierced through the metal cover of the ice machine. It blew a hole into the thin metal cover on the machine while also jarring it loose, allowing the panel to fall, clanging loudly on the floor. He fired his final shot while retreating from the heavy fireproof door that separated the dining room from the adjacent hall.

"Sounds like JD and Peanut found somebody," Blaze remarked to the others outside. "Jacoby, come with me. Miller, Teddy, you two stay out here and keep an eye out for that truck."

"10-4, Blaze. If they come back, we'll handle it," Teddy affirmed to Blaze.

"You sure I should go in? Maybe I should stay out here," Jacoby asked Blaze, his fear evident on his face.

"It's time to step up, Jacoby. We're going in. You need to hunt boy!" Blaze urged firmly, his eyes showing disappointment in Jacoby for even questioning his command.

Meanwhile, inside the restaurant, Kyle had retreated, allowing the heavy metal door to close between the dining room and the hallway. JD, the man who was in the kitchen, had fired several rounds from his black Ruger Wrangler, a small-caliber .22 pistol that looked like something out of a cowboy movie. JD often joked about being John Wayne's brother, JD Wayne, when he carried it. His friends were quick to tease him about it, calling him John's brother, 'Dumbass Wayne'.

The shots from JD's pistol ricocheted wildly, striking the walls inside the restaurant, except for one that had connected with Kyle's body armor. It would have entered his stomach if not for the sturdy metal plate doing its job perfectly. Fortunately for Kyle, JD's pistol required him to cock the hammer between each shot, slowing down his rate of fire. Kyle backed away, peering through the small window of the door leading to the billiards room. He could see the exit door was open and a man standing partially inside. Reacting swiftly, Kyle made a dash to the opposite end of the hallway and entered the west side stairwell. He paused to catch his breath, listening intently as he heard the door between the hallway and billiards room open.

"JD, Peanut?" Blaze called out. "Are you guys in here?"

"No JD or Peanut here," Kyle shouted back to Blaze. "We

don't want any trouble. We're only looking for supplies."

"They call me Blaze, and I lead the Angels. Who are you? How many of you are here?" Blaze asked Kyle, leaning his head to try and see down the dark hallway.

"There are four of us. We don't want any trouble. We just want to leave and go on our way," Kyle said, lying about having four people. He didn't want them to know he was inside alone.

The door from the dining room slowly opened as Blaze twisted his body, aiming his rifle at the door.

"That you Blaze?" JD asked, before poking his head through the opening.

"Yeah, it's me. I got this guy at the end of the hall," Blaze replied.

"He killed Peanut. Shot him. He's dead. Almost got me to," JD said as he stepped through the door.

"You killed one of my guys. You piece of shit!" Blaze yelled angrily as he turned back with the AR15 and fired three rounds, the bullets glancing off the block wall. The sound of each shot blasting inside the small hallway was deafening. "You come out now, or we're going to kill you, boy, just like we did your friends outside."

Kyle gripped his gun tightly and leaned his head back against the wall. It had to be a lie--Arnie knew to leave at any sign of trouble. Kyle clinched his eyes shut, took a deep breath, and exhaled. He could only hope Arnie had indeed escaped in the truck. Unbeknownst to Kyle, Arnie had followed his instructions, driving across Harman Bridge. Well, almost exactly, after crossing the bridge, Arnie had turned onto the gravel road that led by the railroad tracks.

Arnie drove slowly along the small road until he was straight across the river from the old hotel. Miller and Teddy, the two left to guard the door and keep lookout, were talking outside. Neither Miller nor Teddy paid any attention to the direction across the river, focusing instead on the exit door. Arnie stopped the truck, the homemade camo paint job blending nicely with the trees in the background.

4

"Go to my truck, grab a gas can, and bring it here," Blaze instructed Jacoby, his mind set on smoking Kyle out.

Kyle scrambled to devise a quick escape plan. A fire escape in the stairwell led outside, but he hesitated, unsure of the number of adversaries possibly waiting beyond the door. Should he ascend the stairs or attempt the exit door? As he placed his hand on the fire escape handle, he recalled the stack of pallets and wood obstructing it when they scoped out the building. Opening the door would undoubtedly reveal his location with the noise it would create.

"Come out. Maybe we can negotiate for Peanut's life," Blaze shouted out to Kyle.

"That wasn't my fault; they had guns on me!" Kyle shouted back, aiming his light up the dark stairway. "You said you killed my friends; seems you owe me a life now," he added, realizing his companions were safe. This man wouldn't have offered to make a deal if he had in fact killed them. Kyle knew there was no deal to be made regardless, but he felt more secure that his people were alive. He switched off his headlamp and flashlight, choosing to remain silent and hidden for now.

"Here you go," Jacoby said, entering through the door and handing the gas jug to Blaze.

"Good job. Now let's make this asshole squirm. He doesn't have anyone else with him," Blaze said beginning to soak the debris in gasoline. He poured it into a cup and tossed it onto the hallway floor. Using a discarded bottle, he filled it partially with gas, stuffed a hanker chief in, and crafted a makeshift Molotov cocktail. Blaze ignited the hanker chief and hurled the bottle down the hallway. Kyle heard the glass shatter and the immediate whoosh of gasoline igniting in the air. The sudden burst of fire illuminated the western end of the hall brightly. Kyle knew the block walls and fire-retardant ceiling tiles wouldn't burn, but there was enough trash and furniture to fill the air with smoke.

Across the river, Arnie had set up the 6.5 Creedmoor rifle on the hood of the truck. He stood on the ground on the opposite side using the truck for cover as he adjusted his weapon into position. He placed a small, wadded jacket under the barrel for support. Kyle had taught him this simple trick to help stabilize the heavy Ruger Precision Rifle, weighing eleven pounds.

Arnie used his handheld Ranger 1800 rangefinder and found he was only one hundred and seventy-seven yards away. Through the Vortex Viper scope, the high-performance optics gave him a clear view of the two men. Arnie deliberated whether to start shooting or wait for a signal from Kyle. Miller and Teddy stood outside the back door, each armed with handguns. Arnie wasn't concerned about their pistols being a threat, even if they discovered his position. He remained still, focused on the men unaware they were the ones being targeted.

Inside the stairwell, the smoke thickened, irritating Kyle's eyes. To avoid inhaling the smoke, he pulled his face cloth up over his mouth and nose. He knew he was hidden well in the darkness where he had backed underneath the stairs leading up to the first floor. The concrete stairs would provide good coverage from gunfire if anyone started shooting.

"Are you gonna come out and play, stranger?" Blaze shouted to Kyle. Then turning to Jacoby he said, "I bet he went up the stairway. There is nowhere for him to go. It's time to flush him out. JD, you go to the east side and up."

"Hello, can I come out?" Mike asked, his fear running uncontrollably as he stuttered to push the words from his mouth.

"Who the hell is that," Blaze whispered to Jacoby. "Step out slowly, hands up," Blaze ordered as he trained his gun on the hallway. Mike slowly stepped out of the office, facing Blaze. Kyle could see him from the stairwell he stood in.

"Who are you, and who is with you?" Blaze demanded.

"My name is Mike. I'm staying here, I don't want any trouble. I'm not with the other guy," Mike announced. Kyle squeezed his AR tightly, wanting to grab Mike by the throat and choke slam him to the floor at this moment.

"Wrong place at the wrong time huh? Is that what you're saying?" Blaze asked as Mike continued holding his hands high in the air.

6

"Yes sir, that's all it is," Mike responded.

"Yeah, that's too bad for you," Blaze said, squeezing the trigger on his AR and firing one round, striking Mike in the forehead. It happened so quickly, Kyle only witnessed the blood and brain matter spray as it slapped against the nearby door and wall. Kyle watched as Mike's body dropped instantly, his life over.

"Why did you kill him?" Jacoby asked Blazed, shocked at the ease of Blaze's ability to take someone's life.

Blaze looked at Jacoby, his eyes squinting with anger at the question. He breathed him a heavy breath, "because this is my building, and nobody stays in my building without my permission first."

"Yes, sir," Jacoby responded, knowing better than to ask any more questions. "I'm with you, whatever you say."

Blaze and Jacoby began to advance cautiously towards the stairway, Blaze leading with his AR ready to fire. JD ran back to the east stairwell sounding like a horse tromping as his boots clattered against the floor. The concrete stairs on this side were slimy and slippery from years of water draining down. JD cocked the hammer on his pistol and held it upwards along with his light to illuminate the path. Quickly ascending the first flight, he turned at the landing. A chair had been tossed down the stairway, perched halfway up the second flight leading to floor number two. He used his light to shine upwards making sure the coast was clear before proceeding. His nerves taut as he looked higher up the stairwell.

JD, who was never known as the smartest person in the room, nor did he use caution much, reached ahead grabbing for the chair. He gripped a leg on the chair and turned to toss it down the steps. The hard bottom sole of the cowboy boots he was wearing lost traction on the slimy steps, his feet gliding out from under him like a ballerina in flight. He fell hard, landing on his butt and accidentally discharging his pistol in the process. The sound of the gun, even being the small caliber .22, was ear-splitting inside the stairwell. JD dropped the gun allowing it to bounce down the steps hitting each one on the way. He instinctively covered his ears to dull the ringing pain from the gunshot. The chair clattered noisily within the walls of the block and metal stairwell as it tumbled down to the bottom.

"What the hell was that?" Jacoby said to Blaze.

"JD must have found him. I bet that guy tried to get around to the east stairs. You go up and watch that second-floor level in case he tries to double back. I'm going to see if JD has him," Blaze replied, swiftly turning and moving down the hall. Jacoby felt safer now that the threat might be elsewhere and proceeded to the west stairs as Blaze had ordered.

Kyle heard the gunshot and remained concealed under the stairs in the darkness. He wondered if it was Arnie or possibly someone else in the building. As footsteps approached closer, stepping on the fallen ceiling tiles that lay along the floor, Kyle held his breath. Jacoby entered the stairwell, slowly approaching the first step. He shined his light, looking to detect any movement on the upper floors. Ignoring the fact that the stairs had a space behind the first rise of steps, he lifted his weapon. He carried an old single-shot New England Firearms 20-gauge shotgun and slowly began to climb the stairs one by one.

Kyle moved cautiously from under the stairs trying to step softly so as not to alert anyone. He peeked around the corner into the hall, crouching below the dissipating smoke and smoldering debris. Feeling confident no one else was nearby, Kyle followed Jacoby up the stairs. After making the turn on the landing, Kyle could see the man at the second-floor level. The doorway leading into the hallway was propped open and light entered through the window trickling into the stairway. Jacoby was trying to look through the open door to see what danger might await, fearing an ambush. He stood still, so nervous he was almost frozen in fear that someone would jump out from the hallway on him.

Kyle realized he needed to act quick and be swift in his movements, or he would soon be in trouble if the other men doubled back on him. Although it was dark, he could discern Jacoby's silhouette scanning the hall. He removed his Benchmade Infidel Dagger, gripping it tightly in his right hand. With a deep breath, Kyle released the blade smoothly with the slide, its sharpened edges ready for the next move.

Kyle quickly, but quietly climbed the remaining steps reaching the man in front of him. In one smooth and swift motion, Kyle reached around Jacoby, covering his mouth with his left hand and yanking his head back. With his right hand, Kyle slashed across Jacoby's neck with the blade. He could feel the knife slicing through Jacoby's skin and neck tissue with little resistance. A stomach-churning gurgle was all that escaped as Jacoby reached for his neck and struggled at Kyle's tight grip. Kyle could feel the warmth of the blood as it flowed across his hand as he watched Jacoby's shotgun slip from his grip to the floor.

Jacoby gasped, grasping futilely at his neck. He had only seconds before losing consciousness, and moments more before death. As quickly as his blood and oxygen were gone, Jacoby's life would be as well. Kyle held him firmly as he pulled Jacoby away from the door.

Kyle laid Jacoby down slowly looking at the dying man. In the faint light that was illuminating Jacoby's face, Kyle was struck with a sickening realization; this was not a man, but a boy. Kyle could see he was probably no more than fourteen or fifteen years old. Panic and regret flooded Kyle as he tried to apply pressure to the boy's neck. It was an ineffective attempt at this point, there was no taking it back now. The sight of blood on his hands, and the reality of what he had done caused Kyle's stomach to knot, before he could stop himself, vomit spewed from his mouth uncontrollably.

CHAPTER TWO
"Kyle Blaine – Before the Attack"

Kyle Blaine made his decision years ago that he wanted to be a homesteader- a part of his retirement plans once he finished his corporate career in America's heartland. However, life didn't allow it to transpire in the order he wanted, and early retirement would be somewhat forced upon him due to trouble he encountered while working in Kansas. As fate would have it, being forced to start his mini farm early worked out for Kyle in the long run, giving him just enough time to establish his homestead before the impending attack.

Returning home to Buchanan County, Virginia, specifically to the small town of Hurley, felt like coming full circle for Kyle. He was glad to have found his way back, albeit a much different man than the boy who left years ago. Kyle had spent the past two decades living in the Midwest traveling from city to city for work.

During those years, Kyle had immersed himself in learning about prepping, survival, and homesteading. Though he still had much to learn, he had found satisfaction in acquiring these skills. Little did he know, all this research and studying was about to become a crucial part of his life. For those who hadn't started preparing, it would soon be to late. In a post-catastrophe world, only a fraction of the population would manage to thrive and most importantly, survive.

Kyle's plan was to move back and start a homestead gradually before his retirement years, but circumstances accelerated his timeline due to his own actions. Normally soft-spoken, Kyle stood an imposing six feet three inches tall with a solid 240-pound frame. He knew his size could be intimidating to others, so he made a conscious effort to be polite. However, after an altercation outside a Kansas bar one evening, Kyle found himself in trouble. Following a week of investigations by the police, Kyle agreed it was in his best interest to leave the town quietly to avoid charges being filed or his employer being notified.

After submitting his resignation and completing his departure plans, Kyle returned to Virginia. He had worked two decades for Great Sleep and Eats, a hotel and restaurant operation. Kyle had worked his way up to vice president of developmental operations, a prestigious position. It was an impressive job for a single person but not conducive to a family life. His job involved flying extensively, solving problems across the company's various locations, sometimes spending only a day or at other times, weeks in a city.

Over the course of those twenty years, he forged relationships with like-minded individuals across several states. It took time, but he would eventually be accepted into various groups throughout the states where he worked. From these diverse groups, Kyle learned advanced skills in shooting, camouflaging himself and tactical offense and defense. Some classes were much simpler, like with the women of a church on how to can food properly or recipes for making candy. He even took a quilting class once just to learn the techniques of sewing. The added benefit of this endeavor being the earned attention of ladies trying to set him up with their daughters.

Despite the misconceptions that those who disagreed with the government were in some type of cult, Kyle never witnessed anything illegal, maybe questionable, but not illegal. Instead, he learned valuable tools for survival and homesteading from these diverse groups. The more time he spent with them learning, the more he longed to come home to Hurley and build his homestead. He wanted to put his knowledge to work for himself and his family.

Now that he was back in Hurley, Kyle had built a cabin on family property high atop a mountain. The exact location was always a favorite spot of his growing up and playing in the mountains as a kid. He thought the view was breathtaking, especially in the fall and winter seasons. The ridge point was perfect for his home, with only one entrance and one exit. It would be the ideal retreat he would use for self-protection, a secluded sanctuary for his family. He couldn't help but wonder even with his hidden location, how long could they fend off those who desired what he had. At some point even neighbors might turn into adversaries as they battled to survive in this new world. The one thing he was sure of was he needed to keep the dangerous people away, he didn't need enemies in the yard.

Throughout various locations in our country, a plan was being carried out unknowingly too our government and our nation's security. The time had now come that would change the trajectory of this land and the people living here forever. The details weren't all known, due to the breakdown in communications. However, enough information came in the early days to know people were in trouble and the fight for survival would be long and hard. A fight for continued existence by people trying to feed themselves and their children, would soon mean doing unthinkable and possibly despicable acts.

It was a plan that would wreck the façade and shatter the illusion of the American dream and it was approaching completion. A diabolical strategy that would in a coordinated attack, target the infrastructure of America. The growth of cybercrime and cyber terrorism were ready to be unleashed by multiple countries joining forces. Cyber-attacks in combination with a physical attack would be too much to withstand even for a country as robust as the United States. With thousands of planted terrorists across the country, each cell ready to be activated, the imminent threat was clear. Every terrorist in every cell willing to die for a cause. Death to America!

The small unincorporated town of Hurley wasn't filled with the hustle and bustle of larger cities. Hurley was a mere speck on the map that required careful examination to find. Located in Buchanan County, Virginia, one of the poorest counties near the borders of Kentucky and West Virginia, Hurley boasted a population of just over three thousand people, meaning most families knew one another.

Kyle had assured his family and friends for years they lived in one of the better areas should a catastrophe strike the country. It would be nothing like what people in large cities would deal with in a true shit hit the fan scenario. He would often describe traffic in a city and the congestion he would see. A small fender bender could create a paralyzed road system. He warned them to imagine the chaos if hundreds of thousands of terrified drivers tried to flee an area simultaneously. Kyle told them things would still get bad in a small town, even Hurley would face challenges in a crisis, but he believed they stood a better chance at survival. The biggest threats to a small town like Hurley would be power struggles by those trying to control everyone else.

A small town like Hurley with its three thousand residents, could prove dangerous, but cities with hundreds of thousands could become uninhabitable. Hurley would provide an opportunity to recover quickly with the ability to farm, supplying much needed food for families. There were fresh streams coming from the mountains that would provide water and fishing. This would be a necessity that millions in the country would struggle to find. Hurley may be one of the poorest counties in the state, but when the time came, it would be one of the richest for survival.

Whenever Kyle would visit before moving back, he would discuss prepping and survival with his family. There were some eager to learn more, while others wanted him to hush. If they wanted to listen, Kyle stressed the importance of preparing for disasters. Kyle tried to explain it was not only a terrorist attack to prepare for, but a natural disaster as well. Having witnessed past emergencies in their town, some locals understood the necessity for prepping. Grocery stores held three days on average of food inventory, that would go fast when everyone tried to go shopping or looting at the same time. He knew he could not make them plan, but he also knew it would not be on him to save everyone when it happened. Kyle would sometimes question his own sanity, but he remained determined not to sit idly by while disaster loomed.

Kyle had selected his charming little hideaway spot high on the mountain behind his old childhood home. It was accessible by an old mining road from the 1950's that Kyle used to navigate his Can-Am Defender Pro ATV on. The ATV's dark green color helped it blend into the surroundings, a crucial feature for Kyle. The larger than normal cargo box was an additional selling point, capable of hauling one thousand-pound loads. They were often called side-by-sides, these ATVs were popular for traversing mountain trails across the tri-state area.

Off road riding enthusiasts could travel between three states with ease on mountain trails near Kyle's property. Except for a few grumpy landowners who didn't want anyone on their land, it was a common practice among the locals to share private property trails. It was an unwritten agreement between landowners to use their property, with riders ensuring no litter was left behind.

Kyle spent much of his free time at the cabin working on the property. He would ride down the mountain and check in on his mother Rachel a couple times each week. There were a few friends and family members who would visit, allowing regular communication and supply trips. It was usually his Uncle Tom coming up to sit on the porch and tell Kyle what he was doing wrong, but in a joking way. Uncle Tom was a big man, standing a little over six feet tall, and two hundred and twenty pounds. To be in his sixties, Uncle Tom was healthy and could do anything in Kyle's eyes. If Uncle Tom had something to say, Kyle always listened to his advice. He might not always follow his guidance to the letter, but he at least considered it.

Kyle's little buddy and enthusiastic nephew Arnie was a frequent visitor several days a week. Arnie was the nickname he got as a little boy; his real name was Arnold. The young man had not grown the way all his uncle's and grandfather had. Arnie was only five feet, seven inches tall and weighed one hundred forty-five pounds if he had his pockets full. Arnie cherished Kyle moving back home and spent most of his free time with him. He was eighteen years old and a recent graduate of high school. The young man was passionate about riding dirt bikes.

Choosing to live off grid, Kyle relied on solar power, an area he lacked expertise in but fortunately had his friend Knox who was very knowledgeable on the subject. There was no town water, sewer, internet or cable television on the mountain and cell reception was sparse. There was only Kyle and nature, and he embraced it that way. He coexisted with local wildlife, including black bears, coyotes and venomous snakes like Timber Rattlesnakes and Eastern Copperheads. Kyle was always alert and cognizant of these venomous crawlers, constant reminders of the dangers lurking in his mountain habitat. Although Fatalities were low from these snakes, being alone on top of a mountain was not a place you wanted to be if bitten.

CHAPTER THREE
"Crafting A Homestead"

The closer it got for Kyle to move back home, the more he knew he had to start making progress with his ideas. He approached his Uncle Tom about plans to build the cabin, unsure what Uncle Tom would think of it. Kyle was pleasantly surprised by Uncle Tom's reaction and excitement to help. It turned out Uncle Tom had wanted to do this for years but never found the time.

Kyle knew his Uncle Tom was a jack-of-all-trades and he needed his help. The hardest part of the plan would be getting the materials hauled up the mountain. Kyle knew they would need many items, heavy items like lumber and concrete. They would have to do this in numerous loads using both their ATV's and pull behind trailers. A dozer widening the road would have helped, but Kyle didn't want that, he liked the fact that only small ATVs could make it. Uncle Tom never considered a last stand or apocalyptic event, he just wanted to feel like a young boy again, having his treehouse in the woods.

One early spring day, they had walked the area and Kyle explained to Uncle Tom his plans in detail. He expected that Uncle Tom would think he was missing a few marbles as the old saying was. It again shocked Kyle that his Uncle Tom didn't make him feel this way at all, accepting the whole plan and making suggestions on how they could start. Kyle knew Uncle Tom was older now and this would be more of a bonding time for him to spend with Kyle and Arnie doing a project together.

Kyle and Uncle Tom did research and consulted multiple

people in the construction business to gain knowledge. They called companies who specialized in underground bunkers and researched the internet. The plans were reviewed, and Kyle concluded that it would be far too expensive to build an underground bunker like he wanted. They went back to the drawing board, making some deviations to the plan, coming up with a much simpler and less costly blueprint.

Before building any structure, there was a large amount of digging that would need completed. This would be one of the hardest projects as equipment to excavate with would be needed. Kyle rented a small Bobcat mini excavator that Uncle Tom had recommended to do the job. This would be money well spent as they needed other tasks done such as working on areas of the trail restoring ruts or clearing trees. Uncle Tom had operated equipment for years so he would be the one to command the machine, and they didn't trust turning Arnie loose on it. The excavator would be great for helping to clear the site where Uncle Tom's cabin would also go.

Once they had gotten the mini excavator up the mountain, Uncle Tom was as the old saying went, "happy as a pig in shit." It was not work to Uncle Tom; it was an enjoyable adventure. They packed lunches and ate under a shade tree together every day. Kyle cherished this time they spent together talking as Uncle Tom would turn any conversation piece into a history lesson about some part of Hurley. Kyle was old enough to know he was going to miss this one day when Uncle Tom was gone. Arnie was too young to grasp the importance of the moments, just living life each day as a teenager. Uncle Tom had taken Kyle fishing as a small kid, played basketball with him and even helped him learn to golf. Although it wasn't said, Kyle really loved his uncle Tom.

They decided on a plan for an underground tunnel after discarding the bunker idea. Kyle wanted both a hiding spot and additional storage underneath the cabin for food and weapons-a secretive cache. He also wanted to have an escape tunnel that would lead to an exit on the side of the mountain. They would use corrugated metal culvert pipes to create a passageway from underneath the cabin. Arnie just thought it was cool to have a secret escape hatch.

"What in the world do you need an escape tunnel for? Who are you escaping from?" Uncle Tom asked.

"Better to have and not need, than to need and not have Uncle Tom," Kyle replied with a wide smile.

The next challenge was getting the pipes to the building site. This was a slow and careful process as they had to pull the large pipes up the trail. Negotiating twisting turns and sharp cutbacks required cautious maneuvering. Uncle Tom had devised a plan to build dollies that would ride underneath the pipes.

They used the mini excavator and both ATVs to accomplish this part of the project. The trail had some particularly steep sections, they would need all their available horsepower for towing. They had both ATVs connected with a chain to pull from the front while using the excavator to push and steer the rear end when needed. It wouldn't have been easy if it were a paid job but doing it for free had each of them smiling and laughing with excitement the whole time.

Once they had the pipes in place, all that was left was welding the seams together; this along with some concrete, waterproof sealant and textile wrap would prevent water leaking into the pipes. Kyle added battery powered LED touch lights from beginning to end. After adding the door hatch, the pipes would be ready to build the cabin over.

The excavator was needed once again to dig the hole for the 500-gallon septic tank and leach field. Kyle knew of people who had used everything from old refrigerators to junk cars as a septic system. Of course, none of these homemade tanks had approval by the county building official or health department. This illegal type of system had been installed in the farthest parts of the backwoods. Kyle didn't have the approval of county officials either, but he did follow guidelines as closely as possible. They also installed the rainwater collection tank, which was awkward to get up the narrow trail due to its bulky size. The tank was molded from plastic keeping it lightweight but being eight feet in diameter made the slow movement a test of patience. The excavator proved invaluable for these projects.

Once the work was completed for the job at Kyle's location, they moved the excavator to Uncle Tom's site just off the main trail. It was a picturesque spot surrounded by pine trees offering great coverage. If someone didn't know where the cabin was, they would likely drive right by without seeing it. Uncle Tom thought it was perfect overlooking his pond. After clearing the location and getting it prepared, Uncle Tom continued down the winding trail to his last stop at the pond. He used the machine to cut a trail around each side for better fishing opportunities. As the trio watched each step happen, they felt like kids in a candy store. It never felt like work--they were simply having too much fun.

Kyle built his home with a small living area that was open into the kitchen and dining area. Thanks to the septic system, he had a working indoor bathroom. That was one of Kyle's non-negotiables when building the cabin, he didn't want an outhouse. Kyle could remember vaguely growing up as a small boy, his grandmother having an outhouse. He accepted and embraced the idea of living off grid, but he really wanted that bathroom indoors. The kitchen had a small pantry built next to it and two modest bedrooms. The cabin featured a loft that Kyle could use as additional storage space or sleeping quarters if needed.

One of Kyle's favorite things would be a landscaper's nightmare, no grass to mow. He always hated that chore as a kid, always telling his mother she should get rid of it. Turn the lawn into dirt or cover it with asphalt, he would tell her. At his location now, the ground was hard packed dirt with few weeds growing. Kyle would introduce a couple goats to those weeds and they would take care of that issue.

CHAPTER FOUR
"A Flicker of Fear"

"The cabin looks great, Kyle," Ginger said as everyone took a seat for dinner at Rachel's. Rachel enjoyed having her kids and grandkids together anytime she could. Kyle's family didn't always mesh well when everyone was together, and it could be fireworks at any moment. Talking about the wrong subject could be like igniting a fuse and waiting for the show to start. Fortunately, this wasn't one of those times as everyone was in good spirits for the evening.

"Thanks sis. Uncle Tom and Arnie have worked hard helping me to get it done," Kyle replied to Ginger as Arnie smiled while spooning mashed potatoes onto his plate. "You need to eat plenty of those, Arnie. Let's get some meat on your bones." Kyle added, speaking to Arnie, who just shook his head in agreement.

"This looks amazing, Mom! I've been starving all day waiting for dinnertime. I skipped lunch," Susie said to Rachel while pouring brown gravy over her pot roast and potatoes.

"The house has a very aromatic smell this evening," Kyle said as he waved his hand in a circular motion under his nose. He examined the spread of food, looking at the beef pot roast and the large clump of butter making a puddle in the middle of the mashed potatoes. There were green beans, corn, macaroni and cheese, and a big bowl of Susie's coleslaw. He avoided the dessert table as he didn't want to ruin his appetite with sweets. Now that he was living on the mountain, meals like this were rare for Kyle.

"Thank you kids, for showing up. I've missed everyone. It feels as though I haven't had everyone together in months. I wish

20

your brothers Sawyer and Spencer could be here with us," Rachel said, smiling with delight as she watched them fill their plates.

"So, Kyle, now that you got the cabin built, are you going to live in it all the time?" Susie asked Kyle, almost doubting he would do it. She gave him that side-eye and smile they would give each other when some fun ribbing was in order. "I'm just curious how you're going to find me a sister-in-law living on top of that mountain by yourself," Susie added with a giggle.

"Be glad Mom is here, I would have a good joke for you right now. If I'm to get you a sister-in-law, she will have to come find me, I reckon. Those days have passed me by for a family," Kyle said as he spooned every item onto his plate. "I might get a dog. I've been thinking about that. I'll need one to hold the porch down and maybe watch over the chickens," Kyle added with a snicker of laughter.

"Mommy, what do you think about what Kyle is doing?" Ginger asked, always looking for others' approval of anything and everything that came up. Ginger was younger than Susie, but older than Kyle. She usually liked to think about what people said before responding; she was never one for quick comebacks.

"I think he may be going overboard a bit. He has been around and seen more than we have. If Kyle thinks it could get dangerous, he has seen enough to know. Besides, at least we have a place to go if anything bad does happen," Rachel added, smiling at Kyle.

Everyone finished dinner and carried their plates to the kitchen. The next step was like a military exercise as they began forming a line while laughing and prodding at one another as they made their way to the deserts. Rachel had set out banana pudding, her famous strawberry cheesecake that made Kyle salivate, and a Butterfinger delight.

"Let's move it along, people," Susie said, laughing.

Each took a plate, selected multiple desserts, grabbed a cup of coffee, and headed to the living room area. Uncle Tom arrived, having seen Ginger and Susie's cars in the driveway. He wasted no time going to the kitchen to get a plate of desserts before joining the others.

"Well, I see the party started without me," Megan said as she entered the house carrying a box of Coors Light. Megan was Kyle's other sister, who preferred a beer over a hot meal any day.

"Looks like you're bringing the party with you," Kyle said to Megan as she placed the box of beer on the floor next to the couch where she took a seat. Before saying anything else, she pulled out her phone and began taking selfies. The others let her snap away, immersed in her own world.

"Kyle, I have a question to ask. Do you still think anything bad will happen, now that you've been back home for a while and away from the cities?" Ginger asked Kyle, her tone serious. Ginger wasn't the type to be a smartass, she genuinely wanted to know.

"Tell her, Kyle. Tell her some of the stuff you have been telling Arnie and me. Ginger, I thought some of this seemed crazy at first, but the more Kyle has explained, the more it made sense to me," Uncle Tom said, pausing his banana pudding.

"I'm not an expert on national security. I'm not an expert on homesteading or survival either, so take my advice with caution. I'll share my reasons and concerns, but you need to do your own research. I do believe I'm right, but I know there are different opinions as well. I want to see my family safe; that's my top priority. I hope we never have to find out how bad it could be," Kyle said to everyone in the room.

Kyle spent the next hour in an open discussion, providing multiple reasons for his concerns. He talked about natural disasters in their region and the destruction those had caused. He highlighted the mismanagement of FEMA aid by supervisors in the county looking to line their own pockets. People lost their homes and everything they owned in an instant. Insurance companies delayed payouts, reluctant to settle claims. The extended amount of time without electricity and the impassable roads that in some cases took over a year to get repaired. He mentioned all the people that were prevented from reaching a grocery store or obtaining necessary medications.

They discussed people stuck in their homes, surviving on

whatever food they happened to have. The more people relied on restaurants for their meals, the less food they kept at home. Kyle explained how the first step to self-reliance had to come from the individual, not the government. He had never believed in depending on the government, which he viewed as a large corporation run by greedy individuals.

Kyle then brought up the 2003 Northeast Blackout, which left fifty-five million people without electricity in northern states and parts of Canada. The blackout, supposedly caused by a part malfunction or software bug, cost ten billion dollars to repair and resulted in over a hundred deaths during this short period. This was believed by most analysts and experts to have been caused by China.

As Kyle spoke, everyone listened closely, realizing he wasn't on a political rant since he criticized both parties equally. It didn't matter if one was a Democrat or a Republican-disasters happened regardless. When Kyle began talking about cyber-attacks, he knew this was a deep topic, so he kept it simple. He mentioned incidents like the WannaCry virus in 2017, which infected computers to extract ransoms. The virus forced the Taiwan Semiconductor Manufacturing Co. to shut down for three days. It compromised 200,000 computers in the UK National Health System, costing one hundred and twenty million dollars to repair.

"Could cyber-attacks actually shut the country down?" Ginger asked, clearly focused on every word. "And if so, why don't we see more about this on the news?" She questioned, genuinely curious but in a friendly manner.

"The news talks a little about it, but not many people have died from a cyber-attack. If there's no death involved, it doesn't draw good ratings. Regardless of your favorite news station, they're all about ratings, that's what brings the money in," Kyle responded.

"According to the FBI and Department of Homeland Security, they say Russian hackers have infiltrated critical infrastructure like energy, nuclear, and manufacturing sectors."

Kyle explained how the Department of Homeland Security, Department of Energy, and the Department of Defense were all working to block and protect the country from cyberattacks. "The reality is it still happens, and some hackers get through." He brought up the 2021 Colonial Pipeline disruption of oil supply and how they paid five million dollars in bitcoin to the ransom hackers.

The room buzzed with the tension of Kyle's sobering monologue on the vulnerabilities of modern infrastructure and the pervasive threat of cyber warfare. In 2015 and 2016, Ukraine had parts of their electrical grid knocked offline. In 2017 the NotPetya malware got into Ukraine's utility companies, banks and government agencies. In 2010 the Stuxnet virus crippled Iran's nuclear program ruining a fifth of its enrichment facilities. In 2018 shipping ports in San Diego and Spain were hacked. Baltimore's local government had 10,000 computers hacked and frozen. Kyle just went on and on with information spilling from his mouth. He had to stop himself and get a drink as his mouth was dried out.

"I know this is a lot of information I'm giving you. I don't want to overload you. But yes, cyber warfare is a very real thing taking place around the world daily." Kyle said taking a sip of his coffee. His voice carried the burden of his experiences and research, driving home the urgency of the issue. "I haven't told you all this, but I had twenty-six thousand dollars stolen from me in a hack myself. If you add that to the money I've had stolen by family members and so called friends who have swindled me, I've lost a lot of money trusting people."

It was clear that everyone wasn't finished hearing about this so Kyle continued. He explained the reality was that the U.S. energy grid was aging infrastructure that is extremely vulnerable to both cyber-attacks and physical attacks as stated by the General Accounting Office. Kyle told them from his research cyber-attacks are becoming more sophisticated by artificial intelligence. The current power grid has seventy percent of its transmission lines that are over thirty years old and approaching the end of life. Sixty percent of circuit breakers are more than thirty-five years old, making them fifteen years past their useful life already.

As Kyle's words hung in the air, the room was suddenly plunged into darkness. Gasps and shrieks echoed around the room, the sudden blackout sending a jolt of fear through everyone. Ginger's panicked cry for her mother added to the chaos.

"Oh shit! Mom! Mom, where are you? It's happening," Ginger screamed. "Kyle! What do we need to do?"

But just as quickly as the darkness had fallen, it lifted. The buzz of the refrigerator humming back to life and the lights flickering brightness to the room, made everyone pause and look around. Almost everyone, Megan was now asleep on the couch with no idea what was happening.

They all laughed after hearing the laughter of Rachel as she came back from the kitchen to the living room now knowing what she had done.

"I got you all didn't I? I flipped the breaker off and back on. I could hear somebody scream all the way in the laundry room," Rachel said with devilish laughter. "This talk has you all shook up I see."

"Mommy that was mean. I can't believe you did that. What If I would have died from a heart attack?" Ginger asked Rachel.

"But did you die?" Susie said laughing. "I sell that expression on a patch at my store." She continued laughing hysterically.

"Don't be so dramatic Ginger, you're not dead, your just fine. You can't die, if you did, who would make my life hell then?" Rachel said with a snarky comeback. This made everyone in the room bellow out with laughter as it was rare to hear Rachel say a curse word. It also showed that laughter was a good cure to cope with fear as the room's tension eased into a shared laugh.

"Mommy, why do you say stuff like that? Kyle, tell us more," Ginger said as she shook her arms as if to shake out the fear and sudden shock while Susie continued laughing as tears rolled down her cheeks.

Kyle had tried not to chuckle much at his sister, but his body shook with laughter enough that he spilled coffee onto his jeans. He patted napkins onto his clothing to dry the coffee before attempting to continue the conversation. He resumed the discussion, recounting the unidentified hacker who in 2021 had gained access to a network at a water treatment facility in Florida. The hacker had tried unsuccessfully to poison the water supply.

"I've talked a lot, I hope this helped you understand that there are many things that could go wrong, it doesn't have to be one single thing. It could be multi-faceted with several attacks at once. China wants Taiwan which is protected by the United States. Imagine if they did a cyber-attack on our grid system to disrupt this country, allowing them to attack Taiwan in a takeover. The United States worldwide threat assessment report says both China and Russia are capable of such an attack. Top officials say they have been aligning their operations in cyberspace to challenge the U.S. dominance. North Korea and Iran were both mentioned as well as being capable of this." Kyle told them as he was finishing up his discussion.

"Imagine a cyber-attack on the grid system, while at the same time a physical attack happening. This is a very serious fear that could become reality." Kyle painted a grim picture of a potential future where a cyber-attack on the U.S. grid system coincided with physical attacks, crippling the nation and paving the way for geopolitical shifts.

Kyle explained how the United States has continued to show weakness to the world. He discussed how we were getting spread too thin, being the big brother meant we had troops sent all around the globe trying to be the protectors of the world. He felt that the time was coming that these other countries had been waiting for. They were smart, strong, and well financed countries who were no longer scared of the United States.

Kyle's monologue ended with a call to action: "Don't just listen to me, do some research on your own." His parting words carried the weight of his conviction as he prepared to head to higher elevations for a few days of solitude. "It's been great seeing everyone; I've really enjoyed it." Kyle didn't know it himself, but that night was only ten months away from his fear becoming reality.

"It sounds like you have us all covered, so if anything happens, we can move in with you," Deanna, Kyle's neice said, drawing nods of agreement from the others. "We may have to get rid of you then and take over the mountain for ourselves." She giggled at her comment, while Kyle smiled slightly, unsure of how serious to take her.

"Enemies in the yard, that's what I'm saying we have to watch out for. It sounds like I better beware of family in the yard," Kyle said giving Deanna a smile that he knew she was just kidding.

Okay, I'll see everyone later. Bye Megan." Kyle said as Megan let out a loud snore. As the family began to disperse, they all shared in this moment, laughing at Megan's loud snore. Kyle hoped his talk would leave a mark, and his warnings and wisdom would linger in the air long after he left. The future was uncertain, but at least they were a little more aware, a little more prepared for whatever might come next.

CHAPTER FIVE
"A Storm is Brewing"

"Thank you for blessing us with this day, Lord," Kyle murmured, lifting his eyes to the clear, blue sky. He wasn't deeply devout, but he believed in God. His moral compass knowing right from wrong and feeling the conviction of his bad choices. He made it a point to express his gratitude daily, knowing each day was a gift. Kyle acknowledged the fragility of life, as he intended to make the most of every day he was given.

As he walked from the cabin, he inspected the small garden beside his home. It had been a learning process about what grew best, when to plant, and how much water and sunlight was needed. His grandmother had taught him the basics of gardening when he was a boy. The process of removing weeds from the garden was a tiresome chore. Yet, despite the hard work, the reward of biting into a freshly picked, salted cucumber was worth every bead of sweat.

Kyle had taken lessons from his elders on how to preserve his food with canning and storage. He had purchased his own pressure cooker and various size glass jars, as he tried to master the art of canning. He learned how to correctly store produce such as cabbage, green beans, and corn. He was really excited once he had learned to can his meat for long term storage as he built a substantial stockpile. Kyle would pressure cook and can ground beef along with steaks such as ribeye's and strips.

Kyle had never been a traditional farmer, but he had some knowledge about animals. He had one goat, several chickens and two pigs calling his farm home. He enjoyed being able to gather fresh eggs each morning to start the day. He wanted to add cows and horses eventually to his growing farm. Using the help of Uncle Tom, he had a barn constructed and ready for the addition of larger animals once he acquired them.

This morning, Kyle carried a small basket, picking fresh tomatoes, cucumbers, and squash as he walked amongst the rows of growing vegetables. He wanted to take these to Rachel when he went to see her later today. He stopped at the chicken coup and picked up four fresh eggs, adding them to the basket. He tossed a handful of feed onto the ground and opened the door allowing the chickens to roam free during the daylight hours.

He checked his to-do list for the day: "Cut up trees. Go check on mom. Walk fence line." Kyle liked to plan his task the night before, ensuring he could start his day without hesitation. During the sweltering summer days, he tackled the hardest projects in the cooler morning hours before the heat became overwhelming.

Kyle placed the basket of vegetables inside the cabin and walked past the garden to one of his storage sheds. He opened the doors, flipped the switch turning on the solar powered light, and began loading tools into the ATV cargo hold. He attached his utility trailer and set off along the trail. He would try not to let a day pass without being productive at something, and today was for gathering wood for winter. Although winter was months away, Kyle liked to be prepared ahead of time for the cold and snow.

Kyle drove to a clearing where dried trees were down that would make excellent firewood. He spent the next couple hours working at a ferocious pace cutting off tree limbs and then sawing the trees into manageable size lengths. After stacking the cargo area full of wood along with his utility trailer, Kyle let out a deep breath. He removed his hat, wiped the sweat from his head and grabbed his water jug.

There was something calming about being in the mountains. Kyle sat on his ATV, feet propped up on the front dash, feeling the breeze across his face as he finished off his water. He had more to do, and soon started back for the cabin, driving slowly to take in his surroundings. He would watch squirrels jumping through the trees, and occasionally spook a pheasant, seeing it fly up from the brush along the trail. Wild game was plentiful in the area with noise almost nonexistent from people. Kyle didn't mind someone using his trails to gain access to other areas, but it wasn't often anyone did. He didn't want to be the old grouch yelling stay of my lawn to the kids, but he did cherish the solitude.

There had been a few times when Kyle had to force people off his land over building bonfires and leaving trash thrown around. Usually it ended without trouble, but sometimes there was one person looking to push the boundaries. As he drove, he reminisced about such an encounter when he faced a late-night confrontation with a rowdy group he had driven upon.

"Hey guys, I hope everyone is doing well tonight. I'm sorry to say, but this isn't a place for partying, it's private land. I need you guys to load up and find a new place to continue your party. Please be safe and have a good night," Kyle said, turning back to his ATV.

One of the men, close to being intoxicated, threw an unopened can of beer, hitting Kyle's ATV. Kyle jumped to the side and looked back while the group laughed as one man mimicked the throwing motion again to his friends. Kyle picked up the can and walked it back to the man.

"You dropped your can. Please load up and take your party somewhere else now, please," Kyle said firmly.

"We're enjoying the party right here. You can drink this beer and party with us, or you can get your ass out of here," the man slurred his speech.

"This is my land, load up and go. It's not a request," Kyle said, his tone growing stern now.

"Or what, big man?" The man touted with a smile on his face as he swayed side to side in his cocky manor. Two of his friends stepped up and stood next to him, both wearing pistols on their side.

"Or I will punch you in the mouth, I'm not asking

anymore," Kyle warned not intimidated by their weapons.

"I said I'm not..." The sound of Kyle's fist slamming the man in the mouth was like a balloon popping. The man dropped and his body stiffened. The other two men, seeing Kyle wasn't bluffing, held up their hands to surrender.

"We don't want any trouble, friend. He runs his mouth a lot. We'll get him out of here and be gone," one of his buddies said.

"I don't want to see any of you back on my land again. Find somewhere else to party next time." Kyle ordered, watching them pack up and leave. They put out the fire they had burning, grabbed their trash and took off.

Kyle always smiled when passing by this location where that incident had happened. He had not seen those men since that time and was told they were from West Virginia when he had asked around. As he continued, Kyle liked the rare sounds he could hear when mother nature would speak through the birds or bring a soft breeze of wind across his face. He would ride along thinking how could there be a better place to live than this.

After getting back to the cabin and unloading his bountiful haul for the day, he stacked the wood neatly in the woodshed. Kyle felt good about his work for the morning, feeling accomplished in his winter prep. He went inside the cabin to wipe away the dirt, washing his arms and face. He changed into a somewhat clean shirt, picked up the basket of food for Rachel and was on his ATV once again. It was time to go see his momma now and spend some time with her. He hoped she would have lunch made, at least a bologna sandwich. Kyle loved visiting and finding a hot meal on the stove, she was such a good cook. The ten-minute ride down the mountain trail would have his stomach growling once he arrived.

Kyle passed by Uncle's Tom cabin; it appeared like Tom had not been there in a while with pine needles covering the porch. One of the chairs was turned over, most likely from the wind. This cabin of Uncle Tom's was only one room, Kyle called it the "poutin' shack." Just a couple more minutes from the bottom and the trail would lead right up to his mother's house.

"There is my baby boy, coming to see his mom. Did you smell lunch all the way up the mountain?" Rachel greeted him warmly.

"I had to come and see what was cooking, the smell was enticing me," Kyle laughed, hugging her and taking a seat on the porch. "I brought you some fresh veggies and eggs."

"It's looking like we may get some rain, clouds are getting a bit dark moving in," Rachel said as she took the basket and gazed towards the sky.

Kyle looked upwards with her shaking his head in agreement, "we have a storm brewing it appears."

"Thank you son. These tomatoes look wonderful. Did you bring your appetite? I heated a pot of vegetable beef soup I made yesterday. Let's go inside and I'll fix you a sandwich to go with it," Rachel said, opening the door to go inside.

Kyle knew it wasn't a question as much as an order, but he was hungry and ready to comply. The coolness of the air-conditioned house was a welcome relief as he walked in. Kyle washed his hands and joined Rachel in the kitchen.

"Soup smells great, mom. How has everything been the last few days since I was down?" Kyle asked, picking up his plate with the sandwich and bowl of soup.

"Same as always, everybody is still the same as far as I know," Rachel replied as they sat on the couch.

"How about you? What have you been doing with yourself?" Kyle asked, already knowing the answer. She was either watching the news or playing card games on her computer.

"I was playing my card game, but I'm stuck right now. I turned it off and now I've been watching the news," Rachel said. Kyle couldn't hold back from giggling.

"What's so funny son?" She asked.

"Oh, nothing, mom. Just one of those laughs that hit you sometimes," Kyle said, trying to eat his sandwich to hide his smile.

"They're still arguing about the border being open. They

have been discussing how many people are entering the country illegally. They go on about how dangerous it is that we don't even realize the type of people coming in," Rachel spoke softly, looking at the television.

The news channel showed thousands of people lined up, ready to cross from Mexico. It was not just Mexicans, but also Asian and Indians in the line. Kyle thought it was crazy how the country so willingly pushed aside security at the border to gain votes. Other countries had strict borders, but the United States seemed to allow anyone to walk right in and get a free ride.

"This is what I have been talking about, the Democrats have made it no secret they are buying votes. They managed to steal a whole election; they have no fear," Kyle said, looking at the screen. "Many of these people are coming here with support from William Politis, a billionaire who hates America and wants to see its downfall. I fear many of these people are coming here supported by their governments or terrorists' organizations with bad intentions. Our current government is so caught up with counting them as voters that they don't know who is waltzing right on in." Kyle stopped talking to take a bite of his grilled cheese sandwich after dunking it into his soup. He loved his mom's vegetable beef soup; it always hit the spot.

"It's scary. Makes me happy we live here in a small town. I would hate to be in the cities right now with so many people not knowing who their neighbors are," Rachel said to Kyle.

"You can't just blame the Democrats for it; Republicans have allowed it to happen as well. Until we the people stop sending politicians money, nothing will ever get better. Our politicians will allow this country to crumble if they think they can profit from it," Kyle remarked, preparing to leave.

"I know son. It's a mess. You can't blame anyone for wanting to do better for themselves. If this country says, 'come on, we'll give you everything you need,' why wouldn't they?" Rachel said, patting Kyle on the arm. "If they don't get the credit card mess worked out today, nobody will be sending any money to politicians, "she added.

"What do you mean, credit card mess?" Kyle quickly asked Rachel.

"Something is going on with many credit card companies today. They will show it again on the news, it's been on all morning. They say people's cards are being declined," Rachel explained. "There it is again," she said, pointing to the breaking news bar on the screen.

"We continue this morning to follow the story as it develops regarding credit card declines. Many banks are now reporting their systems are down, and they are working to correct the issue. We have no confirmation currently, but a cyber-attack is suspected," the news reporter stated. "We will continue to track this story as more information becomes available."

"This is interesting. Do me a favor, if anything else happens, send Arnie up to let me know," Kyle requested as he hugged Rachel.

"Be careful son. You know where I am if you need me. I love you," Rachel told Kyle.

"I love you, Mom." Kyle headed towards his ATV, started the engine, and drove up the trail. He always had a feeling of loneliness leaving everyone behind, knowing only an empty cabin awaited him.

Pushing aside the thoughts, he quickly returned to the news reporter's comments he had just watched. Kyle had no doubt it was a cyber-attack affecting credit card companies, but who might be responsible for it. He wondered how severe the disruption might be and if any other companies would be targeted. He wondered if this might be part of a bigger scale attack as he had often imagined.

"Hogwash," Kyle muttered as he drove along. "You have yourself so convinced something bad is going to happen. It's time to just relax and enjoy life, enjoy this property you have built." Kyle could tell himself all he wanted to that everything was fine, but his mind wasn't changing. His attempt at self-therapy wasn't going to be enough to make him believe everything was okay.

CHAPTER SIX
"Between Fences and Memories"

U pon his return from Rachels house, Kyle still had work to do. It was time to walk around the property, checking the fence line to ensure there were no openings. Though not a frequent task, he liked to inspect it at least monthly, knowing a fallen tree branch could easily damage a section. Kyle had two separate fences along the property. The first was at the top edge of the property, it was ten feet tall. Along the top was razor wire around three strands of barb wire. This continued all around the entire length of the fence encircling the cabin. The property, shaped like a horseshow on the ridge, gave it the perfect look of a prison site.

The second fence was fifteen feet down the slope of the mountain. It was a much simpler setup, simple farm fencing post with five strands of barb wire that attached and followed around the ridge. It was all Kyle had the first time he installed a fence, and it worked around the steep terrain excellently. Only three months ago, Kyle had debated the cost of installing the larger fence, which Uncle Tom and Arnie helped him with. Uncle Tom saw it as overkill, but Arnie thought it was "super cool," as he had told Kyle.

Kyle was very proud of the new fence after they had finished the installation. However, for now, Kyle needed to check what Arnie had dubbed the "zombie fence." Arnie said the small fence was to keep the zombies out while the large fence was for the bad guys. He proceeded to pass through the gate and descended over the slope, carefully walking down to the fence. He felt for any slack spots the fence might have, before giving it a thumbs up. His legs burned from navigating the steep slope, he was glad to climb back up and stretch them out.

Kyle leaned onto a post and stretched while regaining his oxygen level. He did a daily jog along the trail road, usually a half mile out before turning and running back. It was much easier running on the flat surface than climbing around the steep terrain. The post he leaned against was a leg to one of the two watch towers Kyle had erected. This was another project Kyle was very thrilled with upon seeing it completed. Each tower stood sixteen feet high at the top of the covered roof. This allowed Kyle to be an additional ten feet off the ground giving him an elevated vantage point. It was like the big boy version of a tree house.

On the front side of the cabin the view from the tower overlooked the winding trail that led up the hill. It also showed a distant view of Uncle Toms cabin, although binoculars were needed for clarity. The other tower overlooked the steepest side of the mountain, and although there was little chance anyone would reach the cabin from this direction, it also had a sight line down the main path to the cabin.

At the bottom of the mountain behind the cabin, there was a small farm. It was not easy to see from Kyle's watch tower even with binoculars. Uncle Tom was skeptical, seeing no need to build these lookout towers, but he enjoyed doing it with Kyle and Arnie as a fun project. Arnie on the other hand loved them, he would sit there all-day doing overwatch just for fun and looking for game animals as well.

Kyle had one more thing on his list he wanted to do before calling an end to the day. He went inside his cabin and retrieved a rifle from the gun rack, his Savage .243 caliber rifle with the stock Weaver 3-9x40mm scope. It was a simple but effective gun and didn't break the bank to purchase it. The rifle had a Mossy Oak camo stock which was designed by the manufacturer. Kyle took the rifle with two shells, that should be one more than he needed, and walked towards tower one. Kyle had a wooden ladder built to climb onto the landing that gave him a raised position.

From the elevated platform of the tower, this position

allowed him clear visibility to the main gate. As Kyle got himself situated, he opened the bipod on the rifle, it was the only additional attachment he added to the gun. Kyle placed himself in the prone position and after opening the bolt, he placed one round into the chamber and closed the bolt. As he peered through the scope, he put the crosshairs on a small target near the gate. The clarity of the scope wasn't as clear as he would like at this distance, but it did the job. Kyle inhaled and released his breath.

"Crack!" The gunshot echoed through the trees. Kyle observed through the scope, confirming the impact being exactly where he aimed.

"Perfect," Kyle said, satisfied. He would occasionally fire rounds at the target with different guns to make sure they were zeroed in accurately. Kyle was very meticulous and careful with his firearms so there was really no reason for the scope to be off target. Kyle kept this gun zeroed in at one hundred yards, but already had the MOA adjustments for the shot distance to the gate set using the turrets. This allowed him to quickly adjust back to zero if he needed a hundred yards. It was one hundred and forty yards from the tower to the gate entrance. Kyle was not an expert marksman, but he was a an above average shooter. He had started shooting with his dad during his childhood.

After feeling content with the shot he had taken, Kyle stood up, retrieved his rifle, and went back down the ladder. He sat cleaning his gun on the porch that evening listening to the bird's chirp. After feeling the rifle was ready to go back, Kyle walked inside and placed it on the gun rack. He paused, looking at the gun directly above it. This was a special gun to Kyle, the first gun his dad said was his and the first rifle he had ever shot. The rifle was beautiful, a small .22 caliber. He placed his hand on the stock just to feel it under his fingertips. Kyle closed his eyes recollecting back to when he was a small boy.

"Son, this is a Winchester model 9422 lever action," Kyle remembered his dad saying. His eyes remained closed as Kyle could see his dad down on one knee showing him how to load the magazine tube on the rifle. They set up a target outside the back door. He could remember so clearly the way his dad instructed him to stand and aim at the target. He thought about his dad showing him to lower the lever action and pull it back up, loading his first live round into the receiver. From the first pull of the trigger, Kyle was hooked on shooting. He opened his eyes, breaking himself away from the thought, but missing his dad deeply.

Kyle was now ready for some relaxation after his day's work had been accomplished. It was hard to call it relaxing, as he didn't call it work that he did, enjoying the projects and tasks he took on. Kyle removed a bottle of water from the cabinet at room temperature, pouring a sugar-free flavor packet of lemonade into it, then went outside the cabin to sit.

Kyle took a seat in the rocking chair on his porch, and began a slow rock. These moments were peaceful, but also challenging. It's when all was quiet, that his mind would wander, at times there was no turn off switch for all the thoughts running through his brain. These were the times when he missed his dad the most and imagined how much he would have enjoyed this place. It's when Kyle felt the emptiness of being isolated on the mountain.

He wondered about his brothers, Sawyer and Spencer. Sawyer was likely playing golf and Spencer sitting at a table flipping through baseball cards. He sucked at golf but had finally accepted this fact, which made playing more fun. As a younger man he took the game to serious, often leading to a broken club or one being tossed into a pond. At the young age of forty now, he still enjoyed opening a pack of sports cards looking for a rare find. He no longer collected like he had done as a kid, but he knew Spencer still loved cards and collected regularly.

"And now ladies and gentlemen, prepare to be entertained by the amazing voice of Kyle Blaine," he announced to the chickens pecking the ground. "Well, life on the farm is kind of laid back, ain't much an old country boy like me can't hack. Early to rise and early in the sack, thank God I'm a country boy," Kyle sang as he rocked.

"It's probably a good thing I'm on the top of this mountain right now," Kyle said to the chicken now standing on the porch looking at him. He knew most people would consider his singing to be desecrating on the great voice of John Denver. He did the best thing he knew to do and continued singing into the late evening. After bellowing out a few various tunes and switching his music to songs by Shinedown, he led the chickens to their coup. They obliged without issue and were ready to begin roosting for the night.

"I created the sound of madness. Wrote the book on pain, somehow, I'm still here to explain," Kyle sang by Shinedown as he walked to the chicken coup. "I probably should have been a rockstar, but then I wouldn't be here taking care you girls," he said to the chickens as they marched into the coup.

Kyle went inside and showered quickly, before reading a few pages of his bible, and praying for his family. Arnie hadn't come to see him about the news earlier regarding the cyber-attack, so he thought maybe that had all been resolved. It had been a good day, and he was tuckered out and ready for a night's sleep, unaware of just how much rest he'd need.

CHAPTER SEVEN
"A Sinister Pact"

In the quiet town of Hurley, troublemakers were as much a part of the landscape as the trees and hills. In simpler times, the trouble was minor: a drunken brawl at the pool hall or a petty theft from someone's yard. In the later years, as drugs like oxycontin and crystal meth began creeping into the community, the crimes became more severe. The significant value of items stolen increased and murder, which was uncommon in the small area, even had its share of an uptick.

Two such individuals who frequently found themselves in trouble were Axel and Vince. Axel, as he was nicknamed, was Eli Young, now a twenty-five-year-old aspiring musician. His love for smoking pot had escalated to the much stronger oxycontin pills. He was tall and lanky, more bone than muscle, as his diet consisted mostly of pills. In high school, Axel was usually considered an oddball. After his graduation, Axel soon realized what everyone else knew, without any actual musical talent he had to find a way to survive. He had been given the nickname Axel, not because of any likeness to the frontman for Guns N' Roses, but as a mockery of his rock star fantasies.

Axel wasn't alone in his music endeavors; he had his best friend and sidekick. Mark Thomas was Axel's friend, who went by the name, Vince. Mark, shorter and stockier with a full-face beard, believed his beard made him look tougher and more attractive to girls. A major Motley Crue' fan, Mark eagerly adopted his own nickname Vince, thinking it compared him to Vince Neil.

Despite their lack of real talent, Vince was known as a

respectable fighter in school, unafraid to throw a punch when disrespected. He had the big brother mentality toward Axel and often did his bidding. Vince wasn't known for his intelligence, so he would follow Axel's lead in most situations.

Several years prior, Axel and Vince had made a name for themselves as deadbeats in the area. Most of the locals knew they were usually up to no good, and many suspected them of being responsible for far greater crimes than just simple drugs and petty thefts.

Vince was raised by his grandmother, known by everyone in the mobile home park as Grandma Thomas, after his parents died in a car accident when he was just a toddler. Grandma Thomas had lived in the mobile home park overlooking the school. As a small boy Vince hated living near the school. Grandma Thomas would stand on the porch and watch until he walked into the school, and he hated going to school.

She was a frugal woman who did her best to raise Vince, keeping him away from Axel whenever possible. She never trusted Axel; sensing the bad path he was leading Vince down. It didn't take her long to notice anytime Axel was around, something would go missing from her home. Shortly after their high school graduation, they made a decision that would make them become real criminals.

"Mark, I don't want that Eli Young boy hanging out here. He ain't good people. His daddy is trash!" Grandma Thomas would say, refusing to call either boy by their nickname.

"Grandma, call me Vince, my friends do!" he would sound off back to her with a hateful teenager tone, clearly irritated. "And his name is Axel, I've told you."

"I don't want him here! I've told you and that's final. He's a thief and going to get you in trouble with law." Grandma Thomas expressed herself becoming a little irate with Vince.

"I'm going to Axel's house. You need to wash my shirts tonight. I'll be back later," Vince snapped back before hopping on his bicycle, his primary mode of transportation. Grandma Thomas didn't have a driver's license or a car and couldn't afford one for

Vince, something else he stay angered over.

"What's up man? We ready to jam?" Vince said to Axel as he arrived at the small building behind Axel's house where they hung out, played music and howled at the moon.

"My old man is on my ass again. Get a job is all he tells me. I need out of this house," Axel complained.

"You got a cigarette?" Vince asked. Axel handed him one from his pack. "We need our own place, dude. I'm tired of everyone's rules. Grandma's been on me about hanging out with you. She says you're a bad influence on me."

"I know she's your grandma, but she is always on your back. She has never liked me," Axel said to Vince.

"She don't like me neither. Just puts up with me because my parents died. I'm ready for her to die off so I can take her trailer," Vince joked, taking a drag from the cigarette and holding it, before exhaling a large cloud of smoke into the air.

"Maybe we need to help her along on that journey." Axel said ominously.

Vince let out a slight giggle, looking at the ground and shaking his head. Axel could tell he was allowing the thought to process in his mind. Axel watched silently as Vince continued looking at the ground while using his foot to slide a small pebble around the dirt.

"Let's do it! Let's kill her. We can live there together. I know she has money hidden away. I've seen her with three hundred dollars before," Vince said loudly.

"Hush up big mouth! You can't be saying shit like that out loud," Axel snapped, causing Vince to sulk. "It's okay Vince. I didn't mean to raise my voice at you bro. You know I love you, man. We just can't get caught," Axel said to Vince as he patted his friend on the shoulder.

"Yeah, you're right Axel. I'm sorry dawg, you're always right. I'm just stupid sometimes," Vince said, smiling again. "Do you want to do it? Want to go now?" Vince asked eagerly.

"We need a plan, and you can't ever tell anyone. This will be our moment to shine and get our own home," Axel said, making direct eye contact with Vince as he held him by the shoulders.

The boys went inside the shed and began concocting their plan. Vince mostly nodded and smiled at Axel's suggestions. After putting a mere ten minutes into the plan, they felt ready to carry out the task. Axel felt it was a sure-fire plan that couldn't go wrong. She was an old woman after all, and old people die every day.

Later that evening, Grandma Thomas followed her usual routine. She watched Wheel of Fortune and then took her bubble bath. Vince unlocked the back door and left the house, riding his bike to the neighbor's trailer. He did exactly as Axel had told him, he was going to get his part of the plan correct.

"Hey Gerald!" Vince waved to the old man sitting on his porch. "I'm going to the Family Dollar to get grandma a twelve-pack of pop. Do you need anything?" Gerald shook his head no; the old man could barely speak. The old man just sat on his porch each day, usually alone. This was exactly what Axel had told Vince to do, he wanted to make sure someone had seen Vince leaving for a short time. They knew Gerald could answer the question that he had seen Vince but wouldn't be able to say much else.

Meanwhile, Axel rode his bike to a spot near Grandma Thomas's house, hiding it behind some bushes. He crossed the small stream leading to Grandma Thomas's trailer, slipping on a rock and falling into the water, soaking his shoes and jeans. He scurried up the hill and around to the backdoor of the trailer.

Axel slowly opened the door and entered the trailer quietly. He could hear Grandma Thomas singing "Jolene" by Dolly Parton. He placed his hand on the doorknob to the bathroom and slowly began to turn it, trying to minimize the noise. He picked up a towel and stepped to the curtain. In her joyous singing of "Jolene," she had not heard him enter the room. Grandma Thomas stopped singing, sensing a shadow move on the wall.

"Is that you Mark?" she called out.

She pulled the curtain back just as Axel threw the towel over her face and forced her head down beneath the water. She struggled, inhaling water and trying to kick at her attacker. Axel knelt his knee across her legs pinning her from kicking. She grabbed the shower curtain, pulling it down along with rod holding it. The rod hit Axel's head causing a small cut.

Once Grandma Thomas had finally quit moving, Axel knew she was dead. He didn't remove the towel from her face, unable to look at her. Standing against the wall, he was in a minor state of shock, the gravity of the moment squeezing him tightly.

Axel began to remerge from his transient state, looking at the old woman lying in the tub, the towel still draped across her face and upper body. The shower curtain and rod both lay on the wet floor, drops of blood on the white linoleum. Axel looked in the mirror, seeing a small trail of blood moving slowly down his face. He observed grass floating in the tub, that must have been on his pants when he climbed the hill. There were small amounts of mud on the floor from his shoes. He knew the scene looked bad, but he thought of himself as smart enough to make this work.

Axel tried to put the shower rod and curtain back on top of the shower. In doing so, he noticed the blood smeared on the yellow plastic curtain. While touching his head, Axel had gotten blood on his hand, now transferring it to the curtain. He jerked it back to the floor, taking another look at the chaos in the room.

"Shit!" Axel exclaimed. "Shit! Shit! Shit!"

CHAPTER EIGHT
"Bound by Lies"

"Okay boys, this is Officer Langston, and I'm Officer Ramey. We need you to walk us through what happened," Officer Ramey said calmly, eyeing Vince and Axel intently. "Start from the beginning." Officer Ramey looked into the eyes of Vince; his eyes looked void of any emotion. Officer Ramey, with his years of patrol experience, sensed an unsettling quietness in Vince's demeanor.

"Grandma said she was going to take her bath and wanted me to go to the Family Dollar and get some pop. I rode my bike, after asking Gerald if he needed anything. I came back home, and she was..." Vince hesitated, his eyes moving towards Officer Ramey's sidearm. Ramey turned slightly to the side and placed his hand over the handle of the weapon to block its view from Vince.

"Take your time," Officer Langston encouraged.

"Don't be nervous, I want you to tell us what you found when you arrived back home," Ramey said.

"I brought the pop home, put it on the kitchen table. I called out to Grandma, and she didn't answer. I went to the bathroom and found her...in the tub," Vince murmured, his gaze drifting towards Axel for support.

"The door was open or was it closed?" Officer Ramey asked.

"No, it was closed. I called out to her, and she didn't respond. I opened the door because she never locks it. She just kept the curtain closed when she bathes," Vince explained, avoiding Officer Ramey's eyes.

"If the curtain was closed, how did you see her in the tub?" Officer Ramey pressed gently on the subject.

"I had said her name again and still no answer, so I pulled the curtain back," Vince replied, still avoiding direct eye contact.

"Go on," Ramey urged, glancing at Axel, who was fixated on Vince's every word. His lips seemed to mimic every word Vince said.

"When I called Axel, he said he was coming to help. After he got here, Axel, told me she was dead, we needed to call an ambulance," Vince added, looking upwards at the ceiling, contemplating his next words.

"You're doing fine, tell me more about what happened in the bathroom," Officer Ramey told Vince.

"Axel tried to pull her out of the tub, the shower rod fell, hitting his head," Vince explained, pointing to Axel's head. "But he told me she was dead, and we probably should leave her where she was in case the police needed to see everything."

"Why did you think the police would need to see anything?" a new voice interrupted from the doorway leading onto the porch.

"Boys, this is Sheriff Bascum Gilbert," Officer Ramey said introducing the Sheriff as he stepped aside to greet him.

"Please continue, young man. Why did you leave her for the police?" Sheriff Gilbert asked, stepping forward.

"She was dead, and we didn't know what to do. We called the ambulance," Vince replied.

"I knew she was gone, and I couldn't help her. We got scared is all, Sheriff. We're kids, we didn't know what to do," Axel interjected quickly, sensing Vince might be losing his grip on the story. "I covered her with a towel like they do in movies so Vince wouldn't have to see her like that," Axel continued.

The Sheriff walked past them towards the bathroom, accompanied by Officer Langston. He noticed muddy shoe prints near the backdoor. This seemed odd as the other parts of the home were extremely clean and tidy. Inside, the bathroom told a grim tale-the shower curtain torn down, water puddled on the floor, and blood droplets highlighted by the white backdrop of the floor.

The sheriff removed his notepad from his front left pocket, clicked his pen and began to jot down notes. Despite the chaos of the room, the boys had an explanation for each part of the scene. As the sheriff turned to leave, he noticed the back door was unlocked. He shined his flashlight onto the ground, noticing a muddy path leading into the weeds.

"Been out the back door tonight?" the sheriff asked.

"No, sir, we keep that..." Vince started to explain before Axel interrupted, knowing where the Sheriff was headed.

"I was, Sheriff. I was going to vomit, so I opened the back door and stepped out for fresh air. I walked around and came back inside," Axel told the sheriff as he looked him in the eye while speaking. Sheriff Gilbert noticed Axel's unnaturally calm demeanor, it didn't seem like that of a teenager in this situation.

The Sheriff felt there was more to the story than the boys were telling, but no way to prove it. There was no concrete evidence that could link a crime to this death. He motioned to Officer Ramey and Officer Langston to join him outside and told them this story wasn't adding up.

"These boys aren't telling us everything," Sheriff Gilbert stated firmly. "They should never have been questioned together; they should have been separated from the start."

"They're lying Sheriff, I know they are. That larger kid, the grandson, he is way too calm. The other kid goes by Axel, his real name is Eli Young. His father is a troublemaker, a drug dealer and user I've picked up a few times," Officer Ramey said to the Sheriff.

"It's not what you know, it's what you can prove. Right now, all we can prove is an elderly woman died in the bathtub and two boys tried to help her in a panic," Officer Langston interjected, eager to impress the Sheriff.

"That's true, Langston. It's what you can prove, we need evidence. But those boys are cold, callous and hard-hearted. The torn shower curtain, the towel soaked, there's something not right. There was even grass in the tub, how do you explain that?"

Sheriff Gilbert pondered aloud. "Something happened here tonight, but unless we break one of them, we may never know."

"It'll be a shame if we don't figure it out," Ramey stated.

"Langston, photograph the scene. Apply some pressure in the next few days and see if one of those kids will crack. Do it carefully, as we don't need the community thinking we are trying to railroad two kids," Sheriff Gilbert instructed as he tucked his notepad back into his pocket.

"You need anything from me Sheriff?" Ramey asked as he walked with Sheriff Gilbert back to his police cruiser.

"Keep an eye on Langston. I don't know what it is yet, but I don't trust that guy. He's always kissing my ass," Sheriff Gilbert replied, a hint of suspicion in his voice.

Vince had recently celebrated his eighteenth birthday a few months earlier, and Axel was close. They spent the next three nights at Axel's house while friends mourned Grandma Thomas. Vince was her sole surviving family member. After the burial service, Langston met the boys at the edge of the cemetery.

"You boys get in my car. I'll give you a ride home," Officer Langston said, opening the back door on the police cruiser.

"I knew it. We're in trouble, ain't we?" Vince asked looking at Langston, his voice wavering.

"Not if you get in and listen," Langston said as the boys settled into the backseat.

As Langston drove back to Grandma Thomas's house, he began to speak. "I know what you boys did, and so does the sheriff, we have all the evidence to prove it. Being the understanding guy that I am, you have an opportunity right now," he said to Axel and Vince glancing into his rearview mirror as they shuffled themselves in their seats uncomfortably.

"What's the opportunity?" Axel asked nervously.

"The kind that keeps you out of jail. In return, you help me when I ask. Simple as that," Office Langston explained, pulling over to the side of the road and turning to face them.

"What about the Sheriff? Does he agree to this? He won't lock us up?" Axel questioned, eyes narrowed.

"The Sheriff will go along with my plan. Besides, I'll be the Sheriff soon enough. I'll protect you and keep you out of trouble," Officer Langston assured them, waiting for their response.

"Deal!" Vince said without hesitation. "We'll take it."

"Yes sir, we're in. You call and we'll answer," Axel said, not realizing he was signing up to be Langston's flunky from now on.

"I knew you idiots were responsible. We had no way to prove it, but I knew it," Langston said still looking at the boys.

"You mean you don't have any proof?" Axel asked.

"I didn't but I do now, I just recorded this. Don't worry, do as I say, and nobody ever finds out," Langston said. "Now get the hell out of my car and stay out of trouble until you hear from me."

As the boys entered the home, Vince felt a wave of nausea wash over him. Guilt clawed at his insides. Axel went straight to the kitchen and removed a soda from the refrigerator, taking a long drink.

"That cop lied to us, we could have gone to jail," Vince said, feeling squeamish at the thought.

"We did lie to them first, I guess we're all even now," Axel responded with a devilish grin as he kicked off his shoes into the middle of the room.

"Yeah, I guess you're right," Vince agreed. "Everybody lies."

"We killed your grandma, and we're getting away with it," Axel said matter-of-factly after he finished.

Those words made Vince uneasy, he winced at the bluntness. He could feel his stomach jerk and twist at the thought. His mind churning with conflicting emotions. It wasn't Axel's grandmother they had just killed; it was his. His grandmother was dead, did he do the right thing? Vince was riding an enormous wave of emotions as he looked around the living room to the couch where his grandma used to sit watching her game shows. He wrestled with the guilt as her face smiled at him from a portrait hanging on the wall.

"Let's find the money, Vince!" Axel exclaimed, breaking the hold of her portrait on Vince.

Vince hearing this, looked at Axel with anger in his heart.

He looked at Axel not as his friend, but as the man who killed his grandmother. Vince studied Axel's face, his eyes, he watched as his mouth uttered the words. Axel had been his friend all his life though, he was only looking out for him. Axel was helping him to secure a better future. These thoughts most likely saved Axel from the brutal pounding Vince wanted to give him now. Vince reconsidered Axel's motives, and his anger subsided.

The boys spent the next half-hour ransacking the home in search of money. They rifled through kitchen cabinets and drawers, finding only coupons. They invaded Grandma's bedroom, tossing aside personal items in their treasure hunt. When they found nothing, frustration set in.

"Where else is there to look, Vince?" Axel asked, ready to give up the search.

"I think I know," Vince said slowly, a small smile forming. "Grandma always said one thing she never had to worry about me doing was laundry."

In the hallway, Vince opened the cabinet above the washer and dryer. Moving aside bottles and cleaning supplies, he reached to the back and pulled out an old blue, metal, Maxwell House coffee can. After removing the lid and pulling out a scarf, Vince smiled like a toddler getting candy. He turned to Axel, tilting the can over, showing him the ingredients.

"Hot damn! We're rich Vince," Axel said as he reached for the coffee can. "Let's go count it at the table."

That was eight years ago, and the two young men would now forever be bound by lies.

CHAPTER NINE
"Enemies Within"

Unbeknownst to the population of America who were blissfully unaware, an impending crisis was quickly approaching. Engrossed in their daily routines of school, work, and leisure, they were oblivious to the scheme of a covert group of anti-Americans plotting to change their world. The nation, divided evenly over political issues, was being manipulated by the government. Family and friends were fighting with each other over who was right and wrong in their beliefs. Neighbors were becoming enemies over trivial matters. The borders were open, allowing illegal aliens to enter the United States without consequences, many walking with apparent immunity from the law.

The United States, having made its share of enemies worldwide, was now facing retribution. After many conflicts, countries that had long harbored animosity towards the U.S. were working together on a plan. A clandestine meeting had been convened under the radar, between leaders of American adversaries, including China, Russia, North Korea, and Iran. These countries were devising an operation targeting American's infrastructure through cyber warfare and physical attacks.

The Chinese government masterminded the plan, placing Zhao Wei in charge of the operation. Zhao Wei was a high-ranking official in the Chinese intelligence agency. He was cold, calculating, and highly intelligent. His hatred was fueled by the murder of his parents while in America when Zhao was only a small child. He had dedicated his life to the communist party, quickly advancing through the ranks.

Vladimir Petrov, was a seasoned strategist from the Russian military. Vladimir worked closely with Zhao on the details for the operation. He was known for his ruthless killing efficiency throughout the world, protected by the Russian government who ordered his work to often be showcased. Vladimir had an unwavering loyalty to the cause, he would see it through no matter the cost.

With Zhao and Valdimir as the two lead points for the plan, Iran and North Korea offered their services anyway needed. Reza Pahlavi earned a seat at the table, thanks to his experience as a skilled operative and former soldier for Iran. He was deeply loyal, earning his place with Zhao and Vladimir. His deep-seated hatred for America was well known within the U.S. intelligence community. He was dedicated to the mission and a crucial piece to the manipulation of the Iranian men he would recruit.

North Korea didn't have the resources to attempt any attack on the soil of the United States and it was no secret. However, they had soldiers dedicated to North Korea, that would give their life if asked. Kim Jae-Hwa, a young, passionate agent under the North Korean government looked up to Zhao Wei. His fervent belief in North Korea's cause, and the opportunity to work and learn from Zhao Wei, drove him to follow orders without question.

Infiltrating the United States would not be a challenge for these countries. Over the course of two years, groups of soon to be terrorists were trained for their mission. Instilled from a young age, to hate America, and with promises of care for their families, volunteers eagerly signed up. Once inside the country successfully, they were greeted by handlers and ushered to their appropriate locations.

These cell groups, varying in size from two to seven men, operated discreetly to avoid raising suspicion. They were placed in neighborhoods from the poorest to the wealthiest, supplied with living quarters, food, and all necessary provisions. The handlers' job was to implement the plan for their specific cell, ensuring each participant was mentally ready. Any sign of doubt was met with fatal consequences.

In a dimly lit room in an undisclosed location, Zhao Wei and Vladimir Petrov stood before a large map of the United States. Red pins marked key targets; the White house, bridges, ports, railways, dams, water treatment facilities, oil refineries, and power stations.

"We have our targets," Zhao said, his voice calm but authoritative. "Now, we ensure our operatives are ready."

Petrov nodded, his icy blue eyes scanning the map. "Our men are in place. The weapons are secured. We move forward as planned."

Reza Pahlavi and Kim Jae-Hwa listened intently, their expressions unwavering. "We will not fail," Reza declared, his voice filled with conviction.

Securing weaponry was surprisingly easy. The United States government was preoccupied with political battles, therefor obtaining bombing supplies like C-4 explosives was simple. C-4 could be molded into any desired shape, making it ideal for concealed transportation and placement. It was also very stable allowing it to be carried and planted with ease. The terrorist used vehicles such as moving trucks, catering vans, oil tankers and even funeral hearses to transport their bombs.

The plan, involving over four thousand men, came together swiftly. The command center was disguised as a suburban home outside of Minneapolis, Minnesota. On the inside, it was operated by a seven-man team working tirelessly, its secrets held in the basement underneath, activities coordinated by Ellie Marks. Chalkboard-painted walls were covered with lists of major targets from top to bottom. Names under each heading with a corresponding cell group, larger targets assigned multiple cells.

Ellie Marks, a Liberal Democrat and former political strategist had been covertly working with the adversaries. She had been appointed by the president in 2010, as a Senior Adviser on International Trade Relations. Her duties were never really known, nor her whereabouts at most times. Her strategic mind and insider knowledge made her an invaluable asset to the operation. Her hatred for corporate America and the so-called white privilege, blinded her to the destruction she was about to play a major role in. She was sharp, in her early forties, standing in the middle of the basement command center.

"We are in the final stages," she announced, her voice steady. "Ensure all communications are encrypted and secure. We cannot afford any mistakes."

Her team, a mix of operatives from various backgrounds, nodded in unison. Ellie's leadership was firm and decisive, a result of her years in political strategy. She had once been a rising star within the U.S. government. As the Senior Adviser on International Trade Relations, she had developed strong ties with both China and Russia. Her position required her to navigate complex international landscapes, making her privy to the inner workings of global politics and intelligence.

Ellie had grown disillusioned over time in the American dream and political system, leading her to take extreme measures for what she saw as the greater good. She saw corruption and inefficiency that, in her eyes, were leading the country astray. Her discontent deepened after a series of political defeats and personal betrayals, pushing her to seek more radical solutions. This led her to quietly establish contacts with the Chinese officials, eventually aligning herself with Zhao Wei's cause.

On August 3rd, a message was sent to each handler for translation and relay to their group: "The time has come. We have prepared and will achieve our goal of bringing down America. The United States have for years slaughtered our innocent and controlled our freedoms. This will be no more, and their reign will end now. You are the blessed men to have been chosen for this great deed. You will forever be known as martyrs for the great sacrifices you are making for your countries. You shall be recorded in history as the grand ones who saved the world." The message, met with smiles, handshakes, and hugs, stimulated the cells.

"We will inform the Americans tomorrow of their impending doom. We want them to feel the terror before it happens. Do not be afraid as you will be protected until the finish. The time for judgement is now, you are the executioner! The final steps begin! We are thankful for your heroic sacrifices, my brethren. We will all join you in paradise soon!"

As dawn approached, Zhao Wei made a final encrypted call. "Liang, it is time," he said. "You know what to do."

Liang Chen, a shadowy figure known for his impeccable record, acknowledged the order without hesitation. "Understood," he replied.

Ellie, continued to focus on the mission. Little did she know, the very people she trusted had marked her for death, ensuring no loose ends would remain.

"Purpose?" Ellie asked when Liang later arrived at the front door with a knock.

"You," Liang calmly said as he shot Ellie with two rounds in the chest. Her dishonesty and ruthless attempt at blindsiding her country had blinded her from the reality of the people she had chosen to band together with. Her visions of what the country needed to correct itself, faded from her eyes as did her life.

The United States stood on the brink of an unprecedented catastrophe, its citizens unaware of the terror that awaited them. The clock was ticking down, and the eruption of hell's fire was about to begin.

CHAPTER TEN
"Dawn of Destruction"

The morning of August 4th began like most other summer days had for Kyle. The sun rose, casting a warm glow over the trees, promising a beautiful day ahead. Kyle was outside early, enjoying a hot cup of coffee on the porch while watching two squirrels chase each other along some tree branches. His ears perked, as he began to listen intently, there was a different sound than he normally heard on the mountain each morning.

At first, it was just a faint hum in the distance, a low vibration that Kyle felt like was moving through the ground beneath his feet. Three massive military helicopters appeared crossing over the mountain ridge, dark and hulking shapes against the sky, their rotors chopping through the silence like distant thunder. As they came closer, the sound intensified, a relentless, pounding that rattled windows and seemed to shake the air. They flew in perfect formation, shadows skimming across the landscape below. For a moment, the entire scene was consumed in a whirling thunder, blades slicing through the sky like the beat of some enormous drum.

"Those are Chinooks," Kyle said aloud to himself as he watched the unusual scene. It was rare to see a military aircraft of any kind fly across this part of the country. The helicopters large twin rotors, one on the front and one on the back, cutting through the air with ease. "Why are they flying across here and I wonder what's inside of those? They could be carrying troops doing training missions or some type of cool cargo." Kyle told himself as he thought of all the different types of military gear they could be transporting.

And then, as quickly as they had come, the helicopters passed, the sound slowly fading as they continued onward. Their size and commanding presence dwindling to black dots before finally disappearing beyond the horizon. "That was cool," he said again as he stretched his back and then tossed the remaining coffee from his cup outwards onto the ground.

At the bottom of the mountain, Kyle's mother, Rachel, was glued to the television as usual. She typically tuned in to one of the major networks, as she didn't trust any single news source completely. Rachel often switched between channels, comparing their reports. This morning, she was watching the latest developments in a cyber-attack story that started yesterday, targeting credit card companies.

"As we continue to bring you updates on the developing story from yesterday, it was confirmed to be a cyber-attack. In addition to those attacks, multiple gas pipelines, water treatment facilities, hospitals and emergency systems have been hacked. Officials are asking for patience as they work to resolve these issues. Many banks are expected to be closed today until the situation is sorted out," reported the channel four news station.

Rachel sipped her coffee- a hot cup of Folgers made in her Mr. Coffee coffee maker. She liked cream but no sugar in her coffee. Specifically, she preferred Coffee-Mate powdered creamer, a habit she'd had for years. Kyle's sister Ginger had bought her a fancy Keurig, but Rachel didn't like it as much. She said it was a waste of money when she could make a whole pot for the price of one cup. The single cup portions did cost about the same price as an eight-cup pot so they never argued her point.

Rachel sipped her coffee and continued watching the news as the president blamed Republicans for the problems at the border. He was pointing his finger and trying to look tough, yelling, "Congress must do something now!" It was just a typical play Americans had gotten used to seeing from him. Another speech to push through a pork filled massive spending bill to help pad their pockets and reimburse close donor friends.

Rachel had watched this clip the night before, so it was nothing new to see. She was about to step outside for a cigarette when a loud, ear-splitting buzz burst from the sound bar. It was like the sound warning you that a test of the emergency broadcast system was being conducted. However, this was no test, not this time. She stopped before going outside, assuming they would announce who had committed the cyber-attacks.

"Good morning. This message is of extreme importance. It is with urgency that we bring you this. As you will see in the videos we are about to show, it is known as this time that the country has been attacked. We were given this video showing a masked person speaking. We will play it now and you should know that this video was received by our station nearly twelve minutes ago. We have been trying to authenticate it, and unfortunately, we now know it is a legitimate recording." The screen went blank for a moment before showing a masked figure. It was a hooded person with a black screen over their face, with the number four in white. Their face was hidden behind the dark mask.

This figure's voice was cold and mechanical as it began to speak, sending chills down Rachel's spine.

"To all citizens of the United States, this is four, representing a new alliance of four nations. Your country has been a virus to the world for far too long, spreading its influence and corruption. Today, we take the first step in eradicating your vile ways from this world.

"Already, we have infiltrated your most critical infrastructures. Gas pipelines, water treatment facilities, hospitals, and emergency systems are now under our control.

We have planted explosives in key locations across your nation. Major bridges, power plants, and oil refineries are rigged to detonate. You cannot stop this. It is too late. In ten minutes, we will begin the detonation sequence. Do not attempt to locate or defuse these bombs. Any interference will be met with immediate and deadly consequences.

We have no demands. Our goal is simple: the complete

destruction of the United States as you have known it. Many of you will not survive this day. Those who do will face a choice: submit to our new order or face annihilation.

Let this be your only warning. The era of American dominance is over. The world will watch as your nation crumbles, and a new order rises from its ashes. Prepare yourselves, for the end has come."

On the television screen, the male news anchor was clearly having trouble breathing. It appeared as though he was having a heart attack while on air, perspiration visible on his face and droplets on his bald head. He clutched his hand over his chest before the camera panned to a female anchor at the weather screen. She clearly was being spoken to in her earpiece based on her reaction before beginning to speak herself.

"The situation has been confirmed, and we know the United States military has gone into action. Troops are swiftly being immobilized to deploy, fighter jets have taken off from Nellis, Andrews and Langley Air Force bases. Police are trying to close entry onto several key roadways at this time," the news anchor reported urgently. "We've just received reports of an explosion ripping through a power plant in Baton Rouge. My god I can't believe this is happening,"

She was handed a paper from a staffer, her expression showing the fear overtake her facial expressions. "As news continues to pour in, the George Washington Bridge has been damaged due to explosives, sections have collapsed into the Hudson River. This is just incredibly sad right now. The Golden Gate Bridge in San Francisco has also fallen victim," she said looking off camera for confirmation of what she was reading.

Anyone watching could see the severity of the situation as a medic had run in front of the news reporter going over to the now fallen man. The camera panned, following the medic briefly before quickly returning to the reporter as she continued.

"In addition, we've been told two refineries in Texas are on fire following explosions. You are being told to take shelter without delay. We urge you to please get somewhere secure and remain until we know more. Please do not hesitate, seek shelter immediately. This is a rapidly developing crisis."

"Excuse me Haley, I need to interrupt," a voice said overtaking the reporter who paused nodding her head yes. "We are about to show you disturbing video from the Los Angelas International Airport. You can see, as the plane began to accelerate, the explosion rocked the runway on both sides. Those are chunks of concrete the size of small cars flying into the air. You see the plane veering off the runway, crashing into a ball of fire. We are told that President Hawkins, was indeed on Air Force One just now as it attempted to leave. We do not know his condition at this time, more to follow."

Rachel was looking at the news on the screen, her body frozen in shock. Her brain was telling her to move but her hands, arms and legs weren't cooperating. She took a deep breath and felt her body loosen again. Rachel nervously held the remote towards the tv and changed the channel, looking for more information on the chaos unfolding. Breaking news banners scrolled quickly along the bottom of the screen, confirming the collapses and explosions. Rachel grabbed her cell phone quickly, wanting to record this to show Kyle. She pointed the phone to the television and pressed the red button. There was no cell reception at her home but at least she could record with the phone.

"We repeat, there has been a catastrophic attack on our nation. Please seek shelter. The Golden Gate, George Washington and New River Gorge bridges have all been destroyed," the reporter stated, her eyes filled with tears ready to flow.

Where is the New River Gorge bridge located?" her colleague asked.

"It's in West Virginia, but this list is growing by the second," came the response.

"There are at least five oil refineries that have been attacked in Texas and Louisiana at this time. The Oroville Dam has been breached. Casualties are currently unknown. The country is under attack from terrorists. Please, seek ......" That was it, the screen went black, and the electricity went off.

Rachel momentarily remained standing, staring at the blank screen of the television. She was still holding the remote to the large sixty-five-inch Samsung television, that her kids got her for Christmas. She normally loved the big picture, but right now she wanted to throw it. She aimed the remote at the television and tried pressing the power button over and over as if what just happened didn't actually happen.

"You have to move," she told herself. She placed her cup down on the table, picked up the cordless phone and scanned her contacts. She dialed her daughter Susie's number, held the phone to her ear, hearing only three quick beeps indicating no signal. She was now panicking; how would she contact her daughters to warn them? Cell signal rarely ever worked in the mountains, and they sure weren't working today.

The electricity flickered back on, and Rachel powered up the television. The horrifying reports continued, not only the United States being targeted, but also other countries across the globe. They talked about Japan, Australia, South Korea, and Canada being targeted. She watched as various videos showing massive amounts of destruction from all over flashed across the screen. The urgency of the situation sinking in as repeated warnings to shelter in place continued to be announced. She again tried the phone, even with the electricity back on, there was no signal on the phone line.

Rachel thought of all the people at those locations, how many had been hurt or killed? She watched as one station began scrolling a running list of cities and towns that had been hit with an attack, both small and large. As she was beginning to grasp the reality before her, the electricity went off again.

Rachel quickly went to the front door and out onto the porch, looking towards the sky. "I don't know what I'm supposed to see out here. I've got to think, what do I need to do?" she whispered to herself. Retrieving her car keys, she would get Arnie, he was probably in bed asleep. Arnie, a teenager at eighteen, liked to stay up late playing video games and sleeping late into the day. Rachel slipped her shoes on, coming out the door again, seeing

Arnie running towards her already, out of breath.

"Hey Mamaw, did you see the news? We're under attack," Arnie blurted out while trying to catch his breath.

"I did Arnie, I was coming to find you," Rachel said back to him as he hugged her.

"I'm sure it's real, me and some friends were still online gaming this morning, we played all night. This guy that goes by Southern Discomfort as his gamer tag, said he had just heard a loud boom that sounded like an explosion. He told us there was a huge fire he could see that didn't look far away. Then we lost contact with him. He lives in Louisiana or Mississippi, somewhere like that," Arnie told Rachel before resuming.

"I thought he lost internet service. I turned the tv on, the emergency broadcast message broke in. Kyle told us one day it could happen Mamaw, you know he always said that," Arnie said looking at Rachel, awaiting orders on what to do.

Although he was twenty years younger than Kyle, the two had bonded closely after Kyle moved back. They would go fishing together, many times, not catching any fish, but they wouldn't tell anyone else that. They liked hunting together in the woods for deer and smaller game like squirrels and rabbits. Arnie liked the competition of doing better than his Uncle Kyle, but it was important to Kyle that he slipped a few survival skills into the day. Arnie wanted to go tell Kyle what was happening and get instructions on what they should do now.

CHAPTER ELEVEN

"Wheels of Urgency"

"Arnie," Rachel's urgent voice cut through the tense air, her eyes fixed on him. "Go up the mountain, find Kyle, and let him know what's happened. Take my phone—I recorded some news. He'll come down and help us figure out what to do next. And don't ride that motorcycle too fast; you know what Kyle has told you."

"I know, 'slow is smooth and smooth is fast,'" Arnie replied, already sprinting home to fetch his Honda CRF450 dirt bike.

Arnie had scrimped and saved for the bike after two summers of mowing lawns and clearing brush. Despite a few spectacular crashes in front of friends, he prided himself on his riding skills. Wheelies were his specialty, often earning him more attention than hill climbing. He flipped the kick starter giving it a quick thrust with his foot, the engine roaring to life beneath him. With a firm grip on the throttle and a smooth downshift, he kicked up a trail of dirt and rocks, propelling himself towards Kyle's cabin.

The trail up the mountain, despite efforts with a mini excavator, still bore scars from rainstorms. The deep ruts were dangerous, a lack of caution could catch a bike's front tire and send Arnie over the handlebars in an instant. Kyle had often urged him to trade the motorcycle for a safer ATV, advice Arnie mulled over as he ascended. "Slow is smooth, smooth is fast," he repeated, trying to slow his nerves as the roar of the screaming engine underscored the gravity of the situation.

Approaching the gate, Arnie anticipated it would be closed. As he rounded the final curve, he began easing off the throttle. True to expectation, the slide gate blocked the path. It rolled on wheels, its solar-powered motor humming faintly when it opened.

With no access to conventional electricity, Kyle had opted for solar panels and discreetly positioned battery packs scattered throughout the trees. Knox, a resourceful man in his sixties, had been instrumental in setting up these systems. After his wife left for a man she met over the internet, and his children moved away, Knox had embraced a homesteader's life. Arnie enjoyed Knox being around on projects, especially his ability for language that could rival any sailor's.

One side of the fence hugged the rocky hill where the road had been cut, presenting a daunting barrier to climbing over it. On the opposite side loomed a steep, lengthy drop-off, making any attempt to bypass the gate perilous. The risk of tumbling down the hill, a descent of roughly two hundred feet, far outweighed the possibility of circumventing the gate. This strategic positioning was one of the reasons Kyle had selected this site for his cabin, using these deliberate barriers against the unexpected.

Arnie fondly recalled the day they installed the security code device panel on the fence, laughing so hard that his sides ached the next day. Knox had relentlessly teased Kyle, imitating Arnold Schwarzenegger from his movies.

"Quick! Get to the choppa, Ahnie! To the choppa Ahnie!" Knox would shout in his best Schwarzenegger voice. "You know, Kyle, like the movie Commando."

"Knox, you moron, that line is from Predator, not Commando. The digital keypad you're thinking of is on his gun shed from Commando. Get your movies right, man!" Kyle finally corrected amidst their laughter at his expense.

"Well, slap the piss out of my dumbass for speaking," Knox quipped, adding, "Now, Ahnie, open the fancy digital box so we can get to the damn choppa. Do it before Kyle beats our ass at the no fun zone here at station Assville." Knox's infectious laugh drew Arnie into the laughter once again, earning him a strong side eye from Kyle.

"You jokesters keep clowning, this will come in handy one day," Kyle remarked with a smile, watching as Knox's basset hound dog lounged near the base of a tree. Kyle had been considering getting a dog himself but was undecided on the breed. He wanted a watchdog, yet one not overly aggressive that might mistake a family member for an intruder. He admired the appearance of a rottweiler but hesitated over its potential for mistaken aggression. He also liked Great Pyrenees for their protective instincts, though their size gave him pause.

"I'm going to start calling this place the Assville Plantation. Kyle works us like slaves," Arnie joked with Knox, provoking laughter.

"You can call it the Ass-kicking Plantation if you don't get back to work, 'cause I'm gonna kick both of yours," Kyle retorted playfully to Arnie and Knox.

"Focus, Arnie!" he chided himself as he straddled the motorcycle while leaning over to allow one foot to rest firmly on the ground while he looked at the keypad.. It seemed surreal that frivolous thoughts could intrude at such a serious moment. The country was under attack, yet Arnie couldn't shake the image of Knox teasing Kyle.

Arnie and Uncle Tom were the only ones, aside from Kyle, who knew the gate's access code. Arnie swiftly punched in the four digits on the pin-pad, the motor clicking as the gate began to open. Reflecting on it, the digital keypad, while cool, seemed unnecessary compared to a simple lock and key. It was one of the fun, Batman-like projects Kyle and Arnie had enjoyed developing with Knox's assistance. As soon as the gate opened wide enough for his bike, Arnie gunned the throttle, kicking up dirt and rocks as he sped through the opening.

Meanwhile, Kyle had been tending to his garden and had heard Arnie's bike approaching long before he arrived. They often visited each other, and Kyle was familiar with the sound. His heart raced a bit faster; he prepared himself to scold Arnie for his reckless speed on the trail. Was it just youthful exuberance, or was something wrong? What if his mother was ill? It was out of character for Arnie to ride so fast, especially this early in the morning on the final stretch to the cabin. The gate stood about a hundred and fifty yards from Kyle's cabin, and Arnie arrived abruptly, braking hard and sliding up next to Kyle.

"Hold on, Uncle Kyle, before you get on my shit, listen to me, it's serious," Arnie said urgently, struggling to remove his helmet while trying to preempt Kyle's scolding.

"It better be serious, little man. You looked like Evel Knievel just now," Kyle replied, his tone serious.

"You were right. Terrorists have attacked. Mamaw and I both saw it on the news. Here's her phone; watch it. It was on different stations, all with breaking news that bridges were destroyed, gas refineries were burning, and... and something else got attacked. The electricity went on and off a couple of times, and phones and internet are down too!" Arnie blurted out, his words rushing out faster than his brain could process.

"Hold on, Arnie, calm down. Electricity's out, phones and internet too?" Kyle asked, his tone steadying.

"It all went down while we were watching the news break. They were telling us what happened — a dam got hit. And Southern Discomfort, he saw fire and boom, just like you said, Uncle Kyle! You were right about everything!" Arnie's voice carried a mix of urgency and triumph, as if he'd cracked a puzzle.

"Southern Comfort? You been hitting the bottle, kiddo?" Kyle asked skeptically, half-joking, half-concerned about Arnie's state of mind.

"No, it's this gamer dude, Southern Discomfort, that's his gamer tag. He messaged us about the explosion, then everything went offline. The news broke saying we're under attack, to take cover — and bam, power's out. I ran to Mamaw's, she saw it too, told me to get you. I'm not messing around, Uncle Kyle, I swear. Watch the phone video. What do we do?" Arnie's words spilled out in a rush, I need to find my mom.

Kyle saw the genuine fear in Arnie's eyes, the trembling in his hands. His gut tightened; this was no joke. Something serious was happening, possibly linked to yesterday's credit card incident. Though he wanted more details from Rachel, he believed Arnie. Powering on Rachel's phone, he pulled up the latest video, watching intently.

Kyle swallowed hard, the urgency from the voice in the video sending chills down Kyle's spine. "Oh no," Kyle muttered grimly, replaying the message to ensure he caught every detail before switching off the phone.

"Okay, listen carefully. Drive back to Mom's. I need to grab some things. Uncover my truck, pull it out of the garage. Go on, be safe. I'll be there shortly," Kyle instructed, watching as Arnie fired up the bike and departed, this time without the dramatics of spinning the rear tire.

Hurrying inside, Kyle snatched a green duffel bag by the door, stocked with essentials: first aid, MREs, flashlight, handgun ammo, hatchet, small sleeping bag, and water bottles. Choosing his Kel-Tec KSG pump-action shotgun from the wall, he loaded it with slug rounds and double-ought buckshot from the bandolier hanging beside it. The last thing Kyle did was open a small safe hidden underneath a wall shelf that dropped down to reveal cash and two Glock 17 handguns. He skipped the Glock 17s, having one holstered already on his side, but picking up three stacks of cash, each containing one thousand dollars, tightly held together with rubber bands.

Outside, he tossed the duffel into his ATV's passenger seat and secured the shotgun and bandolier. He fired up the side by side, driving to one of his storage sheds, he removed three of the five-gallon gas jugs he had empty. He always kept twelve jugs cycling through them as needed. Securing them into the cargo carrier, he was ready to go see Rachel. He proceeded to the gate, closing it behind him. This was the moment the digital pad helped instead of fumbling with a key lock. Feeling anxious as to what awaited him, Kyle began to follow the trail to his mom's house. It would take him about ten minutes allowing time to formulate a plan for this situation. He had thought about this moment before, but that all went out the window as his anxiety churned. Kyle rode downhill, mapping out a plan that now felt scrambled amid the unfolding chaos.

CHAPTER TWELVE
"Preparations and Concerns"

Kyle approached his mother Rachel's house and saw that Arnie had the truck ready, just as Kyle had asked. Kyle owned a vintage 1978 Chevy C20 Silverado in a two-tone blue and light blue color scheme. Despite the truck's faded paint and rust spots around the bed, Kyle affectionately claimed they added character. The truck also sported a camper top, referred to by Arnie as an "old man camper top." It was equipped with a resilient V-8 motor that Kyle liked against electromagnetic pulses (EMPs), a precaution he deemed wise given the uncertain times. As of this time, it wasn't known if an EMP had been detonated or not. Kyle parked his ATV beside the garage, tossed his duffle into the truck bed, and placed both the shotgun and bandolier on the front seat.

"Kyle, what do you think is going on? Did you watch the video?" Rachel said, embracing her son. "This is real—it was on the news before the electricity cut out," she continued.

"Arnie briefed me. I saw the video you recorded. Any updates? Casualties?" Kyle asked, anticipating Rachel's response.

"They hadn't reported casualties yet, but that was before the blackout," Rachel replied.

"Uncle Tom swung by; he saw it all and headed to Fred's to top off his gas tank," Rachel added.

"Maybe Fred's got a generator and Uncle Tom can get some gas. That old grump at Creekside definitely has one," Kyle remarked.

"Have you heard from Megan, Susie, or Ginger?" Kyle inquired, concern for his sisters evident in his voice. Their close-knit family bond was more important now than ever.

"Susie stopped by with breakfast; she had no clue what was going on. She's checking on her store now. Ginger was at Stacy's overnight, babysitting. No word from her yet, but she should be heading home soon. Megan was out at a club last night; I'm not sure where," Rachel responded. Ginger rarely stayed away from home long; she often helped out her daughter Stacy, who worked overnight shifts at the jail.

"How much cash do you have on hand? I hope you took my advice and set some aside. Credit and debit cards are useless without electricity. If any stores are open, they'll only accept cash," Kyle reminded Rachel.

Kyle hoped his mother had followed his advice and stashed some cash away. He knew that cash would be invaluable in the immediate aftermath of an event like this. Banks wouldn't operate without power, and electronic money was worthless without access to networks. In these uncertain times, cash was king.

"I've got about two thousand dollars saved up, plus four cartons of cigarettes—enough to last twelve weeks," Rachel replied. "Arnie had mentioned going home to get gear, he said you two might be going somewhere."

Kyle had instructed his mother to rotate her cigarette supply, keeping some on hand for emergencies. Although Rachel didn't smoke much anymore, she still enjoyed a cigarette now and then to calm her nerves. How long would this situation last? Weeks, months, maybe even years? Kyle wasn't fond of his mother smoking, but her happiness mattered most to him. He knew she'd need those cigarettes to keep calm during these trying times.

"Alright, Mom, head to Fred's store. Stock up on cigarettes, water, medicine, canned food—anything you think we might need. If Fred's got generators, grab some gasoline and kerosene too. Load up on essentials like toilet paper, plates, cups, paper towels, baby wipes, and detergent. Spend every dollar you can. Ronald will probably be there to help load your items, we'll handle unloading when I get back," Kyle instructed.

"Okay, I can handle that," Rachel said confidently.

"I'm taking Arnie to check out stores in Hurley. Not many people may know what's happened yet, and those who do won't be able to communicate. Forget Facebook—no one's logging on to see what the neighbors are up to this morning. Head straight to Fred's and back here. You'll be safe; we'll be back in a few hours," Kyle reassured Rachel, who listened intently.

"Stay safe, Kyle, and watch out for Arnie. I know you've got his back, but don't let him do anything foolish," Rachel said, lighting a cigarette and taking a deep drag.

As Kyle walked back to the truck, Arnie emerged from his house. He'd changed into cargo pants like Kyle's, squeezed into a way too-small t-shirt, and had his red Fox racing hat on his head. A movie replica knife from the Rambo series hung on one hip, and a Glock on the other.

"What's with the outfit, Arnie? Looks like you went shopping with The Rock at Baby Gap. And you do know it's illegal to carry that handgun at eighteen, right?" Kyle teased, trying to lighten the mood. He knew the handgun was the least of their worries now. "Get in; we need to get moving," Kyle said to Arnie.

"You always say clothes should fit snug so they don't snag. Got the sidearm for protection, and with a mullet this cool, the hat's essential for keeping it safe. So, where are we headed?" Arnie asked, dead serious about his makeshift mullet.

"Snug shirts might restrict your blood flow," Kyle chuckled briefly before refocusing on the task at hand. He needed to keep Arnie calm; the boy's mother could be on the road.

"We'll hit up Creekside convenience store, the grocery, and the pharmacy. Then we'll swing by Susie's to find out about Ginger," Kyle said. Arnie hadn't mentioned his mother yet, but Kyle knew he was worried. Finding out where she was would ease Arnie's mind.

CHAPTER THIRTEEN

"Fueling Tensions"

Kyle and Arnie rolled into town, their first stop at Creekside Convenience. The small store, known for its reliable generator, was a lifeline during power outages to people of the small town. Pulling up to the pumps, Kyle felt relief seeing lights on inside—an indication they could get the gasoline they needed.

"You stay with the truck, Arnie. I'll be quick," Kyle instructed, stepping out and heading for the side entrance.

The doorbell jingled as Kyle pushed open the door. Inside, Johnny stood behind the counter—a well-known figure in town, respected and feared for his no-nonsense demeanor. His button-up shirt was neatly tucked into dark brown slacks, and the strong scent of Old Spice aftershave permeated the air.

"Good morning, sir. Are the fuel pumps working today?" Kyle asked, hoping for a straightforward transaction.

Johnny eyed him skeptically. "You seen the news? Gas is in short supply."

"Yeah, I heard. I've got cash," Kyle replied cautiously, sensing Johnny's sharp focus on profit.

"I take cash. Gas is ten bucks a gallon today. How much you need?" Johnny's tone was matter-of-fact, assessing Kyle's intent.

Kyle noticed Johnny's hand near the counter—possibly on a concealed switch to the fuel pumps or something else, hopefully not a weapon. He wasn't taking any chances that it was resting on the grip of a pistol, he wasn't looking for an altercation today.

"I need thirty gallons. I'll also take those four jugs on the shelf, plus twenty more gallons. That's fifty gallons total," Kyle stated firmly.

Johnny pondered for a moment. "Those jugs will cost you extra. Let's make it seven-fifty altogether. Show me the money or move on. No free rides here, and don't even think of robbing me either."

"No, sir, I'm not here to cause trouble. I've got the money," Kyle assured, counting out seven hundred and sixty dollars from his wallet. "Keep the extra ten for your hospitality."

Kyle thought to himself, "This old man just raised the price to seven hundred and fifty dollars. That's quite the price hike." It was obvious Kyle was the one about to be fleeced, but he couldn't help but smile at the transaction unfolding.

Johnny watched closely as Kyle picked up the dusty gas containers from the shelf. The jugs, covered in dust, looked like they hadn't been moved in years. Now, in a time of need, their price had skyrocketed. Kyle imagined some urbanite accusing Johnny of price gouging during an emergency, but to Kyle, it was simply supply and demand. Johnny had what he needed, it wasn't going to be cheap, and Kyle understood this. Turning towards the door, Kyle hurried out of the store and ran back to the truck.

"Start filling everything up—truck first, then the jugs," Kyle directed Arnie.

Arnie began pumping gas into the truck while Kyle noticed a newer model Ford F-150 pulling into the lot. The dark grey truck with a crew cab and a lift kit was caked in black coal dust and mud—clearly belonging to miners. Exiting the truck, Kyle confirmed the occupants were indeed coal miners, their reflective neon pants and coal-dusted faces giving them away. The driver, in his thirties, sported a worn trucker hat with a rooster emblem, while the older passenger, about sixty, limped with a hunched posture. His hairstyle—a bald spot with a long mullet—often called a "bullet."

"Good morning," the man with the rooster hat greeted as

he passed Kyle and Arnie. "Time for a cold one after a night of low coal crawling."

"Good morning," Kyle responded, keeping an eye on Arnie as he refueled.

"The power went out as we left the mines," the man with the rooster hat mentioned, a hint of concern in his voice.

"It's been out a couple of hours. Might be down for a while," Kyle added vaguely.

The man with the rooster hat headed towards the side entrance of the store. Kyle heard the bell jingle again and watched them disappear inside before turning back to Arnie, who was almost done with the gas jugs.

"Hurry up, Arnie," Kyle muttered under his breath, knowing there was no speeding up the process.

"I'm trying, it's slow," Arnie replied, glancing over at the miners' truck. "Those guys seemed okay."

"They seem okay, but trust no one right now, Arnie. Assume everyone's a threat until proven otherwise," Kyle cautioned.

Another vehicle pulled into the lot—a battered late '90s Ford Mustang. The white convertible with faded paint and a stained tan top and patched rear window looked like it hadn't seen a wash in years. The rumbling exhaust hinted at serious wear and tear.

In the passenger seat sat a woman in her thirties, though years of hard living made her look older. Her light red hair fell past her shoulders, her thin face and damaged teeth revealing a rough life, likely entangled with meth addiction.

"There is some Meth-Americans," Arnie said to Kyle as the car stopped next to them.

"Meth-Americans?" Kyle asked curiously.

"Yeah, that's what we call them now. The meth heads around here," Arnie replied back.

"Get me some Marlboro Lights," the red-haired woman instructed the towering man climbing out of the Mustang. At nearly six and a half feet tall and solidly built, he wore jeans and a sleeveless flannel shirt, looking over at Kyle and Arnie with a nod before heading into the store.

As he opened the door, the bell chimed again. Kyle glanced over to see the two coal miners exiting the store, clearly displeased the normality of a routine day had been disrupted.

"That bastard wants fifteen bucks a gallon, claiming a shortage," the man with the rooster hat informed Kyle. "And no biscuits this morning. We always grab breakfast here. This is bullshit—I ain't paying fifteen bucks for gas."

Kyle caught the price—fifteen bucks per gallon. The old man had already hiked prices, likely after seeing Kyle pay ten dollars without hesitation.

As Arnie finished filling the last jug, Kyle stood between him and the miners, his hand near his Glock, not wanting trouble, but preparing for it.

"You're buying a lot of gas, my friend," the older man remarked.

"And I paid a lot for it, took all my money," Kyle retorted, not wanting them to think he had more money.

"We ain't paying that. We're heading to Fred's. This old bastard can go to hell," the older man declared loudly.

"How about sharing one of those jugs? Looks like you've got more than you need," a deep voice spoke behind Kyle. It was the flannel-shirted man, now standing beside him.

"You didn't get my cigarettes, Allen," the red-haired woman complained from the car.

"The old man's charging double now. Can't afford it," Allen replied.

Kyle inwardly cursed himself for not noticing the hulking man approach. Arnie stood tensely, unsure of what might happen. The other miners knew Allen Hall—he was trouble, with a rap sheet full of drug-related arrests and assaults on officers. His cousin, the county attorney, always managed to get him out of legal dilemmas.

"Sorry, but we need this. People are counting on it. Hop in, Arnie. Let's go," Kyle said, tightening the lid on the last jug.

"Take it easy y'all," Arnie called out as he climbed into the truck and shut the door.

"How about that gas, buddy? We could use a jug," Allen pressed, stepping onto the concrete pad that separated the pumps and placing his hand on Kyle's door holding it shut.

"The station has gas. Buy all you want. Now, please move your hand. We need to leave," Kyle said firmly, reaching for the door handle.

"We don't have money like you seem to. Hey, Arnie, tell your buddy we need to borrow a jug," Allen continued, moving closer to Kyle. He didn't seem deterred by Kyle's six-foot, two-inch stature, weighing two hundred and forty pounds. Kyle was in great shape for a forty-year old.

"He's my uncle, Kyle. Like he said, it's not all ours," Arnie interjected, his hand moving closer to his Glock.

"Get in the car, Allen. I need some damn cigarettes," the red-haired woman demanded.

"Let it go, Allen. We're heading to Fred's for gas. Follow us. No need for trouble," the older man with the bullet advised calmly hoping to prevent a fight from happening.

"That's right, Allen. Let it go," Kyle added, locking eyes with Allen, a hint of challenge in his voice. It was a side of Kyle he'd left behind—a darkness only he knew the depths of.

"What's it gonna be, Allen? Step aside or try something stupid?" Kyle asked softly, a veiled invitation.

CHAPTER FOURTEEN
"Disrupted Routine"

Susie hurried to her clothing store after Rachel's explanation about the attacks, unsure of the severity. She wasn't one to follow the news or worry much about world affairs, preferring the hustle of her shop where she bought and sold all kinds of apparel, new and used. A social butterfly, Susie loved interacting with people, whether out bowling, playing Bingo, or dancing with friends at Teddy Bears Bar & Dance in Phelps, Kentucky—a nickname given by Kyle for their dance crew, the "Grinding Grannies."

Standing in her shop's center, Susie debated opening without electricity. Cash customers might still come in, but if Rachel was right about the chaos outside, business might be slow. She paced, straightening racks of shirts and dresses, her mind racing with uncertainty.

Deciding to open, Susie unlocked the door and flipped the sign to 'Open'. "The early bird gets the worm," she murmured, rearranging items on shelves in hopeful preparation.

"I better grab a few things for the car, just in case this outage lasts," she reasoned aloud, collecting blankets and candles and placing them by the door. A growing unease gnawed at her stomach, perhaps from the dim, quiet store. There was a small amount of light permeating through the glass door, just enough to maneuver in the space safely.

The door chime jingled, "bumble bee," the sound her son Joel told her it made when going off. Susie looked up to see Alice, a regular customer, enter with a cigarette between her lips—a breach of Susie's no-smoking rule. Alice had the look of a woman who had been through the wringers of life. She was in her mid - sixties and wore a rough scowl on her face showing every year of her age. Alice smoked often, but normally would toss her cigarette to the ground and grind out the burning tobacco with her foot before entering.

"No smoking in here, Alice. Step outside, please," Susie reminded her gently.

"Damn, Susie, why you gotta be a bitch today? Enough's gone wrong," Alice retorted, but complied, tossing the cigarette outside before reentering.

"Bumble bee," the chime sounded again as Alice's daughter, Janet, followed behind, maintaining the family's rugged demeanor. She was thirty-five, good hygiene wasn't something to accuse her of having.

Susie wedged the door open with a stopper, eyeing the increasingly uneasy Alice and Janet. Her tension spiked when she spotted Kyle and Arnie driving by, Kyle honked the horn with Arnie waving from the window. Something felt off, her awareness heightened.

"Now Alice, I'm good to you. But you ever call me a bitch again and I'll make you eat that damn cigarette. Just because the electricity is out don't mean smoking is allowed, and it sure as shit don't mean you're going to call me that!" Susie said as she could feel her face turn red from anger. She would toss this woman to the ground in a hurry and her daughter as well if need be.

"Janet, look around while I talk to Susie," Alice instructed abruptly, surprising Janet with her directness.

"I know you're good, Susie. I'm just on edge. I'm sorry for saying that," Alice softened. "Don at the bank is being an asshole to everybody, he won't let me in for cash. Earl at the grocery store won't give us any credit. We're stuck."

Susie's mind flashed to Kyle's warnings about banks and cash, feeling a sting of regret for not listening better. "Why didn't I pay more attention?" She remembered him telling her how cash would be king, but only for a short period of time. "Why didn't I listen better?"

"What do you mean?" Alice asked, puzzled.

"I was thinking about something. I'm sorry, I don't do store credit, Alice," Susie replied firmly, while watching Robert and Horrace Barker now loitering outside, likely up to no good. The two brothers stood together rocking side to side as they scanned the nearby homes and businesses.

"Morning, Susie," James greeted as he entered, acknowledging the tension in the room and the Barkers' suspicious presence. James was the landlord over Susie's business, and also her friend. He owned a small pawn shop business himself that he hadn't opened today. He mainly opened it for a place to gossip about the local news with his retired buddies who regularly came by.

"Glad to see you, James," Susie replied, grateful for his presence. The situation with Alice and Janet felt increasingly volatile. "I see the Barker brothers hanging out."

"They're trouble, those two," James observed, eyeing the Barkers. "I don't trust them. They asked me to borrow money already, don't let them if they ask you."

"How do rich folks think we'll survive if they won't help?" Alice erupted in frustration. "I'll trade my food stamp card for cash—three hundred on it, I'll take two hundred. Anyone?"

"I'm sorry, Alice. You need to go, get yourself home in case it gets dangerous." James interjected gently, gesturing towards the door.

"Keep your trashy ass shit!" Janet shouted, tossing some clothing towards the counter before moving towards the door with Alice. Once Janet was positioned between James and her mother, Alice snatched up two of the bags containing blankets Susie had planned to put in her car, running off with them.

Susie dashed after them, shouting, "I'll see you again, and

I'll whip your damn ass all around this parking lot when I do!"

"Settle down, Susie," James urged, pulling her back inside. "Lock up. It's not safe. I'll watch your place. There is nothing here worth fighting over, robbed or possibly even killed for."

"I'll wait for Kyle, I'm sure he will stop by when he comes back this way," Susie insisted, scanning the street for her brother's truck, her anxiety mounting.

CHAPTER FIFTEEN
"The Thin line of Loyalty"

"Hey Sheriff, do you need anything before we get started?" Officer Langston asked, glancing at the checklist Sheriff Ramey was reviewing with the receptionist. There was tension buzzing about the room, the weight of unease hanging heavily.

"No, I'm good. Please get everyone into the meeting room. I'll be right there," Ramey replied, his tone firm but weary. The weight of the morning's events pressing down hard on his shoulders.

"Just so you know, Sheriff, several officers are saying they're leaving. They don't care about this office right now," Langston said, turning away, his voice stained with a hint of satisfaction.

"What's Ramey calling this meeting for?" Officer Thompson, with his brow creased, asked Langston as he approached the second-floor hallway after exiting the elevator.

"Because it's what Ramey does. He doesn't care about us. This is about him keeping his job secure in the community. He wants to show voters he has us keeping the place safe," Langston said to the officers gathered outside the meeting room, his words dripping with disdain.

"I'm not worried about Ramey's job. I'm worried about making sure my wife and kids are okay. I don't even want to be here for this meeting," Officer Justus said, his voice cracking with anxiety, his eyes looking towards the exit sign.

"I don't blame you, man. I'd go make sure they were safe. If you want to, take off. I'll tell Ramey," Langston replied, placing a reassuring hand on Justus's shoulder. The hallway felt suffocating, the gravity of the situation weighing on each officer.

"I'm leaving then. Take care of yourself, Langston, and thank you," Justus said, his relief unmistakable. He looked back briefly, seeing the worry and confusion on the faces of his colleagues, preparing to step through the exit door.

"I'll let Ramey know I told you to take off a few days. It will be fine," Langston said with a reassuring nod.

Officer Thompson raced to join Justus, only tossing up his hand for a final wave goodbye. The pressure to be with their families was overwhelming. Traffic tickets and minor infractions were the last things on their minds. Two more officers joined for a brief discussion before walking away together. Langston watched them with a satisfied smile, then walked inside the meeting room. Sheriff Ramey had not shown up yet. Only eighteen officers were present out of the thirty-six on the department staff. It was uncertain how many would come to work versus choosing to stay at home.

"Can you all believe Ramey wants to put us in a meeting right now? He could have said this over the radio. The country is being attacked, and he is worried about covering his ass for votes. I'm not leaving my family to fend for themselves just to protect his job," Langston said to the group, his voice rising with false frustration. The officers nodded in agreement, their faces tense and anxious. The room felt like a powder keg ready to explode.

"What are we supposed to do, quit? I need my job, but I also need my family," an officer in the back spoke up, his voice marked with desperation. He wiped sweat from his face, the fear of the unknown gnawing at him.

"Ramey thinks the job comes first. He isn't worried about our families unless he knows they are voting for him," Langston continued, stoking the flames of dissent, his eyes gleamed with ambition.

"Okay, Samantha, thank you for your help this morning. You get home and make sure your kids are okay. I'm going to go start this meeting. I want everyone checking in on their families, then we can do police work. We will juggle it the best we can," Sheriff Ramey said to the receptionist, his voice softening with genuine concern.

He knew his officers' first concern would be their own families. That was one of the reasons for this meeting. He wanted them to make sure they took care of their families and could help where they could with the job. However, in the meeting room, Langston was manipulating the officers. His ultimate goal was to get Ramey fired and take the Sheriff's position for himself. Even amid an attack on the country, he couldn't see past his own desires.

"Good morning, officers. As everyone is aware now, we had a major attack on our country this morning. We will have to work double time right now as we attempt to keep control," Sheriff Ramey said to the eighteen officers, his voice steady but his eyes betraying his worry. The fluorescent lights flickered overhead, the buildings old generator struggling to keep working, adding to the uneasy atmosphere.

"What are we supposed to do about our families right now?" asked an officer who stood defiantly with arms crossed, his jaw set in a hard line.

"This is a rare event, and I'm sure everyone has questions like this. You need to make sure your family is safe, but we have a job to do as well," Ramey replied, trying to maintain authority. He could feel the tension in the room, like a wire ready to snap.

"Screw this, I'm out. I quit," another officer said, standing up abruptly and walking out. His footsteps echoed in the silence of the hall, a reminder of the crumbling morale.

"Yeah, me too. I quit. State police have already said towns are falling across the state this morning. I have a family to worry about," another one said and followed suit.

"Hang on, everyone. This is not what I want you to do," Ramey said, his voice rising in desperation. He could feel his control quickly slipping away.

"We're out," said two officers together, their defiance clear. They had exchanged glances, their silent agreement to abandon their post clear.

"Everyone, please. This is not the answer right now. The people in our communities still need us; they need our help," Ramey pleaded, his voice breaking. He watched as an officer stood, removed his badge, and tossed it onto the table where Ramey stood. Three more followed suit. Ramey looked down at the floor, shaking his head in disbelief. The weight of the badges felt heavy with betrayal.

With only ten officers remaining, Ramey was at a loss for words. "Why is everyone so quick to quit?" he mumbled, mostly to himself. The silence of the room was deafening.

"Anyone else?" Ramey asked the remaining officers. "For those of you still here, this is going to be a bad situation for everyone. I want you to check on your families. Once your family is secure, please go to your town's center or post office. I'm not sure what is going to happen right now with gasoline, so conserve what you have as long as possible. I don't want anyone putting themselves in a dangerous position; just be a presence."

"Are we making arrests right now?" asked an officer who leaned calmly against the wall with his arms crossed.

"I'm being honest with you when I say this. As of right now, the last communication I received was that the jailors were leaving. The inmates are being set free from Haysi Regional," Ramey said. "And as for the prison at Keene Mountain, I was told they had a plan to handle the hard-core prisoners."

"So what about arrests?" the officer asked again.

"As of right now, I would say no to arrests. I don't want any of you putting yourselves in danger when we can't provide backup or even emergency services," Ramey responded.

"What do we do if we see a crime committed? A major crime like murder?" another officer asked.

"You can attempt to make an arrest, but honestly, I would suggest you defend yourself. There will be no punishment for officer-involved shootings. I hope you understand that," Ramey said, receiving nods in return. The gravity of the statement hung heavy in the room.

"Is Martial Law being declared?" Officer Vanover asked, sipping his coffee nonchalantly.

"No, Vanover, not yet it hasn't. And be aware of this in your communities if anyone tries to do it themselves," Ramey said, feeling the weight of his responsibilities growing with each passing moment.

"If you get in trouble, let us know. If I can get to you, I will be there. I was told we would not see any backup officers from the state or national guard anytime soon. This is a bad situation, folks. Please stay safe," Ramey said, his voice filled with a mix of determination and desperation. The room felt colder, the reality of their situation sinking in more and more.

"I can't believe we lost eight officers just like that," Langston said to Ramey, staying behind after the meeting.

"Go on to Hurley and check on those folks. Be careful about using Supervisor Tate for any assistance. It will come back to haunt us if we do," Ramey said to Langston. He had a gut feeling there was more to the officers quitting, and he didn't trust Langston. The guy always seemed to be up to something; he just couldn't prove it. And right now, he didn't have time to figure it out; there were bigger fires to deal with.

As Ramey walked back to his office, Vanover waited for him. Vanover was a single guy, with no immediate family. He had moved here years ago and liked the county, so he stayed.

"Sheriff, watch your back. I don't trust Langston. I'll be at Garden Creek if you need me. Take care of yourself," Vanover said as he walked away without waiting for a response from Ramey. The Sheriff rubbed his chin as he thought about what Vanover had said; he had felt it himself.

CHAPTER SIXTEEN

"Gathering Storm"

At Creekside Convenience Kyle held his stare on Allen, ready to defend against an assault attempt. "You can keep it, for now," Allen said, stepping back from Kyle's truck and withdrawing his hand slowly from the door. He circled the front of his Mustang with deliberate steps.

"Get in the truck, let's get the hell out of here," the man in the rooster hat ordered the bullet-headed man.

"We'll be seeing you," Allen called out to Kyle, leaning casually against his weathered Mustang.

Kyle climbed into the truck, turning the ignition key while keeping his gaze fixed on Allen. He chose not to respond to Allen's parting words, although his face seemed to say enough.

"Hellfire, Uncle Kyle, I didn't know if things were about to blow up," Arnie exclaimed as Kyle steered away from the station onto the road. "That guy's always trouble, dealing drugs and picking fights. I'm surprised he didn't start one just now," Arnie remarked, eyebrows raised in concern.

"Keep your eyes peeled, buddy. That problem won't vanish. We'll cross paths with him again," Kyle warned Arnie, scanning the road ahead as they approached town. The country road seemed quieter than Kyle would have thought it to be, heightening his unease.

"Here's the list of items to look for. Stick it in your pocket," Kyle instructed Arnie, passing him a folded slip of paper from his shirt pocket. "Maybe we can stock up before things go haywire," Kyle mused aloud as they drove past Susie's store. He honked the horn, and Arnie waved to Aunt Susie.

"First, let's hit the pharmacy and grocery store, then we'll swing by Susie's. It looks quiet now, but who knows," Kyle suggested, eyeing the storefronts cautiously.

"I only saw one lady outside and another at the door, I think," Arnie reported to Kyle.

"Let's make it quick, then, little buddy," Kyle said, ruffling Arnie's hair lightly.

"Easy on the hair dude!" Arnie said pulling his head back from Kyle's hand. "Kyle, look at the bank. Looks like trouble's brewing," Arnie warned as they pulled into the pharmacy beside the crowded bank. A crowd had gathered, banging on the locked doors in desperation.

"You have to give us our money!" a man shouted, pounding the glass door with his fist.

"It's my money! I want it now!" a woman yelled at the bank manager through the glass.

"The electricity's out; we can't access anything. I'm sorry, please come back later," the manager explained nervously to the growing crowd.

"The news said the power won't be back. We need our money now, Don!" another woman protested loudly.

Kyle parked the truck at the pharmacy, keeping an eye on the bank commotion as he stood beside his truck door.

"I'll handle this alone, Arnie. Slide over and keep the truck ready," Kyle instructed, closing the door and moving with purpose toward the pharmacy entrance.

Arnie obeyed, shifting to the driver's seat. The area around the pharmacy was eerily quiet, with only a few futile attempts by passing cars to check the closed pharmacy.

Kyle knocked several times on the pharmacy door, waiting anxiously for a response. Finally, a young pharmacist cautiously approached but refused to unlock the door.

"I need supplies. I have cash," Kyle pleaded, displaying a

handful of twenty-dollar bills through the glass.

"Sorry, sir. No entry without power. Come back later," the pharmacist replied apologetically.

Kyle shook his head, frustrated as he thought about the medicines and supplies just beyond the door. "I understand, thank you." He turned and galloped across the street.

"Arnie, bring the truck. Let's load up," Kyle called out, jogging toward the grocery store entrance.

Arnie parked and locked the truck, joining Kyle at the store entrance. A sign read, "No electricity – Cash only – Perishable Items half price."

"Sorry gentlemen, no weapons inside," Earl, the store manager, greeted them, eyeing Kyle's holstered guns cautiously. His name tag and uniform immediately created an image of a television cartoon character to Kyle. His dingy yellow button up shirt, with a faded brown tie hanging a button too short above his waist.

"I have cash. The guns are for protection," Kyle assured, flashing two stacks of bills to Earl.

"How much are you spending?" Earl asked, eyeing the cash stacks hungrily.

"All of it, if we can keep our guns," Kyle replied firmly.

"Okay, but keep them holstered," Earl agreed, smiling at the sight of the cash.

"Grab what's on the list, Arnie. We're on a tight schedule," Kyle directed, pushing a shopping cart toward his nephew.

"Toilet paper, plates, plastic utensils, and paper towels," Arnie read aloud, swiftly gathering the items. He moved on to canned goods, listing, "Green beans, pinto beans, sardines, canned fruits, and tomatoes. Rice, flour, cornmeal, sugar, coffee, creamer. Got it!"

Kyle filled another cart with medical supplies, toiletries, flashlights, batteries, and duct tape. He added trash bags, charcoal, lighter fluid, bleach, and detergents, glancing at Arnie who eyed the gallon-size jars of hot sausages and Slim Jims with amazement. Packs of Hershey bars and marshmallows completed their list.

"Why the big haul?" a curious young man asked, eyeing their loaded carts.

"Hey, Grady! This is my Uncle Kyle," Arnie introduced proudly. "We're stocking up for a while."

"There's a lot here without scanners," Earl remarked as he attempted to add up their purchases on a calculator, winking at Kyle. "About a thousand bucks worth."

"Phyllis, get me a legal pad from my office," Earl instructed the cashier, preparing for the large transaction.

"We're in a rush, Earl. Also, we'll need four propane tanks. Can you unlock the cage outside?" Kyle requested.

"Grady, bag the loose items fast and take them to their truck. Unlock the propane cage while you're out," Earl instructed Grady, who worked swiftly alongside Arnie.

"Some people are too nosy, I don't have legal pads in my office so that will keep her busy. How much you think? Twelve hundred?" Earl asked Kyle privately.

"Sounds right, but I'll take all those Virginia Slims cigarettes as well. Here is two grand and you can keep the change," Kyle proposed, flashing the cash at Earl, who eagerly agreed.

"Deal. Thanks. Stay safe out there," Earl said, pocketing the extra cash discreetly.

Arnie and Grady loaded the truck as Kyle brought out six propane tanks from the unlocked cage. He stacked them carefully in the truck bed, preparing for the worst.

"Thanks, Grady. Get home safe; things are about to get unpredictable," Kyle advised.

"Arnie mentioned that. I'm loading up and heading out," Grady replied, grateful for their advice.

"You know where to find me if you need anything. Take care, buddy," Arnie said, embracing his friend warmly.

"That's six tanks, Uncle Kyle. You told Earl four," Arnie pointed out sympathetically.

"We take what we can get. If I could have gotten more I

would have, but that's all they had. With no power, stores will be looted soon," Kyle explained, jumping back into the truck.

Bam! Crack! Kyle whirled around at the sound of breaking glass, eyes narrowing as he saw the pharmacy's front door glass shattered.

Kyle watched as an angry man grabbed the anti-theft bars on the door and shook at it wildly. "You can go to hell, Dewayne! Give me what I need!" He yelled, now throwing rocks at the barred windows. The pharmacist stood helplessly behind the safety bars, the situation escalating dangerously. The angry man pulled and kicked at the anti-theft bars protecting the door. Arnie could tell Kyle was pondering whether to intervene and help the pharmacist.

"Let's go, Uncle. It's not our problem. We have people to protect," Arnie urged, tugging gently at Kyle's sleeve.

Kyle nodded reluctantly, proud of Arnie's maturity in a tense moment. He knew emotions could be dangerous, especially now. He had told Arnie so many times how emotions could get him killed, to be smart and tactful in his decisions.

"You're right, Arnie. Let's check on Susie. She needs our help," Kyle agreed, shifting into gear and driving toward Susie's store.

CHAPTER SEVENTEEN
"Tension's Rise at Fred's Gas"

Fred's Gas n Go was a small hometown store that many in the community frequented for their gas and beer needs. The business was a small, rustic establishment that had served as a cornerstone of the community for over forty years. The weathered wooden exterior, covered in faded advertisements, gave the store its charm. Fred advertised three main items, Gas, Beer, and Lottery tickets.

Inside, the store was lined with narrow aisles, stocked with a diverse mix of goods. Colorful racks of snacks and candy flanked the aisles greeting customers as they entered. Refrigerated coolers hummed softly, keeping bottled drinks chilled. The aroma of freshly brewed coffee mingled with the scent of gasoline, creating a unique and comforting atmosphere. Near the entrance, a modern, yet old cash register sat on a worn wooden counter. It was behind this counter that Fred conducted his business with a warm smile and a quick wit.

The store had a deli, a popular spot for locals, featuring a glass display case filled with homemade burgers, hotdogs, and pizzas. The deli's menu, handwritten on a chalkboard, boasted of the best hotdogs in town. Behind the deli counter, a small kitchen area buzzed with activity as Fred and his staff prepared food with great efficiency.

The store's ambiance was enhanced by the cluttered bulletin board near the entrance, plastered with flyers for community events, lost pet notices, and advertisements for local services. A couple of wooden benches and picnic tables outside the store provided a casual gathering spot for patrons to relax, share stories, and enjoy a cigarette. Fred's Gas n Go was more than just a store; it was a social hub where friendships were forged, news was exchanged, and the heartbeat of the community could be felt.

Fred Johnson was a fixture in the community, a man who seemed to embody the spirit of the small town he had served for over four decades. At 70 years old, Fred was a wiry figure with a lifetime of hard work etched into his weathered face. Fred's silver hair was always neatly combed, and he sported a well-maintained beard that gave him a distinguished yet approachable look.

Despite the long hours he put into running the store, Fred was always quick with a smile and a friendly word for anyone who walked through his doors. His voice, gravelly yet warm, had a reassuring tone that made customers feel instantly at ease. He had a knack for remembering names, faces, and the little details about people's lives. Fred's hands, calloused and strong, were a testament to his hardworking nature. Whether he was flipping burgers in the deli, fixing a fuel pump, or jotting down a customer's credit in his old-fashioned ticket book, he did so with a meticulous care that showed his dedication to his craft. He moved with a deliberate pace, unhurried but efficient.

Behind the counter, Fred kept an old office chair, its leather arms worn away to reveal the hard plastic beneath. He referred to its slight wobble as his "trademark old man wobble" and used it to slide around the counter with ease. His revolver, a Taurus Defender .38, was always within reach, a silent reminder that Fred was ready to defend his store and its patrons if ever the need arose. Fred was happy the pistol had collected more dust than fingerprints over the years.

Fred's kindness extended beyond his business practices. He often let people run a tab, understanding that hard times could fall on anyone. His simple credit system was based on trust and a belief in the inherent goodness of people. While some took advantage, most paid their dues, and Fred rarely had to remind them.

Fred knew everyone in the area, their children, and their grandchildren. Despite the volume of beer he sold, he tried to keep the drunks away with a prominent "No Open Alcohol on Premises" sign. Most patrons respected the rule, but there was always the occasional troublemaker who couldn't wait to crack open a cold beer. These individuals often ended up causing altercations, sometimes resulting in a punch being thrown. By the time the police arrived, the trouble had usually passed, leaving only a bit of blood from a smashed nose or split lip on the ground.

Today, however, was different. A steady stream of vehicles arrived at Fred's, their drivers hoping to get fuel and beer. Even in the face of the looming crisis, alcoholics remained focused solely on their next drink. They would be in luck as Fred was open for business, accepting cash only, with a sign stating this fact on his door.

Fred had two small generators to keep the coolers and freezers running for his deli, but he didn't have a backup generator for the fuel pumps, rendering them out of service. A sign on the pumps stated they were temporarily out of gas. The fuel truck, which was supposed to refill the tanks, hadn't arrived that morning, so Fred wasn't trying to sell gas. He assumed the power outage was temporary and would be resolved by tomorrow.

As Fred's customers came and went, news of the day's events spread. Men stood in small groups, discussing what they had heard or seen on television. Others sat on the benches or picnic tables, smoking cigarettes as if the crisis was just a minor inconvenience that would soon pass. While everyone knew something significant had happened, the severity of it had not yet sunk in. Many acted as if the situation would be resolved by the end of the day, unaware of the lives lost and the extent of the damage and devastation.

Glancing out the window at the men standing together, Fred shook his head slowly. He watched as arms flailed and the men laughed and told stories. Fred noticed a lifted, dirty gray truck pull into the station and park at the pumps. When a man stepped out of the driver's side, Fred recognized him. "That's Ricky Taylor's boy," he muttered, watching the young man walk towards the store entrance. The man stopped to speak with the others at the bench in front of the store. Fred assumed from his coal-covered face that he was just getting off work.

An old, dirty white Mustang followed. "That looks like trouble," Fred said, recognizing the car. He knew Allen and that the only time Allen visited his store was to do drug deals in the lot after dark. Fred continued to watch as the young man in mining pants came into the store.

"How are you doing, Fred?" asked the man with the rooster hat. "Got any gas? We're running low."

"Sorry, son. The fuel truck hasn't come today, and even if it had, I have no power to run the pumps. You're one of Ricky's boys, ain't you?" Fred responded.

"Yeah, Ricky's my dad. I'm Samuel, the youngest. Daddy's out in the truck now. He's getting slower with age; the coal mine is tough on his body. We stopped at Creekside earlier, and that crazy ass Johnny wanted fifteen dollars a gallon for gas," Samuel said.

"That sounds like Johnny, always trying to screw somebody over. But at this point, that's your best bet on this side of the mountain. The phones are still out, so I don't know if we're getting a fuel truck today. And again, even if it does come, I'm not sure when the power will be back on," Fred told Samuel as they both peered out the window at the Mustang.

"That's Allen Hall out there, Fred. He can be trouble. I just watched him almost start a fight with some guys at Creekside. He wants gas and who knows what else. You want me to stay in here for a few minutes with you?" Samuel asked, concerned.

"No, thank you, son. I know who that is, and I know he's trouble. I've dealt with his kind before. Take care and stop back in to see me again. Tell your daddy I said hello," Fred told Samuel.

As Samuel left the store, walking towards his truck, he was stopped midway by Allen.

"They got gas here?" Allen asked.

"No, man. Fred said the fuel truck hasn't run today, and he has no power anyway. I'm heading home; I'm beat. I'll figure it out later," Samuel said, starting to walk away. Allen grabbed Samuel by the arm, squeezing tightly to ensure he didn't get away. He jerked Samuel back hard enough that the rooster hat fell from his head onto the ground.

"Give me some money before you go. I'll pay you back sometime," Allen demanded with a menacing look.

"Allen, I don't have any money on me. I have about ten dollars in cash, and that's it. I'd help you out if I had it," Samuel said, choking out the words and looking toward his truck. He saw his father, Ricky, sitting at attention and holding the 30-30 caliber Remington deer rifle, aiming straight at Allen's back. Samuel waved his arm toward his father to put the gun down.

Allen turned his head towards the truck to see the old man holding the rifle. Although Ricky had pulled the barrel to the side, he kept a tight grip, ready to shoot Allen if necessary.

"It looks like your old man means business. You coal miners make plenty of money. Go tell him I need to borrow some," Allen said, slowly loosening his hold on Samuel's arm. The other men had quickly gotten into their vehicles and left when they saw Allen grab Samuel by the arm.

Fred stood up from his chair, pulling his Taurus Defender .38 revolver. Fred had a sign on his door that read, "I carry. I'm too old to fight and too young to die," with a picture of a gun barrel.

"Okay, man, relax a little. I'll go see what I got in the truck," Samuel said, bending over to pick up his rooster hat and knocking the dust from it. He placed it on his head, adjusting the fit as he walked towards the truck. He opened the door, stepped up into the cab, and removed twenty dollars from his wallet.

"Allen is high on dope and wants to borrow money. I'm going to give him this, and we'll leave," Samuel said to his father, still clutching the rifle.

"To hell with that. Shut the door, start this truck, and let's go," Ricky said. "Otherwise, I'll shoot that son of a bitch dead right

94

here."

Samuel looked at his father, knowing he was serious. Ricky was holding the rifle, clearly ready to shoot Allen if needed. It was one of those moments that would be for the best if it happened, yet Samuel didn't want his dad to do it. Allen was not the type of person anyone would want to deal with during a crisis. Samuel started the truck, pulled the door shut, and shouted, "Sorry, Allen, we're broke right now," before exiting the parking lot.

Allen stood motionless, watching them drive out of sight. "You better hope I don't see you again," he muttered.

CHAPTER EIGHTEEN
"Axel and Vince – Seizing the Moment"

"Get up, Vince," Axel said sharply as Vince lay sprawled asleep on the couch. "Wake up, man! The power's going off and on," Axel urged Vince with his foot, his big buddy oblivious to the flickering lights.

"Power's out?" Vince muttered, partially dazed after being awoken from his deep sleep. Slowly, he sat upright on the couch, blinking as he tried to make sense of Axel's words. "How long has it been out?"

"Just went back off again. It's gone off and on a couple of times already. I was watching that show on MTV, with the short girl that likes to party. The news alert came on, saying we were under attack. Then the power went off again. Let's go check it out in town and see what's happening," Axel said, already pulling his shoes on and tying the strings nervously.

"Let's go to the bank and get our money," Vince suggested, sliding his hands down his wrinkled shirt to smooth it out.

It had been eight years since Grandma Thomas had passed, a passing orchestrated by Axel and covered up with help from Vince. The two had been living in her home, enjoying the small monthly check that continued to arrive from the government. Vince had not reported Grandma Thomas's death; therefore, her monthly benefits had continued to arrive in her bank account. Vince would withdraw three hundred dollars daily from the bank's ATM until he had drained all the money from the checking account each month.

Vince and Axel used this monthly income to enjoy their lifestyle. The dirty duo's day usually revolved around watching television, filling the air with the pungent smell of weed, and strumming on guitars they got from the pawn shop. Aside from some gleeful spending, their day was more of a lazy haze than anything resembling productivity.

After killing Grandma Thomas, the boys had ransacked the house looking for any hidden money she may have had. They found an old coffee can hidden in the laundry cabinet containing some money, thinking they were rich. Upon counting their newfound fortune, they had a modest treasure of one thousand seven hundred and forty dollars. Although it wasn't much, it would briefly transform their lives.

Axel and Vince took the money and went straight to James Pawn Shop in the middle of town, each selecting an electric guitar they wanted. After coming into such great wealth, it was time for a housewarming gift. Standing in the middle of the pawn shop, they both stopped after seeing their distorted reflections, a smile covering their faces. On a large stand sat a mammoth flat-screen TV, a surreal indulgence in their newfound wealth.

As Vince stood from the couch, the electricity came back on again. They quickly turned the television on, watching the news anchor relay a message. "The federal government is recommending everyone shelter in place. This is not a test. We have reports of cities across the country being targeted. We are told attacks have happened in Japan, South Korea, Canada, and Australia. News continues to come in quickly from around both the country and the world now. As you can see in this video our producers slowed down of the George Washington Bridge, the detonation of multiple explosion points causing the bridge to collapse."

"This is crazy, Axel. Do you think we are going to be like Patrick Swayze in that movie, with stormtroopers?" Vince asked, eyes fixed on the screen.

"It was called Red Dawn, and they were paratroopers. The

newer version was better with Chris Hemsworth because he was in the Marvel movie," Axel said back.

"He's not better than Patrick Swayze, and those Marvel characters suck, you're so stupid Axel," Vince snapped.

"Anyway, if you start seeing guys parachuting down on us, we will be playing that movie. I'm going to look outside," Axel said, thinking aloud, "what if paratroopers are coming down." He stepped outside onto the porch and gazed towards the sky.

"Looks clear right now. We need to go to town and check things out," Axel told Vince. The heat of the sun was beating down, the sky clear and blue. As Axel scanned the mountains, he heard the distant roar of jet engines. As if targeted, Axel felt his body shake at the suddenness and intensity of three military jets as they streaked across the treetops. The loud thunderous sound, forcing Axel to let out a scream and drop down low, his heart racing.

"What the hell was that? A jet?" Axel screeched out as Vince collapsed back into the recliner chair, laughing uncontrollably. He snorted and wheezed as he mocked Axel's unexpected display of fear.

"Axel. You," Vince struggled to speak through his laughter. "You scream like a little girl!" Vince managed to say before bursting into laughter again.

"Shut up, Vince. That ain't cool, bro. What's the news saying now, be serious?" Axel snapped at Vince, clearly embarrassed.

"This looks bad, Axel. They're saying to stay put. Maybe we should wait a while before we go out," Vince told Axel, pointing to the news anchor on the screen.

"Vince, buddy, this is our time. If we're being attacked, people will be scared. If they keep the businesses in town closed, we might have a chance to help ourselves to a few things. We've got to go check it out, it's our duty," Axel said, pulling on Vince's arm as he picked up a bat they had by the door before exiting. "Just in case, you never know." He said, closing the door behind them and looking up for more jets before leaving the porch.

Axel and Vince took the old car they had and drove the short distance to town. Their first stop was at the grocery store parking lot.

"It looks like the power went out again. Look over at the bank, Vince. People are raising hell over there. You run over and see if you can get some money out of the ATM. I'll go start getting a buggy filled," Axel said as he hurriedly walked to the store entrance.

Axel was met at the door by Earl, the store manager. "Only taking cash right now," Earl told Axel.

"That's what we've got. Vince will be over with it. He's at the bank now," Axel told the man as he pushed a buggy on by and went to the snack aisle.

"He won't get any money from the bank. They aren't giving it out," Earl called out to Axel, who ignored his comment.

"Axel, the bank ATMs not working, and they aren't letting anyone inside. I couldn't get the money," Vince said, exhausted after running from the bank to join Axel in the grocery store.

"What the hell? Where are these people getting their money from?" Axel said aloud as he looked around the store. "Hey, where did you get money from?" Axel said, grabbing a woman by the arm, stopping her as she walked by him. "I know your ass ain't never got no money," Axel said, looking at her with squinted eyes.

"I only got forty dollars. There's a man over at Susie's store giving it out. He told us to come and buy food. He gives everyone forty dollars; you both can get forty each," the woman said as she pulled away from Axel's grip.

"Let's go, Vince. We need to see what this is about," Axel said as he went outside the store. "Hey, look, there's Langston. What the hell is he saying over that megaphone? Let's go this way so he doesn't see us. He'll probably try to make us do something for him."

Axel and Vince exchanged cautious glances as they crouched low behind rows of parked cars outside the grocery store. Langston was notorious for roping them into odd jobs, and his presence now presented a looming threat to their plans for the day. He had indeed called on them over the years as he said he would, often during times when he needed a drug snitch.

"Let's go this way," Vince whispered, gesturing toward the corner of Susie's store. "We can't risk him spotting us. Last thing we need is a job today."

Axel and Vince looked across the road to Susie's store. "If James goes home, we're getting into that pawn shop later," Axel muttered to Vince. "Now come on, let's go," he said as the pair ran across the road to the corner of the pawn store. They peeked around, seeing a man and a teenage boy standing with Susie and James. "Who's that?" Axel questioned Vince.

"I don't know who he is, but that younger boy's name is Arnie. He's a kick-ass dirt bike rider," Vince informed Axel, looking at the group standing by the truck. It was a good thing Arnie didn't hear this comment, as his head would have been too big to fit in the truck.

"Okay, let's go get our money!" Axel told Vince as he stepped around the corner of the building.

CHAPTER NINETEEN

"Final Transaction"

Allen strode purposefully towards the entrance, casting a brief glance back at the red-headed woman still seated in the idling car. Her fingers tapped impatiently on the car's faded dash. The faint trail of cigarette smoke swirling around her silhouette before floating through the partially open side glass. With a nod, Allen motioned for her to join him, and she obeyed, stepping out and falling in beside him as they approached the store. Beads of sweat droplets left wet lines as they glided down Allen's face and arms.

The dim interior of the convenience store greeted them harshly as they squinted, attempting to adjust their eyes from the brightness of the sun outside. Fred, the aging cashier, stood behind the counter with a weariness etched deeply into his features. As Allen crossed the threshold, Fred's voice rang out with a practiced firmness, "No cash, no service, and we're out of gas." Fred hoped to dissuade them from lingering.

The red head leaned casually against the counter, a crooked smile playing on her lips despite the drug-induced haze clouding her eyes. "Come on now, sweetie," she coaxed, her voice honeyed with false sweetness. "I just need a carton of Marlboro lights. We'll swing back later today with the cash, I promise. Help a lady out."

Fred's response was short, his decision firm. "Sorry, no credit today."

Allen's towering figure loomed over Fred, his demeanor hardened with determination. "I'll be taking those cigarettes," he stated, his eyes locking onto Fred's with unwavering intensity. "And anything else we decide we need. You can charge it or not. It makes no difference to me. I don't give a shit either way."

Fred's hand moved with purpose, gripping the handle of his .38 revolver. He pointed it squarely at Allen, the weight of the moment unmistakable in the tense silence that followed. "I don't want to shoot you, son," Fred's voice wavered slightly, betraying his answer. "But it's time for you to leave."

Allen's expression remained emotionless, his eyes narrowing slightly as he assessed Fred's response. The two men stared at each other intensely, before Allen broke the hold. He held out his hand slowly, extended in a gesture of apparent peace, "Mr. Fred," Allen's voice was calm, almost pacifying. "I apologize for the trouble. I'm a little wound up about everything going on today. We'll get some cash and come back. Just set aside those cigarettes for me, please."

For a brief moment, Fred faltered, his grip on the gun slackening gradually. As their hands met in a tentative handshake, Allen's demeanor shifted abruptly. In one swift motion, he yanked Fred forward with a forceful tug, his other arm swinging forward like a battering ram. The sickening sound of fist meeting flesh reverberated through the store, punctuated by the crash of Fred's chair tipping over and hitting the ground as Fred's unconscious body slammed into it. The revolver clattered, its metal frame echoing the sudden violence that had erupted.

"Holy shit, Allen! Did you kill him?" The red head's laughter was combined with disbelief as she looked down at Fred's unmoving form sprawled on the linoleum floor.

Allen's response was short, his movements calculated as he retrieved the fallen gun and tucked it into his waistband. "He's not moving. Maybe I did." He turned his attention to the cash register, swiftly prying open the drawer with practiced ease. Bills spilled out in a disorganized heap as Allen stuffed them into his pockets, a smirk playing on his lips.

"I just hit the jackpot, there is thousands of dollars here," Allen remarked casually to the red head, a glint of triumph in his eyes. "Grab whatever you want from here, we need to hurry."

"Show me the money, baby!" The red head's ecstatic exclamation pierced the tense atmosphere, her excitement intense.

Allen's face hardened, as he dismissed her with a look that she knew meant to get lost, or risk one of his backhands she was all to accustomed with.

"I'm not showing you a damn thing. This is mine. Nothing for you to get excited about," Allen said to her, quickly wiping away the smile from her face.

Her focus shifted to the cooler, where she methodically retrieved a case of beer before going to the cigarette rack. She picked up three cartons of Marlboro lights, squeezing them tightly under her arm. As the red head turned the sign on the door around to show 'closed', a low groan arose from Fred's prone body, still on the floor. Allen's gaze flickered towards the old man, blood dribbling from a split lip and the shards of broken teeth glinting on the floor.

"He's coming to, Allen. We better go, he might remember us," she said with urgency.

Allen's response was swift and decisive. He withdrew the pistol from his waistband, leveling it at Fred's vulnerable chest.

"No need for that, son" Fred's voice was strained, blood pooling in his mouth as he struggled to speak.

"You're not so tough now, are you, old man?" Allen's voice was laced with menace as he cocked the hammer of the pistol, the metallic click slicing through the air.

"No need to make this any worse. Let's just all get back to our business and forget this happened. You can have the money," Fred said as he hoped to relax Allen. He was able to find the strength to hold his eyes open looking at Allen.

The gunshot exploded with an ear-splitting crack, the

harsh smoke curling upwards from the barrel in the dim light. The bullet tore into Fred's chest, entering his heart with little resistance. His body convulsed briefly, a gasp escaping his lips before his eyes fluttered closed, his life draining away.

Allen stood over Fred's lifeless body, watching as the old man's white button up shirt was slowly being turned crimson red.

"Roll-Tide," Allen said as a smile played across his face.

The red head looked at him, not sure of whether it was okay for her to speak or not. Allen let out a hard laugh while looking at her and pointing to his shirt.

"Don't you get it? My team Alabama says roll-tide. His shirt is getting covered in blood like a tide washing over. It was funny," he said as his smile had become more serious now, fading away to a harsh scowl on his face.

"Yeah, baby, that is funny," she said trying to force out a fake laugh. "I get it!"

Allen stood over the fallen man, his expression unreadable as he casually returned the gun to his waistband. "He won't remember us now," Allen's voice held a chilling finality as he rolled his shoulders slowly. He moved towards the door, meeting the red head's gaze, his hand casually flicking open the cooler to retrieve several energy drinks by the door.

"That was badass, Allen! I've never seen someone get dealt with before!" The red head's voice was a combination of excitement and adrenaline as they hurried across the parking lot towards the waiting mustang.

Meanwhile, Ronald had been in the back room, refueling the generators that kept the deli's refrigerators running. Known locally as a friendly alcoholic, Ronald enjoyed a drink often. He was a kind-hearted man who was always nice to anyone around him. He often took odd jobs around town for pocket money, sometimes being paid in alcohol. He was sipping a Coors Light when the gunshot rang out, prompting him to investigate. He quietly approached the front of the store, peering out the large front window. He could clearly see the white Mustang and the large man getting into the car. Ronald watched them prepare to leave, before looking across the counter into the floor.

"Fred? Fred!" Ronald called out, moving around and nudging Fred's shoulder in a futile attempt to rouse him. Ronald focused briefly on the puddle of blood forming on the floor next to Fred, and knew he was gone. He glanced back out the window at the departing Mustang, recognizing both Allen and the red head inside. As the Mustang peeled away, Ronald couldn't shake the feeling that he had just witnessed something straight out of a modern-day Bonnie and Clyde scene.

CHAPTER TWENTY
"The Price of Impulse"

Kyle and Arnie pulled into Susie's, parking the truck in front of the door. A small crowd of six stood outside, their voices a mix of frustration and desperation as they spoke to Susie and James through the glass door. The heat of the day was intense, beads of sweat glistening on their foreheads.

"We just need to get a few things, but nobody is letting us in without cash," a man from the crowd pleaded with James, his voice tight with anxiety. "We're good for the money, as soon as the bank opens."

"There's my brother Kyle," Susie told James. "Let him in."

Kyle approached the crowd, his presence momentarily calming their agitation as they wondered about his intent. Their clothes were crumpled, and their faces drawn with worry, eyes flickering with a desperate hope.

"If everyone calms down, I will help you. Susie doesn't have the goods you need right now. She only has a few clothes," Kyle addressed them, his tone firm yet soothing. "I understand everyone has needs. Go home, get what money you have, and go to the grocery store to get supplies."

"We ain't got no money at home. Nobody is helping us right now," a woman said, her voice cracking.

"I have enough cash to give each of you forty dollars; that is all I can do right now. Get what you can with it," Kyle said, pulling the remaining twenties from his pocket. One by one, he handed each person two of the bills. As quickly as the money touched their hands, they took off, some heading to the grocery store across the street, while others planned to buy a pill or some weed.

"Why did you give them money, Kyle? They will never pay that back to you," Susie said as Kyle entered the store.

"I didn't know they were family," Kyle laughed at his remark, he always said family was where money went to disappear. "It's about to be worthless, Susie, and it won't matter by tomorrow. It gets them away from here for now before they turn into a mob. That money bought us the time we need to leave and get home. This is getting uglier by the minute and will be a riot soon," Kyle told Susie and James.

Crack! Crack! Crack! Three shots rang out from the area of the pharmacy. Although they didn't have a clear view, Kyle recognized the sound of gunfire. He quickly pulled his Glock, moving into a semi-squatted stance with his gun raised. Arnie, not as quick, still managed to get his Glock out of the holster and stepped to the back of the truck for cover. James, clearly nervous, fumbled with his gun, dropping it, before stumbling into the outer wall of the clothing shop. He looked at Kyle, embarrassed, but gave a slight nod to indicate he was okay.

"It's okay, that sounded like it was at the pharmacy or bank. Let's get moving, time is ticking," Kyle said, holstering his gun.

"Pssst, hey James, there is a wall there, buddy, just so you know," Arnie quipped, smiling at James and holstering his own gun. He simply couldn't pass up the chance to make a smartass remark at someone's expense, he was defiantly a Blaine.

"I'm not as young as you, Arnie, I don't have the reflexes," James replied, his face red with embarrassment.

"You're not as good-looking as me either, that's why you don't have the women like I do," Arnie snickered, smacking James on the back.

"Don't pay no attention to him, James. He is always

cracking on somebody, just being a little shit," Susie said.

"Susie, have you talked to my mom?" Arnie asked, changing the subject.

"Just last night I did. I haven't spoken to her this morning. She said she would be at Mom's today," Susie replied, squeezing his shoulder to comfort him.

"She will be okay, Arnie; she probably won't even know anything is wrong until she gets to Mom's house and finds out what happened," Kyle reassured him.

"What do we need to take from here?" Susie asked Kyle.

"Grab all the candles you have. Take blankets, pillows, jackets, and any other clothing you can squeeze into your car. If you have any shoes, throw them in the car, underwear, and socks. We aren't going to be able to come back here and this place will be ransacked by tonight. If anything is special to you, take it now," Kyle instructed.

"James, do you have any ammo or walkie-talkies in your store?" Kyle asked.

"I don't have any ammo or guns, never got into those. Too many requirements from the law. I do think I have a set of walkie-talkies. I'll go look, be back in a minute," James said, hurrying off.

Kyle, Arnie, and Susie gathered anything they thought could be useful, moving it next to the door. They needed to open the door and get the items to the truck quickly to avoid letting anyone in. Kyle had no intention of wanting to kill anyone, so they needed to be quick. James returned, knocking on the door while holding a box containing walkie-talkies. Arnie unlocked the door, letting him in and locking it back after him.

"Here is a set of walkies I hope will work for you. The guy I took them on pawn from still had these in the original box, which as you see, looks to be in good shape. He said he never used them after purchasing. They operate on rechargeable batteries, so if you have a solar charger, you're in good shape," James said, handing the box to Kyle. The box was a brand Kyle hadn't seen before, Topsung. It showed to have six in it with a twenty-five-mile radius. Kyle doubted they would reach that distance, but if he could get a mile from them, he would be happy. They appeared to have different color faces, and the box said water-resistant.

"You need to get out of here, you can't protect this property. It will be overrun by tonight, maybe sooner. Let it go and get somewhere safe where you can protect yourself and your family," Kyle advised James.

"My wife's gone, this is all I have. I worked my whole life here. I'm not leaving it behind without a fight," James replied.

"The attack happened this morning and look around. In this small-ass town, it's already about to turn into a shit show. It will be a fight if you don't leave," Kyle said, trying to encourage him.

"Arnie, you start tossing this stuff into the truck. Susie, do the same and let's roll out in two minutes," Kyle ordered. They quickly carried the items to the truck, with James pitching in to help.

"I need a gun, Kyle!" Susie said, her voice shaking.

Kyle went to his truck and opened the glove box, removing a Ruger American Compact 9mm handgun. He turned to Susie, holding it out.

"It has seventeen rounds in it. There is one chambered and sixteen more in the magazine. This is the safety switch," Kyle explained, showing her the manual safety slide. "When you take the safety off, it is ready to shoot. If you point this at someone, be willing to pull the trigger. Keep your hand clear of the slide, it will take a chunk of meat if not," Kyle instructed seriously.

"This is more complicated than the gun daddy let me shoot," Susie replied, taking the gun.

"That was a revolver, and it was a .38 caliber. It kicked a little more than this will. This is semi-automatic in nine-millimeter. It will shoot smoothly, but you must keep a firm grip on it. Drive straight home and let's hope you won't need it. Go on and be careful," Kyle said.

"Kyle, one more thing. Ginger was supposed to come across Home Creek Mountain and stop by here today. I don't know anything more than that right now," Susie whispered.

"Okay, Susie, we will do what we can," Kyle replied.

After Arnie had loaded the last of the items, they locked the door behind them. Kyle started to walk towards the driver's side when two men quickly approached from around the corner of James's pawn shop.

"Hey there, pal. We were told you were giving out free money over here. How much you got?" A scrawny man asked, his eyes gleaming with wickedness. "What's up, Arnie?" he added, nodding at Arnie. He wore cargo shorts and an oversized T-shirt with a faded Guns N' Roses logo. He looked like he lived on oxycontin pills, with a bony frame and hollow eyes. He held an old aluminum baseball bat low to appear non-threatening but also like he was a tough guy.

"Sorry guys, I gave it all out. We are leaving here now," Kyle said, his eyes narrowing.

"Hold on now. If you don't got no money, we'll take some of that stuff in the back of your truck there," said the other man, stocky with a build hinting at past strength now marred by drug use. He wore a Motley Crue rock shirt with holes and heavily stained jeans.

"Arnie, get in the truck, you're driving. Susie, get in your car and head to Mom's now, no questions, just go," Kyle ordered, his voice tense.

"You just hang on, Arnie. We need to get our fair share before you go. The way I see it, you got three choices. You can either cough up half your stuff, give us some of that free money, or we whip your ass and take it all," said the stocky man, revealing a cheap-looking switchblade.

"And he isn't asking you again," the smaller man raised the bat and smacked it down onto the hood of Kyle's truck.

"Ohhhh, that wasn't a smart move," Arnie muttered.

"And why is that, Arnie, you saying we're dumb?" The scrawny man asked, trying to intimidate him.

"There was no need to hit my truck. I'll give you fair warning; I am going to step around this truck now. If you two asshats aren't gone by then, I will kill you both right here. This is where you will both die today," Kyle said, his look menacing. They glanced at each other nervously as Kyle stepped around the truck with his Glock in hand.

"Okay, hold on now. We weren't serious, just messing around," the guy in the Guns N' Roses shirt said, stepping back.

Susie had already left. James stood at the store entrance with his model 1911 Colt forty-five stainless pistol in hand, ready to raise it if needed.

"We aren't here for any trouble; don't try making it. I'm sorry I don't have money left and can't help you. Good luck to you both," Kyle said, his eyes unwavering.

"Go on, Axel, you too, Vince. Nothing here for you guys right now," James said, naming the men. Kyle watched them walk away, Vince glancing back with anger. Axel pulled on Vince's arm, and they kept walking.

"James, you take care of yourself," Kyle said, getting in the truck.

"You do the same, and it was good meeting you, Kyle. See you, Arnie bug, you keep everybody straight," James said, heading to his store.

"Arnie, that's a good man there. I hope he listens and goes somewhere safe," Kyle said, closing the door.

"Who the hell was that? And why did you have a gun out on us?" Axel asked James.

"I've had it out all morning. People are acting crazy today. That was Kyle, Susie's brother," James said.

"What you got that we can have, James? We need some money or some food. You got any more guns?" Axel inquired.

"You boys go on. I don't have anything, and we're closing all businesses here today," James said, locking the door behind him and watching them from the window.

"Look over there, Kyle. Is that man dead?" Arnie said as they neared the pharmacy. A man lay with his feet on the bottom step, his upper half on the ground, arms sprawled.

"That was the gunshots we heard, Arnie. It's now officially started. Get us home, little buddy," Kyle said as they drove towards home.

"I don't like Kyle," Vince told Axel, watching the truck drive away.

"We will see him again one day when he doesn't have his gun. You can kick his ass then!" Axel replied, patting Vince on the shoulder.

CHAPTER TWENTY-ONE

"Lines of Defense"

As Arnie drove towards home, they once again passed by Creekside Convenience. The gas pumps were surrounded by ten or twelve cars now, where several people engaged in heated arguments, likely over fuel allocation or the exorbitant prices set by Johnny. The tension hung thick in the air as Arnie and Kyle continued on the small country road leading to Rachel's house, now congested with increased traffic. Kyle's mind wrestled with conflicting thoughts—whether to return and await Ginger at Susie's store or ensure Arnie's safety by reaching Rachel's with their acquired items.

"Look, Kyle! It's that Mustang parked up ahead," Arnie exclaimed as they neared a turnoff leading towards Kentucky. Beside the turn, a wide spot often served as a meeting place for illicit exchanges of drugs and money. Here, the merging creeks from Hurley and the Pawpaw section flowed towards Kentucky. The origin of the name Pawpaw was debated, some attributing it to the presence of Pawpaw trees in bygone years. Observing the Mustang parked ahead, Kyle squeezed the KSG shotgun, readying it by the door in anticipation.

"Maintain a steady pace, Arnie," Kyle cautioned as they approached. The Mustang, backed into its spot, had its driver's window rolled down. Inside, Allen reclined, cigarette in hand, his left arm nonchalantly resting on the window frame. When Kyle's eyes met Allen's, the man's expression remained stoic. However, the red-haired woman in the passenger seat didn't hesitate to raise her middle finger and salute as they drove past.

"They're not following us, Uncle Kyle," Arnie said, exhaling with relief.

"They're trouble, Arnie. Stay vigilant around the house. If you see that car pass by, it won't be for a social visit," Kyle warned, impressing upon Arnie the seriousness of the situation. The days of leisurely rocking on the front porch with friendly company seemed a distant memory. Security was about to become a crucial part of their daily lives.

"You going to just let him drive by like that, Allen?" the redhead asked, her voice shaded with impatience as her fingers bounced on her knee. She watched eagerly as Kyle and Arnie's truck disappeared from view. Having witnessed Allen's lethal actions against Fred earlier, she was now excited by the outlaw lifestyle.

"I'm going to follow him. Let's see where they're headed," Allen replied, his voice strong with a newfound confidence. Taking Fred's life had transformed him into a self-assured predator, relishing the lawless realm where there were no police to hinder him. Clinching his jaw tightly, he flicked his cigarette out the window.

"I'm ready, baby," the red head said, a smirk from her lips.

Upon returning to Rachel's house, Arnie pulled the truck into the driveway and parked. They disembarked and found Rachel on the porch, where Susie was filling her in on the day's tumultuous events at her store.

"I'm glad you boys are back safe. Were you able to get anything?" Rachel asked as Kyle stepped onto the porch.

"We did, we had a successful shopping trip. The truck's loaded up with supplies. How about you? Any luck at Fred's?" Kyle inquired.

"I couldn't get any gas, but I managed to gather a lot of canned foods and disposables like you suggested. It's all in the car; Ronald loaded it for me," Rachel said pointing towards her car, feeling accomplished in her task. "I could already smell the beer on Ronald this morning; I don't think he ever stops drinking. As more people were arriving, they were talking about the attack, but they didn't seem overly concerned. They act like it'll be fixed by tonight," Rachel explained, a hint of pride in her voice for now believing in Kyle's words.

"Susie has probably told you how bad it's getting already, Mom," Kyle added, glancing towards the white Mustang that appeared around the curve, the redhead made no effort to hide her gaze as they passed by.

"That's trouble right there. Do you know who that was, Susie?" Kyle asked, his gaze still fixed on the Mustang as it went out of sight.

"I don't know her name, but that's Allen Hall driving. They've been in the store a few times—always strange acting and usually high on dope," Susie responded.

"We had a run-in with him at Creekside earlier while getting gas. They don't seem ready to let it go. He's a big guy, and he'll try to take what he wants," Kyle said, his tone serious.

"Mamaw, have you heard from my mom?" Arnie interrupted, looking at Rachel anxiously. "I wish she would get over here so I know she's safe."

"She'll be here, Arnie. You know how your mom is. She likes to lollygag and takes her time. I fixed sandwiches and wrapped them up; they're in the refrigerator. Everything will spoil soon, so you all should eat something while you have a chance," Rachel told them as she headed inside.

"Kyle, what are we going to do? My brain is all over the place right now. I feel so scrambled, I just can't think straight," Susie said, her voice trembling with anxiety.

"Here it comes back down the road!" Arnie exclaimed, pointing at the approaching white Mustang.

Kyle's hand instinctively went to his Glock, preparing to draw it as he started across the lawn towards the road. His eyes were fixed on the Mustang, his muscles tense with readiness. As the car slowed down, Allen leaned out of the window, his hand forming the shape of a gun. He mock-fired at Kyle, a smug grin spreading across his face, before speeding away.

"Are we going to be fighting people? Shooting people? Is that what's coming? Where are the police?" Susie's voice trembled with a mix of fear and confusion as she rattled off her questions.

"There are no police, Susie. Probably not in many areas at all right now. Everyone, including the police, is scrambling to protect their families. Reality is setting in that this is going to be bad. Yes, there is going to be fighting and shooting," Kyle responded, his tone serious but steady, trying to instill a sense of calm amidst the chaos.

"Shooting who? What are you all talking about?" Rachel asked, her voice filled with concern as she joined them on the porch, her eyes darting between Kyle and the receding Mustang.

Kyle took a deep breath, trying to steady his thoughts. "Mom, things are changing fast. We need to be prepared for the worst. That means defending ourselves and our home."

Rachel's face paled, the gravity of the situation sinking in. She glanced at Susie, who was visibly shaken, then back at Kyle. "What do we need to do?"

Kyle looked at his mother, trying to convey both urgency and reassurance. "First, we need to get you and Arnie to the cabin for safety. It's more secluded and easier to defend. We'll bring supplies up there and make it our base."

Rachel nodded slowly, the weight of the decision evident in her eyes. "Alright, Kyle. We'll do what needs to be done."

"Start packing your bags, mom. Take anything important to you," Kyle instructed Rachel.

As Arnie and Rachel began to prepare for the move, Kyle stood on the porch, watching the road. He knew that this was just the beginning, and they needed to be ready for whatever came next.

Kyle knew that the looting, which had already started in the town of Hurley, would soon spread to people's homes in the coming days. Those who hadn't prepared would need supplies.

Those who had spent their money on drugs instead of food would eventually come down from their highs, find themselves hungry, and become desperate. As the drugs ran out, so would the food, and crime would become rampant.

"I don't want to leave my home, Kyle. What if it gets broken into or vandalized?" Rachel asked, her voice deeply concerned.

"I'd rather it be broken into or burned down with you not inside, Mom," Kyle replied firmly. "This is the best option. We can't protect this place here; it's simply too open."

Rachel sighed, the weight of the situation pressing heavily on her. "Okay, son, I trust you. Do you have room for me up there?"

"Yes, Mom, I have room for several. It's the best option for now. Arnie will drive you up the mountain and get you settled in," Kyle said, his eyes meeting Arnie's, emphasizing the urgency and importance of the task.

"Arnie, you've got an important job to do," Kyle said, his tone firm. "Unload all the items from the truck and store them in the garage for now out of sight. Then, take Mom and her bags to the cabin. If there's extra space, start taking the supplies we gathered. Once you get her settled, hook up the utility trailer and come back. You'll be able to haul more that way."

As Kyle spoke, he saw Uncle Tom approaching on his side-by-side, his expression somber. "The shit is hitting the fan, boys," Uncle Tom announced, smacking his hands together. "I've been up the road to Willie's today, and it's bad. Willie used his ham radio to reach a few people—there's all kinds of chatter going on right now."

"We know a bit, Uncle Tom. I'm getting Mom ready to head up to the cabin. We were in Hurley, and things are starting to break down. Someone was killed at the pharmacy," Kyle replied.

"Killed? We should all be banding together," Uncle Tom said shaking his head in disgust. "I went to Fred's after leaving Willie's. Bad news. Fred was murdered in his store. I picked Ronald up on my way here—he was walking. He said Allen and his girlfriend, Cindy, came in, shot Fred, and left him dead behind the counter. They took the money from the register and left," Uncle Tom explained, his voice heavy with the gravity of the situation. "Ronald was in the storage room, so they didn't see him. He locked the front door and went out the back."

"Fred was killed? I was just there a couple of hours ago. I talked to him. I can't believe this," Rachel said, tears trickling down her face.

"Let me guess, Cindy's a redhead?" Kyle asked.

"Yeah, she is. You should know her—you played ball against her cousins from Haysi," Uncle Tom replied.

"I'm not doing this right now. I don't know who she is, but Arnie and I had a run in with Allen earlier. He drove by here just a few minutes ago." Kyle said, his frustration evident.

Uncle Tom had an uncanny knack for knowing everyone and every road in the area. It was like he had a built-in compass and rolodex. He could drive people crazy with his stories about mutual acquaintances, something Kyle and his brothers, Sawyer and Spencer, often joked about.

Kyle's thoughts drifted to his brothers, Sawyer and Spencer, as he navigated the tense situation at hand. Sawyer lived about six hundred miles away in Florida, a distance that now seemed daunting in the face of the escalating chaos. Despite the miles between them, Sawyer and Kyle often found solace in discussing doomsday scenarios, preparing mentally for the worst. Spencer, on the other hand, was just a two-hour drive away in Wise County, his proximity offering a glimmer of reassurance amidst the uncertainty.

Spencer had taken proactive measures, much like Kyle, investing in land and creating his own secluded retreat. Sawyer frequently reiterated that in a crisis, he would make the journey to either Spencer's sanctuary or Kyle's refuge in the mountains. It was a plan born out of their shared determination to protect their families and weather whatever storm might come.

Kyle held onto the hope that his brothers were safe and making decisive moves to ensure their loved ones' security. In times like these, their shared preparations and unwavering bond offered some semblance of comfort amid the unfolding turmoil.

"Kyle, Kyle," Rachel said seeing his mind was somewhere else right now.

"Yeah, sorry," Kyle responded.

"Ronald said he covered Fred with a tarp," Uncle Tom continued, his voice heavy with the grim news. "He told me the twelve-pack of beer he was carrying was the only thing he took. Poor guy was shaking while telling me, said he needed the beer for his nerves. I took Ronald to his old home place and dropped him off."

"He won't survive without beer, and that isn't a joke," Susie said.

"While I was at Willie's, there was all kinds of chatter on the ham radio about bombs and attacks still going on. One guy said he was watching his entire town go underwater. He lives on a hill that overlooks the town, and he saw the dam blow. He described it like a giant wave crashing through the streets, sweeping away cars, houses, everything in its path. People were screaming, trying to get to higher ground, but the water was too fast. He said it was like a scene from a disaster movie, but this time, it was real," Tom explained as he removed his hat and ran a hand across his head.

"This is so hard to believe it's real," Rachel said as she listened to Tom.

"Another report came in from a guy who said his city had been hit by multiple explosions. He described seeing buildings reduced to rubble, fires raging uncontrolled, and people wandering the streets in shock, covered in dust and blood. He said the skyline was unrecognizable, with smoke plumes stretching high into the sky, blotting out the sun. The hospitals were overrun, and there was no help coming," Tom continued with the terrifying reports.

"Sawyer lives in a big place, do you think he is okay?" Rachel said.

"Sawyer is smart, mom. He knows to take small roads and get out quickly. I'm sure he is on his way to Spencer's now," Kyle added. "That's always been our plan in case of a disaster."

"Someone else chimed in about a bridge collapsing under the weight of traffic trying to escape," Uncle Tom said, his hands moving with his words. "Cars were plunging into the river, and the screams of people trapped in their vehicles could be heard. He was helpless, just a witness to the chaos and destruction."

"We have to focus on our area right now, get our family safe and secure," Kyle said before turning his attention to his go bag, checking his supplies closer.

"It's bad, Kyle. Really bad. And it's spreading. There's talk of martial law being declared in some areas, but no one's seen any troops yet. Everyone's fending for themselves, trying to get supplies. This isn't just a breakdown—it's a full-blown collapse."

"We may figure more of that out later. Are you going to stay at your cabin, Uncle Tom?" Kyle asked.

"I'm taking a few supplies there, just to be on the safe side. But I won't stay until it's my last option," Uncle Tom replied. "You were right, Kyle. It's happened. It won't change anything now, but I'll still say, we should have listened to you better."

"That doesn't matter, Uncle Tom. Arnie is going to be hauling things up to my cabin. Once he's finished, he can help you as well. Watch each other's backs and stay safe. I have one more trip to make," Kyle instructed.

"Remember, slow is smooth and—" Kyle started, but Arnie cut him off.

"Smooth is fast. I know, Uncle Kyle. I can handle this. Where are you going?" Arnie asked.

Kyle had anticipated this question but didn't want to give Arnie too many details. If Ginger was heading to Susie's store, she could be there now. He planned to make the short drive back, and if she wasn't there, he would head towards Grundy. He went inside to explain the plan to Rachel, knowing she wouldn't like him leaving but would appreciate the honesty.

Kyle told Arnie to get the supplies to the cabin as instructed. He told Arnie that Susie had left something important at the store, and they were going to retrieve it. To keep Arnie

120

calm, he added that if Ginger hadn't arrived by the time he finished hauling supplies, he should leave her a walkie-talkie and a note saying, "We're at Kyle's, start walking." This seemed to satisfy Arnie, who got to work.

"You two be careful. I'll keep Arnie busy. Don't worry about us here, go find Ginger," Uncle Tom said.

CHAPTER TWENTY-TWO
"Darkening Horizons"

———————————————

Susie watched out the windshield as the trees zoomed by quickly. Kyle was eager to get back to town and look for Ginger, it showed in him speeding along the way. She finally broke the silence, turning to Kyle, "why did you pick me to go with you?" Susie asked.

"Because you know these people better than I do. I've been gone for the last twenty years. It might help if we get in a dire situation with someone knowing you," Kyle replied.

"I'm not Sister Susie the nun to these people," she replied nervously with a chuckle, trying to lighten the heaviness of the mood.

The drive back to town along the winding country road felt surreal, each familiar landmark now holding an eerie silence. They passed by the empty spot where the Mustang had been parked, now vacant of any signs of life. The coal tipple loomed ahead, its massive structure casting long shadows across the ground beneath. Two men stood by a pickup truck nearby, their movements sluggish, seemingly unaffected by the unfolding chaos around them, as if waiting out the storm for the electricity to return.

Kyle navigated the road with a mixture of familiarity and

unease, his eyes scanning the procession of cars and trucks ahead as they wound their way towards Hurley. Each vehicle seemed to inch forward reluctantly, caught in the same wave of urgency that had driven Kyle and Susie out of town earlier. He drummed his fingers on the steering wheel, a nervous habit born of his growing anxiety. The desire to bypass the slow-moving line gnawed at him, but he remained steadfast, knowing the risks of recklessness in these uncertain times.

Susie glanced out of the window, her brow furrowed in concern as she observed the scene unfolding around them. The normally serene countryside seemed to hold its breath, as if bracing for what was to come. Kyle stole a glance at her, noting the tightness in her jaw and the furrowed lines on her forehead. They were in this together, bound not just by blood but by the unspoken understanding that they needed to find Ginger, whatever it took.

"Let's go people, get the lead out of your ass," Kyle said.

"It looks like word is spreading quickly. Everyone is trying to get a view for themselves or get what supplies they can," Susie observed as they waited in traffic.

Kyle understood the scene as traffic began coming to a stop—the line of vehicles stretched deep towards Creekside Convenience, all waiting for gas. He maneuvered around the traffic, eliciting a shout from a bystander about cutting the line. Kyle waved, indicating he wasn't there for gas, having already filled up. Ahead, a man with a shotgun blocked the road.

"That's Wayne. What's he doing?" Susie asked as Kyle approached cautiously.

Kyle extended his hand out of the window, palm facing outward in a gesture of peace. Wayne eyed him warily, his grip tightening on the shotgun held loosely in his other hand as he watched the truck slow to a stop.

"No skipping the line, pal," Wayne's voice carried a stern but nervous warning.

"I'm not trying to skip. Just heading into town," Kyle replied evenly, his tone calm despite the urgency gnawing at him.

Wayne's demeanor softened slightly as he recognized Susie in the passenger seat. "Oh hey, Susie! What are you doing out here? Things are getting crazy," he greeted her, his voice filled with concern. "Ain't much left in town. Officer Langston just rolled through, talkin' about Martial Law. I'm holding down things here for him. You folks should check on your store and get back quick," Wayne informed them, scanning the surroundings with a mix of vigilance and weariness.

"Thanks, Wayne. We'll make it quick," Susie replied with a grateful nod, her eyes flicking towards the commotion near the store.

"You both watch yourselves out there. Had two fights already," Wayne warned, nodding towards a man slumped on the steps of the store, a bloodied rag pressed to his nose. Beside him, a woman knelt, her expression a mix of concern and submission.

As Kyle eased the truck forward, the tension in the air was noticeable. Around them, the once familiar faces of neighbors now seemed hardened, eyes darting with suspicion and fear. A low murmur of discontent simmered beneath the surface, punctuated by accusatory glares.

Ahead, the line of vehicles snaked towards Creekside Convenience, each car a capsule of uncertainty and apprehension. Kyle navigated carefully through the gridlock, their progress slow but deliberate. Every passing minute seemed to heighten the collective anxiety, transforming the once quiet town into a battleground of simmering frustrations and dashed hopes.

Susie glanced sideways at Kyle, her expression troubled. "This isn't right, Kyle. People turning on each other like this," she muttered, her voice thick with emotion.

Kyle nodded grimly, his knuckles white against the steering wheel. "Desperation does strange things to folks. We'll hopefully get Ginger and get out," he replied, his gaze fixed ahead.

"What if Ginger doesn't show up?" Susie asked, her face showing the worry and fear for her sister.

Kyle hesitated, then replied gently, "I don't know, Susie. I've considered driving to Grundy or waiting at home. I'm not good at waiting."

"What about Megan, Sawyer, and Spencer? I wonder what they are doing and if they're alright?" Susie's eyes welled up, and Kyle felt the urgency to comfort her.

"Right now, let's focus on finding Ginger. After we're all safe, you can let it out," Kyle urged, trying to steady Susie's emotions.

Kyle eased the truck into a parking spot near the church, carefully aligning it between two other vehicles. He had to do some careful maneuvering to fit the truck into the space. As he shut off the engine, the tension in the air was almost visible, weighing heavily on both of them. Susie looked out the window, her expression a mix of worry and determination.

Without a word, Kyle turned to Susie, trying to break the tension that hung heavy in the cab. He managed a half-smile, hoping to lighten the atmosphere. "Well, sis, here we are, parking pros in a crisis. Who knew we'd be doing this today?"

Susie let out a small chuckle, shaking her head at Kyle's attempt to inject some humor into the situation. "You always did find the strangest times for jokes, little brother," she replied, her voice showing both amusement and gratitude. She adjusted the grip on her pistol, a nervous habit that betrayed her anxiety.

"Hey, gotta keep things light, right?" Kyle said, his tone gentle but determined. He reached over and patted Susie's shoulder reassuringly. "We're in this together, no matter what happens out there."

Susie nodded, her eyes briefly meeting Kyle's before looking away. "Yeah," she murmured, more to herself than to him. "Let's find Ginger and get out of here."

Kyle and Susie stepped out of the truck, their boots crunching on the loose bits of gravel on the church parking lot. The heat in the air felt thick, and the distant echoes of shouting and commotion made them more anxious. Surrounding them, other vehicles were parked haphazardly, some with doors left open, abandoned in a hurry.

As they approached the area near Susie's store, the scene

unfolded before them like a grim display of chaos and desperation. Groups of people moved frantically, their arms loaded with goods hastily taken from shelves. The shattered storefronts bore witness to the frenzy, with glass strewn across the pavement and merchandise scattered everywhere.

Susie gripped her pistol tighter, her knuckles turning white, as she surveyed the scene with a mixture of anger and sorrow. "Look at this," she muttered, her voice a low growl. "Teresa and Tina, carrying off my things like it's theirs. Damn dirty thieves."

Kyle glanced around, taking in the devastation. "It's like everyone's lost their minds," he remarked, with disbelief. "James' pawn shop is wrecked," he pointed out, nodding towards the broken windows and scattered items inside.

As they continued, reaching James Pawn Shop, Kyle cautiously pushed open the shattered door. The splintered glass crunching under his boots as he cautiously entered the chaotic scene. Sunlight filtered through the broken windows, casting jagged beams across the chaos within.

The once familiar space was now a scene of devastation. Display cases lay shattered, their contents strewn across the floor—jewelry, electronics, and various trinkets lay discarded and broken. Vinyl records, once neatly stacked, were now scattered like fallen leaves.

Two men, their faces masked by shadows, hurriedly gathered power tools into a duffel bag near the back of the store. They glanced up at Kyle's entrance, their eyes wary but not hostile. Kyle's grip tightened on the KSG, a silent warning of readiness. Ignoring the looters for the moment, Kyle moved deeper into the store, stepping past overturned furniture and broken glass. His eyes scanned the dim corners, searching for any sign of James.

"His office is in the back," Susie whispered to Kyle as she walked next to him, one hand placed on the back of his shoulder as she followed.

Inside the office at the back, he spotted James lying on the

126

floor, curled into a fetal position. A pool of blood had spread around him, soaking into the worn carpet beneath. Kyle knelt beside his new friend, his heart sinking at the sight of the wounds—gashes and bruises marring James' arms and torso.

"He tried to fight back," Kyle muttered grimly. He glanced up at Susie, who stood frozen at the entrance to the office, her pistol clutched tightly in trembling hands. "These are defensive wounds," he added, his tone heavy with sorrow.

Susie's eyes filled with tears, her gaze fixed on James' lifeless form. She took a step forward, as if to reach out, but Kyle gently held her back, his touch a silent comfort amidst the overwhelming grief and anger that hung in the room.

"Ginger," Kyle said quietly, a reminder of their urgent mission. He glanced back at the looters, who had resumed their task with hurried movements. "We need to find her," he continued, his voice firm with determination. "Let's get out of here before things escalate further."

With a last, sorrowful look at James, Kyle stood and guided Susie towards the store's entrance. They moved through the shattered doorway and into the harsh sunlight, leaving behind the shattered remnants of what was once James' livelihood, their thoughts now focused solely on finding Ginger amidst the turmoil that had engulfed their town.

They moved cautiously, navigating through the chaos towards Ginger's car, which stood parked near the corner of a building. Kyle approached cautiously, scanning the area for any signs of Ginger or trouble. His senses were on high alert, every instinct urging him to find her quickly and get out of this volatile situation.

Nearby, a group of people argued loudly over a few remaining items outside another store, their voices rising in anger. A woman shouted, her face contorted with desperation, while a man shoved another, the tension escalating with each passing moment.

Susie glanced nervously at Kyle, her eyes wide with apprehension. "We need to find Ginger fast," she said, her voice trembling slightly. "Before things get even worse. Should we split up?"

Kyle nodded grimly, his jaw set with determination. "Let's stick together," he replied firmly, his gaze sweeping the area. "Keep your guard up."

They moved closer to Ginger's car, their footsteps slow and deliberate, ready for whatever awaited them as they searched for their missing sister amidst the chaos of their once-familiar town.

CHAPTER TWENTY-THREE

"Shattered Silence"

As Kyle and Susie approached Ginger's car, a sinking feeling settled in the pit of Kyle's stomach. The sight before them was stark evidence of the chaos that had engulfed their once-peaceful town. Ginger's car, usually reliable, was now vandalized by the roadside.

The passenger side window was shattered, fragments of glass scattered like fallen stars on the ground and across the driver's seat. The door bore deep dents, evidence of brute force that had pummeled it repeatedly, likely while Ginger had been inside. The car was never pristine, but its current battered appearance was a reminder of the violence that had erupted unexpectedly.

Susie gripped Kyle's arm tightly, her voice barely above a whisper as she pointed towards the nearby grocery store. People hurriedly wheeled shopping carts overflowing with goods, oblivious to the wreckage around them. The bank's windows lay shattered, its doors hanging open and broken at the hinges from the force of the crowd stampeding inside. A similar scene unfolded at the pharmacy, where the lifeless figure of a man lay from an earlier tragic event. Smoke was slowly beginning to billow out of the pharmacy as people carried items away.

"The pharmacy looks to be on fire," Kyle whispered to Susie as he pointed at the smoke beginning to thicken.

"Susie! Kyle!" Ginger's voice called out, cutting through the tense silence and drawing their gaze towards a small shed used for business storage, likely for lawn equipment. Ginger emerged from behind the shed, her face pale and drawn with fear yet relieved to see her siblings.

"Ginger, are you okay?" Susie asked hugging her sister.

"I'm so glad you're here," Ginger said, embracing both Kyle and Susie. "I'm fine. I heard what was happening earlier today, but I never imagined it would be this bad in town. I got stopped on the bridge by two men who flagged me down. They wanted money and my car. When I refused, they attacked me."

Ginger's voice quivered as she recounted the harrowing ordeal. She gestured towards her car, kicking her leg to demonstrate how the assailants had pounded on her door.

"It's okay, sis. We're here now," Kyle reassured her, his voice calm but with an undercurrent of simmering anger. "Tell us what happened."

Ginger continued, her words tumbling out in a rush as adrenaline fueled her memory. She described how the men had smashed her windshield as she tried to flee, only narrowly avoiding a collision with oncoming traffic. Her voice trembled as she recalled how she had swerved, hitting a curb, flattening a tire on the car.

"I ran into James's store, hoping for safety. But they followed me," Ginger explained, her eyes haunted by the memory. "James tried to reason with them, but they didn't listen. They... they killed him."

Tears welled in Ginger's eyes as she spoke of James's futile attempt to protect her. Susie's grip tightened on Kyle's arm, her own eyes mirroring the anguish and anger reflected in her sister's face.

"James dropped his gun, they stabbed him and then shot him with his own gun. It's been chaos," Ginger continued, her voice barely above a whisper now. "Gunshots, people shouting... It feels like a war zone out there. A county cop tried to intervene, but no one listened. They just ignored him and he drove away."

Kyle exchanged a glance with Susie, a silent understanding

passing between them. They needed to act, and get to a safer location. Kyle wanted to be back on his mountain.

"Let's get out of here," Kyle said firmly, taking charge. "We'll talk more once we're safe."

"Wait, what about Arnie, have either of you seen him?" Ginger asked frozen with fear.

"Arnie's fine, he is helping mom get up on the mountain to my cabin. Everyone is fine right now; we'll explain it all to you soon. For now, we need to move," Kyle told Ginger while gently pulling her arm to come with him.

As they walked back past the pawn store, Kyle stopped holding his arm out to stop Ginger and Susie.

"Are those the men who killed James?" Kyle asked looking at the ones who had been looting the store earlier.

"No, that isn't them," Ginger said.

The men, both in the early twenties finally spoke noticing Kyle was looking at them once again. "You all want one of these laptops?" The first man said. "Yeah, we will share man, we don't want trouble, we're just getting it before somebody else does," the other man told Kyle nervously after clearly seeing him holding the KSG shotgun.

"Getting it before somebody else does," Kyle said low to himself. It was the same thing Kyle had told Arnie earlier in the grocery store. He couldn't say anything to these guys for doing the same thing he had done. They just had different needs on their priority list. Kyle was pissed it was James's store they were stealing it from, but he couldn't deal with that now. Although he didn't know James, and had only met him hours earlier, James seemed like a nice man. James had helped Susie and that was good enough for respect in Kyle's book.

"You guys grab a blanket or sheet and place it over James in the back office please," Kyle said to them. The man must have already seen where some quilts were kept, and he ran over picking one up and hurried towards the office. Kyle felt satisfied they would at least do this, and he pulled on Gingers arm to continue moving. Susie followed up the rear watching for any other danger.

The trio moved swiftly towards the church where they had parked their truck, casting wary glances at the unfolding chaos around them. Kyle knew his sister was hurting and he wanted to give her time to soak in the situation, but time was something they didn't have. He motioned for them to continue, Ginger keeping watch for any signs of danger, her senses on high alert. As they approached the truck, Susie paused, looking back at the scene of destruction that had once been her quaint little shop. Her stare was broken quickly by Ginger.

"It's them," Ginger suddenly exclaimed, her voice filled with a mix of fear and anger. "Those are the two men who attacked me and killed James. Right there, breaking into that car," Ginger said to Kyle and Susie.

Kyle's jaw tightened, his gaze fixing on the figures Ginger pointed out. He turned to Susie, a silent question in his eyes.

"Robert and Horace Barker," Susie confirmed, her voice filled with bitterness. "James had mentioned them before. They had a dispute over some equipment James lent them."

"Ginger, get in the truck," Kyle instructed her.

Kyle watched the men for a moment, his grip tightening around the shotgun as he observed the brothers rummaging through the back of a Chevrolet Tahoe. They were carelessly pawing through someone's personal property, oblivious to the world around them. The men focused intently on whatever was in the storage totes in the vehicle's rear, their movements methodical and unhurried. One of the brothers, Horrace, glanced over his shoulder, noticing Kyle and Susie approaching. His eyes widened briefly before he tapped his brother and gestured for him to look.

Kyle's heart pounded in his chest, each beat a drum of impending confrontation. "Hold it, guys! Hands in the air. This is a citizen's arrest." The words spilled from his mouth instinctively, the gravity of the situation lending him a false sense of confidence. He held his KSG shotgun steady, its barrel aimed at the two men as they turned to face him. His mouth was dry, and he could feel the sweat trickling down his back as the hot summer sun unleashed its blaze.

"You assaulted my sister, and you killed an innocent man, you piece of shit!" Susie's voice trembled with rage and pain as she stopped beside Kyle, her handgun raised. Her breath came in short, furious bursts, her eyes wide with a mix of fear and fury. "James never did anything but be helpful to you both."

"He took our money, made himself rich off people like us. He took money from you in rent. Both of you put those guns down and walk away, and nobody will get hurt, Susie." Horrace's voice was cold, his words lacking any genuine remorse. His brother's glare bored into Kyle, a silent challenge in his eyes.

Kyle's mind raced. How did it come to this? He tried to steady his breathing, to focus. "You guys think it's okay to attack a woman in the middle of the street?" he asked, his voice filled with disbelief and anger.

"James was my friend, a friend to everyone in this town." Susie's voice quivered with emotion, the memory of James's kindness cutting through her anger. "You went after my sister!"

Robert, the other brother, slowly slid his hand behind his back, his fingers curling around the grip of a gun. It was the same gun he had taken from James, the same one he had used to kill him. Kyle's eyes narrowed, tracking the movement. The world seemed to slow, every second stretching into eternity.

"Stop right there. Slowly let that arm back down. I'll kill you before you can get that gun around. Please don't force me to do that; this can end peacefully." Kyle's voice was calm, but the tension in the air was deep. He watched as Robert's arm slowly lowered back to his side. His stomach churned with the sickening anticipation of what he might have to do.

"You two just go on, get out of here. We have things to do, mind your business. We're sorry about your sister's car. We'll pay for the damages," Horrace's words dripped with insincerity, a mocking apology that did little to ease the tension. "Besides, ain't gonna be no arrest. Ole' Langston already left here like his ass was on fire."

Gunshots echoed in the distance, the sudden noise causing

Susie to whip her head around, scanning for any immediate threat. Kyle turned his head slightly, just enough to get a glance in the direction of the shots, but his eyes quickly snapped back to the brothers. He caught the movement of Robert's hand reaching for the gun once more.

"Don't!" Kyle shouted, but it was too late. Robert almost reached his gun when Kyle's finger tightened on the trigger.

Boom! The shotgun blast was deafening, the recoil slamming into Kyle's shoulder as nine pellets tore into Robert's chest. The force of the blast threw Robert back into the open hatch of the Tahoe, his body sliding slowly down onto the pavement. The stolen model 1911 pistol clattered to the ground next to him, a grim punctuation to the violent encounter.

Kyle worked the pump action on the shotgun, the spent cartridge ejecting with a puff of smoke, the sound of it bouncing off the asphalt oddly resonant in the sudden silence. He loaded the next round, the action punctuated by a tense stillness that seemed to stretch time itself. The world around them faded away, leaving only the sound of the pump action shotgun, a grim reminder of the lethal force Kyle wielded.

"No!" Horrace's cry was a mix of anguish and rage as he dropped to his knees beside his fallen brother. "Robert! Robert!" He looked up at Kyle, his eyes burning with hatred. "You motherfucker! You just killed my brother."

"He drew on me; he gave me no choice." Kyle's voice was steady, but there was a hard edge to his words. He kept his shotgun trained on Horrace, ready for any sudden movement. His heart ached with the weight of what he'd done. "Don't do anything stupid, and you won't have to join him."

"You will pay for this. I promise you now that you will pay! I know where you live, Susie girl. As for you, I will see you again soon," Horrace's voice was filled with venom, his gaze a promise of future retribution. He stood up slowly, kicking the pistol towards Kyle. "You willing to kill an unarmed man now?"

Kyle bent down, keeping his shotgun trained on Horrace as he picked up the pistol with his left hand. "I could kill you now and end this, but enough has been done already. I didn't want this; it didn't have to happen. I don't advise you to come looking for us, but if you do, dig your own grave first." He began to back away towards the truck, his eyes never leaving Horrace.

Susie mirrored his movements, her gaze locked on Horrace as they retreated. Horrace stood motionless, his eyes tracking them with a mixture of rage and calculation. As they neared the truck, he raised his hand to his face, splitting his forefinger and middle finger in a gesture that showed a promise he would be seeing them again for a future encounter. Kyle nodded in acknowledgment, understanding the unspoken threat.

They climbed into the truck, Kyle starting the engine and pulled away. Horrace watched them go, his eyes burning with a promise of vengeance.

"You just killed a man," Ginger said quietly as they drove. "You just killed a man. He deserved it, but I can't believe that just happened. What the hell is going on with everybody?"

"He knows where I live. You heard him. Maybe we should go kill him too," Susie suggested, her voice shaky but firm.

"I don't know the answer right now, Susie, but we didn't kill him, and we aren't turning around. We're going home." Kyle's tone was final. "And no mentioning what happened just now to Mom. She doesn't need to know that yet."

The two sisters nodded in agreement, the truck falling into a tense silence as they continued to Rachel's house. The weight of the quiet was crushing until Ginger broke it.

"I'm sorry, Kyle, that you had to kill that man. Are you okay?" Ginger asked, her voice filled with concern.

"That wasn't my first, the way things are now, it may not be the last," Kyle replied, his voice distant, eyes fixed on the road.

"What do you mean it wasn't the first? Who else have you killed?" Susie's voice was sharp with surprise and a hint of fear.

"It was some trouble out west a couple of years ago. I've never told any of you about it. Don't say anything to Mom; she doesn't know." Kyle's tone allowed no argument, his jaw set tight against the memories.

As they passed by Creekside Convenience, Ginger noticed the cluster of vehicles there. A hastily scrawled sign on posterboard hung on the front door: "Out of Gas! – store's closed." Wayne stood on the steps, shotgun in hand, waving as they drove by, oblivious to what they had just done. Susie began to fill Ginger in on everything that had happened, recounting the chaotic events as they made their way back to Rachel's house.

CHAPTER TWENTY-FOUR
"A Surge of Responsibility"

Arnie was meticulously loading everything he could onto the ATV cargo hold and utility trailer. The clinking sounds of shovels, rakes, and pickaxes echoed as he arranged them for the next haul. Inside, Rachel was hastily stuffing bed linens and clothing into bags, her mind racing with what essentials they might need. Boxes filled with all the food in the house were stacked high, including cooler and freezer items stowed in an ice chest. They knew these perishables wouldn't last long, but she planned to enjoy them while they could.

As Kyle's truck pulled into the driveway, a wave of relief washed over Arnie. His eyes lit up when he saw Ginger leap out of the truck and run toward him. She threw her arms around him in a tight bear hug, and Arnie, unable to hold back, let tears of happiness stream down his face, knowing his mom was safe.

"Let's give them a minute," Kyle said softly, placing his arm around Susie and guiding her toward the front porch steps. "We need to check on Mom and see why she hasn't left yet." Kyle's voice wavered slightly as he spoke, the weight of the situation pressing heavily on him. Seeing Arnie's raw emotion reminded Kyle just how much fear his little buddy had been carrying all day. He felt a surge of pride for Arnie, who had managed to hold it together and keep working toward their survival. Deep down, Kyle longed for a comforting hug from his own mom, but he knew they had to stay focused.

Inside the house, Uncle Tom was in deep conversation with

Rachel. Kyle and Susie joined them, sharing most of what had happened in Hurley. Arnie and Ginger entered shortly after, and everyone gathered to hear Kyle's plan. He laid out his vision for their next steps, urging them all to join him at the cabin. He explained the vulnerabilities of their current homes and emphasized the need for unity and security.

"I'm not ready to leave my house yet, Kyle. You've been right so far, I agree with that," Uncle Tom said, his voice steady but firm. "But I want to stay as long as I can at my home. I'll get more items to my shack and be ready if I need to move quickly." Uncle Tom's eyes, usually so clear, now carried a hint of stubborn determination. He often referred to his cabin as a shack, a modest comparison to the one Kyle had built. The sign outside, "Tom's Shack," bore testament to his independent spirit.

"You can't stay awake around the clock, Uncle Tom," Kyle pleaded. "If the wrong people come around, I'm afraid you can't defend yourself." Kyle's concern was evident, but Uncle Tom remained stubborn.

"I'm not going, Kyle, not right now. I'll help you get your things and everyone up the mountain. I got my old Honda four-wheeler running; it'll haul two or three people. I have that small buggy for the mower you can hook to the four-wheeler." Uncle Tom's voice softened as he placed a reassuring arm around Kyle, a rare gesture of affection that spoke volumes.

"Okay, let's get everything we can up to the cabin today. We'll figure out the rest as we go," Kyle said, removing his hat and running a hand through his hair, the weight of leadership heavy on his shoulders. He knew arguing with Uncle Tom was futile for now.

"I've got the Can-Am loaded up and ready to go. I can take Mom and Mamaw on this trip and be back for another load shortly," Arnie announced, his youthful determination shining through. Kyle's heart swelled with pride for Arnie, who was stepping up in ways he hadn't expected. It wasn't the time for accolades, but Kyle gave him a nod of approval.

"Mom, you go with Arnie. There's plenty of food at the

cabin and it's safe. It'll be good for now. Once things are back to normal, you can come back home," Kyle said to Rachel, though he privately doubted there would be a return to normal anytime soon.

"What about my kids, Kyle? What do I do?" Susie's voice quivered with helplessness. "Deanna is working in Phelps at the nursing home today and Rocky should have the girls at home." Panic edged her voice. "I know Joel is in bed; he was up playing his game all night, I'm sure." Susie's eyes darted anxiously toward the road.

"If Deanna is in Phelps, that's not far. There's hardly anything between here and there, so she should be fine. Take your car, go to their house, and tell Rocky to pack what bags they need and come stay on the mountain. Do the same with Joel. Wake him up and tell him to come on. I'll be here," Kyle instructed, his tone firm yet reassuring.

"What's up?" Arnie asked, jogging over to Kyle.

"You said you were gaming all night. When did you last sleep?" Kyle's voice was laced with concern for the young man's state of mind.

"I got out of bed yesterday around noon. I'm good right now; I got this," Arnie replied with a determined nod. "I'll get them up the mountain and be back in about thirty minutes." Arnie's confidence was unwavering.

"Here you go, little buddy. Take these walkies with you. I'll give Uncle Tom one and keep one myself. Stay tuned to channel one for now," Kyle said, handing over the walkie-talkies.

Arnie left, the ATV and utility trailer loaded to the brim with supplies. Rachel glanced back at Kyle, tears glistening in her eyes as they pulled away. He gave her a thumbs-up and a broad smile, a silent promise that they would get through this. Ginger sat with her face in her hands, the weight of the morning's events pressing heavily on her. She thought about her daughter in Grundy, hoping she was safe in their secure neighborhood. Arnie was set to drop Ginger off at her house near the base of the trail so she could start packing for them both. Uncle Tom returned home to retrieve his extra four-wheeler for anyone who might need it, Kyle giving him a walkie-talkie with the same channel instructions.

Kyle took a seat on the front porch steps and let out a deep breath. He had prepared for something bad to happen one day, but he wasn't ready for it to be today. No day was a good day for a major disaster. He knew there was so much more to learn, so much more to prepare for. Could he take care of everyone? Was he ready for this enormous responsibility? He had to be strong and set an example for the others, showing them that they would survive.

As he replayed the scene from earlier in his mind, Kyle struggled with the gravity of what he had done. He had taken a man's life, leaving him dead in a parking lot. He wondered if the man's brother would seek revenge. Although Kyle felt a sting of guilt, he had no regrets. He knew that if he hadn't acted, it could have been him, Susie, or all three of them lying dead in that parking lot.

He closed his eyes, finding himself transported back to Kansas. He stood in the parking lot of a bar, rain pouring down as he looked at the lifeless body at his feet. A woman's screams pierced the night as he stood soaked to the bone, the water streaming down his face. The neon glow from the bar's beer signs illuminated the dead man's face. The flickering red and blue lights grew brighter as sirens wailed in the distance. Kyle opened his eyes, his breath ragged and his face slick with sweat. He stood and walked to his ATV, retrieving a bottle of water.

Kyle struggled to clear his mind, recalling the survival course he had taken. The instructor had emphasized the importance of quick, decisive action. Hesitation could mean death. The instructor's stories of lawlessness in third-world countries and his experiences in the military had made a lasting impression. Kyle wished he could thank the man for saving his life, twice now.

The sound of a four-wheeler approaching snapped Kyle back to the present. Uncle Tom rolled into Rachel's yard on the

ATV, something she didn't like to see. ATVs could wreak havoc on a beautiful grass lawn, and although she wouldn't say it, she didn't like them rode on her lawn.

"Here you go, Kyle. Let someone use this," Uncle Tom said, dismounting the Honda. "I'm going to walk back to the house and get my side-by-side. I'll see you soon."

"Okay, thanks, Uncle Tom," Kyle said.

Susie returned without Rocky, but she had her granddaughters in tow. The girls, cute as buttons and feisty as snakes, climbed out of the car. Clara Beth, the older one, was usually reserved and quiet. She liked to keep to herself. Clara Beth got out first and leaned the seat forward to let her little sister climb out.

"Here comes trouble!" Kyle said with a smile, trying to put the girls at ease.

As Coraline climbed out and ran to Kyle, he knelt and opened his arms for a hug, but she punched him in the stomach instead. At six years old, she loved to fight and wrestle. Kyle fell forward, exhaling, and heard Coraline's laughter as she landed on him hard after leaping into the air for a double knee drop.

"That's what you get, buddy boy," Coraline said, giggling.

"You win, you win. I give up," Kyle said, rolling over and pulling Coraline in for a hug. "Coraline the champion!" he exclaimed, and she beamed with pride.

"We don't got no juice, Uncle Kyle!" Coraline complained, her young Appalachian accent thick. "We can't even watch TV, and the dumb internet don't work. I can't get on TikTok or Snap today!" She wagged her finger at Kyle, her frustration clearly shown.

Kyle stood up and gave Clara Beth a hug, ruffling her hair. He could see the worry in her eyes, knowing she understood more than her sister.

"It's going to be okay," Kyle whispered to Clara Beth. "You girls jump on Uncle Tom's four-wheeler. Your grandma is going to take you to my cabin on the mountain. It's great, and when I get there, I'll have a surprise for you." The girls quickly climbed onto the Honda, their spirits lifting at the promise of a surprise.

"What about Rocky and Joel?" Kyle asked Susie once the girls were out of earshot. "Are they coming?"

"Joel still doesn't think it's real. He said he wasn't going anywhere. Rocky asked me to bring the girls, and he's going to get Deanna. He said he'd come up the mountain once he gets back with her," Susie explained, rubbing her hands over her face in frustration.

"We're going to make room. You just get them to the cabin. Be careful; you'll probably meet Arnie on his way back down. He has the trailer, so he shouldn't be going too fast," Kyle advised.

A few minutes later, Kyle saw Rocky drive by on his way to Phelps, honking his horn as he passed. Kyle wished he could have gone with him, but there was no stopping now. He went inside and continued gathering items he thought would be helpful, including a DVD player and some movies for the girls to stave off boredom.

Arnie returned, and they continued loading the remaining supplies, hauling them up the mountain. Uncle Tom helped, picking up Ginger and her luggage in his side-by-side. The men worked tirelessly through the evening, ensuring everyone's safety. As night fell, they were exhausted but determined, knowing the real challenges were just beginning.

CHAPTER TENTY-FIVE
"Mountain Sanctuary"

At the cabin high on the mountain, there was still plenty of settling in to be done. Kyle had convinced Arnie to get some rest on the couch while the others organized their personal belongings. Arnie quickly fell asleep, boots still on, after extracting a promise from Kyle that he wouldn't leave the cabin without him. Kyle marveled at how well Arnie had handled the day's chaos, showing remarkable strength that helped Kyle maintain his own composure through the turmoil.

"Mom, you take the spare bedroom. Decorate it any way you want, make it yours," Kyle told his mother, wanting her to feel she had her own space. He carried in a box of Rachel's pictures and knick-knacks, ready to move furniture if needed. Rachel, however, said it was fine as it was, reluctant to trouble Kyle with additional tasks.

Kyle's bedroom was the subject of a coin toss between Ginger and Susie. Susie won but graciously gave the room to Ginger, opting to sleep in the loft with the girls. It was her plan all along, enjoying the thrill of the gamble more than the room itself. She hoped the loft would feel like a camping adventure for Coraline and Clara Beth. Kyle and Arnie would take one of the bunkhouses outside, giving everyone a bit more space.

"Alright, girlies, I promised you a surprise. I brought a DVD player and a box full of movies. You can watch some tonight if you like, just remember to turn off the TV when you're done to conserve the solar batteries. Tomorrow we start fresh working on the farm," Kyle said to Coraline and Clara Beth. Clara Beth, wasn't interested in farm work, showing little interest, but Kyle hoped she would warm up to it once she bonded with the animals. Coraline, however, had different thoughts.

"This isn't a farm, Uncle Kyle! Where are the cows and ducks? Farms have to have cows and ducks," Coraline insisted, her small hands gesturing emphatically. "And where are the horses? Farms always have horses! And goats too. You can't have a real farm without goats," she added, her brow furrowing in disbelief at the idea of a farm without these essential animals. "What about a tractor?" she added, her eyes wide with excitement at the thought of driving a big tractor.

"Okay, yeah, we might need a tractor, but we do have ATVs," Kyle said trying to keep up with her line of questions.

"And we need a scarecrow. Every farm has a scarecrow!" Coraline finished, crossing her arms as if her case was now undeniably clear.

"Well, sassy pants, maybe we can find a cow and some ducks. Then we'll have a farm like Old McDonald's. I need your help to build it and make us a farm. We'll call it Sassy Pants Mountain Farm!" Kyle said, laughing at her serious expression. "How's that sound to you?"

"Why don't we call it Smarty Pants Farm and name it after you, buddy boy?" Coraline shot back with a cheeky grin.

"How about you go watch a movie, and tomorrow we'll figure it out. I'll get some paint and a board, and we can make a sign," Kyle said, shaking his head with a smile. "She's going to have fun up here," he remarked to Susie.

"I'll have more fun when you get my TikTok working. I've got people who need to see my videos," Coraline responded.

Rachel had brewed a pot of coffee, its familiar aroma filling the cabin and offering a momentary sense of normalcy amidst the chaos. They all gathered around the wooden table, their faces etched with worry and fatigue. Each sip of the hot coffee was a small comfort, a momentary distraction from the heavy burden of their thoughts.

As the minutes passed, they began to share their fears and concerns, their voices hushed and trembling. The weight of uncertainty pressed down on them, an invisible force that made their hearts ache. The absence of family members loomed large, a constant, gnawing worry that none of them could shake.

"I can't believe this is happening. It doesn't feel real," Rachel said, her voice cracking as she struggled to hold back tears. Her eyes, usually so full of strength, now glistened with unshed tears. She had thought she'd faced everything life could throw at her—loss, hardship, betrayal—but this was different. The end of the world was something else entirely, an unimaginable horror that defied comprehension.

Rachel's hands trembled as she held her coffee cup, seeking solace in its warmth. She glanced around the table at her family, seeing her own fear reflected back at her. The children's wide eyes were filled with confusion and anxiety, while the adults wore expressions of grim determination. They were all trying to be brave, to stay strong for each other, but the cracks were beginning to show.

"I keep thinking I'll wake up and this will all be a nightmare," she continued, her voice barely above a whisper. "But every time I open my eyes, it's still here. We're still here."

Kyle reached across the table and placed a reassuring hand on his mother's. "We'll get through this, Mom. We've faced tough times before, and we've always come out stronger. We have each other, and that's what matters most."

Rachel nodded, squeezing his hand tightly. "I know, Kyle. But it's so hard not knowing what's out there, not knowing if the others are safe. I just—" Her voice broke, and a single tear slipped down her cheek. "I just want us all to be together again."

They sat in silence for a moment, the only sound was that of the soft ticking of the clock on the wall. It was a small Bulova clock that Kyle had received as a gift from his company after ten years of service. The reality of their situation settled heavily on their shoulders, a shared burden that bound them even closer together. In that quiet moment, they found a flicker of strength in each other's presence, a glimmer of hope that they could hold on to as they faced the uncertain days ahead.

Kyle explained the solar power system and emphasized the need to be conservative with energy use while they adapted to their new surroundings. They all hoped this situation wouldn't last long, but deep down, they knew it might. Kyle reassured them it wouldn't be easy, but they could persevere. They had all grown up watching "Little House on the Prairie," and in many ways, their new life would mirror that show as they lived off the land. Kyle, having lived at the cabin for nearly a year, knew this change would be challenging for them. He had chosen this life, but now his family was thrust into it.

Kyle took Susie and Ginger outside to show them around the property. Susie hadn't been to the cabin since the early days of its construction, and both were amazed at how much Kyle, Arnie, and Uncle Tom had accomplished. Kyle showed them the bunkhouses he had built, explaining that with a little work, they could house a family.

"These bunkhouses can hold several people once we clear out the junk tomorrow. I can turn one into a living space for Rocky, Deanna, and the girls," Kyle said.

In the dim light of the setting sun, Kyle led them to the small barn, its wooden exterior standing resilient against the elements. The barn's rustic charm was evident in its earthy scent of hay that filled the air. The wide doors creaked open, revealing a cozy yet functional space that had clearly been well-cared for.

Inside, the barn was divided into several stalls, each one meticulously maintained with fresh straw lining the floors. A sturdy wooden ladder led up to a hayloft, where bales of hay were stacked neatly, ready to provide feed and bedding. The soft, golden light filtering through the cracks in the wooden slats gave the space a warm, inviting glow.

"You already have hay stocked?" Susie asked.

"Yeah, I wasn't sure when I would get bigger animals but I wanted to be prepared when I did," Kyle explained as he looked up towards the stacked bales of hay.

Against one wall, various tools hung in an orderly fashion: pitchforks, shovels, and buckets, all essential for the daily chores of a working farm. In another corner, a stack of neatly organized feed bags awaited the animals they had hoped to acquire. Kyle pointed to a large, empty stall that he had intended for a cow, and another space where a horse could have comfortably resided.

"I planned on getting a cow and a horse, but that might not happen now," Kyle said, a hint of regret in his voice. He then chuckled, trying to lighten the mood. "I'll try to find something else for Coraline. She made that clear."

There were shelves filled with jars of various supplies—medicine for livestock and grooming tools. The barn also had a small tack room, where saddles, bridles, and other riding gear were stored, waiting for the day they might be used. A workbench, complete with a vice and an assortment of tools, showed signs of recent use, indicating that Kyle had been busy preparing for his new life here.

The barn's simplicity was comforting, a testament to the hard work and preparation that had gone into making this place a sanctuary. Despite the uncertainty of their situation, the barn stood as a symbol of hope and resilience, ready to support them in their new, challenging reality.

As Kyle showed them the tall fence wrapped in barbed wire and razor wire, they were shocked. The watchtowers he had built also surprised them.

"I can't believe you did all this. It must have cost a fortune," Ginger said, placing her hand on a support beam.

"I thought maybe I was a little crazy when I built them. I hope we don't have to use them for protection, but I'm glad we have them just in case," Kyle said, tapping the beam with his knuckles.

"How much did all this cost?" Ginger asked again, always curious about expenses.

"It wasn't that expensive because we did most of the work ourselves. I saved a lot on labor. Of course, it doesn't matter now; money might be worthless for a long time," Kyle said, exchanging a knowing look with Susie, both aware of Ginger's nosiness.

"I want to climb up there. Can we?" Susie asked, already reaching for the ladder to the first tower.

"Sure, go ahead. It's getting dark, but there are binoculars up there if you want to try them. Just don't fall and break a hip on me, grandma," Kyle teased.

"I'll show you grandma," Susie retorted, trying to climb the ladder quickly.

Ginger followed, and then Kyle joined them. As they stood on the platform overlooking the valley, the dim moonlight cast a serene glow on the treetops below. Kyle pointed out Uncle Tom's cabin location, explaining that they would be able to see it clearly in the daylight. They fell into an unplanned silence, each lost in thought, the weight of their situation heavy on their minds.

"Mom is going to stay shaken up for a while. We need to keep her as calm as we can. Let's keep our secret from earlier today. If any of you get worried, talk to me or each other. Try not to show any panic to Mom," Kyle advised his sisters, who nodded in agreement.

"I agree. But I want to ask you something. What did you mean earlier today about this not being your first time killing someone?" Susie asked.

Kyle leaned against the rough wooded post of the tower's support structure, the memory of that night in Kansas creeping back into his mind. The wind rustled through the trees, bringing with it a chill that matched the unease he felt whenever he thought about those turbulent days.

"It was just outside of Dodge City," Kyle began, his voice carrying a weight of regret. "One night, after a long day at the hotel, I decided to grab a drink at a local bar. I didn't know it then, but that decision would change everything."

"I was just minding my own business, nursing a beer, when things took a turn. This guy, he was drunk and looking for trouble. He mistook my presence as something it wasn't, accused me of eyeing his woman," Kyle continued, his voice frustrated at the memory.

"I tried to reason with him, to defuse the situation, but he wasn't having it. Before I knew it, fists were flying. It was a blur of adrenaline and desperation. In the heat of the moment, he came at me, swinging wildly. I managed to sidestep his blow, knocking him on his ass," Kyle squatted against the support post, wrapping his arms around his knees.

Kyle's gaze dropped to the ground, the guilt of that night still heavy on his conscience. "His friends got him out of the bar, I thought that was going to be the end of it."

He looked up at Ginger, meeting her eyes filled with understanding. "When I left, they were waiting for me in the parking lot. The aftermath was messy. The police got involved, but there were witnesses who corroborated my story. They couldn't prove intent, but it was clear I had defended myself. Still, the incident stained my reputation. I felt unwelcome after that night."

Susie reached out, placing a comforting hand on Kyle's shoulder. "You did what you had to do," she said softly, her voice steady with reassurance.

Kyle nodded, grateful for her understanding. "It was a wake-up call. I realized then that I needed a change. So, I packed up and headed back here, to the mountains."

Silence settled over them, absorbing Kyle's story, understanding the weight of his past and the determination that brought him back to this mountain top he called home once again.

"I've wanted to build this place for years. After that happened, I didn't want to be in large cities anymore. I just wanted to be here and enjoy each day I'm given," Kyle replied.

"I can't believe you never told us about this, I hope you don't have to kill anyone else." Ginger said as Kyle nodded and began climbing down the ladder.

CHAPTER TWENTY-SIX
"The Watchers of the Night"

As darkness fell and everyone settled into the cabin, Kyle decided he needed to go back down the trail. He felt confident everyone was safe for now; only a limited number of people even knew about his place. He loaded shotguns for Susie and Ginger, explaining how to use the firearms. He assured them he would lock the gate as he left and described the large, bright light activated by motion that would come on if triggered. He noted it could be triggered easily so he set the sensitivity to low, meaning it would take a large animal like deer or bears to trigger it.

"I want to check on Uncle Tom and find out about Rocky and Deanna. I thought they'd be here by now," Kyle said to Rachel, Ginger, and Susie as they sat at the small kitchen table. "I'd also like to see Joel and try one more time to convince him to reconsider. I need to wake Arnie; I know he wants to come with me." He glanced at Arnie, who was still asleep on the couch, one leg draped over the back and an arm hanging off the edge, drool soaking the side of his mouth.

Kyle woke Arnie with a firm shake and handed him a bottle of water, which Arnie quickly drank down. Kyle refueled the ATV and prepared a go-bag for both of them. He went over the plan with Rachel, Ginger, and Susie. It had been eerily quiet; there wasn't even the sound of another ATV on the mountain. Most days, Kyle would hear the echo of small engines through the trees.

Kyle added two AR-15 rifles to the ATV for added

protection. The two left the cabin, locking the gate behind them, and headed down the trail. Kyle knew Uncle Tom had chosen to stay in his home despite Kyle's concerns. They continued to the bottom in darkness, the normally lit power pole lights absent. The beams of the ATV headlights cut through the night, occasionally illuminating large spiders in webs between the trees, giving Kyle chills when he saw one. Arnie laughed at his reactions as Kyle leaned side to side trying not to touch or be touched by a web.

As they neared Uncle Tom's house, they saw him in the driveway, holding a lantern. A fire burned nearby, and more people were gathered around it. A green truck and another side-by-side ATV filled the driveway. Three men sat next to Uncle Tom by the fire, watching as Kyle drove closer.

"That's Snaggle's truck. He's a good dude," Arnie said to Kyle as they crossed the small bridge into Tom's driveway.

"His name is Snaggle?" Kyle asked.

"Yeah. He had a crooked tooth when he was younger, they called him Snaggle Tooth. It shortened to Snaggle after he got it fixed. That's what Uncle Tom told me." Arnie shrugged.

"There's little Arnie bug," Snaggle announced.

"What's up, Snaggle? You got things under control yet?" Arnie said with a laugh. "This is my Uncle Kyle. He moved back last year," Arnie added, as Snaggle looked at Kyle.

"Yeah, Kyle, I haven't seen you in a while, but I know you're one of Rachel's boys. This here is Devin, my late wife's brother," Snaggle said, pointing to the man standing with him and extending his hand to Kyle.

"Yes, sir, that's right. I've been living out west for the last twenty years," Kyle said, shaking Snaggle's hand firmly.

"I know Tom has been helping you build a place up the mountain, but he never let me come see it," Snaggle said.

"Uncle Tom has helped me a lot, so has Arnie here. His years of wisdom have been invaluable. I'm glad to be back home now and able to work on it," Kyle replied.

"There you go, throwing old man jokes at me," Tom said.

"You may not be glad you're back now. This place has gone

crazy today. I've never seen anything like it," Snaggle said to Kyle. "Fred's Gas Station is on fire right now. The whole place was blazing, not a fire truck in sight. People were looting it before the fire got out of control."

"Fred's body is burning up in there. He was covered on the floor earlier. I don't think any ambulances or cops ever stopped," Uncle Tom added. He looked at Kyle and told him what they had been discussing before he arrived. "Snaggle was just telling me about his boy Charles getting home from Grundy. Tell Kyle about it, Snaggle."

"When my boy Charles got home, he said only a few policemen were trying to control Grundy. Many of the cops said they had their own families to take care of and left. He said the grocery store was overrun by looters. The Walmart was the same way, people just taking whatever they wanted," Snaggle told Kyle, spitting a stream of tobacco juice onto the ground. "Sorry, Tommy, bad habit, I know," Snaggle said, calling Uncle Tom by his old childhood name. Most of his older friends still did that.

"Charles already went back to the hospital. They told him to go home and check on his family. He's a nurse. He said a lot of the nurses on duty left early," Snaggle continued. "I'll get word back to you tomorrow, Tommy, when he gets home again."

As Snaggle talked more about what had happened during the day, it became more surreal. Kyle told them about his trip to Hurley, minus the part about killing Robert. He mentioned Allen Hall and the trouble they had with him. Arnie explained the dead man on the pharmacy steps, and Kyle described Ginger being harassed along with James being killed. Each story made Uncle Tom and Snaggle shake their heads at the thought of what was happening in their small community.

"I'm going to run for now. I want to check on Joel, Rocky, and Deanna," Kyle said.

"Joel is gone. He said he was going to ride to Hurley and see what the big deal was. I saw him at Fred's watching it burn, and he still acted like it wasn't serious. Rocky's truck went by just a few minutes ago; he's probably home," Devin said.

"Okay, thanks. That sounds like Joel. You guys be safe tonight. How about meeting up tomorrow to figure out a plan for the community? I'd like for Charles to come; sounds like he could help with some information," Kyle said, looking at each of them.

"That sounds good, Kyle. I'll bring Charles. Let's meet back here at Tommy's around noon," Snaggle added as Kyle got back on his ATV with Arnie.

"Keep your eyes open, Kyle. I saw Allen drive by here an hour ago in that Mustang again," Uncle Tom said.

"Thanks for the heads up. I will," Kyle replied.

Kyle and Arnie headed for Rocky and Deanna's house, riding the ATV on the small country road. Kyle told Arnie to keep his AR-15 at the ready in case they ran into trouble. It was only a mile from their home, so it would take just a few minutes. As they pulled into Rocky and Deanna's driveway, they saw a flashlight shining inside the house. Rocky stepped onto the porch, holding a baseball bat.

"Easy, big boy, it's just Arnie and me. We came to check on you. We got worried when you didn't come up to the cabin," Kyle said as Rocky lowered the bat.

"I'm glad to see you two. There are some serious nutjobs out tonight. I went to the nursing home to pick up Deanna. If I'd had a gun, I'd have shot some people," Rocky said frantically as Deanna came out behind him.

"You wouldn't know how to shoot a gun if you had one, Rocky. Lordy, we've had a time tonight. You wouldn't believe what we've seen. Are the girls at your cabin?" Deanna asked.

"They're fine. They're with Mom, Susie, and Ginger. They were watching a movie when I left," Kyle said, as Deanna stepped down from the porch to hug him.

"Rocky came to the nursing home. We had power from a generator for a few hours, but it stopped working. Families picked up patients, which was probably a good thing. Two patients died today, one from a heart attack, the other from an unknown cause," Deanna told Kyle and Arnie, her arms flailing.

"Those sound like natural causes," Arnie said.

"Oh, hell no, that wasn't all. They didn't want Deanna to leave. Somebody even cut her tires down. I think it was someone who worked there so she couldn't leave," Rocky said.

"Yeah, they slashed all my new tires. My car is still there, and it's staying there. I'm not going back. We tried to drive home through Stopover, but there was a huge fight at the intersection where that store used to be. A man shot two others; they were on the ground, probably dead. The road was blocked by cars," Deanna said, her voice rising.

"Look here, this is a bullet hole in my truck bed. I turned around, and someone shot at us. I don't know if they meant to or not, but it hit my truck," Rocky said, pointing to the bullet hole. "I hauled ass to get away. Then we get to the turnoff at Pawpaw Mountain, and there's a roadblock. They charged me thirty dollars to get through."

"You two get what you need and get up the mountain. We can talk more once you're there," Kyle said, wanting to move quickly, not liking the exposure by the road.

Arnie pulled Rocky's ATV from the storage building while they gathered important items. Arnie loaded the ATV as Kyle glanced toward Fred's Gas N Go, seeing the red glare of the fire lighting the sky.

Rocky and Deanna followed Kyle back to Rachel's house. They stopped to check on Uncle Tom once more. He was still out in his shed. Kyle really wanted Uncle Tom to come to the cabin, but he couldn't force him. He could only hope he'd be safe.

"Keep that walkie-talkie close, Uncle Tom. If you need us, use it," Kyle said before they left, Uncle Tom watching their taillights disappear into the darkness.

After reaching the cabin, there were hugs and smiles as Rocky and Deanna arrived. Everyone caught up on their day's events, and Kyle listened, thankful that those who made it to the cabin were safe and secure, at least for now.

"Everyone needs to get some rest. We need to figure this out tomorrow. We'll plan our next steps," Kyle said.

"Are you sure there is enough room for everybody here?"

Deanna asked, looking about the cabin. "I mean, Rocky and I are the only couple here, we could take the cabin with the girls if you all want us to."

Everyone looked at one another, puzzled by the remark. "How about for tonight, we all get some sleep. Tomorrow, we can set the bunkhouse up for the happy couple." Kyle said before exiting the cabin into the darkness.

CHAPTER TWENTY-SEVEN
"Message's in Blood"

The first light of dawn painted the sky in soft hues of pink and gold as Kyle stirred awake. The events of the previous night still echoed in his mind, driving him to act with urgency. He slipped quietly out of bed, careful not to disturb Arnie, who slept soundly on a cot in the corner of the room.

With determination etched on his face, Kyle made his way to the watchtower that overlooked Uncle Tom's modest cabin. With his body aching, he climbed the ladder and stretched upwards, releasing the tightness in his back. Kyle listened as birds chirped from the trees, the sound a reprieve from what awaited Kyle off the mountain. From the platform, he raised his binoculars, scanning the surrounding woods and the clearing where Uncle Tom's cabin stood. There was no sign of movement, Kyle knew he hadn't come to his cabin.

"The coast looks clear," Kyle muttered to himself.

Turning away, Kyle descended from the watchtower, his mind already racing with plans and worries. He returned to the bunkhouse where Arnie was beginning to move, a mixture of exhaustion and determination evident in his young eyes.

"Arnie," Kyle said softly, "we need to check on Joel. Something's not right, I don't like this feeling I have."

"Yeah, sure thing, Uncle Kyle. Let me get my boots on and we'll roll out," Arnie said as he stood, shaking the sleepiness away. He did some quick stretches and bounded out the door.

"Look over there, Arnie. Across the ridge towards town, all

the smoke in the air," Kyle said as he pointed at the thick smoke in the air, the large cloud building as the smoke continued.

"You think they have already burned the whole town?" Arnie asked, before rising back upright, tossing a small pebble to the side. "Let's get going."

Kyle nodded, his expression mirroring Arnie's concern. They mounted their ATV in silence, the engine breaking the morning stillness as they navigated the familiar path towards Joel's house. The crisp morning air carried the scent of pine and damp earth, a sharp contrast to the tension that hung heavy in the air.

As they arrived, Uncle Tom was nowhere to be found, and his doors were unusually locked—a rare occurrence that highlighted the current tension. Kyle guessed Uncle Tom was probably farther up the road meeting with friends, as his ATV was missing. Kyle kept his suspicions about Allen potentially visiting Tom last night to himself, not wanting to worry Arnie.

Kyle left a quick note for Uncle Tom before he and Arnie proceeded to Joel's house. As they approached Joel's house, Kyle's heart sank at the sight of Joel's battered car in the driveway. It was clear from a distance that something terrible had happened overnight. The damage to the vehicle spoke of violence and danger, confirming Kyle's worst fears. Parking his ATV beside Joel's car, Kyle scanned the surroundings with a wary eye. Every rustle of leaves, every creak of a branch made him tense, ready for any threat that might emerge. Arnie, sensing his uncle's unease, stayed close.

"What the heck happened, Uncle Kyle?" Arnie asked, his voice a mixture of fear and disbelief as he took in the wreckage of Joel's car.

Kyle's jaw tightened as he surveyed the scene. The rear bumper was crumpled, the back window shattered, and shards of glass littered the driveway. The passenger side bore the marks of a violent encounter, with broken glass and dents marring the once pristine surface. It was clear that Joel had been through something harrowing.

"Kyle, look! There's Joel on the porch," Arnie exclaimed, his voice rising with urgency as he pointed towards the figure lying still in the early morning light.

Kyle's heart skipped a beat as he saw Joel lying face down on the porch. Without a word, he unholstered his Glock, a reflex born in these uncertain times. His eyes swept the area, scanning for any signs of danger as he moved swiftly towards Joel, Arnie close behind.

"Joel, Joel!" Arnie called out, his voice a mix of relief and concern as he gently shook Joel's shoulder.

Joel groaned softly, rolling onto his back with effort. His battered appearance spoke volumes, telling a tale of violence and confrontation that Kyle dreaded to hear. As Kyle approached, his mind raced with questions, but first and foremost was ensuring Joel's safety.

"Oooooooo. Easssyyyy," Joel groaned, rolling from his stomach onto his back.

"Dang Joel, what happened to you?" Arnie asked, his voice filled with concern as he took in Joel's bruised eye and the dried blood around his mouth.

"Here, let's sit you up," Kyle said, retrieving a bottle of water from his pack. He opened it and handed it to Joel. "Here you go, buddy. Get a drink of this," Kyle said, examining Joel's injuries. "Did you get in a fight?" he asked.

"This is a message. I was told to give it to you," Joel said, peering through his good eye at Kyle.

"A message for me? What are you talking about?" Kyle asked, confusion and anger mixing in his voice.

"I went to Hurley last night to see what all the fuss was about. That place is a disaster by the way, half the buildings on fire. Anyhow, a white Mustang got on my rear really close. I thought he was trying to race me. I stopped at the straight stretch at Kelsey, and he pulled up beside me. He asked if Arnie's Uncle Kyle was my uncle too. I asked why he wanted to know. He just stared at me, then his skanky looking woman laughed like a hyena. I took off and left him," Joel said, sipping the water. His words painted a vivid picture of intimidation and violence, each detail etching deeper worry lines on Kyle's face.

Arnie looked at Kyle, then back to Joel, "that was Allen," he said.

Kyle glanced back towards the road, wary of any surprises. He tightened hard on his jaw as he looked at Joel, "where did the black eye come from? Kyle asked.

"I got to Race Fork on the way back, and the Mustang was parked beside the road. He must have been watching for me. As I drove past, he pulled out behind me, following closely again. I stopped at Kelsey church to let him pass, but he blocked my car instead. He got out and demanded to know where you live, Kyle. When I tried to talk with him, things turned violent," Joel explained, wincing as he recalled the blows he had taken.

"I'm sorry, Joel. He sent his message to me," Kyle said, anger tightening his grip on his fist.

"It's okay, Uncle Kyle. I haven't been in a fight in a while. This was more of a quick ass kicking. He hit my car with a bat and said to tell you it was for the gas. He said you two were even now," Joel said, taking a big drink of water. "What was the deal with the gas?" he asked.

Arnie rolled his eyes and held his hands up, "let me just tell you, so me and Uncle Kyle were getting gas at Creekside. Allen showed up wanting Kyle to give it to him. Kyle tried to be nice, but of course, his smartass side came out," Arnie interjected.

"I'm sorry, Joel. I never thought he'd come after you over it. You're lucky. They say he killed Fred yesterday," Kyle said, patting Joel's shoulder.

"I'll heal. I got home last night and crawled to the porch and passed out. There's more—come inside. I need to get to the couch," Joel said, standing with difficulty. Arnie opened the door for him.

"Arnie, grab Joel a towel and pour some water on it," Kyle said, pointing to a hand towel on the kitchen countertop.

"There's no water in the kitchen. Maybe a can or two of Mountain Dew," Joel said. "I'm going to sleep here for a while. Is it okay if I come up to the cabin later and stay a night or two?"

Kyle was filled with anger and rage, this was his fault for what happened to Joel. He would not let this be the end of it, "yeah, man. Stay as long as you want. We've got plenty of water and food, and your mom and sister are there. Susie's going to kick my ass when she sees you like this," Kyle said with a guilty laugh. "You said there was more?"

"I got to Hurley, and Supervisor Tate had box trucks loading goods at the grocery store. They weren't letting anyone inside; he had guards keeping people out. The pharmacy was burning, what was left of it. There was also a dead guy in front of the pharmacy, the fire charring his body," Joel shook his head thinking of the images. "Tate was talking through a megaphone, saying martial law had been declared. He's taking control and setting up a barter system at his mansion up Lesters Fork. He's trying to control everything," Joel said, covering his eyes with the wet towel.

"Listen, Joel, we're going to lock the door on our way out. We're meeting at Uncle Tom's with some other people. As soon as you feel better, get up to the cabin and rest up. Allen says we're even, but he just added more to his debt, and we're going to take it back with interest," Kyle said, squeezing Joel's hand before walking out the door. "Rest up."

CHAPTER TWENTY-EIGHT

"Rising Tensions"

Kyle and Arnie left Joel's house, riding on to Uncle Tom's where the men from last night we're already waiting. Two additional trucks and one more ATV had joined, amplifying the gravity of their meeting. As Kyle and Arnie approached, the tension was already thick, many getting hungry, being unable to buying their breakfast this morning at Fred's. They both took a seat with the group who were discussing the fire at Fred's and the rumors starting to swirl that Allen Hall had killed Fred.

"Morning Kyle. Hello little Arnie bug," Snaggle said as they approached. "Kyle this is my boy Charles, he has some news about last night, and it's not pretty. We also got some reports over the ham radio and it's terrible everywhere," Snaggle said as Kyle took a seat on a sturdy wooden tree log uncle Tom used around the fire pit. The sight of those logs, usually reserved for roasting marshmallows with friends, now seemed a distant memory.

"Hello Charles, wish we were meeting under better circumstances. You care to tell me what all you learned last night? I'm sure you're ready to get home and sleep, so thank you for stopping here," Kyle said as he shook Charles hand.

"We had power from the generators. Some workers stayed because they had no power at home. Most others left saying they had their own people to take care of, they weren't staying to help and not get paid extra. Some said they were taking a break but went to their car and never came back. One that left was our maintenance man, he said they didn't pay him enough to stay there when the administrator wasn't even around." Charles said as everyone listened to him taking in his every word.

"Was there any other information coming in about this whole ordeal?" Kyle asked Charles, ready to absorb all the information possible.

"Lynn's husband is a county cop. He came by and told her the reports they had gotten said many large cities in the country were destroyed. They expected millions to already be dead and many more to follow over the upcoming days," Charles said, his hands and arms gesturing with urgency as he spoke. "The military was fighting back where they could, but it was mostly hidden bombs that had been blown so they didn't know who to fight with. He said the sheriff's office only had a few officers working, mostly guys that were single with no families." Charles said holding his hands in the air.

As Charles spoke, the gravity of their predicament sank deeper. It echoed Joel's account and painted a bleak picture of the world beyond their hollow.

Charles told them about the drive back this morning. He explained there were several homes that were burning. He told them about the many cars that were parked along the road, possibly from being out of gas. Charles told them about Hurley, and it matched with what Joel had said. He told them about a large sign made from plywood that had been stationed in the center of town. On the board it was spray painted lettering with a large arrow pointing. "If you need gas or food, come to Supervisor Tate's. Bring trade goods. Martial Law in effect!"

This was concerning to each of the men at the meeting. Kyle told them what Joel had said about supervisor Tate taking the remaining food items from the grocery store and declaring Martial Law.

"I did see a water truck at Fred's parked next to the underground tanks this morning. I went to see if Fred's store was all burned, only a smoldering pile of rubble remained. The truck had a hose in the fuel storage tank opening. I knew it was one of Tate's trucks, but I didn't know why he would be putting water in the gas tanks. There were two men there with guns, so I didn't dare go ask," said a young teenager who was the son of a man at

162

the meeting.

An elder at the meeting, removed his pack of cigarettes from his pocket, placing one between his lips and flicking on the bright red Bic lighter he carried. "He wasn't putting water in them. He was siphoning the remaining fuel into the water truck," he said taking in a heavy draw, blowing his smoke up into the air. "Hopefully he didn't get much, I know Fred said yesterday morning when this first happened that he was expecting a delivery that hadn't arrived. Tate is going to control all he can, I should have stayed there yesterday," the man said taking another draw from the cigarette.

"If everyone agrees, I think we need to get a coal truck and block the road down at the mouth. Stop traffic from getting up this way until we know more. We need to keep at least two guards at the truck, block off this part of the hollow. Everybody knows each other, we don't need no strangers up this way," Kyle said as the men were nodding their heads in agreement with this.

Snaggle stood up, adjusting his belt one notch tighter around his waist, "I agree with Kyle on this one guys. If we don't look out for each other, none of us will make it long. As soon as people start running out of food they are going to come looking. It won't matter how long you have known someone, if they need to feed their family, they're going to do whatever they have to," Snaggle said wagging his finger around at each man. "We may not all be blood, but we're all family in this holler. I'll fight for every single one of you," Snaggle added as he slammed his fist against the open palm of his other hand.

Continuing to discuss this plan it was agreed upon that Harold would drive his coal truck there and park it. They would all pass the news of this plan on and get as many people as they could to volunteer for guard shifts.

"What about food and water?" asked one of the men. He was sixty-five, a full white beard covering most of his face.

Kyle didn't have all the answers yet, but he looked around, feeling the eyes starring back at him, waiting for his guidance. The sun was in full glare by now, sweat soaking into the pits of Kyle's shirt. "I hope you have some food on hand, ration it as much as possible. If you have gardens, share items. Fuel will be gone soon, try to conserve as much as possible. Water storage and filtration will be important. Many of the elders here know how to do these things, we need everyone to share their knowledge," he finished.

"I'm just not sure this will last long enough to get so worked up about it," J-Rod stepped into the conversation after being quiet and listening so far to everyone. J-Rod was young, early twenties and worked in the coal mines. "Maybe we all need to relax a little and give this a few days to see how it goes."

Snaggle was one of the elders to quickly shake his head no to this thought. "I'm going to start covering my butt now. I'll do what I can to be ready, if it passes by quickly, good. We'll meet back here in a year and talk about how scared shitless we all were and laugh about it. But until then, I'm on board with survival," Snaggle said to J-Rod and any others who might be having doubts.

"I'm with Snaggle and Kyle on this one. I'm going to prepare for the worst the best I can. I wish I had done so sooner but I can't cry about that now. I recommend everyone go home and take inventory of what you have. If anyone needs help with gardening, water, even building an outhouse, let's all work together. Between us we have the knowledge to figure this out," Uncle Tom said as he stood up ending the discussion. He was never one with a lot of patience, he liked to get to the point.

"Charles are you going back to the hospital?" Kyle asked as Charles started to walk away.

It was easy to see the thought dancing in Charles head as he pondered the question. He rubbed his hand over his chin, before looking back at Kyle. "I don't know. I don't know how to get more gas and I don't want to get stuck," Charles answered.

"I understand, nobody would blame you if you don't. If you do be sure to keep an eye open for any medical supplies you may be able to get your hands on. Everything is important now; nothing is worthless except money," Kyle said to him, shaking his hand again before going to speak privately with Uncle Tom.

"Uncle Tom, I want to go see old man Hadley. You think he would sell us some cows?" Kyle asked Uncle Tom. "He has several that graze close to the cabin property, it would be easy to walk them over."

"Old man Hadley is a tough nut. You better let me go with you. He may not even know about the attack yet and he still doesn't like strangers. Let's ride across the mountain on the ATV's and stay off the main road. We will follow the trail down to him, just be prepared to duck in case he shoots first," Uncle Tom said to Kyle and Arnie about the old farmer.

"Those cows are just out the trail a little ways from the cabin, we could just go get us a few of them," Arnie said.

"No sir we aren't doing that. Those are still Hadley's cows. We aren't stealing his cows," Kyle told Arnie as Uncle Tom shook his head in agreement.

"Now hang on a second. I remember us taking more propane tanks than we paid for. That was stealing as far as I have been taught. What's the difference?" Arnie asked scrunching his head down and holding his hands in the air.

"Yeah Kyle, explain to us what's the difference you dang thief," Uncle Tom said jokingly.

"Speaking honest, the difference is that stealing is depending on how we choose to justify it right now. You're right, we technically stole those tanks. I also gave them two thousand dollars at the grocery store. Everything that happens will be justified by each person and their needs. I'm not saying it's right or wrong, but that's just what will happen," Kyle told them.

"I can't argue with that, I have to agree," Uncle Tom said.

"When someone is willing to kill one of us in need of our food, they won't think of it as murder, it will be survival. I will shoot back if I have the chance," Kyle said. "This is a different set of rules we're living by, basically there will be no rules for now."

"It's like the wild west again, I need to learn how to ride a horse! I need to get a horse first!" Arnie said as he squatted his knees and pretended to bounce along on a horse.

CHAPTER TWENTY-NINE
"Sassypants Farm Preperations"

Kyle, Arnie, and Uncle Tom rode to the top of the trail and parked Uncle Tom's ATV at the cabin. Kyle talked to Susie about what had happened to Joel, and she was furious.

Seeing her face turning red, her breathing heavier, he placed his hand on her shoulder, "it will be handled in due time, sis. Acting on emotion isn't the way to get anywhere. I talked to Joel about coming up to the cabin as soon as he feels rested today," Kyle said, putting his arm around her, giving a light squeeze to calm her down.

The girls were in the garden pulling weeds, and Coraline's little face was already covered in dirt and dust. She waved at Kyle with a huge smile and went back to pulling the weeds. Rachel sat on the porch in a rocking chair and listened to the plans being made. Rocky offered to ride with the guys to see old man Hadley, but Kyle told him to stay at the cabin. Kyle went inside and picked up three bottles of water and a small, locked box from a cedar chest. Kyle opened the box; it was the last of the cash he had, eight thousand dollars. He came back outside, tossing a water bottle to Arnie and one to Uncle Tom.

The three of them loaded onto Kyle's ATV and set off from the cabin to see Mr. Hadley. They exited through the gate and followed the winding trail that snaked around the backside of the mountain. The trail was narrow, hemmed in by dense underbrush and towering trees whose branches reached out like skeletal fingers. Sunlight filtered through the canopy, casting dappled shadows on the ground.

As they descended, they passed by several of Hadley's cows

grazing freely on the mountain's grassy slopes. The sight of the large, sturdy cows and their playful calves brought smiles to their faces. Kyle pointed at the animals, giving a thumbs-up to Uncle Tom and Arnie, who nodded in agreement at the prospect of bringing some of these creatures back.

The trail was challenging, demanding careful navigation. It was a rarely traveled path, overgrown with a tangle of weeds and branches that scratched at their arms and faces as they pushed through. Deep ruts and hidden holes caused the ATV to jolt and lurch, making progress slow and cautious. They maneuvered around fallen logs and avoided patches of loose, rocky soil that threatened to send them sliding.

Upon reaching the bottom of the path, they came to a closed, rusty, weathered gate leading onto the property. The gate hung on it's hinges, surrounded by a perimeter of wildflowers and tall grasses swaying gently in the breeze. Beyond the gate, the landscape was littered with old cars and trucks, their rusted frames sinking into the overgrown grass. Piles of discarded machinery parts and broken tools were scattered around, giving the place a chaotic, lived-in feel. Tom opened the unlocked gate, pulling it back as Kyle drove through. As Kyle slowly drove towards the house, old man Hadley walked out onto the porch.

The farmhouse itself was a weathered structure, with peeling paint and a sagging roof. A few chickens clucked around the porch, pecking at the ground. Hadley held a shotgun down by his side as he tried to recognize the people on the approaching ATV. His eyes, sharp despite his age, squinted against the sun, scanning the visitors.

Holding his shotgun was how Hadley would have greeted them whether an attack had happened or not, so it wasn't clear if he knew about it.

"Easy, Hadley. It's just me, Tom. I got my two nephews with me," Tom shouted out as Kyle held his hand up, waving.

"Well, hello, Tommy. I haven't seen you in a few days," Hadley said, with a few days meaning more like two years. His voice was gravelly, a result of years spent shouting over the noise of farm machinery and the elements. "What have you boys been up to on the mountain? I heard a lot of noise up there last year," Hadley, slowly placing his shotgun against the porch railing.

"We built a cabin out on the ridge," Uncle Tom told Hadley, pointing up the mountain in the direction of the cabin. "I'm surprised you didn't come check it out."

"I thought about it a time or two, but I figured it was something you were involved in, so I wasn't concerned. I knew it was either on your land or your Rachel's from the sound's location. What brings you down here to visit me? Does it have something to do with what happened yesterday?" Hadley asked Uncle Tom, who also liked to get to the point. A little small talk was fine but keeping it brief and moving on to the main topic was how these older men went about their business.

Kyle removed his hat, wiped a handkerchief over his forehead, and stepped up to Mr. Hadley, extending his hand. "Hello Mr. Hadley. I'm Kyle, Rachel's son. You probably don't remember me, but I used to come here with my dad as a small boy. He always liked visiting with you and talking about the Bible. You let me run chickens around the yard," Kyle said with a smile as he remembered the moment.

"I do remember you, son. You sure could run them dang chickens around. Your dad was a good man; loved the Lord, he did. I hate that he got sick. I do miss him visiting," Hadley said to Kyle as he returned the gesture, shaking Kyle's hand.

"Yes, sir, he was," Kyle said. "You taught me what the white stuff on top of chicken shit was," Kyle said, letting out a laugh, getting a snicker from Uncle Tom at the comment.

Arnie looked puzzled, glancing between Kyle and Uncle Tom, before turning to Mr. Hadley. "What is the white stuff on it?" Arnie asked.

"Well, son, it's chicken shit too," Hadley said to Arnie as he and Uncle Tom joined in Kyle's laughter. Arnie just shook his head and mumbled, "I guess I stepped in that one."

"Now you know, Arnie," Uncle Tom said allowing one louder laugh to roar out. He then turned his attention back to

Hadley, "Hadley, it sounds like you've seen the country has been attacked. We expect it to be a hard road ahead for the immediate future. Do you still have that hateful bull I gave you a few years back? You're the only person I knew that could handle that one," Tom asked to remind the old man he had once given him a bull free of charge. It was a bull Uncle Tom couldn't keep in his fenced lot, getting out every day until Uncle Tom got tired of dealing with it. It was a smart move by Uncle Tom to help break the ice.

"You boys are buttering me up, so let's go ahead and split the biscuit. Tell me what you're after," Hadley said, allowing a smile to show through his thick white beard and mustache.

"We wanted to see about buying some cows from you, Hadley. In case whatever is happening does last some time, we would like to have a few to get us started," Tom told Hadley.

"We would like to get some cows, goats, and ducks if you'll sell them. I see those rabbit cages; I would love to get some of those as well. And if you're feeling like making a deal, I'm in the market for a couple of horses," Kyle said, getting it all on the table for Hadley to consider.

"Shewww weeeee! That's a long list you got, son. How long you fellers think this outage will last?" Hadley asked, stepping down from the porch.

"Well, sir, to be honest with you, I think this may last a while, a year or longer. I have no knowledge as communications are out, but that would be my best guess. There are going to be major parts and repairs needed that won't be done easily. And that's just from what information I was able to gather so far," Kyle said, trying to be honest; he didn't want to lie to him.

"A year, you say," Hadley said, rubbing his hand through his long beard. "I'm not sure money is going to be worth much if that's the case."

"Money is money; it's always good to have," Arnie jumped into the conversation. Arnie had yet to learn that he wasn't as slick as he thought when it came to dealing with the elders. As the old farmers like to say, putting sprinkles on manure is fine, but it's still manure.

"Sir, I can't tell you that money will be worth anything before long or when it would be again. It's all I have right now to barter with, other than offering myself to work some for you. We can pay cash or come help you around here once we are set," Kyle said to Hadley, wanting Arnie to see the truth was sometimes the best option.

"I'll give you two cows and two calves. They're already up on the mountain grazing. You can take two of those rabbit cages and fill them as full as you can. If you can catch any ducks, take all you want of them. I'll give you four goats. As for the horses, I better hang on to those. How you feel about five thousand dollars? That's a fair deal on them cows," Hadley said to Kyle as he looked him straight in the eye for an answer.

"Yes, sir, we can do that. It's fair to me, and I know you're doing me right," Kyle said back to Hadley.

"How are we going to get the money? Banks aren't open," Uncle Tom said to Kyle with a questioning look.

Kyle removed his small pack and unzipped it. Reaching in, he pulled out five small bundles of twenties, each wrapped with a thousand-dollar bank band. Kyle stepped to the old man and held out his hand with the money in it. Arnie looked at Uncle Tom and smiled widely as Tom had a look of disbelief.

"You didn't come to talk; you came to buy," Hadley said with a laugh. "I tell you what, let me think about the horses. Maybe come back in a few days and I'll let you know an answer," Hadley said to Kyle, accepting the cash from his hand.

"Arnie, load the rabbits on the ATV. I'm going to catch some ducks. Do you have any bread, sir?" Kyle asked Hadley.

"I already have some for you," Mr. Hadley's wife, Opal, said as she came from the farmhouse. Although the years had piled on, her long black hair now faded to silver, she was a beautiful soul, a woman of God keeping Mr. Hadley in line.

The pond where the ducks gathered was a picturesque spot, surrounded by tall weeds and dotted with lily pads. The ducks, a mix of mallards and Pekins, quacked loudly as Kyle and Arnie approached, their eyes keen and watchful.

"Let's get started," Kyle said, breaking the bread into pieces and tossing them near the water's edge. The ducks waddled over eagerly, their curiosity overcoming their wariness. Slowly, Kyle and Arnie crouched down, spreading more bread closer to themselves.

"Alright, Arnie, on the count of three, we grab," Kyle instructed. "One, two, three!"

Both men lunged forward, grabbing as many ducks as they could. Feathers flew, and the ducks squawked in protest, but Kyle and Arnie managed to secure five ducks, their webbed feet flapping in the air.

"Got 'em," Kyle said triumphantly, holding up a squirming Pekin. "Let's get them caged."

Meanwhile, Uncle Tom and Hadley sat on the porch, catching up on the neighborhood gossip. As they talked, Kyle and Arnie worked quickly, placing the ducks in makeshift cages. They turned their attention to the rabbits next. The rabbit cages were sturdy but worn, each holding a few nervous bunnies, their noses twitching and ears perked up.

"Easy now," Kyle said softly as he reached into one of the cages. He gently lifted a large Flemish Giant, its grey fur soft and warm against his hands. "These guys will be great for breeding."

Arnie followed suit, carefully handling a smaller Lop with distinctive floppy ears. They put the rabbits on the ATV, securing the cages to ensure they wouldn't tip over during the ride back.

Next, they approached the goats. The goats were agile and alert, their eyes glinting with mischief. "These ones might be a bit of a challenge," Kyle muttered, eyeing a particularly feisty Nubian.

"She looks mean," Arnie said laughing.

"Come here, girl," he coaxed, holding out a handful of feed. The goat hesitated, then trotted over, nibbling from his hand. Kyle swiftly attached a rope halter and led the goat to the ATV. Arnie did the same with another goat, and soon they had four goats tethered and ready for transport.

"Thank you, Mr. Hadley. I'll be back about the horses, I hope you sell, but no hard feelings if not," Kyle said as he shook the man's hand. "Come visit us anytime, we'll have coffee."

"Sounds good, Kyle. Take care," Mr Hadley responded.

The guys left on the ATV with the rabbits, ducks, and goats. Hadley loaned Kyle some small cages they squeezed the goats into, with the promise he would return them. They waved goodbye and drove away to the back of the farm, passing by the old junk cars. Carefully, they slowly began to climb the trail back up the mountain in an effort not to bounce the animals around.

After reaching the cows grazing, Kyle stopped the ATV. The cows were a mix of Hereford and Holstein, their coats a patchwork of brown, white, and black. The calves stayed close to their mothers, their big eyes filled with curiosity.

"You think we can get a rope on these? We will tie them to the back of the ATV and slowly lead them back to our side," Kyle said to Arnie and Uncle Tom.

"Yeah, these girls are calm cows," Uncle Tom said as he walked towards them with a handful of straw grass. The cows graciously walked up to Uncle Tom to eat the straw from his hand. As they did, Uncle Tom slowly slipped a piece of rope over their necks. Uncle Tom walked them over and tied the ropes to the ATV, leaving roughly ten feet of rope to give them slack to walk away from the exhaust fumes.

With their new livestock secured, the trio began their return journey to the cabin. The cows, roped and tethered, plodded along behind the ATV, causing small puffs of dust to rise from the dry earth. Kyle navigated carefully, keeping the pace slow to avoid startling the animals. The path was a well-worn track, bordered by thick underbrush that occasionally encroached on their route, requiring Kyle to maneuver around branches.

Every so often, they had to stop and adjust the ropes, ensuring the cows and calves remained calm and secure. The cows' hooves made a rhythmic clop against the rocky ground, a sound that mingled with the rustle of leaves and the distant calls of birds hidden in the trees.

Arnie, tasked with holding the rabbit cages, held on tightly as the ATV bounced over ruts and dips in the trail. The rabbits, nestled in their temporary homes, huddled together, their noses twitching in curiosity and mild alarm. The ducks, meanwhile, quacked softly from their makeshift pen, occasionally flapping their wings as if trying to make sense of this strange journey.

The final stretch of the trail was in view and the guys looked at one another with delight. Uncle Tom walked alongside the cows, murmuring soothing words to keep them calm, while Arnie occasionally glanced back to ensure none of the animals were struggling.

Finally, the cabin came into view. Coraline's delighted squeals of "You got cows! You got cows!" echoed through the clearing as she saw the procession of animals. The sight of the cabin, with its rustic charm, brought a sense of relief and accomplishment.

"Look what else we have back there," Kyle said to her.

"It's rabbits and ducks, Coraline, come look," Clara Beth said, showing excitement for the first time since arriving at the cabin. Kyle knew this would be hard on Clara Beth and countless other young kids. Attempting to adapt to what this world might become would be a hard transition from the smartphones and internet.

"Now we just need to make our sign," Kyle told the girls.

"What kind of sign?" Coraline asked.

"Our Sassy Pants Mountain Farm sign I told you about," Kyle said as he laughed with the girls.

"Well hot damn! We got a farm!" Coraline shouted as she smacked one of the goats on the rear end.

"Coraline!" Deanna said looking at the little one who quickly dropped her head and covered her face with her hands.

"Daddy says it," Coraline said as she attempted to fake some tears.

"Rocky!" Deanna shouted.

"I gotta get to the barn. Talk to you in a bit," Rocky shouted as he ran to the barn while everyone else laughed hysterically.

"I agree, hot damn!" Kyle said helping Coraline, who quickly peaked under her hands giving Kyle a wide smile.

CHAPTER THIRTY
"The Price of Blood"

"On the morning of the second day, Horrace was exhausted after spending the night sitting next to his dead brother's body. With no emergency services in town, Horrace had brought Robert's body home. He wrapped it in an old quilt their grandmother had made. Promising Robert he would avenge his death, Horrace attempted to dig a grave at the back of the house, but the hard ground and thick tree roots made progress slow. After considering his options, Horrace thought of Supervisor Tate, who had a backhoe that could quickly dig the grave. Horrace was determined to lay his brother to rest properly, six feet under. He knew it was time to visit the supervisor and ask for help.

"Horrace, how are you today? Where's that shady brother of yours?" Miran Tate asked with a chuckle as he walked into the large metal garage building at Tate's house.

"Robert's dead. He was killed yesterday," Horrace replied, his voice heavy with sorrow as he lowered his eyes to the ground.

"Dead! Who killed him, and why?" Tate asked, flicking on his butane lighter to toast the foot of his cigar.

"We didn't do anything, sir. We were trying to help people in need. This guy said he was taking our car, and Robert tried to stop him. He shot him dead over it. I don't know the man, but he was with Susie from the clothing store in town. I know where she lives, but not him," Horrace said, without hesitation, lying about how the incident had unfolded.

"I'm sorry, Horrace. I know things got rough in town yesterday, I was there myself. Rumors are swirling that you and Robert were involved in James's death. Any truth to that?" Tate asked Horrace, now puffing on his cigar and blowing smoke into the air.

"No sir, we didn't kill James. We went into the pawn shop to see if he needed any help. He was dead in his office. We did take a few things, knowing he wouldn't be needing them anymore," Horrace explained, looking earnestly at Tate. "I want revenge for my brother now. I need your help."

Meanwhile, at the other end of the garage building, Tate had already opened a barter store. One of his men was handling transactions. Anyone who came in with something valuable to trade could make deals for food and gasoline. Word was just starting to spread about the barter store, and Tate was eager to capitalize on the opportunity. The trading terms weren't fair, but for some people, it was their only option. For instance, a man in need of gasoline accepted one gallon in exchange for eight small boxes of .223 ammunition, each containing twenty rounds. Before the attack, this ammo would have been valued close to a hundred dollars, making it a take-it-or-leave-it deal where Tate knew he had the upper hand.

Tate, who owned a construction company, was well-off with a range of equipment and tools. He had insider knowledge about upcoming county projects, enabling him to buy and resell property at significant profits. By greasing a few palms, everyone involved was satisfied. Most content of all was Miran Tate, who was banking substantial profits on these deals.

He had one of the sheriff's officers in his pocket as well. Officer Langston did whatever Tate needed or demanded. Langston had been corrupt for years, and most people knew it. They were afraid to speak out against him, fearing Tate's retribution. Those who crossed Tate often found themselves facing increased property taxes or, in some cases, inexplicable house fires. Tate hadn't always been this way, but the reasons for his transformation remained a mystery.

Tate glanced up at Horrace, holding his cigar to the side. "What would you like me to do, Horrace?" he asked.

"The first thing I need is to use a backhoe to dig a proper grave. Robert's body is at the house, and I want to bury him. I tried digging with a shovel, but the ground is too hard," Horrace explained. "Next, I need a few of your men to come with me and help me kill that bastard." He paused, his voice edged with determination. "I'll be in your debt."

"Well, I'm not getting into the business of credit, but I'd be willing to help you for a trade," Tate said to Horrace as he leaned forward in his chair. Tate could read people well enough to know Horrace was lying straight to his face, but he was okay with it if there was something in it for him.

"I don't have anything to trade, Miran. You know this," Horrace replied, doubt evident on his face that Tate would actually help him.

"You have yourself, and that's what I need. I want you to go with Lucas to Creekside and Fred's Gas n Go. He will drive the water pumping truck there and empty out the fuel tanks. You go help him. He's going to visit a few people that owe me and do some collecting. He will collect by any means necessary. You got a problem with that?" Tate asked, his gaze intense as he stared at Horrace.

"No sir, I will do it. And then you will help me?" Horrace asked Tate.

"While you're gone, I'm going to send someone to dig the grave for you. I'll get Langston to find out who this guy is, and then we will handle him," Tate assured Horrace, watching him perk up at the offer.

Tate used a walkie-talkie to radio Lucas to bring the truck around. He handed Horrace a shotgun and enough shells to fill both pockets. Lucas quickly maneuvered the large truck with bold "WATER" markings around the garage. Horrace climbed into the cab and placed the shotgun by his leg. Lucas gave a brief honk of the horn and followed the long drive from the garage to the main road.

Lucas and Horrace spoke little on the drive, eventually arriving at Fred's Gas n Go, or what was left of it. They saw the smoldering remains of Fred's store, now reduced to a pile of blackened debris. Lucas parked the truck next to the underground fuel tanks and halted. He glanced at Horrace, tossed a piece of paper onto the dashboard, and said in his rough voice, "We won't be needing this now." Then, Lucas climbed down from the truck, gun in hand, scanning the area to ensure it was clear.

Horrace picked up the paper and read the handwritten note: "Upon appointment of Martial Law by authority of the government, all gasoline and items of necessity are to be appropriated by local power." He couldn't help but shake his head at the blatant abuse of power implied by Tate's actions. He knew Supervisor Tate was corrupt, seeing such a broad statement of authority didn't disturb him. He placed the paper back onto the dashboard and climbed down from the truck.

Lucas had already uncovered the tank opening and was now attaching the large hose from the truck. "Let's hope there's still some fuel in these tanks. You keep watch while I get this started," Lucas said to Horrace as he lowered the hose into the tank opening. He swiftly activated the pump to start siphoning the fuel. The truck's tank had a capacity of six thousand gallons and he hoped to fill it full.

The two men watched the dial as it indicated the amount of fuel in gallons being transferred. Horrace could hear the hum of tires approaching on the road pavement, signaling an ATV nearing the parking lot. He turned to see the ATV rider stop briefly upon noticing Horrace and Lucas by the truck, then quickly turn around and speed away.

As the tanks neared empty, Lucas switched the hose from unleaded to premium fuel to maximize their collection. By the time they finished, they had managed to extract only eight hundred and fifty gallons, a disappointing amount compared to the potential twenty thousand gallons they expected could be in the tanks.

"Damn! I thought there would be more in here," Lucas muttered as he tossed the hose back onto the truck. "Let's go, we got more to do."

The men hurried back into the cab and left the charred remains of Fred's Gas n Go behind. "We need to head up Guesses

Fork Road now. Tate wants us to retrieve a .50 caliber gun from Travis McMurray. You've got my back, right?" Lucas asked, glancing over at Horrace as the truck rumbled along.

"Yeah, I've got you covered. What does McMurray owe Tate for?" Horrace asked, turning to Lucas for an answer.

"Technically nothing, I reckon. Travis has a .50 caliber rifle. This piece of paper says Tate needs it, and he knows Travis has one," Horrace explained to Lucas as they drove towards Travis McMurray's home.

"This is all bullshit," Horrace said as he eyed Lucas. "These rich people take what they want."

Lucas glanced at Horrace, feeling the anger in him. "That isn't my decision, Horrace. I just do what I'm told, I want to stay alive." He turned his gaze back forward on the road.

Upon arriving at Travis's house, Lucas parked the water truck and stepped out with his gun in one hand and the paper from Tate in the other. Horrace grabbed his shotgun and joined Lucas as they approached Travis's front door. Travis intercepted them before they reached the front door.

"What are you guys doing here with those guns?" Travis demanded, emerging from his two-car garage, his hands caked in dirt, oil, and grease.

Lucas handed Travis the paper from Tate, "it's all right here, Travis. Read for yourself."

Travis took the paper, looking confused at Lucas and Horrace. He opened it, smudging grease from his hands onto it in the process. "Upon appointment of Martial law by authority of the government, all gasoline and items of necessity are to be appropriated by local power," Travis read aloud, clearly infuriated. "What in the hell is this supposed to mean? I don't have any gas, and this handwritten note isn't worth the paper it's written on." As Travis continued to voice his displeasure to Lucas, Horrace walked into the garage to look around.

"It means you have a .50 caliber rifle, and the local government will be, I think they say commandeering it at this time," Lucas said, attempting humor and using a big word out of

178

the ordinary for his everyday language.

Travis's face darkened with anger. "Lucas, I've known you for some time now. You mean to tell me you actually thought you were going to take my gun with this piece of paper? Let me see, I think they say it like this, you ain't commandeering shit! Now get the hell off my property."

Lucas tried to maintain his composure. "I understand Travis, but this is the law right now. It's martial law, Supervisor Tate told us. He is in control, and he needs the .50 caliber and all the ammo you have for it. So go get it, and we'll be on our way."

Travis crossed his arms, glaring at Lucas.

"Lucas, you aren't hearing me. I'm not giving ....."

Booooommmmm!! The splatter of red chunks and warm blood covered Lucas's face as he fell back to the ground. He opened his eyes and swiped his hand across them to look ahead. As he slowly sat up and began patting to feel his face and chest, it wasn't he who had been shot. Horrace had stepped up behind Travis, pointed his shotgun at the back of Travis's head, and pulled the trigger. It was Travis's flesh, brain matter, blood, and skull fragments that sprayed onto Lucas. Travis's motionless body lay face down on the ground in front of him, or what was left of his face, at least.

"I ain't got time for chit-chatting, we've got work to do," Horrace said, reaching his hand down for Lucas to pull him back to his feet.

A loud scream exploded from the front door as Travis's wife, Shelia, looked out to see her husband dead on the ground.

"What did you do? Why?" she screamed, running off the porch and falling on her knees next to Travis. She placed her face in the middle of his back, continuing to scream. "Travis! Travis!" she yelled, pleading for him to come back to her.

"Bring her inside," Horrace said, giving a clear order to Lucas that now showed who was really in charge between them. Horrace had already started walking into the house.

"Come on, Shelia, let's go. He's not messing around; he will kill you if you don't," Lucas said to Shelia, shocked at what

Horrace had done. Lucas had known both Travis and Shelia for years, having grown up in the small town. His hands were shaking as he reached for Shelia's arm. "Come on, let's go," Lucas said, pulling at Shelia. The young woman jumped up, slapping Lucas as hard as she could, blood and flesh from her husband attaching to her hand from Lucas's face.

"I'll kill you!" Shelia screamed at Lucas as he tried to block her additional swings. "I'll kill you both!" Lucas stepped back, tripping and falling over a landscaping timber that lined the walkway to the porch.

"I'm sorry, Shelia. I didn't mean for this..." Lucas managed to get part of the thought out.

"Booooommmm!" The sound of the shotgun once again filled the air. Lucas had an up-close view of Shelia's small frame flying violently backwards. She landed across part of Travis's already fallen body. Horrace stood on the porch, holding the shotgun as smoke rose from the barrel. Lucas jumped back up, looking at Horrace in disbelief.

"What are you doing? We weren't supposed to kill them!" Lucas shouted at Horrace, tasting the blood that covered his mouth from Travis. Lucas jerked his shirt off, wiping his face with it as he looked at Horrace; the crazed look told him not to push it. Horrace opened the door once again and stepped back inside. He picked up the .50 caliber rifle and pointed to a can of ammo.

"This is what we came for. Carry the ammo can and let's move. I've got more killing that needs to be done, and daylight's burning," Horrace said calmly, walking back to the water truck.

Lucas had two more stops he was told to make, but he said nothing to Horrace about them. The men climbed back into the truck, and Lucas struggled to press the clutch in, his leg shaking wildly. Lucas thought he was ready to carry out Tate's orders, but he didn't expect it to go like this.

"Inhale, Lucas. This is the new way of doing business. Now press the clutch like a big boy and start this truck," Horrace said, biting into a honey bun he had taken from Shelia's kitchen.

180

CHAPTER THIRTY-ONE
"Goats, Guns and Giggles"

As everyone gathered to meet the new animals, Kyle felt a sense of satisfaction wash over him. He watched Coraline excitedly interacting with each animal, trying to give them names.

"Your name is Spot, and you're Shorty," Coraline declared, petting two of the goats.

"I've got an idea for names. How about Breakfast, Lunch, and Dinner?" Kyle suggested with a grin, looking at Coraline, awaiting her reaction. She promptly placed her hand on her hip and wagged her finger at him.

"Shame on you, Uncle Kyle. Shame!" Coraline scolded, before turning back to Shorty. "You're not breakfast, lunch, or dinner, Shorty. You're Just Shorty. Don't listen to Uncle Kyle. I think he needs a whoopin'."

Everyone at the cabin pitched in to care for the newly acquired animals. Rocky had been busy securing the barn, preparing for the possibility of cows or horses. He spread hay in the stalls and completed some unfinished tasks Kyle had not gotten to. Ginger and Susie helped with the rabbit cages, while Uncle Tom quickly built a bin for them. Clara Beth eagerly joined in, especially excited about the rabbits.

"Can I name the rabbits?" Clara Beth asked.

"Sure, you can take charge of the rabbits," Kyle replied.

"You're not naming my goats. You go name your little dumb rabbits," Coraline retorted, her head moving from side to side sassily.

"I don't want to name your goats; they're ugly," Clara Beth teased, grinning at Coraline, who retaliated with sass.

"Well missy, my goats can kick your rabbits' ass!" Coraline shouted at Clara Beth, immediately realizing her slip. She covered her mouth, eyes widening. "Oops," she muttered softly, glancing at her mother.

"I'd say 'oops' if I were you, Coraline! Where did you learn to talk like that?" Deanna's voice was sharp, her face flushed with anger as she confronted the little girl.

"Okay, hold on, everyone. Let's all calm down. They're just excited about the new animals," Rachel interjected, trying to diffuse the tension before Coraline got into deeper trouble.

"Oh no, young lady. Mamaw isn't going to get you off that easy. Now, I asked you, where did you learn that?" Deanna pressed again.

"If I may interrupt, Deanna. Have you met her parents, or her Mamaw Susie, her Uncle Kyle, or Uncle Joel?" Arnie chimed in, unable to contain his laughter at the unfolding drama. "Maybe we should let the girls settle it in the pig pen," he added, now doubled over with laughter.

"Well, you're not wrong. She definitely picked that up from her daddy. Rocky! You won't believe what your daughter just said," Deanna shouted towards the barn, her frustration evident as she marched in Rocky's direction like a woman on a mission. Everyone sympathized with Rocky; they knew he was about to face the consequences. He could only put his hands on his head and look skyward in resignation.

Amidst the laughter and commotion, Coraline felt confident she had escaped any punishment. To ensure her safety, the little one quickly grabbed her big sister Clara Beth's hand and said, "Come on, Clara. Let's help you name your sweet rabbits." Clara Beth smiled and took her sister's hand as they walked over to join Uncle Tom at the new cages.

Meanwhile, Kyle and Arnie observed as the goats and cows freely explored their fenced area. "We'll need to graze them outside the fence often. They'll eat up this grass in a few days,"

Kyle remarked to Arnie.

"Not to mention we don't want cow patties everywhere. Try not to step in them," Arnie added amusingly.

Ginger went to check on the pigs in their pen, where a small mountain spring provided water. Kyle had ingeniously diverted the water two ways: one line into the pig lot and the other to a cutoff valve. The continuous flow kept the pigs' area wet and muddy, ideal conditions for them.

Inside the cabin, Rachel was busy preparing a pot of stew using beef from her thawed freezer stock. She found herself impressed by the amount of food Kyle had stored away. "Not hoarding, just stockpiling, I suppose," Rachel murmured to herself as she stirred the stew. It wasn't typical to make stew at this time of year—usually a winter dish—but these were far from normal times.

The sound of an engine along the trail instantly grabbed everyone's attention, causing them to pause their activities. All eyes turned towards the direction of the noise, except for Rocky, who dashed straight to the watchtower for a better view.

"You trying to get a better look or just escaping Deanna's wrath?" Arnie teased, chuckling at Rocky's quick retreat. Rocky simply shook his head, opting not to reply.

"What do you see up there, Rocky?" Kyle called out, craning his neck to see the platform. Rocky adjusted the binoculars, scanning the area until he caught sight of an ATV through the trees.

"It's Joel, I see him. You can't miss that ugly red and black paintjob on his side by side. He should be here in about five minutes," Rocky answered, hanging the binoculars back on their hook and descending the ladder.

Arnie headed out to the gate to greet Joel, opening it just as Joel approached on his ATV. Once Joel had driven through, Arnie closed the gate behind him. Susie hurried over to Joel, visibly relieved to see him at the cabin.

"I was hoping it might be lunchtime; I'm starving," Joel exclaimed as he dismounted from his ATV. Susie enveloped him in a tight hug before stepping back to notice his new black eye.

"We've got stew ready and hot," Rachel called out from the cabin doorway. "Someone better clean up that little wild one over there," she added, pointing to Coraline, who was now standing in the pig lot, grinning and waving.

"It's break time, let's grab some food and water," Uncle Tom announced, and everyone formed a line to eat. The meal was a welcome relief, and conversation was sparse as they savored the food. Rachel, Susie, and Ginger sat on the porch enjoying their meal. Rocky, Kyle, Arnie, and Uncle Tom found shade under a tree. The girls opted for the barn to relax, while Joel wandered around the property, exploring as he ate.

"You've really got a nice place here, Kyle. I should've come up more often to help," Joel commented as he joined the group. "I thought you had a small shack going on but this is awesome."

"It's okay, buddy. I knew you were busy. Uncle Tom and Arnie were a big help, so we managed fine. Just glad you're finally here," Kyle replied, though he knew Joel hadn't been occupied with much beyond video games in his spare time. At least Joel had a job in the coal mines, which Kyle was glad about for his nephew. "How's the eye feeling?" Kyle asked, concerned.

"I'm alright. Can't believe I let that happen, I should have been paying better attention. You always said to be aware of our surroundings. I'd love to take a lug wrench to that guy's head," Joel replied, staring off into the distance beyond the trees.

"Once we get everyone settled and things squared away here, we're going to track down that guy later. I promise you, if someone else hasn't already taken care of him, we'll make sure he gets what's coming to him," Kyle assured Joel with a wink and a determined smile. "But for now, we've got to be smart about it."

Deanna had made her way over to the guys, listening to their conversation before adding her two cents. "You like my house, Joel? I'm going to move Kyle and Arnie down the mountain and use them as bodyguards. They can build some smaller huts near Uncle Tom." Deanna laughed.

"We're getting evicted already?" Kyle asked with laughter

184

as he tossed a small twig at Deanna's foot. "You're a mean landlord."

"Enemies in the yard, Kyle, enemies in the yard! Throw her out!" Rocky announced playfully as Deanna gave him a mean scowl in return.

Throughout the day, Kyle enlisted Arnie to assist with firearm safety and training. Rocky, who had no prior hunting or firearm experience, joined Deanna, Susie, and Ginger as they headed to a small clearing on the trail to practice shooting. Kyle focused on pistol training while Arnie coached them with long guns. Knowing their scopes were zeroed for one hundred yards, Kyle and Arnie guided them through proper technique, emphasizing efficient use of ammunition due to limited supply.

Kyle found pistols to be trickier, especially with Ginger. She initially handled the pistol awkwardly, her movements erratic after each shot. It took repeated corrections from Kyle to break her habit of turning immediately to check with him about her target with a loaded and cocked firearm in hand. After a couple of hours of practice, Ginger finally grasped the basics—loading a magazine, chambering a round, and safely clearing the weapon. Kyle felt proud of her determination to learn.

In contrast, Susie quickly adapted, drawing on childhood memories of her father teaching her to shoot. She only needed to adjust to operating a semi-automatic pistol after her previous experience with revolvers. Rocky, meanwhile, struggled with accuracy when using a pistol but excelled with a rifle. As the saying went, "he couldn't hit the broad side of a barn" with a pistol, but his marksmanship with a rifle at one hundred yards was spot on.

As the training session progressed, Kyle ensured everyone gained confidence and competence with their firearms, preparing them for the challenges ahead.

"I probably needed a .45 caliber; I think I'd shoot better with that," Rocky remarked, examining the pistol in his hand.

Deanna burst into laughter, snorting as she spoke, "You just need to open your eyes when you shoot, jackass." Her comment elicited laughter from everyone, including Rocky himself.

"Thanks for the spousal support there, darling," Rocky replied, playfully putting his arm around Deanna.

"I usually prefer nines because they tend to have more rounds compared to larger calibers," Kyle chimed in, trying to steer the conversation away from Rocky's shooting woes. "In a real situation, more rounds can be crucial since you might not hit your target with every shot. It's not like in the movies—on 'The Walking Dead,' they hit zombies in the head from fifty yards away while running with a pistol."

"I love that show, but shooting a gun isn't as easy as they make it look. You only had to shoot one-time yester," Ginger said before Kyle cut her off.

"I only fired once to scare them off, and it worked," Kyle swiftly interjected, preempting Ginger from revealing more than necessary about the incident involving Robert. Rocky and Deanna remained unaware, and Kyle preferred to keep it that way. "But that's not always how it goes. In a real shootout, people aren't stationary targets, and they're shooting back at you. There's no time for perfect stance or aiming," Kyle cautioned, turning his gaze toward the trail road.

Susie sensed where Kyle's thoughts had drifted, recalling the grim scene in the parking lot with Robert lying lifeless on the ground. The weight of the recent events hung intensely in the air as they continued their firearm training, mindful of the real dangers they might face.

Kyle took the time to demonstrate proper stances to each of them, emphasizing the importance of accuracy and stability.

"You have to maintain your position. Don't let anything distract you from your target. Stay focused," Kyle instructed, his tone serious and focused.

"How did you learn so much about guns, Kyle? Did Sawyer teach you all this?" Ginger inquired, her confidence growing as she absorbed the training.

"I spent time with groups who trained more intensely than

our military. They taught me a lot. I owe them a great deal for the knowledge I gained," Kyle explained to Ginger, reflecting on his past experiences and the valuable skills he had acquired from rigorous training sessions. His gratitude for those who had imparted that knowledge was evident in his words.

CHAPTER THIRTY-TWO
"Tate's Law and Order"

"We've got a problem child in the community. I need you to find out a little information about him and gather a group to remove him," Miran Tate instructed Officer Langston.

Langston, gripped tightly on his belt, knowing Tate wasn't going to like his answer that was about to come. "Okay, but we need to wait. Sheriff Ramey said he'd be driving over today to pay you a visit. Grundy is chaotic, and Ramey plans to meet with supervisors about starting community help centers," Langston said, noticing Tate's unease.

Tate sat upright quickly in his chair, squeaks crackling loudly. "Why is he coming to see me already? He needs to stay in Grundy and leave this area to me," Tate retorted.

"Well, sir, you know Ramey doesn't care for you. He always says you're a crook who shouldn't be in office. Not my words, just telling you what he says," Langston replied nervously.

"Killing has already started. That nosy bastard may need a taste of it himself. Radio him and tell him this area is being secured, no need for him here," Tate ordered, rising from his chair and placing his hands on his hips.

Langston immediately pressed the mic on his police radio. "Sheriff Ramey, come back. Sheriff Ramey, you out there?" he called into the radio, letting Tate listen.

"This is Ramey, go ahead, Langston," came the response.

"Hey, Sheriff, I'm in Hurley. I stopped at Miran Tate's place. He says he has everything under control. No need to waste a trip over here," Langston relayed.

"Stay there, Langston. I'm already en-route. Be there in thirty minutes. I'm out," Sheriff Ramey responded.

"10-4, Sheriff," Langston replied.

Miran Tate picked up a coffee mug, with one of those popular slogans, "Deez Nuts" and flung it against the wall of the large metal garage. The glass mug shattered as it hit, pieces bouncing across the smooth concrete surface of the floor. He didn't like Ramey's response and would not be welcoming the Sheriff with open arms upon his arrival.

"You with me or with the Sheriff?" Tate demanded, placing his hands on the desk and glaring at Langston.

"You know my feelings about Ramey. That should have been my job. I'm with you, Miran," Langston assured him, holding eye contact. "Whatever you want to do, we'll do it."

Miran Tate leaned back in his chair, the leather creaking softly as he took a few contemplative puffs on his cigar. His eyes narrowed thoughtfully as he spoke, and Officer Langston listened intently, knowing that Tate had a detailed plan in mind for dealing with Sheriff Ramey. Killing a few local troublemakers was something Tate considered routine, but eliminating a police officer would undoubtedly invite intense scrutiny. He understood that if these recent events were resolved too quickly, it would only prompt deeper investigations that could uncover their darker dealings. He didn't anticipate a return to normalcy anytime soon.

During their conversation, Tate disclosed Horrace's desire for vengeance against Kyle, the man who had killed his brother. He outlined his agreement to support Horrace in tracking down Kyle, emphasizing the potential risks and rewards. Langston was familiar with Kyle, Susie's brother, and knew that Kyle had come under police scrutiny when rumors surfaced about his off-grid cabin in the woods. This had prompted a brief period of police surveillance and background checks.

In Langston's view, Kyle shouldn't have been subjected to investigation, but acknowledged that in a police state, such precautions were standard procedure. Sheriff Ramey had personally intervened after learning about Kyle's incident in Kansas, prompting Kyle to visit the Grundy police station for a thorough discussion. Kyle openly recounted the events at the

Kansas bar to Ramey, who, finding no cause for concern, opted not to pursue the matter further. Satisfied with Kyle's explanations and with no additional complaints against him, Ramey closed the case.

"Axel and Vince. I'll get those two clowns to go with Horrace," Langston suggested, his voice low but determined, as if calculating the logistics in his mind. He paused briefly, looking out towards the distant outline of the mountain. "Let them use a side-by-side; it's quiet and maneuverable. They can ride up that mountain trail to find the guy. If they catch him, well, they'll do what needs to be done. Leave him there, let nature take its course. It'll be clean and quick."

"You think it will be that easy?" Tate asked, his eyes questioning the plan.

"It's just a guy living on the mountain, how hard can it be?" As Langston spoke, his eyes flicked towards the approaching vehicle, a reflexive response honed through years of vigilance.

"That wasn't thirty minutes. He's trying to catch us up to no good," Tate said letting out a deep laugh. "Quickly, go out the side door. Be ready to come in from behind him if this goes bad," Tate instructed Langston, who scurried to the side and exited.

"Sheriff," Tate greeted as Ramey walked into the open door at the front of the garage.

"Miran, how've you been? Where's Langston? His cruiser is here," the Sheriff asked, looking around the open garage.

"Langston went out back to relieve himself. Probably on my hydrangeas. I'm sorry you wasted a trip here, Ramey. I've got this area supervised," Tate said holding his arms in an embracing gesture of the area. "I'm sure Grundy and the rest of the county need you right now. I have people restoring order in our little town of Hurley and the surrounding communities," Tate said.

"That's what I'm afraid of, Miran," Sheriff Ramey said somberly, his gaze sweeping across the large garage, taking in the scattered items that hinted at both preparedness and suspicion. His eyes settled on the assortment of gas jugs, guns gleaming in racks, and crates of ammunition stacked against the walls. The presence of large quantities of food caught his attention as well, a stark contrast to the scarcity prevailing elsewhere in the county.

"I don't want to scare people any more than they already are," Ramey continued, his voice laced with concern. "The rest of the county is broken right now. I need to rally community leaders to set examples of unity and mutual support. We can't afford any hints of racketeering or lawlessness," he added firmly, casting a pointed glance at the sign that read, "Take it or leave it," suggesting an alternative economy based on barter and community sharing.

"I don't get into racketeering, Sheriff. I'm bringing the people back with the hope of a better tomorrow," Tate said with a wide smile. "I even have my community help center started here where people can take something or leave something to help each other in these troubling times," Tate added, knowing Ramey had seen his sign and goods set up for trade.

"I'm calling in National Guard troops to help you get it under control. This has the potential to be a long-term catastrophe, so I want it contained," Ramey said, clearly looking around for any additional signs of Tate's misdeeds. "I tell you what, Tate, if you've got room, how about I stay here and help you plan?" Ramey added, making Tate clearly uncomfortable.

"There won't be any National Guard coming, Ramey. We both know that," Tate replied firmly, his voice, a mix of defiance and resignation. His eyes bore into Ramey's, challenging the Sheriff's authority. Tate gestured broadly at the radio on his desk, where sporadic transmissions crackled through the airwaves, a testament to the breakdown of centralized authority.

"You like being the man don't you, Tate?" Ramey asked.

"You've heard the radio calls, same as me. We've been sent back to caveman days," Tate continued bitterly. "You're trying to stick your nose where it doesn't belong, and that's the kind of action that can get a man hurt."

Ramey's jaw tightened visibly, his eyes narrowing as he met Tate's gaze head-on. "Is that a threat, Tate?" he asked sharply, his hand hovering near his pistol. "I know what kind of underhanded deals you're a part of. By law, I can remove you from your post right now. This isn't going to be a free-for-all."

The tension in the garage thickened, each man silently assessing the other, their stances poised for action yet restrained by the weight of the situation.

"I am the law, Ramey. These people need me, far more than need you," Tate said, his stare a dagger through Ramey.

"I'll have Langston arrest you, Tate. We can hold you until we figure out what to do with you," Ramey responded, sliding his cuffs from his belt.

"Join us, Langston," Tate signaled, his voice commanding in the tense air of the garage. Langston, already gripping his gun, keeping it trained on Ramey, stepped cautiously forward. The Sheriff turned to face him, his expression a blend of acceptance and disappointment. It was evident he had long suspected Langston's allegiances to Tate, even linking him to the tragic car accident that had claimed the former sheriff Bascum Gilbert's life.

"Keep those hands away from your sidearm, Sheriff. I see you're not surprised," Langston remarked, his gaze unwavering as he circled around Ramey, maintaining his awareness.

"I think I've known for a while you were on Tate's payroll. Knew you were dirty, Langston. Just didn't want to believe it," Ramey responded bitterly, his voice edged with betrayal.

"I could've been straight and narrow. I could've had your job, been making the big bucks," Langston countered, a hint of regret underlying his words, though his stance remained firm.

"What's your plan now? How do you think you'll get away with this?" Ramey challenged, his gaze piercing.

"It'll be easy, Ramey," Tate interrupted, his tone chillingly calm as he retrieved a revolver from his desk drawer, handling it with practiced ease. "You brought this on yourself. Should've stayed away. You said you'd stay here tonight. Looks like your soul's gonna rest in Hurley forever, Sheriff."

The tension in the room thickened with each word, the air heavy with unspoken consequences. Tate's determination was clear, his demeanor unyielding as he faced off against the man who dared challenge his authority.

Ramey's hand twitched towards his holster in a desperate bid for his weapon, but before he could draw, Langston's gun was already leveled and firing. The first shot found its mark in Ramey's chest, the impact absorbed by the Sheriff's body armor with a dull thud. The second bullet tore through his arm, shattering bone and exiting through the back, leaving a trail of crimson in its wake. The fatal blow came swiftly, a third bullet piercing Ramey's neck, severing the carotid artery in a burst of arterial spray.

The Sheriff staggered backwards, a strangled gasp escaping his lips as he clutched at his throat, blood pulsing between his fingers. He collapsed heavily onto the cold concrete floor of the garage, his body convulsing with the shock of mortal wounds. Pain etched across his face, mixing with disbelief and the chilling realization of his impending death.

"He's bleeding out; drag him outside," Tate's voice cut through the chaos, devoid of remorse or hesitation.

"I'm sorry, Ramey. You're a good man," Langston murmured, his tone filled with regret as he steadied his aim and fired a final shot into Ramey's forehead, mercifully ending his suffering.

"Damn, Langston, you didn't have to shoot him again. He was finished," Tate remarked with a grim chuckle, the sound echoing off the walls of the garage. The air was filled with the scent of gunpowder and the weight of irreversible actions, marking the end of one man's life and the sinister beginning of another chapter in Hurley's troubled history.

"He caught us, Tate. That's all he did wrong. Ramey was a good man, and I disliked him for it. He didn't deserve a slow death. I wanted to end it quick for him," Langston said as he slid his pistol back into its holster.

"Whatever makes you feel good about it. Now get him out of here and clean this mess up. Take him up Home Creek, put him in the driver's seat, and set fire to his cruiser. On your way back, radio out asking for him just in case any deputies are left working.

Just say he hadn't shown up yet. I doubt anyone is working now. Take somebody with you to drive his cruiser," Tate instructed.

Langston nodded and moved quickly to drag the Sheriff's body outside. The weight of the dead man was substantial, but adrenaline spurred him on. He took the Sheriff's car to the top of the mountain and parked it in a spot next to the road. He heaved the body into the driver's seat of the cruiser, arranging it to look as natural as possible. Then, he doused the vehicle with gasoline and struck a match. The flames roared to life, consuming the evidence of their crime, at least as much as needed for now.

As Langston drove back, the smell of burning flesh and metal filled his nostrils. He pressed the radio button and called out, "Sheriff Ramey, come back. Sheriff Ramey, do you copy?" There was only static in response. He knew it was unlikely anyone would be listening, but the charade had to be maintained.

"This is Vanover," the radio chirped surprising Langston. "Ramey is supposed to be in Hurley. I can come that way," Officer Vanover replied, his voice calm.

Langston quickly grabbed his mic, squeezing it as he responded. "No need, Vanover. I'm already here, I'll watch for him. Save your fuel."

"10-4," Vanover replied, a tinge of accusation in his voice.

Lanston slammed the mic down, "nosey son of a bitch."

Returning to Tate's garage, Langston felt a strange mix of relief and dread. The deed was done, but the consequences loomed large. "It's done. Cruiser's burning, and there's nothing left of him," Langston reported.

"Good. Now, we focus on the next step. Get Axel and Vince ready. We need to deal with Kyle before he becomes a bigger problem," Tate said, lighting another cigar. "How about this Vanover, is he trouble?"

"I don't think so, we call him Joe Cool at the office, he thinks he is Perry Mason." Langston said, the weight of their actions settling heavily on his shoulders. Hurley was now a town on the brink, and the path ahead was fraught with danger and deception.

CHAPTER THIRTY-THREE

"Dark Alliance"

———————————————————

Upon returning to Miran Tate's compound, Lucas maneuvered the water truck beside two towering fuel tanks, their metallic surfaces gleaming in the harsh light. After witnessing Horrace's capabilities, Lucas politely asked him to begin transferring the fuel from the truck into the tanks. The sound of the liquid rushing through the hoses filled the air as Lucas made his way down to the garage to report to Tate.

As he stepped inside, a sense of dread washed over him. The dimly lit garage felt heavy, the scent of iron thick in the air. A large puddle of blood stained the concrete floor, its deep crimson color stark against the grey surface. Drag marks, smeared and grotesque, led toward the door, suggesting a violent struggle. The sight was haunting, and Lucas knew something terrible had occurred in this very spot.

"How much fuel did you get, Lucas?" Tate asked, carrying a bucket of water and tossing it onto the blood.

"We got about eight hundred and fifty gallons. Fred's store was burned to the ground," Lucas responded, looking at Tate with a mix of weariness and concern.

"Burned to the ground? Damn scoundrels around here. Were you able to obtain the other items I told you?" Tate asked, handing Lucas a deck brush.

"You aren't going to like this, Tate. We did go to Travis McMurray's and collect his .50 caliber," Lucas said, beginning to push the deck brush over the blood.

"And why am I not going to like it? Did they give you any trouble?" Tate asked, a hint of impatience in his voice.

"He wasn't going to give it to us. Then Horrace blows his head off right in the front yard. Just walks up behind him and pulls the trigger. Blew his head damn near clean off," Lucas said, scrubbing harder at the blood. He looked behind him before saying anything more. "He is crazy, Mr. Tate. I mean craaa-zzzzzy. He killed McMurray's wife Shelia too. Shot her in the chest and walked away eating a damn honey bun like it was break time."

"Where is he now? Did you make the other stops? How did they go?" Tate asked, noticing Lucas's visible nervousness.

"He is emptying the fuel into the tanks. And no, sir, I didn't make any more stops. I didn't think you wanted anyone killed. I wasn't taking him around nobody else," Lucas said, shaking his head. "Looking at this blood, I guess killing was the thing to do today," he added, glancing back up at Tate.

"Lucas, you've been with me a long time. You're safe with me, and I'll take care of you. Sometimes, though, men just need killing. No way around it. We did what was needed here, and it sounds like Horrace did what was needed with you today. No crying over spilt milk, or should I say spilt blood," Tate said laughing deeply, his body convulsing. As Tate regained his composure, he tossed another bucket of water onto the blood, rinsing away the memory of Sheriff Ramey.

As Lucas finished cleaning up the blood, Tate walked away from the garage. Horrace was just finishing up the fuel transfer from the truck into the tanks. Approaching him, Tate handed Horrace a beer.

"I'm told you did a good job today taking care of my business. I'd like to keep you on if you're good with that. I will see to it that you have food and water," Tate said as Horrace eagerly accepted the beer, twisting off the cap and taking a long drink.

"Yes, sir. We had some people who didn't want to abide by the rules. I wasn't giving them time to take us out, so I shot first. I'm not looking to die yet," Horrace said, showing the look of a man willing to kill on order.

"I had your brother's grave taken care of. When you're ready, you can use the backhoe to fill it. I thought you might want to say some words over him first," Tate said.

"With Robert gone now, I have nobody left. I have nothing but the old home place, and it's in desperate need of repair," Horrace replied, continuing to enjoy the cold beer.

"I also found out who your guy is. The name is Kyle Blaine, and he lives up on a mountain top now. We haven't gotten the exact location, but we know the vicinity," Tate told Horrace, watching as he chugged the remainder of the beer.

"I appreciate that, Mr. Tate. Can you help me get on that mountain? I owe him, and I intend to pay," Horrace said, his calm demeanor chillingly reminiscent of a serial killer, making Tate wonder if he had killed anyone else in the past.

"I have three men that will go with you. You can bury your brother tomorrow. I'll have some work here that needs to be done. Let's give it a few days, then I'll send the three of them with you. I'll give you a four-person side by side, guns, and ammo," Tate said, pointing to the large vehicle parked next to the garage. "You can use that to get back and forth from home to here. Sound like a deal?" Tate extended his hand for a shake.

With the agreement in place, Tate felt a surge of satisfaction. He had secured a true killer for his team, someone whose loyalty seemed unwavering. Horrace, on the other hand, viewed the arrangement purely as a means to exact his vengeance. Tate's grand schemes were of no interest to him at the moment.

Langston soon returned, changing his clothes after the messy task of disposing of Sheriff Ramey's body and police cruiser. His face bore a grim expression as he walked into the garage. Tate quickly briefed him on the newest member of their group, Horrace.

"Langston, meet Horrace," Tate began. "He's joining us."

Langston's eyes narrowed slightly, recognizing the name. He knew Horrace's history—minor drug offenses and a few breaking-and-entering charges. But there was something about

Horrace that suggested a far darker past.

"Horrace, welcome," Langston said, extending a hand.

Horrace didn't take it. "I know who you are. As long as you're going to act like a cop, expect me to treat you like one, you can kiss my ass," Horrace said, his voice flat and his stare cold.

Langston bristled at the blatant disrespect but tried to maintain his composure. "Look here, pal. The law doesn't matter anymore; only Tate's martial law does now. This uniform is for show. If I wanted, you could have been arrested long ago, and you know exactly why. But that doesn't matter now; you're a free man," he said, attempting to reassert his dominance.

Horrace's expression didn't change. He didn't flinch, didn't blink, just continued to stare at Langston. Langston felt a chill run down his spine, realizing he may have underestimated this man. Tate watched the exchange, a smirk playing at the corners of his mouth. He liked the tension; it meant both men were on edge.

"Then you know that son-of-a-bitch had it coming to him," Horrace said as he turned and walked away.

"What the hell did he mean by that? Maybe he did kill someone," Langston said to Tate.

Tate leaned back against his desk, the dim light of the garage casting darkness across his face. He spoke in a low, measured tone, outlining his plan to Langston. "We'll let Horrace take the lead on finding Kyle up on the mountain. He's got the drive and the grudge to see it through."

Langston nodded, Kyle wasn't on his list, yet.

As Langston spoke, Tate's mind wandered to the bigger picture. Sheriff Ramey was no longer a threat, and the chaos spreading through the county played perfectly into his hands. Tate envisioned a new order, with himself at the helm. He could sense the fear and desperation among the people—an emotion he could exploit. Offering them security, or imposing his will through brute force, was the key to seizing control.

"We've removed the biggest obstacle," Tate continued, his voice filled with a cold confidence. "With Ramey gone and the county in disarray, we'll move in. First, we'll offer them protection. They'll come to us willingly, seeking safety. And those who resist?" He paused, the flicker of a smile matching Langston's. "They'll learn quickly that resistance is futile."

The garage fell silent, the gravity of Tate's words hanging heavily in the air. Langston could see the vision unfolding in Tate's eyes—a vision of power, dominance, and unchallenged rule. This was no longer just about survival; it was about conquest.

CHAPTER THIRTY-FOUR
"A Place of No Return"

Snaggle wasted no time getting the big coal truck positioned to block the road leading into their small neighborhood community. The truck, an imposing barrier, stood as a guard against any unauthorized entry. Snaggle, a burly figure with a rugged appearance, took his place next to the massive vehicle, his eyes scanning the horizon with a wary intensity. The goal was clear: no one was getting through without his say-so.

Stationed beside him was Herbie, a volunteer watchman eager to prove his worth. Herbie, slightly smaller and younger, mimicked Snaggle's stance, his eyes darting around nervously. Both men knew the importance of their task; the community's safety depended on their vigilance.

As Snaggle squinted against the afternoon sun, a glint caught his eye. A white car approached from a distance, the sunlight reflecting off its hood. The vehicle slowed as it neared, and Snaggle's grip tightened on his rifle. He could feel the tension in the air, an obvious sense of anticipation. On the other side of the truck, Herbie mirrored Snaggle's alert posture, scanning the surroundings with a mix of excitement and apprehension.

The white car inched closer, and its details became clearer—an old, rugged and battered Mustang. Snaggle didn't know the driver, Allen, personally, but he recognized the car from descriptions given by the community members. It was a vehicle associated with someone potentially troublesome.

Swallowing hard, unsure of what might happen next, Snaggle stood his ground. The car came to a stop a few feet away.

The engine idled, the hum of the motor the only sound breaking the tense silence. Snaggle took a step closer, his rifle held firmly but not yet raised. He glanced at Herbie, who gave a slight nod, indicating he was ready for whatever might unfold.

"What's your business here?" Snaggle called out, his voice strong and unwavering, carrying the authority of someone who was used to being obeyed.

The driver's side window of the Mustang rolled down, and Allen leaned out, his expression a mix of determination and frustration. "I need through. I'm going to check on friends," he replied, his tone firm but not aggressive.

"Everyone is good this way. No entry for anyone who doesn't live here. You need to move on," Snaggle responded, his voice allowing no argument.

Allen stared at Snaggle for a moment, assessing the situation. Realizing there was no point in arguing, and knowing he was currently outgunned, he nodded bluntly, then put the car in reverse. With a swift, practiced motion, he backed up, pulled the emergency brake, and spun the car around in a dramatic maneuver. The Mustang's tires screeched as he accelerated away, the rear wheels kicking up dust and gravel.

"That looked like something you see in a movie," Herbie remarked with a chuckle, relaxing his stance now that the immediate threat had passed.

Snaggle allowed himself a small smile, but his eyes remained focused. "Yeah, but this ain't no movie. Stay sharp," he replied, his tone a reminder of the seriousness of their task.

Herbie nodded, the gravity of the situation sinking back in as he resumed his vigilant watch. The dust from the Mustang's departure slowly settled, leaving the two men standing guard, ready for whatever might come next.

Allen set a new plan in motion, needing to find a place to stay for a while. He made his way down the narrow, gravel one-lane road, the sun beating down relentlessly, casting heat waves over the landscape. The road wound its way up a holler, flanked by dense woods and stifling heat. Tall weeds lined the roadside, their dry stalks rustling faintly in the occasional breeze. The house ahead appeared weather-beaten and neglected, its paint faded and peeling, surrounded by an overgrown lawn.

As Allen's Mustang rattled down the driveway, its engine sputtering with the last of its fuel, he leaned on the horn several times. The sound echoed through the stillness, a signal to the man inside. The front door creaked open, and a figure emerged—a thin man with tattoos covering his arms and a cautious gaze. He smiled and approached Allen with a nod, slapping his hand in a familiar greeting before pulling him into a quick hug.

"Good to see you, bro. Where you been?" the man greeted Allen, his voice gravelly with a hint of suspicion.

"I've been around. Just trying to stay out of trouble," Allen replied, his tone casual despite the brutal crime he had committed just the day before.

"What you think about all this shit?" the man asked, taking a long drag from a half-smoked joint he held between his fingers.

Allen glanced around, his eyes searching for any sign of fuel. "I need some gas and a place to crash tonight," he said bluntly, cutting straight to the point.

The man's demeanor shifted slightly, his expression hardening as he considered Allen's request. "Sorry, bro. I ain't got no gas. Maybe a quarter gallon in that jug for the mower," he replied, pointing to a small red jug tucked under the porch steps.

Allen frowned, frustration bubbling beneath the surface. "They got the road blocked up a few miles with a coal truck. Two guys with guns standing guard. Wouldn't let me through, I seen a guy with gas," he explained, his voice expressing clear frustration.

The man raised an eyebrow, his interest piqued. "Who's got gas?" he asked, his tone shifting to one of cautious curiosity.

"Some dude in an old blue truck. Had that Arnie kid with him, the one who rides dirt bikes. Arnie said it's his Uncle Kyle. You know 'em?" Allen replied, hoping for a lead that could get him out of his current predicament.

The man scratched his chin thoughtfully, exhaling a cloud of smoke. "I know of Arnie. Seen him ride by here sometimes. His

Uncle Kyle, though? Never heard of him. I do know there's a place up at the top of the mountain where some guy's been hoarding supplies," he said, as he recalled bits of local gossip.

"I know he's got fuel. We need to find him," Allen said firmly, his mind racing with possibilities.

"I might know where we can score some gas. Up the holler a bit, the last house is a farm. If we cut through his property, it leads to the trails up the mountain—probably the same area that guy Kyle's at," the man suggested, gesturing farther down the narrow road.

Allen nodded, his determination growing. "Sounds like our best shot. Let's go," he said, glancing at the man expectantly.

"Where can we get the gas, Allen?" Cindy asked walking up to the men reaching out her hand for the joint.

"Cindy, this is Ronnie, my boy from way back," Allen introduced, his voice carrying a hint of weariness from the day's events.

"We've been friends for twenty years now," Ronnie chimed in, offering a friendly smile to Cindy despite her standoffishness.

Cindy responded with a nod, her expression bordering on impatience. "Hi. That's nice. What are we doing, Allen? Does he have any gas?" she asked abruptly, her eyes flicking dismissively over Ronnie.

Ronnie shot Allen a bemused glance, his eyebrows raised in disbelief at Cindy's attitude. Allen, feeling the tension rise, acted swiftly. With a sudden, controlled motion, he delivered a light backhanded slap across Cindy's cheek. The sound echoed briefly in the quiet air, startling Cindy into a stunned silence as she spun around.

"Show some respect," Allen commanded sharply, his voice allowing no argument. "Get your ass back in the car." Cindy, taken aback, hesitated only for a moment before turning on her heel and scurrying back, her cheeks flushed with embarrassment.

"Still keeping them straight, I see," Ronnie chuckled, giving Allen a playful slap on the shoulder. Ronnie, grinned and called out to another figure lingering nearby. "Tricky! Let's roll," he shouted, motioning for Tricky to join them.

Tricky, a clear friend of the oxycodone, with a mischievous grin, hurried over and hopped into the back of Ronnie's beat-up truck. Allen jumped in his Mustang, ready to follow. The truck rumbled to life, its engine growling as Ronnie steered it onto the dusty road.

They continued down the winding path, the trees casting shade across the road. Each bump and dip in the gravel sent vibrations through the truck's chassis. As they approached Mr. Hadley's property, Ronnie slowed the truck to a stop, eyeing the gate ahead that blocked their path.

"We're gonna talk to old man Hadley," Ronnie muttered to himself, his tone full of determination. "This old man has everything we need, I'm sure of it."

Allen followed, as sweat trickled down his brow in the oppressive heat, but he remained focused on the task at hand. This was their chance to secure fuel and continue their journey, no matter the obstacles in their way. If they chose, this could possibly be a place to stay for a while.

As they pulled up to the gate, Ronnie could see it was chained and locked. He honked his truck horn a few times, the sound echoing in the still air, before getting out and climbing over the gate. The metal clanked as it swayed under his weight. He began walking toward Hadley's house when he heard the screen door slam shut. Hadley appeared on the porch, looking every bit as weathered as his home, a trusty shotgun at his side.

"That's far enough. What are you doing on my property?" Hadley called out, his voice gravelly and stern.

"Hello, Hadley. It's me, Ronnie, from down the road. I wanted to come by and check on you," Ronnie called back, raising a hand in a friendly gesture.

"I know who you are. One of them drug dealers at the mouth of the holler. Nothing for you here. Just turn around and head on back," Hadley replied, his grip tightening on the shotgun.

Ronnie could see Allen moving through the tree line behind Hadley's house, slipping behind an old woodshed that provided ample cover. Trying to keep Hadley's attention away from that direction, Ronnie called out again, "Come on, Hadley, don't be like that. I just wanted to make sure you were okay. Is there anything I can do for you?"

"I said I'm good. Now you go on back the way you—" Hadley's words were cut off abruptly as Allen struck him across the back of the head with a thick piece of wood. The sound of the impact was sickening, and Hadley tumbled forward, falling down the steps of the porch. His shotgun clattered to the ground as he rolled to a stop in the grass at the bottom, groaning in pain.

"If he wasn't a saved man before, he is now, because you knocked the hell out of him!" Ronnie said to Allen, a twisted grin on his face. Hadley struggled to his hands and knees, his eyes darting toward the barn.

"What are you doing?" a woman shouted from the barn, her voice filled with panic. "Leave him alone!" she screamed, rushing toward them.

Hadley's eyes widened with terror as he saw Allen pull his gun and aim at the woman. "Opal, run!" he shouted, his voice hoarse with desperation. "Run, Opal!" he shouted again as she turned and bolted back toward the barn.

Ronnie kicked the old man in the side, his boot digging into Hadley's ribs with a thud. Hadley gasped, clutching his side in agony, the pain etched deeply into his tiresome face. A cruel smile shown on Ronnie's lips as he watched the old man crumple back to the ground, a pathetic, broken figure.

Pop! Pop! The sound of Allen's gunshots shattered the tense silence. Opal's scream pierced the air as she stumbled, the impact throwing her to the ground. The deadly echoes bounced off the trees, as birds were flushed from the branches.

Hadley's eyes, filled with a mixture of pain and helpless rage, locked onto his wife's fallen frame. The love and years they had shared flashed before his eyes, now marred by blood and violence. He reached out a trembling hand toward her, his heart breaking as he watched the life drain away.

The scene descended into a deadly silence, broken only by

the labored breaths of the dying and the triumphant. Hadley watched Opal, hoping for another movement, hearing the heartless chuckles of their attackers. The weight of the brutality hung heavy in the air, a chilling testament to the depths of human cruelty.

CHAPTER THIRTY-FIVE

"Whispers in the Barn"

It was a scorching day, and Kyle and Rocky were dressed in cargo pants and long-sleeve shirts to protect themselves from the relentless sun. Kyle's family had spent the past few days settling into the cabin and adjusting to their new way of life. They had been helping Uncle Tom prepare his cabin for daily living, even going old school by digging a hole for Uncle Tom's new outhouse. Kyle was surprised at how proud his Uncle Tom was of what Arnie liked to refer to as the "shit shack."

"I told old man Hadley I would be back to see him about the horses. I'm going to ride down and see what he decided," Kyle said, picking up his backpack and sliding it over one arm. "Keep your fingers crossed that he's going to sell us a couple. He may have changed his mind by now."

"You want me to go with you, Kyle? I can help you with the horses if he does sell," Rocky offered. Rocky had a lot of experience with horses, and Kyle knew it.

"I'd be glad to have you go, Rocky. You know way more about horses than I do. You can even make sure if he does sell, we get healthy ones," Kyle said, nodding his thanks.

"I'll go with you too, Uncle Kyle. I can ride horses; I have before," Coralina said, pulling on her boots. "Mom! Get me a snack to take," she added, yelling for Deanna.

"I'm sorry, little one, but we can't take you on this trip. It may be dangerous, and we can't let you get hurt. Your mommy will whip your daddy and me both if we do," Kyle said, kneeling down for a hug.

"If I can't go, you don't get no hug," Coralina pouted, crossing her arms and lowering her head in pretend tears.

"I'm hugging you anyway," Kyle said, quickly grabbing her up while she tried to act mad and twist away. "And here is a big kiss too," he added, kissing her cheek.

Kyle went out and got in his ATV, waiting for Rocky. Rocky quickly hugged the girls and Deanna before joining Kyle. "We'll be back shortly, hopefully with horses!" Kyle said as he began to pull away. As they drove down the narrow trail, they talked about the horses and what would be needed to care for them.

"You got about everything we'll need," Rocky said to Kyle as they discussed it. "You got a tack room full of gear, how did you even know what to buy?"

"I just told those guys at the horse ring one night I wanted horses, to show me what all I needed. Then I started buying it a little at a time," Kyle said with uncertainty that he was buying the right items.

Rocky mentioned he had another saddle at home they could retrieve if it hadn't been stolen. He also suggested they try to get some more hay bales from Hadley, as the animals would use plenty during the winter, depleting Kyle's stock quickly.

About halfway down the trail, Kyle stopped in a clearing and used binoculars to look at old man Hadley's farmhouse. He was quickly drawn to the side of the house where he could see the front end of a white Mustang parked next to it. "You've got to be kidding me," Kyle said aloud, catching Rocky's attention.

"What do you see? Something wrong?" Rocky asked, trying to see in the same direction without binoculars.

"There's Allen's Mustang parked by the house. Take a look for yourself," Kyle said, handing the binoculars to Rocky. "That's the guy that beat Joel up a couple of days back. I wonder what he's doing there."

"Here, take another look. Over by the barn, is that what I think it is?" Rocky asked, handing the binoculars back.

Kyle looked where Rocky had indicated and saw a body on

the ground near the barn. It wasn't old man Hadley; it looked like a woman with long, silver hair lying face down in the grass. Kyle knew it was Mrs. Hadley. He hoped it wasn't, but who else could it be?

"Okay, let's ride down a bit farther and then I'm going to park and walk in," Kyle said, moving slowly down the trail. "I'll go in alone. I don't need you getting hurt. If there is any sign of trouble, head back up to the cabin and get the defense in place," Kyle instructed, thinking about what he might be walking into. If Allen had indeed hurt the Hadleys, he would make him pay. He already owed him for what he had done to Joel earlier. Sometimes people needed to be put in their place, and Kyle saw Allen as one of those people.

"Okay, stay here. I'm going to go in for a closer look. Any sign of trouble, get your ass up that trail," Kyle reiterated to Rocky.

"You sure you don't want me to go with you? Who knows what you're walking into," Rocky said, holding Kyle's arm before he walked off.

"I'm going to scout it out. If I do something stupid, you just get back up the mountain," Kyle said, slipping his pack over both arms onto his back. He took his AR with him and continued down the trail. The summer season provided great concealment with trees and weeds grown up all around. Combined with the old junk vehicles, he had plenty of cover to maneuver. Once near the gate, he slipped off to the side of the trail and moved through the trees. Rocky lost visual on Kyle but could see the house and barn clearly, waiting anxiously for Kyle to reappear.

Kyle hopped over the fence and made his way closer to the barn. He stopped to look toward the house for any sign of movement. He could hear voices talking but couldn't see anyone. He could make out at least two male voices. Kyle made his way to the back of the barn before stepping out of the tree coverage. He ran over to the barn, reappearing in Rocky's view. Kyle looked at the body lying in the grass and saw she had been shot in the head.

Kyle wiped his sleeve across his face, the sweat running

over him like a waterfall in the dry heat of the day. He opened the side door of the barn and slowly stepped inside. Natural light shone through the cracks of the old sawmill lumber used on the barn years ago. He moved around the side of one stall and saw old man Hadley lying on a pile of hay. Kyle moved over to him and whispered, "Mr. Hadley, are you okay?" When no answer came, Kyle stepped closer. He placed his hand on Mr. Hadley's shoulder and gave him a light nudge. "Mr. Hadley," Kyle repeated.

The old man let out a low groan as he opened his eyes, looking up at Kyle. The man held both hands over his abdomen. "Hey there, son. You came back for them horses, I see," Mr. Hadley said, trying to catch his breath.

"What happened, sir?" Kyle asked, pulling Hadley's hands up from his stomach. He could see Hadley had been shot, his coveralls heavily stained in red. The large amount of blood loss and Hadley's pale face showed he had little time left.

"There were some fellers who showed up a couple of days ago, maybe yesterday, I don't really know now," Mr. Hadley began, his voice weak but determined to share his story. "One snuck up on me, I didn't even hear 'em till he was right behind me. Next thing I know, he hit my head, and I'm seeing stars. Opal, bless her, she was in the barn tending to the horses, brushing down Midnight, her favorite. She heard the commotion and came running out. I could see the panic in her eyes when she spotted me on the ground, blood pouring from my head. I told her run, but before she could take more than a few steps, they shot her. Cold-blooded. No warning, just bang! She fell right there, by the barn door."

Hadley's breathing grew more labored, and Kyle could see the pain etched deep in his wrinkled face. "I tried to get to her, Kyle. I tried so damn hard. I could hear 'em laughing, these sick, twisted laughs. They let me crawl, inch by inch, getting closer to Opal. I was so close I could almost touch her hand, but then... then they shot me in the back. I felt the bullet tear through me, burning like fire. I collapsed. I got back up, somehow. I turned around to face 'em, maybe to beg or to curse, I don't know. That's when they shot me again, right in the belly."

Hadley coughed violently, a deep, wet sound, and blood began to leak from the corner of his mouth. Kyle knelt beside him, feeling helpless. "They just stood there, watching me suffer, enjoying it. I laid there for hours, I think. Maybe it was days. I finally crawled in here, trying to get to my rifle, but I couldn't make it that far. I thought maybe if I could get my hands on it, I could at least take one of 'em down with me. But this," he gestured weakly to his blood-soaked abdomen, "this is as far as I got. It's time for me to go meet my Opal. She's waiting for me. If I see your dad up there, I'll let him know you turned out alright, son. He would be proud," Hadley said giving Kyle's hand a slight tap.

"You just relax now, Mr. Hadley. I will get you some help," Kyle said, holding the man's hand. Kyle felt Hadley's strength fade away as his hand softened. He pulled Hadley's eyelids down as the old man passed away. Rage flowed through Kyle as he wanted so badly now to kill Allen for this.

Rocky continued watching the barn, waiting for Kyle to reappear. He bounced his gaze between the barn and the house. He saw two men walking around to the front of the house, stopping to look toward the barn. One man pointed toward the barn, Rocky wondered if they had seen Kyle.

As the two men approached the barn, they noticed old man Hadley wasn't laying on the ground as he had been the night before. Rocky watched anxiously, his own sweat filling his eyes, burning like a hot match to them, as the men closed in on the barn doors. Kyle could hear the voices nearing and stepped back behind one of the stalls for cover. He heard the barn door open and one of the men speak.

"There he is. I guess he wasn't dead. He must have crawled inside last night," one voice said. This wasn't Allen's voice.

"Looks dead now," the second man said, removing his pistol and firing another shot into old man Hadley's chest. "He's dead now for sure." Laughter filled the barn, but this voice wasn't Allen's either. Kyle remained still, the horses became disgruntled, stomping around the stalls and snorting loudly.

Rocky heard the gunshot and looked to the barn, hoping it wasn't at Kyle. He saw another man leave the house, tromping down the porch steps heavily and moving quickly to the barn. This was a large man with a pistol out. "What was that?" the big man said loudly as he approached the barn.

There it was, that was Allen's voice, Kyle thought to himself. He debated on what to do. Should he rise from behind the stall and unleash a hail of bullets on the men? He would be putting himself at risk in doing so. He felt a surge of anger, not just for the killing of Hadley, but the extra shot they put into the man's dead body for fun. Kyle slowly exhaled and briefly closed his eyes to think, he needed to find a place of calmness, his emotions running away now.

"This place is going to be good for us, Allen. You did a good job here. All that food in the basement, we won't have to leave for a long time," one of the voices said.

"When are we going to visit your new friend, Kyle?" the other voice asked.

"I'm thinking tomorrow night. I want to go look around and see their place. We will figure out exactly where they are and what they have. Maybe in a couple nights we will go hit them. We're going to do it when they aren't expecting it," Allen said with a laugh. "I'm going to beat him senseless. I want to make him beg me to kill him. But tonight we're going to party and eat like the kings we are."

Kyle, hearing this, slowly began to rise from behind the stall. As he peered over, pulling his rifle in line with his eye, the men had turned back towards the house, walking out of the barn. Kyle wondered if there might be more inside or if it was only these three. He could probably shoot all three in the back as they walked away, but what if there were more? He watched as the men went back to the house, disappearing inside.

Rocky, still watching and becoming more impatient, thought the shot he heard was Kyle being killed. He was not sure how he was going to go back and tell everyone, but he knew it was what Kyle had told him to do. He rubbed his hands over his face quickly a few times and, as he prepared to leave, saw the side door open on the barn. Rocky stopped, squatting back down in the brush and weeds. Kyle stepped out the side door and ran back into the tree line. Rocky was relieved but still unsure about what the gunshot was about.

Rocky climbed back into the ATV and waited for Kyle to reach him. Hearing a slight rustle, he knew it was Kyle who soon appeared from the trees with a look of both guilt and disappointment.

"What happened, man? I heard the gunshot," Rocky asked, watching Kyle as he opened a bottle of water and took a long drink before pouring the remaining amount over his head and neck.

"Old man Hadley was inside the barn," Kyle began, his voice tight with suppressed anger. "I found him sitting against a pile of hay, barely clinging to life. We talked a bit before he passed. He told me everything. Those bastards showed up out of nowhere, beat him down, and shot Opal right in front of him. The last man who came into the barn was Allen. They killed Hadley and his wife to take their property."

"That's crazy," Rocky said, his face pale with shock.

"It gets worse," Kyle continued, his eyes dark with determination. "They know we're up on the mountain. I overheard them talking. They're planning on coming to attack us, and Allen's got it out for me. He wants me dead. They're not just thieves, they're killers, and they're coming for us next."

Rocky clenched his fists, his jaw set in a hard line. "What are we doing? Are we going back and kill them now?" he asked, his voice filled with a fiery determination, ready for a fight.

Kyle shook his head, his mind working quickly. "No, we're not rushing in blind. We're going to watch them first. We need to see how many there are, what kind of firepower they have. Then we go back and round up the troops. Everyone needs to be aware and ready for a possible attack. We'll fortify our defenses and make sure they can't catch us off guard. Once we know what we're dealing with, we'll bring the fight to them on our terms."

Kyle sat down on the ground, the weight of his

responsibility pressing heavily on him. "I will see to it that man dies," he vowed, his voice a low, dangerous whisper. "He has crossed the line of no return. He's not just a threat to us, he's a rabid dog that needs to be put down. We'll make sure he never harms anyone else again."

CHAPTER THIRTY-SIX

"Impending Storm"

Kyle and Rocky arrived back at the cabin to a flurry of questioning faces and one clearly disappointed little girl. The air was thick with tension, the gravity of the situation pressing down on everyone. Kyle's heart sank, knowing the grim news he had to deliver. Coraline stood next to the porch, her small figure almost dwarfed by the wooden porch post. Her eyes, usually bright and full of mischief, were now dark with disappointment and confusion.

Her face was streaked with dirt, evidence of her day spent playing with the animals, little smudges marking her cheeks and forehead. Her hair, wild and tangled, framed her face in a way that only emphasized her pout. She twisted her lips in frustration, her lower lip quivering slightly as she fought back tears. The sight of no horses in tow made her eyes narrow in a mixture of sadness and betrayal.

Kyle's thoughts drifted as he looked at her, wondering how they could ever slaughter an animal now that she had made friends with them. Coraline had a way of bonding with the creatures around her, her innocent heart forming connections that made the harsh realities of their survival all the more difficult. He imagined her earlier, giggling as she chased the chickens or pigs. The innocence in her eyes was a painful reminder of the world they were trying to shield her from, a world filled with violence and loss.

As she stood there, her small hands clenched into fists at her sides, Kyle could almost hear her unspoken question: "Where are the horses?" The weight of her unasked question added to his burden, making the truth he had to share even more unbearable. He took a deep breath, hardening himself for the conversation that was to come, knowing that the innocence in Coraline's eyes might never fully return once she learned of the horrors that awaited them.

Rocky knelt down to Coraline's level. "Hey, sweetheart, why don't you go with Clara Beth to the barn and make sure the stalls are clean?"

Coraline huffed, but Clara Beth took her hand, leading her away. As the girls ran off to the barn, Kyle gathered the adults. "We need to hold a family meeting."

In the living room, the group assembled, their faces tight with concern, the room heavy with anticipation. Kyle and Rocky stood at the center, their expressions grim as they recounted the horrifying events at old man Hadley's farm. Their voices were low and steady, but the weight of their words hung in the air like a dark cloud.

Kyle spared no detail, his words painting a vivid picture of the brutality they had witnessed. He described how the attackers had ambushed Hadley, beating him mercilessly before gunning him down in cold blood. Rocky added to the narrative, recounting the senseless killing of Hadley's wife, who was shot down as she tried to flee. The callous cruelty of the attackers was evident in every word, their laughter echoing in Kyle's memory as they toyed with their victims before delivering the final blows.

Rachel's tears flowed freely, her body shaking with sobs. She had known the Hadleys for years, their families intertwined through countless shared moments and memories. The thought of their violent end was too much to bear, and she covered her face with her hands, her shoulders heaving with each sob.

Susie and Ginger clung to each other, their faces pale with terror. They listened in stunned silence, their minds struggling to process the horror. Susie's eyes were wide, glistening with unshed tears, while Ginger's lip trembled, her grip on Susie tightening with each gruesome detail. The room seemed to close in around them, the walls pressing down as if to crush the hope out of their hearts.

The moment was full of fear and sorrow, each person grappling with the stark reality that their world had changed permanently. The vivid recounting of the Hadleys' fate served as a brutal reminder of the dangers they now faced. The group sat in silence, the true reality settling heavily upon them, knowing that the fight for their survival had only just begun.

"Where are Arnie and Joel?" Kyle asked, scanning the room.

"They went off the mountain to check on the houses. Joel said he needed to gather some supplies," Susie replied, nervously running her hand through her hair.

Kyle sighed, feeling the weight of his next words. "I think it might be a good idea if we take you to Uncle Tom's house, Mom, at least down to his cabin away from here."

Rachel covered her mouth with her hand, her eyes wide with fear. "I thought this was supposed to be the safe place for all of us. That's why we came here, to ride this out. Are there no police we can get involved to help?"

Kyle shook his head, his voice heavy with frustration and sorrow. "It is the safest place, Mom. I mean, it was. It's supposed to be! But there are no police now. I'll take the fight to them, but if it goes wrong, I have no way to protect you all." He looked to Susie and Rachel, his expression grim.

"I can't do it by myself," he continued. "That means I must take Arnie, Joel, or Rocky with me. This isn't paintball, and there is a chance one or all of us may not be coming back. Honestly, Rocky has two young girls here; he needs to stay with you all."

"Bullshit!" Rocky interjected, his face flushing with anger. "I'm not staying behind while you or anyone else fights for me. I'm going with you."

Before Kyle could respond, the shrill chime of the motion alarm cut through the tense silence, jolting everyone into alertness. The sound signaled that someone was at the perimeter gate. Kyle's heart pounded as he quickly grabbed his rifle, the cold metal reassuring in his grip. He moved swiftly to the porch, the wooden boards creaking under his boots.

The gate's mechanical hum as it opened brought a momentary sense of relief; it meant the approaching vehicle was known. Kyle squinted against the fading daylight, straining to see who was coming through. The familiar growl of the ATV engine soon grew louder, and as the vehicle came into clear view, Kyle recognized Arnie and Joel. Arnie, usually steady and deliberate in his driving, was coming in a little faster than usual, kicking up a cloud of dust and gravel in his wake.

Kyle's eyes scanned the perimeter, ensuring no one else had slipped in under the cover of the ATV's arrival. Rocky, Susie, and Ginger emerged from the cabin at the sound of the engine, their faces etched with a mix of hope and apprehension. They joined Kyle on the porch, the collective tension unmistakable. The once serene mountain cabin now felt like a fortress under siege.

As Arnie brought the ATV to a halt, Joel jumped out, his face flushed with a mixture of anger and frustration. Arnie's usual calm demeanor was replaced by a look of urgency, a clear sign that their errand had brought troubling news. The dust settled around them as they dismounted, and the magnitude of their expressions told Kyle that whatever they had discovered was serious.

Kyle tightened his grip on the rifle, his mind racing with the possibilities of what Arnie and Joel might report. He took a deep breath, readying himself for the next wave of challenges that was surely coming their way.

"Somebody trashed our houses!" Joel said, getting off the ATV and slapping his hat against his leg in frustration.

"What do you mean they trashed the houses?" Ginger asked, hugging Arnie as he got off the ATV.

"I mean they trashed them. I don't know if they stole anything. Most of the windows were knocked out, and the rooms were ransacked. Just a complete mess," Joel explained.

"They hit Joel's house and got Rocky and Deanna's too. Snaggle has a roadblock set up and nobody could get to Mamaw's house. They are not letting anyone by that doesn't live in this

218

holler," Arnie added.

"We gathered up a couple of boxes of food items on the ATV," Joel said. "I don't know if it would have helped to have been there or not. Looks like it was more than one person that did it. I'm already hating people. This is freakin' nuts."

"Don't say anything to Deanna and the girls yet," Rocky said, shaking his head in disgust. "Let me talk to her about it."

"We got bigger problems right now to deal with," Kyle said to Arnie and Joel. "We may need to get Uncle Tom's help."

"Uncle Tom was working around his place. He said he was going to stay at his cabin tonight. He told us he would probably ride up here later," Arnie said.

"Try to radio Uncle Tom, let him know to bring his gun and come on up here. We have a problem," Kyle said to Rocky.

Everyone filed back inside the cabin, their steps heavy with the grim reality they faced. Unspoken fears and the deep tension of impending danger filled their thoughts. They gathered around the worn wooden table, each person taking a seat with a sense of urgency and dread.

Kyle took a deep breath, trying to steady his voice as he continued the interrupted meeting. The thought of one of them possibly being killed was agonizing, a heavy burden that hung over them like a dark cloud. He glanced around the room, seeing the mix of determination and fear in their eyes. This was the harsh reality they were living in, where every decision carried the weight of life and death.

Turning to Rocky, Kyle spoke with a mixture of determination and compassion. "Rocky, you have your wife and daughters here that need you," he began, his voice steady but laced with emotion. "They need you safe. We all do." He paused, letting the words sink in. "But more than that, you're a crack shot with the long rifle. We need someone we can trust to cover the gate, to watch over them from the tower platform."

Rocky's jaw tightened, his eyes flickering with conflicting emotions. He felt it was his duty to be on the front line with Kyle, to face the danger head-on. The thought of staying back, even for the sake of his family, gnawed at his sense of responsibility.

Kyle saw the hesitation in Rocky's eyes and leaned in closer, his voice dropping to a more personal tone. "Rocky, you're the best shot we have. Up there, you can protect all of them, make sure no one gets through. It's the most important position. We need you there."

Rocky nodded slowly, the logic of Kyle's words battling with his instinct to fight alongside his friend. He accepted the decision hesitantly, understanding the crucial role he would play. "Alright," he said, his voice gruff with suppressed emotion. "I'll stay on the tower and watch the gate. But you make sure you come back, Kyle. We need you too."

The room was silent for a moment, each person absorbing the roles that would be needed for the situation. They all knew the risks, the possible sacrifices. But they also knew they had no choice but to face whatever came their way, together, as a family. Kyle's heart ached with the weight of leadership. They would fight, and they would protect each other, no matter the cost.

"You will keep this walkie on you. I will take Joel and Arnie with me," Kyle instructed everyone.

"Wait a minute. I've never fired a real gun," Joel said, looking nervous.

"What? Never ever?" Arnie asked incredulously. "You're just the dang paintball, call of duty champion of the world," he added with a snicker.

"Okay, that changes things. I'm going to put this plan together. Be ready in one hour to move out," Kyle said, walking away to create the plan of attack.

Everyone was anxiously awaiting Kyle to produce a plan that would be successful. Kyle worked on the strategy with much apprehension as to who he would place where. It wasn't something he took lightly, but he knew that everyone would be needed to make this a winning battle. Kyle knew winning a battle didn't mean they would win the war, but he sure didn't want to lose this one.

As everyone waited impatiently, they began pacing in and

out of the cabin. Rocky and Joel walked around the perimeter of the fence. Susie and Deanna had a walk together out to the front gate and back, sharing a moment of mother and daughter bonding. Although it wasn't being said aloud, everyone knew they could lose one or all of the family members taking part.

Uncle Tom came riding up to the front gate at a faster-than-normal pace for him. He quickly keyed in the code and drove up to the cabin. Kyle was the only one who remained inside, continuing to figure out the battle plan.

"I just came from Willie's. We got some more news over the radio. They found Sheriff Ramey's police cruiser burned on top of Home Creek Mountain. Ramey was inside, burned to a crisp but with a hole in his skull!" Uncle Tom told them, his voice shaking slightly. "Where is Kyle?"

"He is inside. He went to Hadley's this morning. Tom, the Hadleys have been killed. Kyle overheard the people that did it say they were coming here for us next," Rachel explained, her voice trembling.

"What? We were just there a couple of days ago. Who killed them, and what do you mean they're coming here for us?" Uncle Tom asked, visibly alarmed. "What do I need to do?"

Kyle appeared at the door, a determined look on his face. "Hey, Uncle Tom, good to see you. If I could get you all together, let's go over this."

Kyle placed a crisp sheet of white paper onto the table, motioning everyone to gather around. "I heard Uncle Tom say the Sheriff is dead. I told you there are no police anymore. For the foreseeable future, we're on our own. It's going to be the old west for now."

On the paper, Kyle had a rough sketch of the area surrounding the cabin, with trails drawn out leading down one side to Hadley's farm and down the other to Uncle Tom's.

"Mom, you keep the girls and stay inside the cabin. If you want or need, drop into the tunnel, do as I showed you and follow it to the end. You will not be detected; stay quiet and stay down," Kyle instructed, his eyes meeting Rachel's as she nodded, worry etched into her features.

"Rocky, you take watchtower one and cover the main gate. If anyone comes, that is their only way of getting in. If you don't know them, shoot them. Got it?" Kyle asked, looking at Rocky.

"I understand. I got this," Rocky responded with a firm nod.

"Ginger, you will take tower two behind the cabin. You will have visuals on the backside of the barn, down the backslope, and part of the main trail inside the gate. You are overwatch. Shoot to kill! Got it?" Kyle asked, awaiting a positive response.

"I understand, Kyle. I can do it," Ginger replied, her voice steady despite the fear in her eyes.

"Deanna, you take the barn with Susie. Stay quiet and keep the lights off. We'll turn the motion lights on at the gate and there are two on the trail from the gate to the cabin. They have enough solar power and will work fine. If you see one turn on, be ready to shoot. Got it?" Kyle asked, his tone firm.

"We got it," Deanna and Susie said simultaneously, their hands gripping their weapons tightly.

Kyle looked at each of them, all holding their weapons, looking terrified but brave at the same time.

"What am I doing?" Joel asked, looking to Kyle.

"You're the driver, Joel. You're going to take Arnie and I down the mountain. You will park the ATV and take cover. I have a rifle and I'll explain the plan on the drive down. Arnie will set up one hundred yards out, and I will move in undetected if all goes well," Kyle said, his eyes scanning the room.

"But what if all doesn't go well?" Rachel asked, her voice trembling. "This is most of my family here. I don't want to lose anyone."

"You all just be alert here. Once we return, you will hear the gate open and know it's us. We can do this," Kyle said, shaking his fist to emphasize his determination.

"What about me? Where do you want me?" Uncle Tom asked Kyle.

"If you could stay near the top of the trail where we turn

down, that would be great. You can be a line of defense there just in case they get by us. We really should have gotten some gates and fencing up at the trailheads," Kyle said to Uncle Tom.

"We'll fix those gates tomorrow, once you boys get back and are rested," Uncle Tom said, not wanting to put any doubt in the mission ahead. "I'll cover the top of the trail."

"You will be ten minutes away, but if you hear gunshots, be ready. Thanks, Uncle Tom," Kyle said, giving him a quick hug.

"I promise I will be there. I need thirty minutes. I'll be back and get in place," Uncle Tom said as he got into his ATV and took off towards the gate and down the mountain.

Kyle outfitted Arnie and Joel with bulletproof body armor, the weight of responsibility settling heavily on his shoulders. The vests, cumbersome and rigid, carried four steel plates each. Kyle had found them on eBay, labeled as tactical level III protection, and ordered five sets, thinking they were a bargain. He hadn't anticipated the sheer weight and discomfort of wearing them, but any protection was better than none in their perilous situation. The vests covered the chest, stomach, sides, and back, offering a measure of security against the unknown dangers they faced.

As Arnie and Joel slipped the vests on, their movements slow and deliberate, the weight of the armor a constant reminder of the life-and-death stakes. The cabin was filled with tension, punctuated by the occasional nervous glance or whispered reassurance. Kyle adjusted the straps on Arnie's vest, ensuring a snug fit. "It's heavy, but it will protect you," he said, trying to inject a note of confidence into his voice.

Joel tugged at the edges of his vest, testing its fit. "Feels like I'm wearing a brick house," he muttered, attempting to lighten the mood. The corners of his mouth lifted in a strained smile, but his eyes betrayed his anxiety.

As they loaded into the ATV, the moment really began to sink in. Hugs and kisses were exchanged with a mix of urgency and tenderness. Ginger's embrace was tight, her eyes glistening with unshed tears as she clung to Arnie. "Be safe," she whispered, her voice trembling. Arnie kissed her forehead, trying to convey a sense of calm he didn't entirely feel. "We'll be back shortly. We got this," he said, his words meant to reassure, but carrying an undercurrent of uncertainty.

Joel's smile was forced but determined as he settled into the driver's seat. He looked back at the gathered family, giving them a thumbs-up before turning his attention to the path ahead. Just as Joel was about to pull out, a deafening crack of thunder split the sky, making everyone flinch. Within seconds, the heavens opened up, and rain began to pour down, quickly soaking everything underneath the clouds.

The downpour was relentless, the water pounding the trails and quickly turning the ground into a muddy, slippery mess. The ATV's tires dug in for traction, kicking up clumps of wet earth as they started their journey. The rain hammered against the roof of the cabin, a relentless drumbeat that matched the pounding of their hearts.

Rocky stood in the doorway, watching them disappear into the storm. He felt a knot of anxiety tighten in his chest. The weather added another layer of difficulty to an already dangerous mission. He knew the trails would be treacherous and visibility poor, but the sound of the rain would mask the potential threats to Allen and his crew.

As the ATV faded from view, swallowed by the curtain of rain, Rocky took a deep breath and turned back to the others. "Let's get ready," he said, his voice steady despite the turmoil within. "We need to be prepared for anything." The storm outside mirrored the storm in their hearts, but Rocky knew they had no choice but to face it head-on. Pulling the zipper to encase himself in a large rain coat, he took off to the watch tower.

CHAPTER THIRTY-SEVEN

"Storm of Vengeance"

Kyle had Joel stop at the top of the trail before descending toward Hadley's farm. He took a moment to survey the path ahead, his mind racing with unspoken thoughts and unvoiced fears. The weight of responsibility bore down on him, making it difficult to find the right words to say to Arnie and Joel. He wanted to reassure them, to offer wisdom and courage, but the right words seemed elusive.

As Kyle opened his mouth to speak, the sound of an approaching ATV caught their attention as the rain continued to fall. They turned to see Uncle Tom's vehicle cresting the trail, the engine's growl a familiar and somewhat comforting noise. Uncle Tom, ever the character, approached with a wide grin, waving a mason jar of clear liquid. The sight of it brought a momentary lift to their spirits. The contents of the jar were unmistakable—white lightning, mountain dew, pure moonshine.

Uncle Tom pulled up alongside them, the tires of his ATV spitting up mud as he came to a stop. He swung his leg over and hopped off, protected by the rain poncho he wore over his clothing, the mason jar sloshing slightly in his hand. "Thought you boys might need a little something to steady your nerves," he said, his voice raised a few decimals in the mix of the thunder and rain. He held up the jar, the liquid clear inside, "A sip of this, and you'll feel like you can take on the world, at least kick some ass tonight."

The jar was passed around, each of them taking a small swig. The moonshine burned as it went down, a fiery warmth spreading through their chests. Kyle winced at the intensity, but it did indeed help to calm the frayed edges of his nerves. Joel took his turn, his eyes watering slightly, but camouflaged by the rain, as he handed the jar to Arnie. "Smooth," Joel said, coughing a little, a hint of a smile on his lips.

Arnie took a longer sip, his face remaining stoic. "Just like the old days of last week," he said, wiping his mouth with the back of his hand and passing the jar back to Uncle Tom. The moment of camaraderie did more than the alcohol to bolster their spirits.

"Listen boys, I went to see Snaggle at the roadblock. I told him what was going on, pay attention to who you get into it with as they may get there with some back up." Uncle Tom said.

"Okay we'll take any help, but hopefully we make this quick. It's time to roll. See you soon Uncle Tom." Kyle said.

"Later Uncle Tom." Joel said as he started the ATV and eased down the trail.

"See you soon old man and don't forget to load your gun!" Arnie shouted to Uncle Tom.

Kyle finally found his voice as they began to go down the trail. "Listen, you two. This isn't just about Hadley's farm. It's about us, our families, and everything we've worked to protect. We need to be smart and careful. Stay alert, watch out for one another, and we'll get through this."

As they continued their descent, the storm seemed to intensify, the rain pelting them with renewed ferocity. The ground was slick and unstable, every bump a reminder of the danger they were heading into. But with the burn of moonshine still warming their insides and the solidarity of shared purpose, they pressed on, ready to face whatever awaited them at Hadley's farm.

After a ten-minute ride that felt like an hour, they had reached the spot where Kyle wanted Joel to park the ATV. The rain had slowed to a slight drizzle falling now, Kyle wasn't sure which would was better, rain or no rain.

"Joel, get behind that fallen tree. Keep your gun ready." Kyle said pointing to a location on the trail where it made a horseshoe cutback.

"Are you sure about this? This feels like a military exercise, and we aren't military," Joel said, his face churning out expressions of fear.

"I wish we had military training right now, Joel. We are what we are, some guys trying to protect our family. We do what we can now," Kyle said as he squeezed the grip on his rifle, his nerves bouncing throughout his body.

"We're going to do this, Joel. There is no time for second guessing anything. Do your job!" Arnie lashed out, suddenly looking like a member of the Navy Seals or Delta Force.

"Arnie, you push a hundred yards on down and to the right. You can get a vantage point on that ledge overlooking the house and barn." Kyle told Arnie as the young man listened and nodded his understanding. "This could get scary, really quick. If anything goes wrong, get back up the hill and go defend the family."

"We can do this Uncle Kyle, all of us. You just do your job and stay safe. Joel and I will provide overwatch." Arnie said to Kyle raising his fist to Kyle for a bump.

"I'm proud of you both, keep your heads down and stay safe, I love you guys." Kyle told them as he quickly turned and began to move on foot.

Joel attempted to move quickly into position behind the tree Kyle had told him. His old days of paintball would come in handy with his ability to move quietly. This would have worked had he not immediately tripped over a rock falling into some shrubs and dropping his gun. He landed flat on his stomach letting out a loud grunt that caught Kyle's attention, stopping him in his tracks. Kyle looked back to see Arnie shaking his head and pointing into the shrubs and brush where Joel lay.

"Paintball ninja my ass," Arnie said as he turned to continue to his position while laughing at Joel.

"What have I done?" Kyle said to himself as he went on down the trail by foot.

As Joel got up and behind the tree, his face flushed red with embarrassment, he threw up his middle finger to Arnie. He knew if they made it out of this Arnie wouldn't let him forget this one, it would be joked about as long as they lived. Of course, the joking would also mean they had made it out of this, that was a good trade off. Once in position, he did what Kyle had shown him with the rifle, lowering the lever action down and back up, loading a live round. Kyle had given him a Remmington 30-30 rifle that was zeroed in at one hundred yards. He didn't want Joel to attempt a shot any farther than this as Joel knew nothing about adjusting the turrets for distance. Joel breathed in and out slowly as Kyle had told him to do.

Kyle worked his way back through the trees on the same route he used earlier to get to the barn. Arnie moved through some thickets getting pricked by thorns as he worked his way to the ledge. Arnie reached his destination and dropped down into the prone position. He removed his pack from his back and placed it next to him. He opened the pack and removed an extra magazine for the Ruger Precision rifle he carried. The rifle was heavy, and Arnie moved the pack underneath the rifle for support. He quickly pulled the bolt back, then forward loading a round in the chamber. He used a green tarp he had taken from his bag to spread it out overtop his body and the rifle.

As Kyle arrived at the edge of the tree line, he stayed in cover not moving to the barn yet. Kyle carried a Sig Sauer AR15 for this trip and he used his optics to get a visual on the house. Kyle had only seen one person so far, a man smoking on the porch. This made him anxious as he wanted to get a visual of each one at the house. Kyle could see Opal Hadley's body still lying in front of the barn. These people didn't have the common decency to even cover her up. He decided then he would see to it that she got a proper burial, which meant he had to come out of this alive to do so.

The rain was starting to fall hard once again, the humidity thick and heavy. Each step Kyle took felt like he was wading through a swamp, the weight of his gear pressing down on him, making every movement a struggle. His anger simmered, the memory of Hadley's lifeless body fueling his desire for revenge. He could taste the bitterness of it on his tongue.

Kyle made his next move, scurrying across the lawn between the trees and the barn, his boots sloshing through the soggy grass. The added weight of the water-soaked gear made running difficult. Kyle now felt like a forty-year-old man as he struggled to breathe, each gasp feeling insufficient, his lungs burning with the effort. Reaching the barn, he slipped through the side door, his heart pounding in his chest.

Once inside, Kyle leaned against the wall, desperately grasping for oxygen to fill his lungs. His leg and shoulder muscles screamed in agony, the lactic acid buildup making every fiber of his being ache. He fought off the urge to sit, knowing he needed to stay alert. The barn was suffocatingly stuffy, the air heavy, like molasses. The buzzing of flies filled the air, and Kyle's stomach churned at the sight of them crawling on Mr. Hadley's face. He grabbed an empty feed sack and gently draped it over Hadley's upper body, covering his face in a small act of respect.

Kyle scanned the barn, debating his next move. The edge of darkness was approaching, the rain beating off the metal roof of the barn heavier now, and he knew he had to act soon. Should he create a sniper's nest in the barn and pick off Allen and his crew one by one, or should he go in guns blazing? The weight of the decision pressed on him as heavily as his soaked gear.

With determination, Kyle left the barn and moved near the porch of the house, staying low to the ground. He crept around the side, hoping for a better view through the window. Peering inside, he saw Allen, Cindy, and another man loading rounds of ammo into shotguns and revolvers. They had gained access to Hadley's firearms. Spread out on the table were a couple of pump-action shotguns, two deer rifles, and three revolvers. The sight made Kyle's blood boil.

He clenched his jaw, the anger and frustration nearly overwhelming him. He wanted revenge, but he knew he had to be smart about it. His heart pounded in his chest as he weighed his options, the rain continuing to pour down, masking the sounds of his movement. The tension in the air was intense, every second feeling like an eternity as he prepared to make his next move.

"I'm going to get that four-wheeler next to the barn running," Kyle heard a voice say as the man came onto the porch. He could hear the flick of a lighter and then someone else speaking.

"Dude, you're not going out in this monsoon, are you? It's nasty out there," the man said as he puffed on his cigarette.

"It's too stuffy in the house, I'd rather be working with something. I'm going to start on the four-wheeler," he said as he quickly ran off the porch into the rain.

Kyle watched as the man went under the lean to shed on the side of the barn hoping on the parked four-wheeler. He attempted to start the machine, without success. The man opened the fuel cap on the four-wheeler, he must have found it empty of gasoline. Kyle watched as he went inside the barn, disappearing behind the door as it closed. The man reopened the door, preparing to run back to the house, suddenly stopping next to Opal's body. He quickly turned, going back inside the barn once again. This time, he pushed the door open in a haste, running with all his speed towards the house.

Kyle continued trying to listen, the rain falling hard and fast on him as he tried to clear his eyes. Kyle realized why the man was in a hurry, his mistake suddenly apparent.

"Damn Tricky, what you in such a hurry for?" Ronnie asked, glancing up from loading the magazine as Tricky came barreling into the house, water dripping all over the floor.

"Has anyone been in the barn?" Tricky demanded, his eyes darting nervously around the room.

"Not since earlier today," Allen replied, his brow furrowing in confusion.

"Somebody's here. I didn't see them, but they're here," Tricky insisted, his voice edged with urgency.

"Why do you say that?" Allen asked, standing up and looking towards the front door.

"Because there's a feed sack over that old man's face, and I'm pretty sure he didn't put it there himself," Tricky responded, his tone grim. "I went into the barn to look for some gas, and that's when I noticed it. It wasn't there earlier today when I was in the barn."

Tricky picked up an older Smith & Wesson .38 caliber

revolver from the table, his fingers trembling slightly as he checked the chamber. "Whoever it is, they're close. We need to be ready."

Allen's expression hardened, and he exchanged a quick glance with Ronnie. The atmosphere in the room grew tense, the realization of an unseen presence weighing heavily on them. They moved with purpose now, their senses heightened, every creak and shadow suddenly suspect. Cindy looked out the window, seeing nothing but the falling rain.

"Maybe the wind blew it on him, this storm is bad," Cindy said as she looked towards the barn.

"The wind? Where did you find her, Allen?" Ronnie asked, shaking his head at the thought. "Did someone hold the barn door open for the wind to blow it on him?" he asked sarcastically.

Kyle crouched beside an old pump house shed he moved his position to, roughly thirty feet from the house. He assumed it was only Allen Hall, two unknown men, and Cindy inside, the same four he and Rocky had observed earlier today while surveilling the house. Kyle had already killed one man since the attack, so he knew he could do it again, but this was going to be a small war.

From his hidden position, Arnie watched Kyle move from the barn to the house and now to the water shed. "What is he doing?" Arnie whispered to himself, his breath barely audible.

Kyle's mind raced as he weighed his options. Should he start shooting through the window, catching them by surprise? Or should he call them out, confronting them directly like a scene from a Clint Eastwood movie? He took a deep breath, closing his eyes to steady his nerves. Instantly, images of Opal and Mr. Hadley's lifeless bodies flashed in his mind, fueling his tenacity.

Determined, Kyle stood up, pressing his AR-15 against the corner of the water shed. He peered through the optic, lining up one of the unknown men in his sights. His finger moved to the trigger, ready to pull, when the sound of an approaching vehicle broke the silence. The rumble of tires on gravel grew louder, and the sloshing of water from potholes the car hit, coming from the other side of the house.

Kyle froze, his senses on high alert. The rain, which had begun to fall harder, drummed a relentless rhythm on the metal roof of the shed. Anger bubbled up inside him, a fiery determination to avenge the Hadleys. He lowered his rifle slightly, shifting his focus to the approaching threat. He couldn't afford to make a move without knowing who was in that vehicle. The rain pounded harder, masking some of the sounds, but Kyle's ears were finely tuned to every subtle noise. His heart raced, the tension coiling within him like a spring ready to snap.

It wasn't only Kyle who heard the car as he seen the men quickly move from the room. Kyle went to the other side of the shed for a glimpse at the car. He wasn't sure if this was Snaggle or if it was more of Allen's people. They left the headlights of the car on as two men exited. There was still enough light through the rainstorm for Kyle to see the men exit the car.

"Anyone in there?" A voice said but it didn't sound to Kyle like Snaggle. "Are you home Hadley?" The voice added, shouting through the rain.

"The Hadley's went on vacation. I'm watching their house for them," Allen said as he came onto the front porch. He watched as one of the men from the car looked towards the barn. There would be no way he couldn't have seen Opal's body on the ground, even with the torrential downpour that was happening.

A gunshot pierced the approaching darkness hitting the car hood. Kyle had no view of where the occupants in the house had gone, but he knew they were somewhere on the opposite side. He was not able to see the front porch clearly and had to move. Gunshots rang out from the car firing towards the house and vice versa. Kyle ran from the water shed towards the barn jumping into a baseball slide bringing him behind a large tree. It was like sliding into second base and it worked perfectly, especially with the soft and wet grass beneath him. Kyle quickly went up to one knee aiming his gun towards the house and firing hastily as Allen smashed through the screen door getting back inside. Kyle's rounds hit all along the house as his nerves had him uneasy, shooting almost blindly through the thickness of the rain.

"I'm hit!" Kyle heard a voice from the car say, looking over to see someone slump to the ground in a heap.

Arnie and Joel could hear the gun shots, but neither could see a target from their locations. Arnie stayed in place keeping his eye on the house. The tarp worked to shield him from the falling rain as he peered through the rifle's optic. Kyle spotted a figure in the house and fired several rapid shots into the window, towards the silhouette inside. It was Ronnie who caught one of the rounds just under his right arm, piercing through his ribs and lung. He fell to the floor gasping for oxygen, he needed help, help that wasn't going to come.

The second man that had been at the car was knelt at the rear of it appearing to be reloading. More bullets continued to come from the house but not as fast now. Kyle continued firing more shots to provide cover for whomever was behind the car. Although he wasn't sure who it was exactly, he was grateful to be getting the help. He emptied his magazine and pressed the ejector letting the empty mag fall to the ground. He slammed another into the gun, hit the paddle releasing the bolt and continued to shoot.

As Kyle rapidly fired hot rounds of lead, he failed to see the man who had exited through the kitchen's back door. It was Tricky, he had run over to the water shed seeing Kyle shooting from behind a tree. Tricky went into pursuit, running towards the barn, stopping to give himself a line of site to Kyle. Carrying the .38 pistol, he began firing quick shots at Kyle, as fast as he could squeeze the trigger. One round hit the tree near Kyle's head, another hit Kyle right in the center of his back. The force of the round colliding into Kyle's plate carrier pushed him forward. The taste of wet grass and mud filled his mouth as his face collided with the ground. He had come so close to removing the plate carrier, the weight almost too much to tote, but it now saved his life. The armor did its job, stopping the bullet instantly before it could do any damage to Kyle. He flipped onto his back, raising his gun towards Tricky, who had also turned to look behind him.

Arnie had eyed Tricky running to get position behind Kyle. He put his sights on Tricky and fired, but the bullet missed Tricky and hit the ground to the left of his foot, close enough for Tricky to feel the vibration next to his foot. Tricky turned his attention, looking into the trees with no idea where the bullet had come from, blinded by the rain, looming darkness and cover of the trees. It was all Kyle needed to get a lock on Tricky, but he paused unsure of Arnie's position in the darkness behind him. Arnie's next round that he had chambered wouldn't miss his target, striking the center of Tricky's chest knocking him onto his back, killing him immediately. Kyle watched Tricky fall to the ground, his body limp an still as the rain fell on him. Kyle gave a thumbs up towards the tree in case Arnie could see him, then turned his attention back to the house.

There was no shooting from the house or the car now, it was silence, only the sound of rain landing on the metal roof and cars. A candle lit up one room of the house where they had been loading weapons, the other parts of the house growing increasingly dark. With both headlights now shot out on the car, Kyle looked to the house, back to the car, then to the tree line.

"Anyone left inside? This is your chance to come out now!" Kyle shouted towards the house. "Come out, hands up where we can see you."

Kyle looked over to the car seeing the man who had been shot still not moving, lying in a puddle of water. He had Tricky to his left on the ground, dead from the accuracy of Arnie's 6.5 Creedmoor bullet. "Nobody else needs to die here. Come on out." Kyle again shouted, knowing there was indeed someone who needed to die, if he wasn't dead already.

There was still no movement from inside as the glow from the room seemed to be brighter than it had been. Realizing a fire was now burning inside the house, most likely from the candle falling during the shootout, he needed to know if Allen was still alive. Kyle dropped his pack, and moved to the porch, quickly climbing the steps to kneel beside the broken screen door. He clicked on his flashlight and shined it through the shattered front window. Kyle could see one man lying on the floor dead, but it wasn't Allen.

This was two of the men Kyle had a visual on, however, Allen remained unaccounted for. Kyle pushed open the remaining part of the broken door and stepped inside. He let his AR hang from its sling while he pulled his Glock from his leg holster. Kyle glanced towards the dining room where the fire was growing, going the other direction through the living room where the man lay dead. He shined his light into a bedroom there as he passed by it, moving down a small hall leading to an empty bathroom. "Where the hell are you?" Kyle said in a low voice.

Kyle turned his attention back to the living room, his heart pounding in his chest. The room felt thick with tension, the air humid and heavy with the scent of rain and sweat. There was Allen standing silently, a menacing presence, the glow from the fire illuminating his face. Rainwater continued to roll down Kyle's cheeks, his hair and clothing thoroughly soaked, adding to the weight of the moment.

"All you had to do was give me a jug of gas," Allen growled, his voice low and dangerous.

"That wouldn't have done it. You're a bully, a prick, the type who wants to take from others," Kyle replied, his voice steady despite the adrenaline coursing through him. His hand tightened around the Glock. "Why did you kill the Hadleys? They were innocent people. They were good people."

"I'm trying to survive like everybody else. They didn't want to help me, and they paid the price. The same as you're about to do," Allen said, his eyes dark and unforgiving, his face hard as stone.

"Looks like I have the advantage here, big boy. Damn, you are a big boy," Kyle said, his eyes narrowing as he sized up the large man, his grip on the Glock tightening.

"Let's settle this like men," Allen proposed, letting his pistol fall to the floor with a dull thud. "Whoever takes the ass whipping will agree to leave this area," he continued, peeling off his flannel shirt and slapping his closed hand to his chest multiple times, his muscles tensing in preparation.

Kyle lowered his Glock and let it slide back into the holster on his leg. He unclipped his AR-15 rifle from the sling around his neck and placed it upright against the wall. Unfastening his body armor, he pulled it over his head, letting it drop heavily to the floor. Allen bellowed out a roar and charged at Kyle, knocking him hard against the wall, their weight caving a large hole into the paneling. Allen swung a heavy punch that Kyle ducked, countering with a right fist into Allen's rib cage, followed by a left across Allen's chin, sending the giant staggering. Pain shot through Kyle's hand, but he ignored it, focusing on the fight.

Arnie heard a loud commotion, tossing the tarp back to see Joel sprinting down the trail toward the house. Joel wasn't slowing, and Arnie jumped from his position, pulling his Glock and falling in behind Joel.

"I'm right behind you, Joel! Keep your eyes open!" Arnie shouted as the two raced towards the house.

Allen regained his balance and charged again, tackling Kyle onto a coffee table that splintered under their weight. Kyle grabbed Allen's throat, squeezing tightly, and punched the big man twice in the face. Allen struggled to recover from the blows, and Kyle quickly rolled them over, jumping back to his feet and stepping away. Allen slowly climbed back up, blood streaming from his nose and mouth. He pulled a knife from his pocket and grinned at Kyle, his eyes filled with malice.

"It's time to settle this like it's the apocalypse, which it happens to be," Kyle said, his voice cold and unbendable.

"What the hell does that mean?" Allen smirked, his confidence unshaken.

"It means I do this!" Kyle snapped, pulling his Glock and squeezing the trigger. The bullet spiraled out of the barrel, hitting Allen's left knee. The large man fell back, collapsing against the wall and sliding to the floor. Kyle stepped closer and fired again, this time hitting Allen's right knee, ensuring he wouldn't get up.

"Fuck you!" Allen shouted at Kyle as he grimaced in pain.

Kyle could feel the heat as the fire had fully engulfed the

dining room and was closing in on the living room now. Allen pushed himself backwards out the front door onto the porch. Kyle took aim again firing his third round into Allen's right shoulder making the big man scream out in pain.

"Stop! No more. I'll go, just let me get out of here," Allen said to Kyle as the pain was becoming unbearable.

"That first one was for Fred. The second one for Joel. The third for Mrs. Hadley," Kyle said before squeezing off a fourth round that went into the left shoulder of Allen forcing the giant to tumble down the steps into the yard. He let out a yell of pain before trying to catch his breath.

"That one was for Mr. Hadley. Now, if you can save yourself, you're free to go. Kyle said as reentered the house, collecting his armor and rifle.

"I'll kill you for this. I'm going to find you and kill you!" Allen screamed out at Kyle as he came down the porch steps.

Kyle stopped before walking away. "This isn't the movies, dumbass." Kyle said as he turned back looking at Allen. "You will have to find me in hell, because you're on your way there now," Kyle fired three rounds into the chest of Allen watching him close his eyes for the last time and take his last breath of air.

"Don't shoot, I'm coming over," a voice said from the car. Kyle could see the man approaching carrying a flashlight now. Kyle shined his light towards the man to get a better look not recognizing the man approaching. He looked towards the tree line seeing Joel and Arnie running towards him, he held up a hand to show them he was okay.

"We appreciate the help, but who are you?" Kyle asked as the man stepped up to him reaching for Kyle's hand.

"I'm Herbie. Snaggle sent me and Carl. We were at the roadblock today volunteering. I knew Allen, pure trouble, always has been. It was Allen or one of his guys that killed Carl, he is over by the car. Carl was a young man, maybe eighteen to twenty years old." Herbie told Kyle as they shook hands.

"I really appreciate your help. I'm sorry about Carl. We'll need to get him in the car and take him back to his family," Kyle said as he turned to see Arnie and Joel approaching.

"I'm glad you're okay," Arnie told Kyle with a fist bump.

"Yeah, we're glad you're alright. Did you get everybody?" Joel asked as he looked at Allen on the ground and then towards the burning house now giving light in the darkness. The rain continued to fall but was no match for the fire that now lit the sky.

"Allen's girlfriend!" Kyle said as he looked at the house. "I didn't see her inside," Kyle raised his gun to scan.

"Let's spread out, stay alert," Herbie said as each began shining flashlights around. They searched the perimeter.

"I found her!" Joel's voice cut through the night, desperate and urgent, as it echoed from the back of the house. The others sprinted to join him, their breaths labored and hearts pounding. There, sprawled on the wet grass behind the house, lay Cindy, her lifeless body illuminated by the flickering flames. A revolver rested beside her, its metallic surface glinting with its final deed. She had taken her own life, her final act of despair.

"She deserved it for what they've done," Arnie muttered, his voice thick with a mix of anger and resignation.

"This was someone's daughter, maybe a sister, possibly even a mother," Kyle said, his voice heavy with sorrow and fatigue. "She got tangled with the wrong guy, and this is how it ends for her. It's really a shame." He bent down, his hands trembling slightly, and grasped her cold, wet arms, dragging her body away from the house and the spreading flames.

The fire roared, casting an eerie glow that danced on the charred remains and the wet ground, creating an almost surreal scene. Kyle's face was set in grim determination as he turned to Joel and Arnie. "Tell everyone on the mountain they're safe. Send Uncle Tom to pick me up; I've got things to do before leaving."

"I thought this would be an all-night fight," Joel said as he looked at the house burning, the heat forcing them back. "I didn't expect it to be over so quickly."

Arnie nodded, their faces reflecting the exhaustion and relief of surviving the night. They hurried off, leaving Kyle alone with Herbie to complete the grim task at hand. He moved with purpose, getting Hadley's old tractor. The machine sputtered to life with a groan, its engine cutting through the night's silence. Using the tractor and the fire's light, Kyle began to dig a grave next to a large oak tree near the barn. The soil was heavy and wet, each bucket scoop a reminder of the weight of his promise.

Kyle worked tirelessly, his muscles aching and his clothes soaked with sweat and rain. He placed Hadley and his wife Opal together in one grave, their bodies now at peace. He then dug a separate grave for Cindy, Tricky, and Allen, their fates intertwined by violence and desperation. As for Ronnie, the raging house fire would be his final resting place.

Cindy had chosen a path of drugs and darkness, and though Kyle felt sadness for her, he was also relieved that the threat to his family had been eliminated. He thought of Arnie and the burden of taking a life, knowing he would need to speak with him about it, but that conversation could wait until tomorrow.

The sound of Uncle Tom's ATV grew louder, its headlights cutting through the night as it approached. Tom drove up close, the additional light revealing the freshly dug graves in stark clarity. He stepped off the ATV and walked over to Kyle, placing a comforting hand on his shoulder.

"I don't even know Hadley's first name," Kyle said, his voice barely above a whisper as he looked at the fresh grave. "He was always Mr. Hadley or old man Hadley."

"It was William. William and Opal Hadley," Uncle Tom said softly, his voice carrying a note of respect. The two men stood in silence, the weight of the night's events pressing down on them as the flames continued to burn in the background, a testament to the harsh world they now lived in.

"You physically hurt?" Uncle Tom asked.

Kyle glanced at him, before shaking his head no. "I'm not, Uncle Tom. We we're lucky tonight."

Uncle Tom nodded in agreement, "you did what you had to do Kyle. Being shot would probably hurt less than the memories you're going to live with now."

CHAPTER THIRTY-EIGHT
"Whispers Before Dawn"

"Good morning, son." Rachel said softly as she stepped out of the cabin, the early morning warmth touching softly on her face. She handed Kyle a cup of hot coffee, the steam curling upwards. Kyle placed the cup on a log stump he used as a makeshift table, its rough surface worn smooth by countless mornings like this, however, always alone before. Rachel noted the dark circles under his eyes; he looked like he had been up all night. The shootout from a few nights before with Allen still haunting him.

"Good morning, Mom. Thank you for the coffee. I didn't want to come inside and wake anyone." Kyle replied, his voice thick with fatigue.

"Do you want to talk about it?" Rachel asked gently, watching as Kyle rubbed his hands together slowly, staring at the ground.

"I do, and yet I don't, Mom. It's just how things are now. But I'm worried about Arnie. He had to take a life at Hadley's that night. He seems fine, but I'd appreciate it if you could keep an eye on him for a while," Kyle said, his voice barely above a whisper. "And I keep thinking about Megan, Sawyer, and Spencer. I wonder if they have their families protected. I'd like to know if Megan is alright and where she is. Sawyer lives in such a large area; there are so many things he'll have to deal with. I just wish we were all together."

"I do too, son. I wish we could talk to them. I'd like to know if my kids are all safe. A mother has an intuition for some things, and I haven't gotten the feeling they are hurt. I think they are so much like you; they are taking care of those around them." Rachel said before taking another sip of her coffee, the warmth spreading through her body.

Megan was Kyle's sister, adopted by Rachel when she was just a young child. She could be a handful at times, but Kyle loved her like they were blood siblings. Sawyer was Kyle's brother living in Florida, and Spencer was another brother, also not by birth, but adopted as a toddler. The three boys grew up together like full-blood brothers, always looking out for one another. If anyone asked, adoption was never mentioned; they were brothers, pure and simple.

"I know you want to be home, Mom, but I hope you're getting settled in here okay. It wasn't as ready as I would have liked it to be," Kyle said, still staring off into the distance, his mind a whirlwind of worries.

"You've been through a lot already, Kyle. You're worrying more than you need to about us. I'm going to tell you something I've never brought up before, and I wasn't going to unless you did. I know why you left your job; your boss called me when you turned in your resignation. I know about Kansas, and I know you've been carrying that with you for some time now."

"I'm sorry, Mom. I had no idea Dean had called you. It's all been settled and over though, don't worry about it." Kyle said, a hint of defensiveness in his tone.

"He was once my boss too, son. That's why he called me. It wasn't to tattle on you, but he wanted me to watch over you, just like you said about Arnie," Rachel said, placing a comforting hand on his arm.

"We're going to make it. I won't let anything happen to you or the family," Kyle said, finally taking a sip of his coffee, the bitterness grounding him in the present moment.

"Look over there at the mountain top. The sun is about to rise, and we are alive to see it. We may be alive for many reasons right now, but one for sure is because you are here and have helped us," Rachel said, patting her son on the knee, wishing she could take all his worries and bear them herself.

"This isn't going to get better anytime soon, Mom. These kids deserve so much more than what they will face now. I want to help as much as I possibly can, but I'm afraid I can't bear all the weight that may come," Kyle said as the sun began to peek over the treetops, casting a golden glow on the land.

"You just take one day at a time right now, Kyle. Matthew 6:34 tells us, 'Therefore do not be anxious about tomorrow, for tomorrow will be anxious for itself. Sufficient for the day is its own trouble.' What the kids and everyone else may go through tomorrow, next week, or next year isn't something we can worry about today. We have got to take it one day at a time," Rachel said, quoting from her old days as a Sunday school teacher.

Kyle knew Rachel was right. Their main focus had to stay on the present. The two spent the next few minutes watching the sun rise higher into the sky, warming their faces and lighting the land. They each enjoyed their coffee and slowly rocked in their chairs, the quiet morning bringing a moment of peace.

Susie and Ginger joined them, bringing their coffee out and taking a seat. If only briefly, they all sat together quietly, enjoying the moment. It was going to be a beautiful day, and Kyle hoped it would be a peaceful one as well.

"I can tell you one of my biggest fears right now," Kyle said, breaking the silence.

"And what might that be, little brother?" Susie asked, already smiling to start the day.

"If things don't get back to normal soon, I see a problem developing. How are we going to handle Ginger when the caramel and whatever other stuff she fills that coffee with are gone?" Kyle said, laughing as they looked at Ginger, who was stirring up her concoction of ingredients.

"Kyle! You just drink your coffee the way you like it, and I will drink mine the way I like," Ginger said with a giggle.

"Oh, mercy, you are right about that. She will be a handful when she doesn't have all that sugar," Susie said, laughing at Ginger, who gave them all a firm middle finger salute.

"Do you have to do that, Ginger? That is so vulgar," Rachel

said, shaking her head.

"Yeah, Ginger, why are you being so vulgar towards us?" Kyle asked, laughing along with Susie.

It wasn't long before Coraline came bursting out the front door, delivering a playful punch to Kyle's stomach. So much for peacefulness today, Kyle thought to himself. "Give me a hug, you little rugrat," Kyle said, pulling Coraline into his arms. "I hope you got plenty of rest because I'm about to work you like a plow mule today." He added, kissing the top of her head.

"I'm not working today. I'm feeding the animals and cleaning the barn for them," Coraline said back to Kyle, hands on her hips in a stance that said, I told you how it is. He was glad she didn't see farming as work but something she enjoyed doing.

"Good morning, gang," Arnie said as he came from the bunkhouse, joining everyone else.

"Morning, Arnie. Did you get some rest?" Kyle asked.

"I'm all good, recharged, and ready for more," Arnie replied, but the exhaustion was still evident on his face. Kyle knew Arnie needed more rest; he had been helping the last couple of days getting the barn ready to handle the coming arrival. They had all taken turns going to Hadley's over the last two days, feeding the horses and animals. Kyle knew they couldn't continue this, as it was burning fuel with each trip back up the mountain trail.

"Okay, little man, I need you to stay around here and help today. I'm taking Rocky with me to help get those horses at Hadley's barn and bring them up. I'm not comfortable with horses yet, but that's right up Rocky's alley," Kyle said, giving Arnie the opportunity to remain close to the cabin and his bed. Kyle himself was worn down, but that didn't matter at this time. There were simply too many things that needed to be completed. Kyle figured he would rest when he was dead. Arnie didn't question him on this, clearly not wanting to go off the mountain.

"We're going to get those horses today. Maybe tomorrow, you and Joel can go check in at Mom's house. I'd like you to get the spray paint in the garage and throw a camouflage paint job on the truck. You can park it in the trees and cover it with that camo netting I have in Mom's garage," Kyle said to Arnie. He wanted to ensure Arnie felt necessary to the overall mission, even if it wasn't for today.

Arnie nodded, understanding the task and its importance. The idea of camouflaging the truck was practical, providing a hidden escape route or a concealed supply vehicle if needed. Kyle hoped it would also keep Arnie's mind occupied, giving him a sense of purpose amidst the chaos.

Kyle geared up, fastening his rugged leather gloves and adjusting his hat to shield his eyes from the morning sun. He grabbed his backpack, filled with essentials: some rope, a couple of tools, and a water bottle. The thought of transporting the horses and finding a safe grazing area occupied his thoughts.

Rocky soon emerged from the cabin, stretching and yawning, but ready for the day's tasks. His lanky frame moved with a casual grace, but there was a spark of determination in his eyes. Kyle appreciated Rocky's resilience; the man had a natural knack for handling animals.

"Let's get you loaded up," Kyle said, patting Rocky on the back as he helped him onto the ATV. The engine roared to life, the sound cutting through the morning silence. Kyle could feel the vibrations under his hands, a reminder of the work that lay ahead.

Kyle's mind wandered to the logistics of housing the large animals. The main fence around their property was solid, but it wasn't large enough to accommodate both the horses and the cows. They needed more space to roam and graze.

"We'll need to do some quick work in the coming days to create a larger barrier for the animals," Kyle said, mostly to himself, but Rocky nodded in agreement.

In the shed, there were various sizes of barbed wire fencing, remnants from previous projects. Kyle mentally cataloged their supplies: enough wire to start but not enough to finish. "Once the barbed wire is gone, we can go old west style," he said, his mind conjuring images of rough logs forming a sturdy fence. The idea of cutting trees to make a fence seemed daunting, but it was necessary.

As they made their final preparations, Kyle couldn't help but feel the weight of responsibility pressing on his shoulders. Each task, each plan, was a step towards ensuring their survival in an uncertain world. He took a deep breath, the morning air filling his lungs, and readied himself for the day ahead.

"How was life at your cabin the last couple of nights, Uncle Tom?" Arnie asked as Tom drove up for the first time in the last two days. They had been able to check in on each other with the walkie-talkies they had, which was helpful and saved on burning fuel.

"It was okay, just takes a while to clear my head at night and fall asleep. It's just a shame this is what it's turned into already," Uncle Tom said.

"You got plans today for anything, Uncle Tom? Rocky and I are about to go to Hadley's and get the horses and hay. We will try to gather up whatever animals remain," Kyle said. "You're welcome to go with us; we could use the hands."

"That sounds good to me. I made a headstone we'll take for them," Uncle Tom said to Kyle.

"I just want to see everything stay calm for a while. No more shooting," Kyle said to Tom as they rode along the trail.

"I've been going up to Willie's and listening in on the radio waves. There's more information circulating now," Uncle Tom began, his voice a mix of weariness and urgency. "It appears terrorists planted bombs in every major shipping lane—ports, highways, you name it. They used moving trucks to store these massive bombs and then detonated them at key structures, bringing down buildings and bridges."

Kyle's eyes widened in disbelief. "Just unbelievable they were able to put that together under the nose of this country," he responded, shaking his head slowly. He pictured the chaos, the devastation—cities crippled, supply chains severed, lives lost. The sheer scale of the operation was mind-boggling.

"They even had oil tankers hauling huge bombs," Uncle Tom continued, his face etched with concern. "They drove right into refineries and detonated them. The destruction was immense. But, the reality is, it shouldn't be so hard to believe. Our country's been so divided, fighting within itself for so long, it was probably an easy task for them to pull off." His voice was somber, reflecting the grim truth of his words.

Kyle nodded in agreement, feeling a cold chill run down his spine. The image of burning refineries and collapsing buildings flashed in his mind, a stark reminder of their precarious situation. "We've been so distracted with our own issues, we didn't see it coming," he muttered, his voice barely above a whisper.

Uncle Tom looked off into the distance, the lines on his face deepening as he thought about the broader implications. "The country's infrastructure is in shambles. They've hit us where it hurts the most. Now, it's every man for himself. We've got to be smart, resourceful, and stay one step ahead if we're going to survive this."

Kyle clenched his fists, a surge of determination rising within him. "We've got to continue with life. This will be the last place that gets repaired; we must survive on our own," he said, his voice firm. "As for now, we've got animals to get up the hill. It shouldn't be hard, but it will take us some time."

Uncle Tom nodded, the gravity of their conversation settling between them. "You wait until you see Rocky climb on one of those horses. He'll have all of them up the hill before you and I can get up there on the ATVs. That boy can ride a horse," he said, a small, proud smile breaking through the grimness.

Kyle managed a chuckle, appreciating the momentary lightness. "He is still no John Wayne as he can't hit a thing with a pistol," he said, the laughter providing a brief but welcome distraction from the heavy reality they faced.

CHAPTER THIRTY-NINE
"Barter and Blood"

———————————————

At Miran Tate's garage, he reveled in the barter system he had put into operation. The garage, once a simple repair shop, had transformed into the nerve center of Tate's burgeoning empire. Tools and spare parts were pushed aside to make room for shelves stocked with canned goods, fuel canisters, and an array of weaponry. The scent of motor oil mingled with the musty odor of stored supplies, creating an atmosphere of gritty survivalism.

Tate was, as the saying went, sticking it to the people with trades. Knowing they had no choice but to pay if they wanted food or gas, he acquired not only weapons and ammo but also agreements for work services as needed. In one corner, a chalkboard listed the day's trades: "3 gallons of gas for 8 hours of labor," "1 rifle for 10 cans of food." His method was ruthless but effective, ensuring his dominance over the community.

Quickly, he was becoming the local mafia boss, a role he eagerly embraced. Tate liked to sit back with an unlit cigar in his mouth, embodying the image of power and control. His office, situated in the back of the garage, was adorned with reminders of his ascent: a polished wooden desk, a wall of confiscated firearms, and a map marked with territories and routes.

Tate preferred to stay out of trade negotiations himself, leaving it to Lucas to make the deals. Lucas, a thick man with a knack for coercion, stood at a makeshift counter, haggling with a desperate woman over the price of a bag of pasta noodles. His sharp eyes missed nothing, and his voice carried the cold assurance of someone who held all the cards.

As Langston approached the parking lot in his police cruiser with two men, the crunch of gravel under the tires echoed in the quiet afternoon. The sun cast shadows across the rows of parked cars, many of them stripped for parts. Langston's presence commanded respect, his uniform a stark reminder of the authority he wielded.

He walked into the garage where Tate sat, the door creaking as it swung open. Tate looked up, his eyes narrowing at the intrusion but relaxing when he recognized Langston. The tension in the room shifted, the workers pausing momentarily before resuming their tasks, knowing better than to eavesdrop on a conversation between the two most powerful men in the area.

"Hello, Miran. Word around town is there was a big gunfight recently. Apparently, Allen Hall, who stays in trouble, got himself killed. My understanding is he killed some old couple and tried to take their house. He was killed along with some other lowlifes," Langston told Tate. "There are quite a few bodies piling up," he added, taking a seat.

Tate leaned back in his chair, the leather creaking under his weight. He took the cigar from his mouth, rolling it between his fingers as he considered Langston's words. "You know anything else about it? Who killed Allen or who the old couple was? Hell, truth be told, we probably need a few more old couples knocked off. They're hoarding some good supplies, I'm sure of that," Tate said with a boisterous laugh.

Langston smirked, though his eyes remained cold. "That's the part I thought you'd find interesting. It was the same man Horrace is after—the guy named Kyle. Kyle Blaine. There's a roadblock outside Hurley, and they're not letting anyone through unless they live that way. Word is spreading from some volunteers there who had a part in it," Langston continued as Horrace walked in, hearing his name mentioned.

"When are we going to get this guy, Tate? I want to see him die a slow and painful death," Horrace said, his face reddening with anger at the mention of Kyle Blaine.

"Easy, Horrace. I know you want him. Allen was trash, we

248

all know that. He was a tough dude, though, so if this Kyle fellow killed him, maybe we need to rethink our plan. Who are these two yahoos you got with you, Langston?" Tate asked, eyeing Axel and Vince.

"These are the boys I told you about. This is Axel and Vince," Langston said, pointing to each.

"Can you boys actually help us? Looks to me like you spend a lot of time helping yourselves with drugs. We don't need anyone who snorts a pill in the middle of a fight," Tate said matter-of-factly.

"No, sir. We don't need a pill. I won't turn one down if you've got it. Maybe we can get a little weed for helping out," Axel said with a smile.

"If you get the job done and survive, I'll see to it you get a little weed," Tate replied.

"If we survive? Can we get killed?" Axel quickly blurted out.

"You aren't going to die. He's just messing with you," Langston said, giving Tate a wide-eyed look.

"It sounds like we might need a few more reinforcements before we go charging in on this guy. How about you round us up a few more willing to fight? You only got the four of you; try to get that number to ten or twelve," Tate instructed, pointing to a rack of guns on the wall. "We can equip a small army, so get us one."

Horrace stormed out of the garage, his footsteps echoing loudly against the concrete floor, clearly upset that Tate wanted to increase their numbers before going after Kyle. His face was flushed with anger, jaw clenched tightly. Horrace felt he could do it on his own, believing that a larger group would only slow him down.

The midday sun was blinding as Horrace burst into the open air, and he squinted against its harsh glare. He kicked a loose rock in frustration, sending it skittering across the gravel. Langston quickly followed him out, his boots crunching on the ground, calling after him.

"Horrace, wait up!" Langston's voice was firm but measured. He caught up to Horrace, placing a steadying hand on his shoulder. "Listen, I know you want Kyle, and we'll get him. But think about it—more men means more firepower, more eyes watching our backs. It's an advantage we can't ignore."

Horrace shrugged off Langston's hand, his expression a mix of anger and thought. He paced back and forth, the gravel crunching beneath his heavy boots. "I don't need a damn army, Langston. I'm more than enough to take down Kyle."

Langston crossed his arms, leaning against the side of his cruiser. "I know you're capable, Horrace. But this isn't just about taking Kyle down. It's about making sure we don't lose anyone in the process. We've got to be smart about this. Tate's right—we need more men."

Horrace stopped pacing, taking a deep breath. He stared out at the horizon, the rolling hills and distant treeline blurring in the heat. Slowly, he nodded, though reluctance still shown in his features. "Fine. But we move fast. I don't want Kyle slipping through our fingers because we're too busy recruiting."

Langston gave a tight-lipped smile, a glint of approval in his eyes. "Agreed. We'll start gathering men today. There are plenty around town willing to fight for a good cause—or a good reward."

Horrace turned to face Langston, his determination unwavering. "We'll get him. And when we do, he'll wish he never crossed me."

Langston nodded, his eyes cold and calculating. "I'll spread the word. We'll have our reinforcements soon enough. Let's make sure everyone knows what's at stake."

With a final nod, the two men parted ways. Langston headed back inside the garage to relay the plan to Tate, while Horrace stood for a moment longer, staring out into the distance. The wind rustled through the trees, carrying the promise of the hunt to come.

"Here you go, boys. Go have yourselves some fun with this," Tate said, tossing a small bag of marijuana to Axel and Vince from his desk drawer. "I want to see you both back here in two days, and you better have something to offer. I don't care where or how you get it, but have me something of value."

Axel and Vince thanked Tate and ran back to Langston's police cruiser to wait.

"What are we going to get him, Axel?" Vince asked.

"We'll steal some guns maybe. James is dead now, so let's go to his house later and see what we can scrounge up. We could become Tate's number one guys," Axel said, giving Vince a fist bump. Langston shortly joined them, giving the guys a ride back to their home.

"You make sure you find something good for Tate. If you do, he will take care of you; if you don't, he may kill you," Langston said, receiving a chuckle from Vince. "It's no joke, guys. He will kill you and dispose of your bodies as if you never existed."

"You know what everybody is saying? Horrace and his brother killed James," Axel spoke up, breaking the tense silence in the cruiser. His voice was low, almost conspiratorial. "I don't know how it went down with his brother being killed, but the people we've talked to said they were causing problems. They attacked that guy's sister too—probably deserved what they got."

Langston's grip on the steering wheel tightened as he listened, his knuckles whitening. The interior of the cruiser was hot and stuffy, the midday sun beating down through the windshield. Axel and Vince sat in the back, their eyes darting nervously between each other and Langston.

"That won't matter now," Langston said, his voice a mix of irritation and authority. "Horrace is on Tate's favorite list, so don't even bring that up again. Just do what he says, and you will both be fine." He glanced at them in the rearview mirror, his eyes cold.

As they pulled up to the curb, Axel and Vince exited the police cruiser, the door hinges creaking in the harsh heat. They stood on the cracked pavement, adjusting to the brightness outside. Langston leaned out the window, stopping them with a sharp command.

"Hang on, one more thing," he said, his tone making it clear this wasn't a request. "Tate wants you to collect all the bodies you can find around town. Take them to lower Knox and dispose of them in the river. They can float on to Kentucky."

Axel and Vince exchanged uneasy glances, the significance of the task settling in. The thought of handling corpses sent a shiver down their spines, despite the heat.

"How the hell are we supposed to haul bodies around? We don't got a hearse," Vince said, his voice cracking slightly. He looked at Langston with a mixture of confusion and fear.

Langston's lips curled into a smirk, his eyes narrowing. "Figure it out, dipshit. Just make sure it's done by tomorrow. Otherwise, face the consequences." His words hung in the air like a dark cloud, the threat unmistakable.

Vince nodded reluctantly, swallowing hard. Axel clenched his fists, trying to mask his own apprehension. They turned and began to walk away, the weight of Langston's words pressing down on them.

"We better get this done, Vince. Tate doesn't make empty threats."

Vince nodded, his mind racing with thoughts of what lay ahead. They had no choice but to comply, knowing that failure was not an option. The reality of their task loomed large, each step bringing them closer to the grim duty that awaited them.

Axel and Vince went inside their home for a little fun, smoking their newly acquired marijuana.

"Nothing like a free smoke, Vince. Everybody loves us. You and me will probably be running this town before long. We will have Tate watching our backs. Once we are in charge, we can rename the town in our honor," Axel said as he puffed on the joint.

"You're crazy, Axel. But that would be cool if we do become the boss. Which one of us would be the boss out of me and you?" Vince asked.

"It would have to be me. There can't be two bosses, and if you were the boss, how could I be the boss? You see what I'm saying? But you would be my vice-boss. That sound good?" Axel said, taking another deep draw.

"Yeah, that makes sense. Vice-boss. I like that," Vince said, leaning back on the couch, taking a hit from the joint and letting the smoke roll slowly out of his mouth. After smoking two joints, they were ready for a little nap time. Although they each had a bedroom, they usually ended up asleep on the couch and recliner. After a couple of hours passed by, the boys awoke and scrambled about the room.

"We got to get going, Vince. Grab your shoes and come on," Axel said, rushing Vince out the door.

The boys got into the old car they had stolen from town, its engine sputtering to life with a reluctant growl. The vehicle was a relic, rusted and creaking, but it served its purpose. They drove toward James's house, their minds racing with possibilities. They needed to find something that would impress Tate, though they had no idea what that might be. The task of removing bodies around town loomed over them, a grim duty they'd have to tackle later.

As they crossed the rickety bridge leading to James's house, they scanned the surroundings. The area was eerily quiet, the only sound the rustling of leaves in the gentle breeze. The house itself stood solemn and still, showing no signs of life. They parked the car behind the house, out of sight from any potential onlookers.

"Alright, let's make this quick," Axel said, his voice a low whisper. He glanced around nervously before taking a deep breath and smashing a window on the back door with his baseball bat. The glass shattered with a loud crash, and they both winced, before Axel quickly reached inside to unlock the door and slipped in.

The interior of the house was dim and musty, the air heavy with the scent of neglect. The kitchen was eerily tidy, as if frozen in time. An empty coffee cup sat on the table next to a neatly folded newspaper, remnants of a morning routine now abandoned.

"I didn't know people still got newspapers," Vince muttered, looking around the room with a mix of curiosity and unease.

"Me either," Axel replied, already moving towards the pantry. "Let's see what we can find and get out of here."

The pantry was a treasure trove of goods. Axel's eyes lit up as he spotted a fully filled and unopened black and white box labeled "Jim Beam" on the side. He hefted it out, feeling the weight of twelve bottles inside. Next to it was another box, this one containing a variety of wine bottles. Axel knew nothing about wine, but he figured Tate would appreciate the find. He moved the boxes next to the kitchen door and continued searching. He grabbed a couple of boxes of Little Debbie snack cakes and two bags of chips, leaving behind the canned foods that filled the shelves.

Meanwhile, Vince had made his way through the rest of the house. He tossed a few pieces of jewelry into a pillowcase—a couple of watches, several sets of earrings, and necklaces that had belonged to James's deceased wife. In a closet, he found a small safe and a larger one bolted to the floor. The small safe was light enough to carry, so he took it with him, leaving the larger one behind.

In the living room, Axel opened a glass gun cabinet and removed four hunting rifles. He wrapped them in a small rug, creating a makeshift bundle. Vince joined him, showing off the pillowcase full of jewelry and the small safe he had found.

"Hey Vince, do you think we should keep some of these things here? Maybe this would be a good place for us to move. It's not like James is going to be needing it now," Axel suggested.

"I think that's a great idea, Axel. Let's hide some guns and keep the safe here. We'll ask Tate if we can have this house now," Vince replied, putting the small safe back in the closet.

"Take the other items and put them by the door. Let's go check the garage," Axel said, heading towards the door that led to the garage.

Their eyes widened with excitement when they saw the new model Dodge Ram pickup inside. The truck was black with chrome wheels and a chrome toolbox bolted in the bed.

"Oh yeah, baby! Look at this, Vince," Axel said, running his hand along the sleek exterior. "We're about to upgrade our ride."

"The body mobile," Vince said, trying to elicit a laugh from Axel. "You know, because we got to haul those bodies off."

"Yeah, whatever, man. That sounded stupid. Just start loading our stuff in the truck. I'll figure out how to get the garage door open," Axel said, shaking his head as he walked back inside the house and out the back door.

"That sounded stupid, Vince," Vince mocked Axel under his breath. "You don't know anything, Vince. Vice-boss," he muttered to himself as he loaded the items into the truck.

Axel eventually managed to open the garage door, flooding the space with light. As he stepped back, he noticed fresh white paint on the truck. He grabbed a spray can from Vince's hand and examined it.

"What in the hell did you do, Vince?" Axel demanded, shaking his head. A large "BM" was scrawled on the driver's side door, and over the rear tire on the truck bed, Vince had painted "Body Mowbeel."

Vince grinned and chuckled at his handiwork. "Now we're official body collectors, Axel. We look like a legit company."

"Yeah, we look legit alright," Axel said sarcastically. "There's paint running off crooked letters. And you spelled this wrong—there's no 'w' in 'mobeel.'" He enlarged the 'o' to cover the 'w,' shaking his head at the mess.

CHAPTER FORTY
"Guardians of the Roadblock"

The mid-summer heat bore down relentlessly, making the air thick and heavy. Waves of shimmering heat rose from the asphalt, distorting the view down the deserted road. Despite the sweltering weather, the roadblock had proven effective in keeping trouble away from the small community. A steady flow of volunteers, working in shifts, helped maintain order and control.

It had also become a hub of information, with people often stopping to share news and rumors. To combat the scorching heat, a makeshift canopy had been erected to the side of the roadblock, providing limited shade. It was set up near the creek, where the sound of flowing water added a semblance of coolness to the otherwise stifling air.

Snaggle, enjoying the role he had carved out for himself, had become the self-appointed leader of the roadblock crew. With his ever-turning grey hair, constantly tanned skin, and a grin that rarely left his face, he was a comforting presence. The volunteers didn't mind his self-imposed leadership; Snaggle's humor and light-hearted banter kept the atmosphere relatively upbeat, even in the face of the ongoing crisis.

Herbie, who had helped at old man Hadley's farm the night Kyle killed Allen, was stationed at the roadblock. He was a burly man in his mid-forties, with calloused hands and a sunburned neck, a testament to his years of hard labor. Herbie had shared the story of the shootout with people, unaware that there were more threats looming over Kyle. He didn't speak with bad intentions, but rather from pride in what Kyle had done.

"You should've seen Kyle that night," Herbie would say, his voice animated. "He stood his ground like a true warrior, going inside a burning house after Allen. We need more folks like him around here."

His stories painted vivid pictures of Kyle's bravery, making him a local hero in the eyes of many. Men nodded with admiration, finding a glimmer of hope in Kyle's actions, a feeling of self-worth they could also stand up to the bad guys, whoever they may be.

Willie, who operated the ham radio, regularly relayed news to Snaggle, which was then passed on to others at the roadblock. Willie was a tough old man with keen ears and quick fingers, always tuned into the crackling static of his radio, hoping for any scrap of news.

"Anything new, Willie?" Snaggle asked, peering over his shoulder.

Willie shook his head, his hands steady as he adjusted the dials. "Same old, same old. FEMA might set up operations, but that's still a year out possibly. We're on our own for now."

The country had been decimated by the attacks. It was becoming clear that no help was coming. The sparse broadcasts emphasized that people needed to fend for themselves. Each grim update Willie received was shared with a heavy heart, knowing it dashed the hopes of those who longed for rescue.

"Hang in there, folks," Willie would say to the volunteers, his voice heavy with concern. "We're tough, and we can make it through this. Just gotta stick together."

The volunteers at the roadblock would gather around, their faces somber as Willie relayed the latest updates. The flicker of hope in their eyes dimmed with each passing day, but they kept going, driven by the necessity of survival.

Today, two volunteers were set to relieve Herbie and Blackout, the nickname for Ian Lester, a Hurley native. Ian had earned the nickname Blackout during his military service after inadvertently poisoning a platoon with spoiled chicken, causing a bout of intense food poisoning. The soldiers' misery had led to his unfortunate nickname, a constant reminder of his blunder. Despite the passage of time, the name stuck like a stubborn stain, a testament to the military's dark humor and the lasting impact of a single mistake.

Under the relentless summer sun, the air shimmered with heat waves, making the roadblock feel like an island of parched earth. Traffic had dwindled as fuel supplies ran dry, and the once-busy roadblock had become a somber checkpoint. The sight of an approaching vehicle always heightened the tension among the volunteers.

As Herbie and Blackout neared the end of their shift, they spotted a black truck coming down the road. The vehicle's dark, gleaming surface contrasted sharply with the dusty surroundings. It slowed to a stop at the roadblock, and the driver, leaning out of the window, gave a casual wave, signaling his intent to pass through.

"What's your business here?" Herbie asked, walking around to the side of the truck. He didn't recognize the vehicle or the driver. He read the letters on the door aloud, "BM... Body Mobeel?"

"We're working for emergency services under Supervisor Tate. It's martial law now. We're collecting dead bodies for disposal. You got any?" Axel, the driver, responded.

"We don't have any dead bodies here," Herbie replied. "You say Tate has declared martial law? Has he placed himself in charge?"

"Supervisor Tate is in charge. Everybody has to listen to him and the people he appoints, like us. If we need something, you have to comply, that's the rules," Axel said.

Blackout walked towards the passenger side to get a better view of the occupants. "That you, Vince?" he asked, recognizing the passenger.

"Why, hell yeah, it is! How you been, man? I thought you were still in the army," Vince said, slapping Axel's arm. "Look here, it's Ian from school."

"How you doing, Ian? We thought you were still in the army," Axel said.

"I got out six months ago. Probably left at a good time. I'm not sure the army even exists now," Blackout replied.

"Hey, I heard you made a bunch of soldiers sick or something like that," Vince said.

"Something like that," Blackout said dismissively. "I hate to run, but we're changing shifts. I'm heading home for supper."

"Before you go, we're going to need your guns for Tate. He wants them confiscated. Just toss them in the back," Axel said with a tone of expectance, clearly misunderstanding the citizen's acceptance of martial law.

"No, that's not happening. We're keeping our guns. But it was good talking to you. Good luck with the body collection," Herbie said, laughing at the thought of handing over their weapons. "There's no other business for you here, so you can turn around and go back the way you came."

"Tate isn't going to like this. He may come to visit himself, and if he does, it won't be good. He's not as nice as we are," Axel warned.

"Tell Tate if he wants to come, we'll tell him the same thing. He's not getting our guns. Now go back and tell him 'mobile' is spelled M-O-B-I-L-E. Somebody really jacked up this truck," Herbie said, stepping back and brushing dust off his shirt.

Axel's jaw tightened, but he didn't respond. He carefully maneuvered the truck in a three-point turn, the engine's low rumble resonating in the stillness of the summer afternoon. As he shifted into reverse, Vince leaned out the passenger window, waving. "See you, Ian. Glad you made it home safe!"

"Hush, Vince. Don't talk to them. They're not on our side," Axel snapped, the words sharp as he stomped on the gas. The truck's tires squealed in protest, kicking up a cloud of dust before speeding away, leaving a trail of frustration behind. "I'll deal with that smartass one way or another."

Herbie watched the truck disappear down the road, then

turned to Blackout with a smile. "So, what's the story about you getting soldiers sick?"

Blackout's eyes shifted briefly, and he let out a chuckle. "It's a long story. Maybe another time," he replied, clearly not in the mood to revisit old wounds. He shrugged off the conversation and began preparing for the shift change, the heat of the day mingling with the tension still lingering from the encounter.

CHAPTER FORTY-ONE
"Fortifying the Path"

At Uncle Tom's house, Snaggle had joined him to unload a new haul they had managed to get their hands on. Arnie and Joel had ridden down the trail to Uncle Tom's, and their eyes widened upon seeing what Snaggle and Uncle Tom had in their possession. The boxes were clearly marked dynamite and blasting caps.

"Holy crap, Uncle Tom, is that dangerous to handle? Can I have one?" Arnie asked, both worried and excited.

"No, it's not. I mean, it is, but it's not if we handle it correctly," Snaggle told Arnie.

"Handling it correctly, means keeping it out of your hands," Joel said laughing while smacking Arnie on the shoulder.

"Where did you get it?" Arnie asked, slowly sliding his hand across the box, feeling the dust on the cardboard beneath his fingers.

"Let's just say we don't think the mines will be needing this right now. We don't want anyone getting hurt by unattended explosives," Uncle Tom said with a snicker in his voice.

They carefully moved some of the boxes to Uncle Tom's ATV cargo hold. He placed a roll of fuse in as well while leaving the remaining fuse roll in Snaggle's ATV.

"We're going to blast large gaps in the trails coming up the mountain from Hadley's direction and from Kentucky. This will prevent anyone from sneaking up on the mountain that way," Uncle Tom told Arnie and Joel.

"Kyle is up there now putting some gates up too. He'll be glad to see this. There will only be one way up now, unless someone wants to climb," Arnie said to Snaggle and Uncle Tom.

"I'm heading back up the road, Tommy. Don't forget to talk with Kyle, tell him I would really appreciate it," Snaggle told Tom as he climbed back onto his ATV.

"I sure will, and I know he will want to help you," Uncle Tom said to Snaggle before he drove away.

"You better get up there and let Rachel know about her other kids as well," Snaggle added before driving away.

"What is that about, Uncle Tom? What does he need Kyle's help with? And what about the other kids?" Arnie asked quickly after listening to the exchange between Tom and Snaggle.

"Snaggle's boy Charles hasn't been home in a few days. He went to work at the hospital, and Snaggle hasn't seen him since. He wants Kyle to go to the hospital and look for him," Uncle Tom said to Arnie.

"Okay, that sounds like it could be dangerous, but Kyle will probably do it. What about the other kids?" Arnie said to Tom.

"I'll see you guys a little later. I'll have news for everyone, and then we're going to blow some trails up," Uncle Tom said with a smile.

"You can say 'blow some shit up,' Uncle Tom. I'm grown now," Arnie said with a big smile on his face.

"Get out of here, you little hoodlum," Uncle Tom said back, laughing at Arnie and pretending to kick him in the rear end.

Arnie and Joel went to Rachel's house to see how it was holding up. The house was still as they left it, there hadn't been anyone there. Arnie checked on Kyle's truck in the garage, finding it as they last parked. He opened the garage door to allow additional light to shine in. He scanned the shelves, finding the paint Kyle had told him about.

Arnie and Joel each grabbed a can of paint and started spraying the truck. Arnie took the black and Joel used brown. Kyle had told them to paint the truck in a camouflage design. He then wanted them to bring the truck as far up the trail as they could before it narrowed. There was a location where they could pull the truck off the trail and hide it amongst the brush and trees. Kyle thought the added camouflage would help in concealing it.

They also had a camouflage netting to toss over the truck.

Arnie enjoyed painting the truck in the wild, overlapping patterns. They let the paint dry before attempting to move the truck. The guys relocated it to the new hiding spot, got it parked, and covered it with the camo netting. Kyle had purchased the twelve by twenty-foot netting for fifty dollars online. He purchased ten packages of netting. When he purchased it, he didn't know if he would ever have a need for it, but now there was.

"There goes Uncle Tom. I wonder what news he has," Arnie said to Joel as Uncle Tom waved on his way by.

"I don't know, but I don't think it's bad. He didn't seem upset about it," Joel said to Arnie.

"And what's Kyle going to do with all these other packs of netting? Maybe we are going to cover the cabin so we aren't seen by anything flying over," Arnie said, laughing at the thought.

"I'm not sure that's a joke, Arnie. I think Kyle might try something like that eventually. I'm going to work at the roadblock if anybody needs me," Joel said, laughing himself.

Joel left after they had finished covering the truck to go work a shift at the roadblock. He wanted to be helpful and, not really knowing how to tend to animals, thought the roadblock was better suited for him. Arnie went back up the trail, catching up with Uncle Tom, who drove slower. He followed closely behind, Tom having no idea he was there. Arnie giggled as he watched Tom slow down to sightsee repeatedly.

Once they had reached the top of the mountain, Kyle waved as he saw them approaching.

"What are you guys doing?" Kyle asked as they came to a stop with Tom still oblivious to Arnie being behind him.

"What do you mean by 'you guys'? Who do you think is riding with me, the Holy Ghost?" Uncle Tom asked, looking puzzled at Kyle and holding his arm open over the empty seat.

"Well, it might be good to have the Holy Ghost riding with you, but I was talking about Arnie behind you," Kyle said, pointing to Arnie who was giggling as Uncle Tom looked at him bewildered.

"You better be glad I wasn't a bad guy, Uncle Tom. I would have had the drop on you," Arnie said, pretending to shoot Tom with his thumb and forefinger.

"Dag gummit. You sure would have. I got to pay better attention than that," Uncle Tom said.

"Unless the bad guy shoots like Rocky, then you would be safe," Kyle said, looking at Rocky with a grin.

"We were getting along just fine, no reason to throw a jab at me. You just wait, I will shoot every bullet you have until I get good with that pistol," Rocky said, punching Kyle on the side of his arm.

"I got hold of some dynamite, Kyle. We can blast some big cuts into the trail to keep anyone from riding ATVs from the other directions to get here," Tom said to Kyle, showing him the explosives he had brought.

"Hell yeah!" Rocky said, high-fiving Arnie.

"I got some great news for everyone I need to share. Let's get everybody together for a moment," Uncle Tom said.

"That's what we need, some good news. Is this over with?" Rachel asked.

"I wish that were the news, but no, that's not it. Willie got word yesterday from Sawyer that they're all doing okay. They were able to get communication out from somewhere in North Carolina. He is attempting to make his way to Spencer's now. He wanted you to know the family was with him," Uncle Tom said as Rachel couldn't get a word out before the tears streamed down her face.

"Oh thank God! Thank you! Thank you! Thank you!" Susie shouted.

"That's wonderful news, Tom. Does that mean Spencer is okay too?" Rachel asked Tom.

"Willie heard from Spencer this morning. He wanted to let you know Sawyer was on his way to Spencer's house, and they were all doing well. Megan is already with Spencer; she made it there on the day of the attack. Willie told them you all were on the mountain with Kyle," Uncle Tom said as Rachel hugged him.

"That is fantastic news, and much needed as well," Kyle said clapping his hands together.

"Alright, let's go to work. It's a good day," Uncle Tom said as they got into the side by side. "Let's blow some stuff up."

"Say it, Uncle Tom. Let's blow some shit up!" Arnie said, smiling and nodding to Uncle Tom. It was like peer-pressuring a friend in school to say a bad word.

"You better watch it, Arnie bug. You say that in front of your grandma, and she might beat your butt," Uncle Tom said before looking back, "Now, let's blow some shit up!"

"Wooooooo hooooooo, Uncle Tom!" Arnie shouted as he laughed hysterically hearing Uncle Tom say a four letter word.

Uncle Tom showed Kyle, Rocky, and Arnie how to assemble the dynamite stick with a blasting cap and fuse. They placed small charges to blow out large chunks of the trail. Once they had their charges in place, they took cover and lit the fuse. Arnie liked to yell, "Fire in the hole," as the dynamite blasted dirt into the air.

Kyle had attached the gates as well for added protection at the trail entrances. There would be no ATVs coming in this way without making a great deal of noise clearing out a new path. That would require taking down trees to make the route accessible. Kyle felt comfortable with this; he wouldn't be as worried about anyone getting into their camp while he was away. If someone did try, he knew Rocky or Ginger would be ready to snipe them from the watch towers.

The guys all worked together like they did before the attack, knowing that Sawyer, Spencer, and Megan were all safe. Kyle was disappointed that none of them had learned to operate a ham radio, although they had discussed it multiple times. He was glad to know that Spencer had found someone with the ability to get word out. He was concerned that Sawyer may find trouble getting to Spencer's house, but he knew his brother could take care of himself.

CHAPTER FORTY-TWO
"Whiskey and Warfare"

"I'm going to do reconnaissance," Langston told Tate.

"What's your plan for that?" Tate asked.

"I'm taking a ride to check out the roadblock and ask some questions. I'll take Horrace and the rockstars with me," Langston said.

Axel and Vince arrived at the garage in the Dodge truck they had taken from James's house.

"A truck is a nice gesture. I would prefer it didn't have spray paint misspelling words on it," Tate said to Axel and Vince as they got out.

"The truck isn't the gift, Mr. Tate. We got that in the back," Axel replied. They dropped the tailgate, and each removed a box.

"Tell me that's Jim Beam in the box!" Tate exclaimed, clapping his hands together and grinning widely at the sight of the Jim Beam print on the box.

"Yes sir, it is. We also brought some wine. One bottle inside got broken," Vince said, placing the box on Tate's desk.

Tate opened the box of Jack Daniels, admiring the case full of sealed bottles. "Let's see the wine you got," he said, opening the other box and lifting the bottles for further inspection.

"Yes sir, Mr. Tate. We thought you might like them," Axel said with the enthusiasm of a child.

"These are run-of-the-mill cheap wines. Wait a moment,

this bottle of Champagne is a decent find. Dom Perignon Brut, probably three hundred dollars. You boys did a good job," Tate said, starting to close the box but pulling out the broken bottle first. "Why, you stupid jackasses. The best bottle in the box, and you break it. This was a 2002 Napa Valley Reserve red wine, probably worth three thousand dollars, and you idiots break it," he said, shaking his head in disgust.

"We're sorry, Tate. We tried to be careful with them all," Vince said, looking at the floor.

"I believe you, Vince. It is a good thing I'm a bourbon man. I am happy with this offering," Tate said, patting his shoulder.

"We good to go, Tate?" Horrace asked, eager to get started.

"Go hunting, gentlemen. Good luck finding us some information," Tate said, motioning them to carry on.

"Let's take the police cruiser. It has a hitch, and we can connect the trailer for the side-by-side," Langston suggested, eyeing the sleek black Ford Explorer parked nearby. The cruiser, despite its recent wear and tear, still exuded authority. "Horrace, put Vince and Axel in the back, and you sit up front with me."

Langston hoped the gesture would act as a peace offering, easing the lingering tension between Horrace and himself. Ever since the catastrophic events had upended their world, Horrace had become increasingly resistant to taking orders, preferring to act autonomously. Langston thought offering Horrace the front seat might show respect and camaraderie. Horrace, however, perceived it as an order disguised as kindness, fueling his growing resentment. He was willing to work with Tate, but his patience for being commanded by anyone else had worn thin.

The group moved with purpose, connecting the trailer to the cruiser and securing the side-by-side vehicle, a rugged, versatile machine built for the rough terrain. Axel and Vince climbed into the back seat, their presence filling the confined space with a mix of nervous energy and anticipation.

As Langston drove, the heavy silence was soon filled with Axel and Vince recounting their harrowing encounter at the roadblock just days before. They spoke in rushed, overlapping sentences, the memory still fresh and vivid.

"We got stopped by these guys, real rough-looking types. They said we couldn't go through unless we lived around there," Vince explained, his voice filled with frustration.

"Yeah, they had this makeshift barricade and everything. Told us to turn around unless we had some kind of local ID or proof we belonged," Axel added, shaking his head.

Langston listened intently, his eyes fixed on the road ahead. "Typical territorial behavior," he muttered, more to himself than to the others. "They're trying to control who comes in and out, probably out of fear and desperation."

"What are we going to do? They won't just let us through," Vince said, a note of worry creeping into his voice.

"We'll get past a couple of hicks," Langston replied confidently. "I've got a plan."

Langston's mind was already working through various scenarios. He knew that brute force wouldn't be the best approach. Instead, he planned to leverage his uniform and the cruiser's intimidating presence to bluff their way through. The badge still held some weight in these lawless times he thought, and Langston intended to use every ounce of that lingering authority to their advantage.

The cruiser rumbled along the winding mountain roads, the landscape a blur of green and brown as they descended towards the valley. Langston's grip on the steering wheel tightened. He was aware of Horrace's menacing silence beside him, the man's eyes scanning the surroundings with a guarded intensity.

"We'll approach them with calm authority," Langston said, glancing at Horrace. "No unnecessary violence. We need information, not a bloodbath."

Horrace grunted in response, his gaze never wavering from the passing trees and rocky outcrops. Langston hoped that once they reached the roadblock, his plan would hold up under pressure and Horrace's simmering defiance wouldn't boil over.

As they neared their destination, the tension in the cruiser became intense, a silent current of unease running between them. Langston knew that the success of their mission hinged not just on their strategy, but on their ability to work together despite the cracks in their alliance.

At the blockade, Joel and Snaggle laughed, as Joel told him about Arnie falling in the pig pen, his face getting covered in manure. Snaggle loved the story, slapping his hand against his leg several times. Joel had stepped down to the creek, dipping his handkerchief in the water and dabbing it onto his head. The coolness of the water a welcome relief to the sun's penetrating heat.

"Hey Joel, there's a vehicle coming," Snaggle said, interrupting his moment of joy with the wet cloth on his head.

"It looks like a police cruiser," Joel said as he climbed back up the embankment from the creek. "Why are they stopping down there?" Joel asked as the vehicle had stopped several hundred yards away from their checkpoint.

"How far do you think it is from here to that coal truck? I'm thinking two hundred yards," Langston said.

"Yeah, that seems about right to me," Horrace replied.

"Are we going to kill those guys and break through the roadblock?" Vince asked Langston.

"No, we aren't breaking through it. We want to get by without killing anyone. We need to gather some information on these people," Langston said.

Langston drove closer to the roadblock as Snaggle and Joel stood next to it.

"Let me do the talking, Horrace. We want to get by here peacefully," Langston said.

"What can we do for you, officer?" Snaggle asked Langston, who was still wearing his police uniform. Snaggle held his rifle but kept it pointed downward to show he wasn't a threat. "We haven't seen any police in some time now."

"I understand that, my friend. We are reestablishing a presence in the communities. We're out checking every area to see what the people need," Langston told Snaggle, watching his hands on the rifle. "You can put the gun away; no need for that with us."

"It's just a part of me now, officer. I prefer to hang onto it. This community is doing well. We are working together and keeping it safe," Snaggle said, trying to see who was inside the police cruiser.

"We're going to need to get through. We need to inspect it ourselves for an official report. Not that I think you would lie to me," Langston said, noticing Snaggle's intense scrutiny of the cruiser.

An ATV approached the coal truck. It was Blackout and Scott, bringing some food from a rabbit Scott had killed to the day crew at the roadblock. Vince, not thinking, raised a hand and waved at Blackout.

"Put your hand down, dumbass," Horrace said to Vince.

"I'm sorry. Don't call me that again, or our friendship is over. And I'll hurt you," Vince shot back.

"All of you hush a minute. My god, you're like dealing with kids," Langston said as he stepped out of the police cruiser.

Blackout called Snaggle over to the ATV and whispered to him. Snaggle looked back at Langston as Blackout spoke low.

Snaggle nodded and then walked back to the cruiser.

"How about you park your police cruiser, and we will escort you for a look-see. No need for everybody to enter," Snaggle said, clearly irritating Langston.

"I tell you what, maybe you can help me with some information, and I'll be on my way. An old couple was killed a few days back, their house burned. There might have been more of the community's underbelly types killed as well. Do you know anything about this?" Langston asked Snaggle while Joel stayed quiet.

"Can't say that I do," Snaggle replied.

"Do you know a Kyle Blaine living up this way, somewhere on the mountain?" Langston asked.

"I know of him. Good kid that sticks to himself," Snaggle said, keeping his answers short. This was clearly getting to both Langston and Horrace.

"By the authority of martial law declared by the highest enforcement of this region, put your guns down. Then I want you to move your truck and let us through," Langston said, now clearly attempting to enforce his power.

"We have declared martial law here as well, deputy. As I said, we'll take care of this community. You can go take care of somewhere else that needs you more," Snaggle said.

"You aren't making this easy on yourself. I can arrest you now for interfering with a police investigation, obstruction of justice, menacing, and illegal weapons," Langston said, getting louder as the conversation continued.

"Let's cut the shit, son. Your uniform and police cruiser don't mean a thing anymore. Those idiots in your car that can't spell don't mean a thing either. Turn around and go on your way; you're not welcome here," Snaggle said before spitting on the ground next to Langston's foot.

The passenger door opened on the cruiser, "Tell Kyle his friend Horrace was asking about him. Let him know I haven't gotten that dug yet. He will know what it means," Horrace said, showing his face before closing the door again.

"You're going to regret this. You didn't do yourself any favors today," Langston said, opening his door and getting inside. He backed the cruiser to turn around, getting the trailer jackknifed. His face turned red as he saw the men around the truck laughing at him. As Langston pulled the shifter to drive, Horrace grabbed his arm.

"You drive fifty feet away slowly and stop this car," Horrace commanded, his grip like a vice on Langston's arm. There was a clear determination in Horrace's eyes that Langston couldn't ignore, even if he didn't fully understand his intentions. Complying, Langston pulled out and let the cruiser roll slowly along the road before bringing it to a stop as Horrace had asked. The silence in the vehicle was thick with tension. Langston's mind raced, questioning why he was deferring to Horrace, yet there was an unmistakable authority in Horrace's voice that made him fall in line without protest.

As they stopped, a voice broke the tension. "Get cover!" Joel yelled out, his voice urgent, as he and the other men at the roadblock watched the cruiser halt. The passenger door swung open with a suddenness that sent a jolt of adrenaline through everyone. Horrace stepped out, his movements swift and deliberate, an AR-10 clutched firmly in his hands. The sleek, black rifle gleamed menacingly in the sunlight.

Without hesitation, Horrace raised the AR-10 and began firing towards the men at the roadblock. The sudden burst of gunfire shattered the stillness. Several rounds struck the coal truck, the metallic clang echoing through the air. One round found its mark, catching Snaggle in the back just as he turned to duck behind the truck, the impact knocking him forward onto the ground with a sickening thud.

Chaos erupted as Joel, driven by instinct and fear, pumped rounds from his twelve-gauge shotgun as quickly as he could work the action. The shotgun's booming retort punctuated the air, and some of the pellets made contact with the cruiser, shattering the light bar on top and peppering the vehicle's exterior with a spray of plastic shrapnel. The trailered ATV took most of the pellets, but did no real damage.

Langston, still behind the wheel, felt the cruiser shudder with each impact. The air was thick with the smell of gunpowder and the tension of a situation spiraling out of control. Horrace continued to fire, his face set in a grim mask of determination. Each pull of the trigger was executed with cold precision, a stark contrast to the chaos unfolding around them.

"Get back in!" Langston shouted, his voice barely audible over the ringing of the gunfire. Horrace, with a final burst of shots, let himself fall back into the passenger seat, his sinister laughter echoing through the confined space as Langston slammed the gas pedal and sped away.

The tires kicked up gravel and dust as they tore down the road, the cruiser's engine roaring with the sudden acceleration. Horrace's laughter filled the vehicle, a dark, chilling sound that contrasted sharply with the tense silence of Axel and Vince in the back. The two younger men exchanged wide-eyed glances, their hearts pounding with a mix of fear and excitement.

"That was so badass, Horrace. Way to go, bro!" Axel shouted, unable to contain his adrenaline-fueled exhilaration. Vince joined in, laughing nervously as Horrace's sinister chuckle reverberated through the cruiser.

Langston, his jaw set and eyes fixed on the road ahead, remained silent. He felt a mixture of anger and frustration boiling inside him. Horrace's actions had escalated the situation far beyond what he had planned. The images, in a moment of chaotic violence, played repeatedly in his mind. Yet, despite his inner turmoil, Langston knew they had to keep moving. There was no turning back now.

"Snaggle, are you okay?" Blackout asked as they rolled him over onto his back. The damage from the exit wound showed the force of the large round.

"I'm not going to make it," Snaggle croaked, his voice barely above a whisper. Thick splatters of blood trickled from his mouth, staining the ground beneath him. His eyes, once full of life and determination, were now dimming. "Joel, please tell Kyle to find my boy Charles," Snaggle pleaded, his voice faltering as he took his last breath. The words were a final request, a desperate plea from a man whose life was slipping away on the hot, sticky, unforgiving road.

As Snaggle's eyes glazed over, Joel, Blackout, and Scott knelt beside him, their faces etched with a mix of grief and helplessness. They stared at the lifeless body of a man who had become more than just an ally in their struggle; Snaggle had been a friend, a beacon of kindness and reliability amidst the chaos. He was the kind of person who deserved to live, to find peace in this shattered world. The sight of him lying there, motionless, was a painful reminder of the harsh reality they faced.

Joel's heart sank as he gazed at Snaggle's lifeless form. The thought of breaking the news to Uncle Tom filled him with dread. It was a burden he wished he didn't have to carry, knowing the pain it would bring to someone who had already suffered so much.

The minutes ticked by with an agonizing slowness as the men remained by Snaggle's side, though it felt like an eternity. The sun began to dip below the horizon, casting shade over the scene. With quiet determination, they lifted Snaggle's limp body and placed it gently in the cargo hold of the ATV. The weight of their grief was intense as they worked, their movements slow and deliberate.

Blackout and Scott, their faces hard and determined, urged Joel to take Snaggle's body home while they continued to man the roadblock. "Get him home," Blackout said, his voice rough with emotion. "We'll hold the line here. Make sure to send more help in case that cruiser comes back."

Joel nodded, his own voice catching in his throat. He covered Snaggle's body with a tarp, his hands trembling slightly as he tried to maintain his composure. The sense of finality weighed heavily on him as he prepared to leave.

He drove to Uncle Tom's place, his mind racing with thoughts of what he was about to do. Pulling into the driveway, he parked the ATV underneath the carport with a heavy heart. The familiar surroundings of Uncle Tom's home were a stark contrast to the grim reality of what he was carrying. Joel took a deep breath, strengthening himself for the difficult task ahead.

Langston arrived at Tate's garage, pulled in quickly, slammed the cruiser into park, and got out. He stormed inside the garage like a man on a mission.

"What's going on, Langston? Why so pissed?" Tate asked as he walked inside.

"You got a bottle of liquor?" Langston asked.

"Sure, help yourself to one," Tate said, motioning to a large cabinet.

"I'm going up to the guest house. I'm going to have a few drinks tonight, and we'll talk tomorrow," Langston said, opening the cabinet and removing a bottle of Jameson's Irish Whiskey before walking out of the garage.

CHAPTER FORTY-THREE
"The Price of Loyalty"

Uncle Tom had gathered everyone at the cabin for some family time. Rachel had been recalling tales of the old days, captivating Susie and Ginger the most. They reminisced about events from fifty years ago, offering a welcome diversion from the current grim reality.

"Kyle, I need to talk to you about a request from Snaggle," Uncle Tom said. "I know you want to stay on the mountain and maintain your peace, but he's asked you to check the hospital for Charles. He hasn't been home for days, and Snaggle is worried sick."

"I'm going to take a shower," Arnie announced, excusing himself and heading inside the cabin.

"That could be dangerous, Uncle Tom," Deanna interjected before Kyle could speak. "There are a lot of roads to cover between here and there."

"I agree, and from Willie's radio chatter, it's clear that Grundy has been ravaged. There are lowlife criminals committing horrific acts, much like here. A group calling themselves Blaze's Angels is trying to control parts of Grundy. People are terrified to be on the roads and even more so to stay home," Uncle Tom explained, his words sinking heavily into the group.

Kyle watched as Ginger's eyes welled with tears. She hadn't heard from Stacy in nearly two weeks since the chaos began. She kept silent, but Kyle could see the anguish she felt for Stacy and her grandbaby, Jackson.

"I don't think it's a good idea to venture that far," Rocky voiced his concerns. "It's not my place to decide, but if it were me, I wouldn't go."

Seeing Ginger's distress made Kyle's decision clear. She was his sister, and he couldn't bear to see her suffer. He worried about his brothers, who were full-grown men. If he had a child out there, he knew what he would do. The decision was simple.

"I'll do it. I'm leaving tomorrow. I need to find Stacy and make sure she's alright also," Kyle declared. Ginger looked up, her face brightening as she wiped away her tears. She embraced Kyle tightly, while Rachel offered silent support, understanding both sides of the situation.

"Kyle, you've protected us so far, and I have no doubt you'll continue to do so. Stay smart and don't do anything reckless. We'll manage things here until you return," Rachel said firmly.

"Kyle, are you there?" came Joel's voice over the walkie-talkie. "Uncle Tom, it's Joel."

"I'm here, Joel," Tom replied.

"I need you to meet me at your house. We had a problem at the roadblock today," Joel's voice crackled through.

"What happened, Joel? Are you okay?" Tom asked, concern evident in his voice.

"I'm fine. I need you to come now. Bring Kyle if you can," Joel insisted.

"We're on top of the mountain. Give us about ten minutes," Tom responded.

Without hesitation, Kyle revved up his ATV. "I'll be back," he said, speeding off with Uncle Tom in tow.

"What do you think that's about?" Susie wondered aloud.

"I don't know, but I hope nobody got hurt," Ginger replied,

her worry evident.

Kyle and Uncle Tom drove down the trail, navigating the rough road with urgency. It felt like no time had passed before they reached Tom's home. Joel had been waiting with Snaggle's body, and it seemed like an eternity to him. Kyle pulled in first, with Tom following closely. It was clear that Joel had a covered body in the back of his side-by-side, but the identity was still unknown.

"Who is it?" Kyle asked, approaching Joel.

"We got ambushed at the roadblock. It's Snaggle," Joel said, his gaze fixed on Uncle Tom.

Tom closed his eyes briefly, taking a deep breath before stepping over to the covered body. He pulled back the tarp and looked at Snaggle. "I'm sorry, my friend. You deserved so much more. I hope you're at peace now." He gently tapped Snaggle's shoulder in a gesture of farewell.

"Tell us what happened, Joel," Kyle prompted, pulling his attention away from Snaggle's body.

"Snaggle and I were working when Blackout and Scott arrived just before the incident. They saw everything and insisted I bring Snaggle home," Joel began, pausing for Tom to turn around. Tom wiped his face and looked at Joel, his expression grim but ready to hear the details.

"A cop showed up—one who works for Tate. He demanded to be let through the roadblock, claiming martial law and needing to check on the community. Snaggle refused, telling him to turn around," Joel continued, glancing between Kyle and Uncle Tom.

"How did Snaggle get killed?" Kyle asked, his voice tight with concern.

"After some arguing, the cop said he was leaving. Then a man named Horrace said he wanted you to know he hadn't dug it yet. After that, they turned, but the cop car stopped, and Horrace jumped out, opening fire. I fired back, not sure if I even had my eyes open. They eventually fled," Joel explained. "Who was Horrace?" he asked, looking at Kyle.

"A guy I hoped I would never see again," Kyle said, his face hardening. "On our first day in Hurley, Horrace and his brother attacked Ginger and killed James. I ended up killing his brother."

"You killed his brother? Why didn't you tell us?" Uncle Tom's voice was sharp with hurt. "We could have warned everyone."

"I'm sorry, Uncle Tom. We didn't want to scare everyone. There was so much happening that day. I told Ginger and Susie to keep it quiet to keep everyone calm," Kyle said, leaning against the side-by-side.

"Snaggle asked me to tell you that he wanted you to find his son Charles," Joel said, placing a hand on Kyle's shoulder.

"I'll look for Charles tomorrow. I owe it to Snaggle, and I'll see it through," Kyle vowed.

"Snaggle was a good, honest man. He didn't deserve this. I'm taking Snaggle to his family. I won't mention your part in this, but it's disappointing. You should have told us about this," Uncle Tom said. He knew Tom was deeply upset, not just about Snaggle, but about the whole situation. He sat quietly as Uncle Tom drove away with Snaggle.

"Let's head back up the mountain. I need to plan," Kyle said to Joel.

Back at the cabin, there was an unspoken tension as Joel began to recount the grim events of the roadblock. He detailed the ambush that had claimed Snaggle's life. Kyle opened up about his own harrowing involvement in the conflict with Horrace, revealing for the first time the full extent of his actions. As he spoke, his voice was steady, but the gravity of his confession weighed heavily on him.

The room fell into a stunned silence. Each person absorbed the revelation, their faces etched with a mix of disbelief and understanding. The secret that Kyle had kept hidden since the first chaotic day of their ordeal now lay bare, and the shock was obvious. While the truth had initially seemed like a betrayal, the context and urgency of the situation made the revelation more comprehensible.

"It sounds like you put us all in danger by not telling us about this," Deanna said, her eyes squinted, her anger almost seemed fake. "Maybe you should consider going to Grundy and staying that way, leave us to being safe here." Deanna added before storming out of the cabin.

Susie broke the nervous silence, her voice trembling but firm. "Kyle saved our lives that day," she said, her eyes meeting each of theirs in turn. "Without his quick thinking, we might not have made it through. We're here now because of him. Ginger and I knew the truth, but we didn't speak up because we wanted to protect everyone from the fear and panic. Kyle made a tough decision in a dire situation, and he isn't to blame for that."

Her words hung in the air, a declaration of loyalty and gratitude. The group, although still shaken, began to process the gravity of Susie's statement. The harsh light of the truth had unveiled Kyle's sacrifice, shifting the mood to a recognition of the heavy burdens they all carried. Understanding began to replace accusation, and although the pain of the revelations remained, there was a new sense of solidarity in the room, at least with those remaining in the room.

"Damn right we kept it quiet, Susie and I are just as guilty if anyone wants to put that on Kyle," Ginger added, her voice firm.

"It's going to be alright. We'll face this challenge and overcome it," Rachel reassured everyone.

Rocky reached for Kyle, placing a hand on his shoulder.

"Look over Deanna, she is just scared."

"Yeah, it's fine, no worries," Kyle said as he stood and stretched his arms upwards. "Let's just get cleaned up and get some rest."

One by one, the men trickled into the cabin's small bathroom, each taking turns to wash away the grime of the day's events. The sound of running water mingled with quiet murmurs of exhaustion. Once cleaned, they each found a spot to unwind, their bodies succumbing to the day's weariness as they settled into chairs or sprawled on makeshift beds. The cabin's dim light cast soft shadows over their faces, their breathing soon deep and rhythmic as sleep claimed them with surprising speed.

Kyle, however, remained awake a little longer. He held and watched as Coraline, full of boundless energy, played with a small doll in her hands. Her innocent laughter and curiosity were a fleeting reminder of normalcy amidst the chaos. After a few minutes, he gently set her down to rest and then made his way to the table where the remaining women were gathered.

As darkness deepened, Kyle pulled out a chair and sat down, joining them in their subdued conversation, before being joined by Rocky. The weight of the day's events hung heavily in the room, but the presence of his family offered a semblance of comfort and connection. The cabin was quiet now, except for the soft murmurs of the group and the occasional creak of the old wooden structure settling into the night.

"Arnie and I need to leave tomorrow. Snaggle asked me to find his son. It's something I have to do," Kyle said, scanning the faces around the table.

"Kyle, I understand you feel obligated, and I think you should," Deanna said, never one to shy away from sharing her opinions.

"I know, Deanna. Snaggle gave his life helping us. I feel I

owe it to him. Just keep things running here, keep the girls calm, and lock the main gate. We're leaving at six in the morning. Allow us twenty-four hours; we might have to move slowly. We'll also look for Stacy," Kyle said, noting the concern on their faces.

"I don't think you should, I'll leave it at that," Rocky spoke up, drawing a look of trouble from Deanna.

"If Langston plans to return, he'll likely get better equipped first. That could take time since he knows we'll be on high alert now," Kyle added.

"I want to know Stacy and the baby are safe. I also know Arnie looks up to you and will do anything you need. Just keep him out of trouble," Ginger said, placing her face in her hands.

"I promise to keep Arnie safe. He's a great shot and can provide backup from a distance," Kyle said, offering Ginger a comforting touch.

As they accepted Kyle's decision, the debate ceased. They discussed their plans for the next day, focusing on necessary supplies like food, first aid, and books. Although they had plenty, they planned to grab more whenever possible.

Ginger, looking for a way to slow her mind from racing, stood at Kyle's bookcase. She noticed the books Kyle had and asked, "Who is Franklin Horton? He wrote a lot of these."

"He's one of my favorite authors. You'll enjoy his Locker Nine series," Kyle replied, handing her the first book. "They're not romance novels, they can be quite intense. I also have some do-it-yourself books on gardening, canning, and construction if you need something more calming."

Kyle packed go-bags for Arnie and himself with essentials: water, protein snacks, MREs, bandages, gauze pads, and extra flashlights and ammo. He and Arnie headed to the bunkhouse for some rest, anticipating a long day ahead.

"Wake up, little man. It's time to go," Kyle said, shaking

Arnie awake.

"Oh crap, is it already time?" Arnie groaned, sitting up and rubbing his eyes. "How do you old folks get up so easily?"

"I'll show you old folks. You don't want me dragging you through the pig pen before we leave," Kyle joked, chuckling. "Yes, it's time. There are clean pants, two shirts, and your boots. Coffee's ready in the thermos. I'll be at the cabin when you're set."

Kyle made his way to the cabin, his steps heavy with the weight of the day's events. The kitchen light spilled out as he opened the door, casting a warm glow in the morning air. Inside, Rachel and Ginger were busy with last-minute preparations, their movements reflecting a mixture of anxiety and determination.

Rachel turned as he entered, her face illuminated by the soft light. Her smile was both warm and bittersweet, the lines of worry etched clearly despite her attempt at cheerfulness. "We're not crying," she said, her voice slightly wavering. "We're just hoping you stay safe and bring us back something nice."

Arnie followed closely behind, his face set with a smile of determination. He wrapped his arms around both Ginger and Rachel, pulling them into a heartfelt embrace. "I love you both," he said, his voice thick with emotion.

Ginger's voice cracked as she spoke, "You have twenty-four hours before we come looking. I love you both so much." Her arms lingered in an embrace, unwilling to let go just yet.

Susie, her eyes reflecting both pride and fear, offered a small but sincere smile. She held Kyle and Arnie tightly, her arms encircling them in a protective hug. "We love you too. Be careful out there," she said softly.

As the emotional farewells continued, the living room became a gathering of shared concern and support. Everyone had come together to offer their best wishes and heartfelt goodbyes, the cabin thick with unspoken fears that this might be their last moments together. Hugs were exchanged, each one a mixture of comfort and desperation, as Kyle and Arnie prepared to leave.

Rocky approached, his expression serious but filled with unspoken affection. He clasped Kyle's hands firmly, his grip a physical promise of support. "I need to work with the horses a few days," Rocky said, his voice steady. "Don't make me come looking for you boys. Get back and help me with the work."

Coraline, still rubbing the sleep from her eyes, looked up at Kyle with a mixture of concern and hope. "Be careful, Uncle Kyle," she said, her small voice trembling with emotion. "I love you. And if you find any goats, bring them back. And maybe a slime licker too, if you can find one. And bring Clara Beth one as well."

With the final goodbyes said and the weight of their expectations heavy in the air, Kyle and Arnie made their way outside. The ATV was loaded and ready, the engine's hum a low promise of their return. Despite the uncertainty of their journey, the support and love of those they left behind fortified their mission.

CHAPTER FORTY-FOUR

"Beyond the Barricades"

The early morning darkness cloaked Kyle, Arnie, and Joel as they descended the mountain. Joel expertly maneuvered through the winding paths, leading them to the base where Kyle's truck was parked, hidden with the trees. Arnie and Joel had disguised it with a makeshift camouflage paint job, and as they removed the netting, Kyle's was pleasantly surprised at their work. The truck, his trusted companion, now bore a coat of homemade paint that altered its familiar appearance. Though the change was needed, not wanted, he had to admit the job was impressive.

They quickly loaded their gear into the truck, refueled, and stowed extra gas cans in the back. Kyle turned to Joel, his expression serious.

"Joel, make sure everyone's okay if we don't come back," he said, his voice heavy with unspoken worries.

Joel clasped his shoulder. "Let's keep it simple. I'll handle things until you guys return," he replied, his tone solid. With a firm hug, he did the same with Arnie, watching as they climbed into the truck.

Kyle and Arnie sped away, passing the roadblock where they briefed the guards on their plan. As they drove down Hurley Road toward town, the morning light revealed a scene of devastation. The Creekside Convenience store, once bustling with life, lay in ruins, its shattered windows and overturned shelves a testament to the chaos that had unfolded.

They continued into town, the devastation growing more pronounced. Burnt-out vehicles and vandalized storefronts painted a grim picture. The pawn shop, its charred remains barely visible in the dim light, hinted at a fire that had consumed it.

The grocery store's parking lot was a mess of abandoned buggies, trash, and derelict cars. Steering through the maze of obstacles, Kyle and Arnie passed the school. Flickering lights inside suggested it had become an emergency shelter, its once welcoming halls now dimly lit by lanterns or candles.

As Kyle and Arnie navigated their way to Slate Creek Road, the landscape grew more chaotic. They soon came upon a makeshift roadblock that spanned the road. Three men, their faces shadowed by the brim of their hats and the flickering flames from barrels nearby, stood watch. The barrels, crudely fashioned from fifty-five-gallon drums, held roaring fires that crackled and popped, sending occasional sparks into the early morning darkness. The fires cast a sinister, uneven light, creating a dance of shifting shadows on the asphalt.

The roadblock itself was a haphazard arrangement of debris and scrap metal. A rusted movable gate, mounted on wheels and painted with bold stop signs on the front and back, blocked their path. The gate swung lazily, its chains clinking softly.

One of the men, clad in a tattered military jacket and gripping a rifle with a white-knuckled hand, stepped forward as Kyle's truck approached. The man's eyes were hidden behind sunglasses, but his posture was rigid, a clear sign of authority. The other two men, positioned on either side of the gate, kept their weapons trained on the approaching vehicle, their expressions unreadable. The scene was a stark reminder of the new world's harsh realities, where even basic travel required confronting armed strangers and their crude fortifications.

"We're headed to the hospital," Kyle announced as he approached the guards.

"The hospital can't take you. Turn around," one guard replied, gesturing to the truck.

"We're not seeking medical help. I'm a former Navy corpsman offering assistance," Kyle said, fabricating his credentials in hopes of gaining entry.

The guard studied him for a moment, then nodded. "Alright, go ahead. They could use the help. No power, though. Stay safe," he instructed, signaling his colleagues to open the gate.

"Nice lie, Kyle. How'd you know that would work?" Arnie asked, chuckling as they drove past the checkpoint.

Kyle shrugged. "Most people in need will accept help. It's a safe bet."

As they neared the nursing home, Kyle slowed the truck and pulled into the parking lot. "This place was already in bad shape. I'd be surprised if there's anyone alive," he commented to Arnie.

The nursing home stood in darkness, the air thick with a foul stench. Kyle pulled his face covering over his nose, but it did little to block out the odor. The early morning sunlight began to filter through the windows, casting an eerie glow on the scene. Evidence of drug use—spoons, tin foil, syringes—littered the floor. The medical supply room had been stripped bare.

Determined to find something useful, Kyle made his way to the kitchen. The stench grew more unbearable. Many doors along the corridor were closed, and he was reluctant to open them for fear of encountering danger.

Just as he was about to enter the cafeteria, a messy woman in her thirties, looking far older, emerged. Her skinny frame and vacant expression revealed her dependence on drugs.

"Who are you?" she asked, eyeing him with a mix of curiosity and suspicion. "You moving in? Got any pills? Need a girlfriend?"

"I'm with FEMA. I'm here to assess the supplies so we know what to send," Kyle blurted, hoping his lie would be convincing.

"Great. We're out of pop and snacks. The pantry's through that door. Don't open the big silver one; that's where the bodies are stored. It smells terrible," she said, pointing toward the kitchen.

"Bodies?" Kyle echoed, his stomach churning.

"Yeah, all the old folks who didn't make it. There might be some alive in their rooms, but I doubt it," she replied, rubbing her hand absently on her face. "I'm heading back to bed. Don't forget the candy."

Kyle watched as she shuffled away, then quickly moved into the kitchen. The silver door she mentioned was unmistakably a walk-in cooler, and the stench emanating from it was overpowering. Ignoring it, he focused on the pantry. Despite his reluctance, he considered the possibility that there might be survivors who needed the food more than he did. But the thought of scavenging under these circumstances left him conflicted. He grabbed nothing and stepped back outside, breathing in the fresh air.

Back at the truck, Arnie greeted him with a grimace. "Man, what's that smell? You reek."

"It's a place of pure death. Nothing salvageable. Let's just head to the hospital and find Charles. We've got to do this for Snaggle," Kyle replied.

As they drove away, the weight of their mission pressed heavily on their shoulders.

CHAPTER FORTY-FIVE

"Letters and Labor"

As the first rays of sunlight began to crest the horizon, Rachel stood on the cabin porch, her gaze fixed on the mountain trails. Joel approached, carrying a folded letter. He handed it to Rachel, his expression a mix of seriousness and sympathy. "Kyle left this in the bunkhouse," he said quietly.

Rachel accepted the letter, her fingers trembling slightly as she turned it over. The only mark on the outside was the single word "Family" scrawled in Kyle's familiar handwriting. Feeling the weight of what it might contain, Rachel hesitated before heading inside.

Deanna sat at the table with Rocky. Rachel called for Ginger and Susie to join them, and soon they were all gathered around the table, the letter a silent question in the center.

"Kyle left this for us in the bunkhouse," Rachel said, her voice wavering. "I can't handle a goodbye letter if that's what it is. I need you to read it, Deanna."

Deanna took the letter from Rachel's outstretched hand, unfolding it carefully. Her eyes scanned the words as she began to read aloud:

"Somebody tell Mom to stop crying. It's not my going-away letter. It's a work list you all need to get started on today. I fully intend to be back no later than tomorrow morning. There's plenty of food that will last a long time, but you need to be able to defend it. Take shifts today with someone in the watchtower overlooking the main trail—Arnie calls it Tower One. I don't expect trouble, but don't take it for granted. Shoot to kill."

Deanna paused, handing the letter to Rocky. He continued reading, his voice steady:

"Have the guys go off the mountain and get with Uncle Tom. The trail road will need to be blasted in at least two more places. Have Uncle Tom help find suitable spots where you can make access routes that aren't easily visible. Avoid muddy areas; make sure the ground is firm to leave no tracks."

Rocky glanced at Joel. "That's a good idea. We don't want anyone getting to us easily."

Rocky handed the letter to Susie to finish. She cleared her throat and read the final instructions:

"When the girls are fully awake, tell them Arnie and I had to run some errands. Have them take care of the animals today. Susie and Ginger, get in some target practice—work on being smooth. Smooth is fast." They all repeated the last three words together, a mantra they had heard from Kyle many times. "Tell Mom I'll need a cup of coffee first thing tomorrow morning. Go about your business as usual today. Don't spend all day watching the trail for us. Stay safe, and we'll see you soon. We love you."

Susie folded the letter back up, and the room fell into thoughtful silence. Despite the necessity of the measures Kyle outlined, the sense of unease was intense. They knew the importance of staying vigilant but struggled with the reality of it.

Deanna took the powdered milk and mixed it with water, creating a makeshift milk for the girls' cereal. The girls grimaced at the taste, but they knew it would sweeten as the cereal softened. Ginger heated water for instant oatmeal, adding dehydrated blueberries to it.

Outside, Joel and Rocky performed a thorough walk-around of the fence line, checking for any weak spots or damage. They inspected the watchtowers and checked on the animals. The sun was already casting a fierce heat, making their chores more demanding. They filled the gas tank on the ATV and readied it for the trip to Uncle Tom's.

"Look over there," Joel said, pointing toward the edge of the fence. "See that big buck standing outside?"

Rocky squinted in the direction Joel indicated. "Yeah, I see it. Never shot a deer before. Not sure what I'd do with it if I did."

"I haven't shot one either," Joel admitted. "We'll definitely need Kyle and Arnie back to teach us how to hunt and process game."

The buck, sensing their presence, bounded off into the trees, disappearing down the trail.

Back inside, Coraline frowned at her cereal. "This milk tastes awful!" she complained. "I need different milk. I've got work to do today. I need to be fed!"

The table erupted in laughter at Coraline's dramatic declaration.

"Well, a hard worker like you does need to be fed," Mamaw Rachel said with a smile. "What would you like this morning?"

"Sausage McMuffin," Coraline replied with a cheeky grin.

Rachel chuckled. "There's no McDonald's on this mountain, sweetheart. How about pancakes instead?"

"Okay, I'll settle for a stupid pancake. But make me two! It's going to be a tough day," Coraline said, taking another bite of her cereal and scrunching her face in disgust.

"There's nothing wrong with that cereal. Quit being a brat," Clara Beth chimed in, finishing her own breakfast.

"Mommy! Tell Clara I'm not a brat. I'm just a hungry farmer," Coraline retorted, glaring at Clara Beth across the table.

"Well, I think the cereal is fine. I'm going to play with the rabbits," Clara Beth said, slipping on her shoes and skipping out onto the porch.

"Her and those damn rabbits," Coraline muttered, not realizing she had spoken aloud.

"Coraline!" Deanna called out as she approached the table. But Coraline was already up and darting outside before Deanna could reach her.

"Lord!" Rachel exclaimed, shaking her head. "The mouth on that child." Ginger and Susie's laughter was infectious, spreading through the room and lifting everyone's spirits.

Rachel turned to the others with a thoughtful expression. "We've got to think about shoes and clothing. The girls are going to outgrow their shoes soon. How are we going to get more?"

"That's a good point, Mom," Ginger said. "We might need to plan a run to loot a store like JC Penney at some point," she said laughingly at her remark.

Meanwhile, Joel and Rocky set off for Uncle Tom's place, the ATV rumbling steadily down the mountain trail. The morning sun was already climbing higher, casting heat waves across the landscape. As they drove, the dense forest gave way to an open meadow, leading them to a serene pond nestled in a small clearing.

They parked the ATV on the edge of the pond and stepped out, the air thickening with the rising heat. The surface of the pond was a shimmering expanse of blue, interrupted only by the occasional ripple as fish darted beneath. The surrounding trees created a natural canopy, their leaves rustling gently in the light breeze.

Joel scanned the water with a practiced eye, spotting several fish gliding lazily through the pond's depths. The fish were well-fed and healthy, their scales glinting in the sunlight as they moved. The sight of them stirred a primal hunger in Joel, who could almost imagine the rich, succulent flavor of a fresh fish dinner.

Rocky, equally mesmerized by the scene, broke the silence. "Man, look at those fish. They'd make for a fantastic meal."

Joel nodded, his gaze lingering on the pond. "Yeah, they would. A nice change from our usual rations."

Despite the tempting prospect, both men knew that their mission took precedence. The reality of their situation loomed over them, reminding them that there was important work to be done.

Joel pulled his gaze away from the pond, turning to Rocky with a determined expression. "We've got to stay focused. Let's get to Uncle Tom's place and take care of what needs to be done."

Rocky agreed, casting one last longing look at the pond before they climbed back onto the ATV. The hum of the engine resumed as they continued their journey, leaving the peaceful pond behind.

As they approached, Uncle Tom was already hard at work, his figure outlined against the backdrop of the trail where he was setting up new metal posts. The scene was a stark contrast to the quiet pond, underscoring the urgency of their task. Joel and Rocky dismounted the ATV and approached Uncle Tom, ready to tackle the day's work with renewed focus.

"Morning, Uncle Tom," Joel greeted him. "You're starting early. What are you working on?"

"I'm putting up some new posts and steel cable to create another gate," Uncle Tom replied, wiping sweat from his brow. "It'll slow anyone down trying to come up the mountain. Needed to keep busy, clear my head."

Joel picked up a bag of concrete and began pouring it into a freshly dug hole, the weight of the heavy bag taking all his strength to control. "Kyle wanted us to get your help with the trail.

He wants to blast a few more spots and create secret pathways around them. He said you'd know the best locations."

Uncle Tom looked up, his eyes weary but determined. "Where's Kyle and Arnie?"

"They went to the hospital to look for Charles. Left early this morning," Joel explained.

"I wanted to talk to Kyle before he left. I was too hard on him yesterday," Uncle Tom admitted, his voice filled with regret.

"He understands, Uncle Tom. He knows you were upset, but he's been beating himself up enough over Snaggle. No one can make it any worse," Joel reassured him.

"I need to tell him it wasn't his fault. He was ahead of the rest of us with all this," Uncle Tom said. "I'll get some dynamite sticks and the chainsaw. We'll get this done."

Despite his fatigue, Uncle Tom's determination was unshakable. He would work tirelessly, unwilling to give up until the job was complete.

CHAPTER FORTY-SIX

"Ruthless Alliances"

Miran Tate stood in the entrance of the garage, sweat staining the armpits of his shirt as the early morning sun turned the space into a sweltering oven. He took a long drag from his cigar, the pungent smoke mingling with the smell of gasoline and oil. The small desk fan beside him whirred ineffectively, its breeze barely cutting through the heat. Tate poured a splash of water onto a rag and dabbed it across his forehead, trying to cool down. Leaning back in his creaking office chair, he closed his eyes and took a few thoughtful puffs from the cigar.

Langston entered, his expression tight with frustration. He flopped down on the worn-out couch next to Tate's desk, his face lined with worry. "We need to talk about Horrace. The guy's out of control."

Tate kept his eyes shut, enjoying the fleeting relief from the fan. "Tell me what happened yesterday. I didn't bother asking the others; I just sent them home."

Langston sighed deeply, his irritation evident. "Horrace was a loose cannon. We tried to negotiate our way through the roadblock they set up. I was about to come up with a new strategy when he just lost it."

"Lost it how?" Tate asked, finally opening his eyes to gaze at Langston, the flicker of the fan's light sending ripples of dark shades across his face.

Langston rubbed his temple. "He jumped out of the car and started firing on them. I don't know if he hit anyone, but the guards returned fire. That's how the light bar on the cruiser got broken."

Tate's brow furrowed as he absorbed the information. "So the situation's deteriorating. This isn't just some random guy on the road; it's a whole community banding together."

Langston nodded. "Exactly. They're organized, and we're at a disadvantage. Even if we get past the roadblock, we still need to navigate through the mountain. We need a solid plan and a lot more manpower."

Tate leaned back, his eyes narrowing as he considered the problem. "Can we shoot our way in?"

Langston shook his head. "That's too risky. Even if we break through, we'll still be lost once we're inside. We need a foolproof strategy and a large force to pull it off."

"Alright, start recruiting an army then," Tate said decisively. "Offer food, supplies—whatever it takes to get people on board. We need better intel before we make another move."

Langston nodded, already pulling out his phone despite the lack of signal, his contacts were listed. "I can work on that. But what about Horrace?"

Tate's gaze hardened. "Let me handle him. He's got issues with authority. I might be able to rein him in better than anyone else."

Langston's pen scratched furiously across the notepad as he began jotting down names and ideas. The pages were already filled with hastily scribbled notes, phone numbers, and potential contacts. His eyes darted between the list and Tate, seeking affirmation.

"I'll start reaching out to potential recruits," Langston said, his voice shaded with a mix of determination and urgency.

"There's a group causing quite a stir in the Grundy area, going by, Blaze's Angels. They've been making a mess on Route 460—raiding, looting, and generally wreaking havoc."

Tate's interest piqued. He leaned forward, his large frame blocking out the light in the dim garage. His eyes, sharp and calculating, fixed on Langston. "Blaze's Angels, you say? I've heard rumors about them. They've been moving from Grundy toward the Kentucky line, right?"

Langston nodded, his pen pausing mid-air as he considered the implications. "That's right. They're known for their brutality and have been stirring up trouble wherever they go. If we can make contact with them, there's a chance we can form an alliance. They're already causing chaos, so they might be receptive to joining forces with us."

Tate's expression shifted to one of intense focus. He rubbed his chin thoughtfully. "That's a promising lead. If they're already on a rampage, they could be a valuable asset. We need to leverage their aggression and create a formidable force."

Langston's eyes narrowed as he wrote down the details. "Exactly. If we can get them on our side, it'll bolster our position significantly. But we need to approach them carefully. They're unpredictable and might not be easy to control."

Tate's gaze hardened, his mind clearly working through the ramifications. "True. But we can use their unpredictability to our advantage. If we make an example out of those who defy us, it'll send a strong message to the rest. They'll see that we're not to be trifled with."

Langston looked up, his expression serious. "You're thinking of making a few examples?"

Tate nodded slowly, a cold smile curling on his lips. "Exactly. Show the community that defiance has consequences. We'll need to demonstrate our strength decisively. If Blaze's

Angels are as ruthless as they say, they'll understand the necessity of our actions."

Langston finished his notes and folded the notepad, his mind already racing with strategies and potential alliances. "I'll reach out to them and see if we can arrange a meeting. If they're willing to work with us, it could turn the tide in our favor."

Tate's eyes gleamed with approval. "Good. Keep me posted on any developments. We need to be ready to act swiftly. The sooner we consolidate power and show our dominance, the sooner we can control the narrative."

Langston nodded, understanding the weight of the task ahead. He left the garage with a renewed sense of purpose, ready to navigate the treacherous landscape of alliances and power plays. Meanwhile, Tate remained seated, the hum of the fan a faint backdrop to his thoughts, already plotting the next moves in a high-stakes game of control and domination.

CHAPTER FORTY-SEVEN
"Candles in the Corridor"

The sun had risen high, Kyle and Arnie drove across the bridge into the hospital parking lot. The once bustling area was now eerily quiet, littered with abandoned cars and debris. Kyle considered whether he should stop at the YMCA next to the hospital to search for supplies. The building bore the telltale signs of early use as a shelter—broken windows, makeshift barricades, and scattered belongings. Surveying the trash-filled parking lot, he assumed any useful supplies had long been scavenged.

He thought about Charles and the mission he was on. Until he found Charles, he couldn't afford unnecessary stops. The nursing home could have gone much worse than just a horrible smell. He had to stay focused. They drove to the backside of the hospital near the emergency room entrance. It was calm and quiet; no one seemed to be around. Only someone that appeared to be sleeping by the door of the entrance. Kyle parked the truck in front of the doctors' offices in a nearby building.

"Okay, little man. We're going to go in through the emergency room. We'll play this by ear. If it gets hairy, we get back out. If we get separated, head back to the truck," Kyle said, pulling the charging handle on his AR and loading a cartridge.

"I'll let you lead and stay right behind you," Arnie said, mirroring Kyle's actions with his own AR. They got out of the truck, the crunch of broken glass beneath their boots the only sound in the stillness. The parking lot was filled with vandalized cars, their windows shattered and doors ajar. As they moved closer to the entrance, it became clear that the figure by the door wasn't sleeping. Two dead bodies lay slumped over each other, partially covered by a sheet, their lifeless forms a morbid image in the harsh daylight.

Kyle manually slid the doors apart since there was no power. Inside, an eerie atmosphere settled over them. The corridor leading to the patient examination rooms was dimly lit by candles, their flickering flames casting a ghostly dance on the walls. The admissions desk was unattended, and the waiting room was empty except for some blood-stained sheets and towels scattered on the floor.

"It looks deserted," Arnie whispered.

"Someone is here. These candles didn't light themselves," Kyle whispered to Arnie as they cautiously moved down the hall. "Keep your eyes peeled."

"May I help you?" a woman's voice called out from an open doorway. She cautiously kept her body inside the room, only peeking out with her head. "You can't have those guns in here," she said, eyeing their rifles.

"We're not here for trouble. We mean no harm, just looking for someone. We want to leave as badly as you want us out of here. My name is Ted; this is Jamie," Kyle lied, not wanting to reveal their real names as he walked closer to the woman. They remained several doors apart, making it difficult to get a clear look at her.

"Well, Ted, what can I do for you then?" she asked, stepping slowly out of the room and moving a bit closer. Kyle was charmed by her voice. She seemed close to his age, maybe a little younger. Her black hair hung from underneath her hat. Her voice was soft but carried a hint of exhaustion.

"I'm looking for a guy named Charles. He works here," Kyle said, offering her a bottle of water from his pack.

"Thank you. That's very gentlemanly of you, but I'm okay. We have water here. How do you know Charles?" she asked. Arnie stood, bouncing his eyes back and forth between Kyle and the woman as they inched closer.

"He is the son of a friend. I promised to look for him. He hasn't been home in a couple of days," Kyle explained.

"I'm sorry to be the one to tell you this, Kyle, but Charles was killed. We had an argument here two, maybe three days ago. Charles tried to calm the situation, and a man shot him multiple times. We tried to save him, but we had no power and no surgeons. He was badly injured; I promise you we tried. It was fast; he suffered very little, if at all," she said as Kyle tried to see her face better in the dim light.

"Wait, you called me Kyle. You know who I am?" he asked, stepping closer to see her better. "Oh my, no way."

"Your name isn't Ted. Kyle Blaine, I know exactly who you are. Do you think I could forget that voice?" she said with a slight smile. "It's good to see a familiar face, even after all this time."

"April! Is that really you?" Kyle said, a smile spreading across his face.

"It's me. It's been a long time, but I haven't forgotten you. How could I after you left me the way you did?" April said, smiling and sighing simultaneously.

"April, I can't believe it's you. You stayed around here all these years?" Kyle asked, still smiling like a schoolboy.

"Yes, I'm still here. I moved to Wise County for a while, tried nursing school at the community college. That didn't work out. I had a bad teacher there who enjoyed seeing us fail rather than teaching us. She was only doing it for the money. I went to Wytheville next and got a degree in physical therapy," April said, smiling more now.

The sound of a plastic wrapper tearing caught their attention, and they both turned to see Arnie sitting in a chair, opening a Slim Jim. He motioned with his hand and said, "Keep going, this is getting good now. Days of Our Lives hasn't been on." He crossed his leg and leaned back, taking a bite of the beef stick. The words snapped Kyle and April out of the moment, and Kyle cleared his throat.

"Is Charles's body here? I'd like to take him back home to his family. His dad was also killed helping me. I want to get them back together for their family. Why are you here, April? The place looks deserted," Kyle asked, looking past her down the dark hall.

"Yes, he is. We moved him down to the morgue. The refrigeration isn't working, so the smell has gotten really hard to stomach. We lost four patients who were on ventilators. We have had a dozen or so brought in with gunshot wounds that passed. We just kept putting them in the morgue. The funeral home had been coming to pick up bodies, but they haven't been here in a week or so," April said, a look of sadness crossing her face at the thought of all the death.

"And what about you? Are you alone here?" Kyle asked, glancing over to see Arnie still eating the beef stick.

"We were trying to keep services going. It got down to me and one more nurse, Jenny. She was an RN. I'm not even a nurse; I'm a therapist. I'm just doing what I can to help. There hasn't been anyone coming in for treatment recently. The other nurse hasn't been back either," April said.

"Why are you staying now? This is getting bad, April. It's not safe to be here. Things are only getting worse by the day," Kyle said, unknowingly taking her hand in his.

"I have nowhere to go, Kyle. You know I only had my grandma growing up. She passed away five years ago. I tried marriage, but that didn't work out. I'm just on my own now. My car is out of gas in the parking lot. Someone cut the tires on it, so I couldn't leave even if I wanted to. I figured this was the safest place to stay," April said, holding eye contact with Kyle.

"This place will eventually be invaded by people looking for a place to stay. And not good people either. Food will run out. What then?" Kyle asked, sincere worry in his heart for her safety.

A tear slipped from April's eye and rolled down her cheek. "I don't know, Kyle. I'm trying to stay positive. There are already people staying on the upper floors. They said they were moving in whether we liked it or not. They said we could keep the emergency room open for now, but they were staying. There is just nowhere to go or no way to get there. The food is already gone from the kitchen; it's been picked through and stolen," April said, more tears sliding down her face.

"What if there was a place to go and a way to get there?

Would you go then?" Arnie spoke up, asking April as Kyle looked over at him. "Go with us. Uncle Kyle has a home built for this. It's not five-star accommodations, and the owner can be an asshole, but it's where we are staying. Uncle Kyle is single, so you don't have to worry about pissing off any woman."

"Uncle Kyle, you say. I thought maybe he was your son," April said with a grin, wiping her tears away. She realized Kyle had been holding her hand and let go.

"I'm not his son. Look at that giant and look at me. Kyle says he shits turds bigger than I am," Arnie spouted.

"Arnie! I'm going to break a foot off in your... I'm not saying it. I'm going to get murdered by your mother if you don't get that dirty mouth under control," Kyle said, shaking his fist at him. April smiled and let a small giggle slip from her mouth.

"I'm so sorry about him. And this isn't Jamie. His name is Arnie, and he is my foul-mouthed nephew. Is it okay if we get Charles's body now?" Kyle asked, trying to change the subject.

"You can, but you have to be careful. There are some shady people already staying here, and they have been lurking around the basement," April told Kyle. "Come on, I'll show you the way."

"Let's go, jackass," Kyle whispered to Arnie, smiling.

CHAPTER FORTY-EIGHT
"Echoes of the Morgue"

April led Kyle and Arnie to the stairwell entrance, the flame from her flickering candle moving to the beat of their steps on the grimy walls. The faint, unpleasant smell of mold and mildew permeated the air, a prelude to the decay awaiting them below. Kyle and Arnie unclipped their flashlights from their belts, their beams cutting through the darkness with pure efficiency. The cold, familiar weight of Kyle's AR-15, equipped with a tactical light, provided a sense of readiness. Handing his flashlight to April, he offered her a steadier, more reliable source of illumination.

Kyle took the lead, his footsteps echoing in the confined space, each one cautious and deliberate. The stairwell seemed to swallow the light, its depths unknown and menacing. April followed closely, the candlelight flickering wildly, reflecting her unmistakable anxiety in her widened eyes. Arnie, bringing up the rear, cast frequent, nervous glances over his shoulder, the sense of being watched gnawing at him.

"I really hate going down here. It's so dark and creepy," April said as she slowly pushed open the door, the rancid smell of decomposition oozing out. They all looked up, hearing a faint voice and the sound of a door closing several floors above them. They quickly aimed their lights, seeing no movement. Kyle held his position for a moment before continuing their descent.

"I told you, people are living on the upper floors now. I feel like I'm being watched constantly," April said, her hand resting on Kyle's shoulder.

"Keep moving. Let's get this done," Kyle urged.

They descended each step with measured caution. At the bottom, Kyle pushed open the door, and the full force of the stench of death and decay enveloped them. It was an overpowering, nauseating mix of bodily fluids and rot. Kyle and Arnie pulled their face coverings up, trying to filter the foul air, while April pressed a cloth from her pocket against her nose. The hallway ahead was a dark, foreboding tunnel, their flashlights casting narrow beams of light that barely penetrated the gloom.

"It's here," April said, stopping at a thick wooden door labeled "MORGUE." "Are you ready for this? It's really bad."

"Did you hear that?" Kyle said, quickly aiming his rifle down the hallway. It looked empty except for a few gurneys against the walls. The gurneys lay bare, only the stainless-steel metal showing, however, remaining ready for use.

"You're freaking me out, Uncle Kyle," Arnie said, pushing the door open. "Let's just get in here and get back out."

Inside, the morgue was a scene from a nightmare. Bodies lay on tables, covered with sheets stained with the fluids of decay. More bodies were piled haphazardly on the floor, also covered in blood-stained sheets. The heat accelerated the decomposition, filling the room with a stomach-churning stench that burned their nostrils and triggered their gag reflexes. Some of the bodies were grotesquely bloated, blood and foam oozing from their mouths and noses, forming dark, sticky puddles on the floor.

Kyle and Arnie swept their flashlights over the deathly scene, searching for Charles.

"He isn't with those. We put Charles in one of the holding vaults. He was a good man; he deserved better than being left on the floor," April said, guiding Kyle to a wall of vaults.

Kyle carefully pulled the handle, the loud click echoing ominously in the metal room. As the door opened, a fresh wave of putrid air burst forth, making Kyle bend over, gagging and struggling to keep his stomach contents down.

"Here, rub some of this under your nose," April said, handing him a small container of Vicks Vapor Rub. She dabbed some on her upper lip and passed it to Kyle.

Kyle, still coughing, did as instructed, then handed the container to Arnie. He pulled the metal bed out, the wheels screeching against the railings, the sound reverberating harshly in the room. Arnie, his nerves fraying, kept scanning the room with his light, as if expecting one of the bodies to rise and speak to him.

"Calm down, Arnie. These aren't the people we have to worry about. It's the living that concern me," April said, trying to soothe him.

Kyle fully extended the metal bed, revealing Charles's body. He picked up a black body bag and spread it open on the floor. Arnie handed out pairs of nitrile gloves. They worked gently, respectfully handling Charles's remains despite the circumstances. Each creak of the old building kept them on edge.

"You sure about this, Kyle? He looks like he's swelling," Arnie said, his face pale.

"Let's get him in the bag and zip it up," Kyle said.

They carefully placed Charles's body into the bag. April held the flashlight, the cloth still pressed against her face. Kyle grabbed the bag's strap with his left hand, his right hand holding his AR at the ready. Arnie used both hands to carry his end.

"April, open the door. I'll go first. When we get to the stairs, do the same," Kyle instructed, eager to leave the room of death.

April opened the door, and they quickly moved into the hallway. The air was thick and stale, the walls amplifying every sound. Kyle felt the hairs on his arms stand up, a cold chill running down his spine. The metallic clanging sound startled them, like a bedpan sliding across a table. His pulse quickened as he thought he heard faint laughter in the darkness. He turned his light towards the noise, the beam cutting through the blackness, but it revealed nothing but empty space and shadows.

Exhaling deeply, Kyle turned back towards the stairs just as April opened the door for him. His muscles tensed, and he gripped his rifle tighter, the anticipation gnawing at him. Suddenly, a tall figure materialized in the doorway before him, a silhouette against the dim light. The man's presence was unnerving, his face impassive, eyes fixed on Kyle. He made no move to harm them, simply standing there silently, his expression unreadable.

"Whoa!" Kyle exclaimed, almost freezing, his gun trained on the man. His senses quickly heightened as a jolt of adrenaline flooded his body with the eerie encounter.

"What? What is it?" Arnie asked, his voice quick with panic.

The man remained silent, stepping aside to let them pass. Kyle led the way up the stairs, followed by April and Arnie. As they ascended, Kyle turned his light back, ensuring the man wasn't following. April shielded her eyes from the beam, and Arnie quickly looked away. Just before they rounded the corner, Kyle took one last glance down the stairs. He saw a small child standing in the doorway by the man, waving before the door closed with a soft thud.

Once they made the turn on the stairway, Kyle refocused and moved to the door. He quickly opened it, stepping into the emergency room hallway. He gasped for air, yanking down the face covering quickly trying to inhale. The familiar yet unsettling smells of disinfectant and decay greeted them. Kyle eased the body bag down, feeling the burn in his bicep as the weight was relieved. His breaths were heavy, the tension still coursing through his body. Arnie and April took a moment to catch their breath, the dim candle lights offering a glimpse of relief in the otherwise uncomfortable hospital hall.

Kyle swept his light in both directions, seeing no one. He took several deep breaths, allowing Arnie and April time to do the same. When he felt they were ready, he picked up the bag again. They hurried toward the exit doors, stopping once the hallway brightened with sunlight.

"Have you seen those two before?" Kyle asked April.

"Seen who? Who are you talking about?" April asked, puzzled.

"The two people downstairs as we left. A man and a child," Kyle said, confused.

"We were probably in such a hurry we just didn't notice,"

April said, seeing Kyle's confusion.

"I'm just glad we got out of there. That was a creepy place," Arnie said, wiping sweat from his face, he was puzzled himself about Kyle's comment.

"I could have sworn I saw two, ah, nevermind... never mind. Let's get ready to leave," Kyle said.

"Maybe it was a ghost," Arnie said, not cracking a smile, uncharacteristically serious.

Kyle didn't mention it again, though he was confident he had seen them. He briefly considered going back to check, but the thought was short-lived. They heard voices at the other end of the hallway. Arnie was the first to look up, seeing three or four people watching them. He quickly raised his weapon, locking onto a man in front.

"You can't be back there. This area is for patients only," April said, her voice soft yet firm.

"Says who?" a man shouted back, a pistol at his side.

"Please, that was the agreement. This area is for patients only," April insisted.

"For now, it will be," the man shouted, motioning the others to move on. "We'll be back, see you soon sweet thing." They turned and disappeared down another corridor.

CHAPTER FORTY-NINE

"Raiders of the Fallen"

Route 460, once the bustling artery of Grundy, now lay empty and deserted, a stark testament to the ravages of time and chaos. The road, a vital conduit stretching from the vibrant towns of Pikeville, Kentucky, to the distant reaches of Suffolk, Virginia, had once pulsed with life and purpose. The highway, once filled with the roar of engines and the flow of commerce, was now an empty pathway to nowhere. Scattered with abandoned vehicles that stood as silent witnesses to a time before. These forsaken cars, many with their windows shattered, lined the roadside like skeletal remains. Dust and debris swirled in the occasional gust of wind, a visual echo of the emptiness that encompassed the area.

The scarcity of fuel had rendered travel a distant, almost impossible goal. Gas stations, once bustling with activity, now stood empty, their pumps dry and their lights out. The few remaining vehicles, if any, were left with their tanks running on empty as their owners struggled to find even the barest essentials.

For the residents of Grundy and other communities ravaged by the collapse of society, survival was an unrelenting battle. Every day was a struggle, a dangerous balance between finding food and water and defending against the ever-present threat of criminals. The constant vigilance had become a way of life, as people lived in the shadow of fear and uncertainty, their once-comfortable homes now fortresses against an unpredictable world. The once-familiar landscape of Route 460 had transformed into a bleak, haunting reminder of what had been lost.

In the early days of the attack, chaos had unfurled like a storm across the land, sweeping through towns and leaving devastation in its wake. As the social fabric unraveled, thieves descended with a voracious appetite, stripping businesses and homes bare. The elderly, isolated and vulnerable, found themselves at the mercy of these predatory scavengers. Among the chaos, Blaze's Angels emerged—a gang whose predatory instincts had been ignited by the breakdown of order.

Initially, Blaze's Angels' crimes were petty but insidious. Their early heists involved pilfering lawn mowers, power tools, and jugs of gasoline—items that seemed inconsequential compared to what was to come. Their audacious thefts, though minor, set the tone for the escalating violence that would soon follow.

As days passed, the Angels' criminal activities grew bolder and more brutal. Their petty thefts evolved into full-blown home invasions, marked by terrifying acts of violence and cruelty. Unchecked by law enforcement, their audacity turned into a reign of terror. They operated in groups of three to five normally, striking swiftly and ruthlessly. Each attack was meticulously planned, with members of the gang assigned specific roles: some would force entry, others would subdue and terrorize the occupants, and a few would ransack the premises for valuables.

The transformation from ordinary criminals to monstrous predators was swift and alarming. The Angels' brutal tactics continued to escalate, although they weren't experts yet. Their crimes included arson and assault. Blaze's Angels didn't just steal—they burned. They set fire to houses after robbing them, leaving behind charred remains and a trail of destruction. The flames were not just a means to cover their tracks but a chilling statement of their dominance and disregard for human life.

Their assaults were often accompanied by extreme violence. Anyone who resisted was met with brutal force. Stories emerged of homeowners being beaten with blunt objects or even shot in cold blood. The brutality was a tool of intimidation, ensuring that the Angels' victims would not dare to confront them.

The Angels took a sadistic pleasure in psychological

torment. They would often leave taunting notes or graffiti on the walls of the homes they robbed, mocking their victims and further deepening the sense of helplessness and fear within the community.

The presence of Blaze's Angels was a relentless nightmare for the residents. The fear they instilled was evident, with communities living in constant terror of the next attack. The once-safe confines of homes became virtual prisons, with families barricading themselves in an attempt to avoid the gang's brutal reach. The Angels' reign of terror was a stark reminder of how quickly the appearance of civilization could be stripped away, revealing the raw and savage instincts lurking beneath.

"Hey Blaze, we need to head up to Popular Creek and see what those wealthy folks have stashed. I bet we'll find some real treasures up there," JD suggested, his voice dripping with greedy anticipation. His eyes gleamed with a predatory glint as he spoke, envisioning the riches that might await them.

Blaze Stiltner, a man whose name was synonymous with fear and evil in the area, had once been known as Ellis Stiltner. The name Blaze, however, had become a part of him, a remnant of his dark past. In his coal mining days, the mines were his personal "pit of hell," a place where he felt he was the devil's gatekeeper. He liked to boast that he controlled the fiery blaze of hell with the coal mined, a story so deeply ingrained that it became his nickname. The name Blaze stuck, even after he had orchestrated a back injury to claim disability benefits—a deceit that only added to his reputation for manipulation and greed.

Blaze's imposing figure was a stark contrast to the dim, dilapidated setting they were in. His rugged face, marked by a lifetime of rough living, bore scars that told tales of countless confrontations. His eyes, cold and calculating, flickered with the promise of violence as he contemplated JD's suggestion. The remnants of his coal-stained past were evident in the grit and grime that seemed to cling to him, adding to the appearance of danger that surrounded him.

"Sounds like a plan, JD, but we got to be careful. A lot of

those folks got money, and that means weapons," Blaze replied, his voice a gravelly rumble that seemed to echo with the weight of his past transgressions. He glanced over at his son, Jacoby, who was aimlessly shooting hoops by the garage—a waste of time in the eyes of Blaze. The game was a fleeting escape for Jacoby from the grim reality of their existence.

"Jacoby, put that ball down. I told you, it's time to grow up and contribute. Get your shotgun and get ready—we're heading out on a search," Blaze barked, his tone tolerating no argument. The command was delivered with an authority that was both feared and begrudgingly obeyed.

Jacoby, visibly intimidated by his father's harsh demeanor, dropped the ball and hurried to comply. The once-innocent game of basketball was now a mere distraction from the harsh lessons of survival that Blaze imposed. As the boy retrieved his shotgun, the weight of his father's expectations hung heavy on him.

Blaze's gang, a ragtag group of individuals bound by their shared lust for power and wealth, had become a force of terror in the region. Their exploits were not merely criminal—they were acts of deliberate cruelty and intimidation. The gang's reputation was built on a foundation of fear, with Blaze at the helm, orchestrating their reign of terror with a ruthless efficiency that left a scar on the community.

"Hey Dad, maybe I should stay and help Mom. She could use an extra hand," Jacoby suggested, returning from the house with a hint of reluctance.

"What are you, a fairy boy? You'd rather stay here, doing dishes and cooking, than go with the men and earn your keep? If you can't handle it, maybe we'd be better off without you," Blaze sneered, delivering a sharp smack to the back of Jacoby's head as he walked by.

"We can manage this one without him, Blaze. If he's not ready, let him stay," Peanut suggested, his tone cautious.

A loud slap echoed as Blaze spun Peanut around, his rage unmistakable. "Don't ever question me in front of my son or anyone else. You understand? Or there will be one less mouth to feed," Blaze growled, grabbing Peanut by the shirt and pulling him close.

"I'm sorry, Blaze. I didn't mean anything by it," Peanut stammered, fear evident in his eyes.

"Let's get going. Jacoby, get in the truck," Blaze said, his anger momentarily subsiding. Jacoby, wanting to avoid further conflict, quickly joined Peanut in the truck's bed.

"I'm sorry about that, Peanut. Dad can be rough, and I don't want him taking it out on you," Jacoby said, his voice filled with concern as he patted Peanut's arm.

"Let's get out there and see what we can find," Blaze said as he climbed into the driver's seat, starting the truck with a rumbling roar. The vehicle jolted forward, leaving behind a wake of dust and despair as they drove off into the fading light.

CHAPTER FIFTY
"Unbroken Ties"

"We need to get Charles into the truck. April, you're welcome to come with us. This isn't a safe place to be by yourself," Kyle said, his voice laden with genuine concern. April, standing in the dimly lit hallway of the hospital, clutched her hands tightly on her hips, her gaze fixed on the worn tiles beneath her feet. The offer, though made in the midst of a crisis, felt like a bittersweet echo of the past—a past where she had hoped for an invitation like this, but never received it.

"I can't go with you, Kyle. You take care of yourself," April replied, her voice trembling with a mixture of resignation and old wounds. Her heart ached with an emotional exhaustion that went beyond the physical strain of her situation. The invitation, while appreciated, seemed tainted by the passage of time and the weight of his guilt. She wanted to feel Kyle's comforting embrace, to be enveloped in a sense of security that had eluded her for so long. But now, accepting his sympathy felt like a bridge too far.

"It's not safe here, April. Please, come with us," Kyle urged, his eyes scanning the shadowy hallway with unease. His voice carried a note of desperation, the kind of sincerity that spoke of past regrets and unspoken emotions.

"Yeah, April, come on and go with us. We have shelter, food, and security," Arnie added, his tone supportive but urgent.

April shook her head slowly, a single tear escaping down her cheek despite her best efforts to remain composed. "I'm sorry, Kyle. I need to stay here. I'm really glad I got to see you again."

Her heart was heavy with the weight of this unexpected reunion, her emotions tangled in a web of nostalgia and longing.

Kyle's gaze fell to the floor, his frustration evident in the tightening of his jaw. "Okay, April. I can't make you go. Please get out soon and keep yourself safe. You can keep my weapon; it's easy to use." He removed the sling from his neck and placed the rifle on the counter, along with two fully loaded magazines. The gesture was more than practical; it was a token of his lingering care and concern.

"Let's go, Arnie. Grab the bag strap; we need to move," Kyle said, his voice stubborn but mixed with an undercurrent of regret as he lifted his end of the body bag containing Charles's remains.

"Goodbye, April," Kyle said softly, the words heavy with unspoken emotion, a farewell that was more than just a departure.

"It was good meeting you, April. I hope you stay alive," Arnie said with a grunt, struggling under the weight of the body bag.

"Goodbye, Arnie. I hope you stay alive as well," April replied, her smile wavering with the strain of the situation. The moment felt surreal, the stakes higher than they had ever been.

As Kyle and Arnie moved across the parking lot, the weight of Charles's body bag seemed to drag at Kyle's heart. He opened the rear hatch of his camper top and lowered the tailgate, shuffling items to make room. The hot metal of the tailgate seemed to echo the heat of his decision. With the tailgate closed and the engine running, Kyle's thoughts were troubled. He pulled onto the bridge and stopped before turning onto Route 460, his mind racing with what-ifs.

"Are you really going to drive away and leave her, dude? I don't know what I was seeing, but I saw something in that darkness," Arnie's voice broke through Kyle's trance.

"I tried, Arnie. She's an old friend from school. I can't make her go," Kyle said, his voice strained with the weight of past regrets and current desperation.

"The hell you can't. Hogtie her, throw her in the back like

the old Western days. Or maybe you just ask again. She needs us, Uncle Kyle. You heard what she said. She has nobody except for the creeps starting to stay there." Arnie's eyes were intense, reflecting his concern and the unspoken bond he saw between Kyle and April. "This will be the first time I've seen you give up, and it's probably the one time you shouldn't."

Kyle gripped the steering wheel tightly, his knuckles white. The weight of Arnie's words pressed heavily on him. With a deep breath, he reversed the truck, the tires crunching against the loose pieces of pavement as he backed off the bridge. He sped back to the emergency room, his heart pounding in his chest.

"Stay here and keep your eyes peeled, Arnie. I'm going to give it one more shot. If she doesn't want to go, then that's it," Kyle said, his voice a mix of determination and anxiety.

Kyle ran back into the hospital, the eeriness of the empty emergency room amplifying his sense of dread. The weapon he had left for April remained, a stark reminder of the danger. As he walked past the reception counter, the sound of muffled sobs led him to a room ahead. He hesitated before peering inside, finding April seated in a chair, her face buried in her hands.

The sight of Kyle's familiar face was like a lifeline. April's tears flowed freely as she sprang into his arms, the embrace a mix of relief and longing. The warmth of his presence was a stark contrast to the cold reality surrounding them.

After a moment, Kyle gently stepped back, his hands lingering on her shoulders. "April, I must ask you again to come with us. This place isn't safe. You're not safe here! Twenty years ago, I was a scared kid who ran away when I wanted so badly to be with you. I didn't know how to handle those feelings. I know this isn't a movie, and I can't promise you anything more right now than my life. I will give it to protect you today and every other day. I'm not asking you to get married, just to be my friend and trust in me. I'm a different man than the boy who left here years ago."

April's eyes met his, and for a fleeting moment, the years seemed to fall away. "Kyle, I hated you for leaving me all those years ago. I hated you for years after. I thought I still did. But when I saw you today, it was like stepping back into the past, feeling like we were in high school again. I was so in love with you. Deep down, I probably still am. But Kyle Blaine, I'm not looking for a knight in shining armor. I would just like to have hot food and a soft bed. I want to sleep for a night without worrying about getting murdered before daylight."

"I don't have shiny armor, but I do have a homemade camouflage paint job on my truck outside!" Kyle said with a soft laugh, trying to lighten the mood. "I'm not offering or asking for anything other than your safety right now. There's a good chance we may be in a shootout before we get back home. But if we make it home, I have bunkhouses with somewhat soft beds. My family is there, and my mom still cooks country food like a five-star chef." His words were heartfelt, each one a promise of a measure of normalcy and care.

April's arms wrapped around his neck, her embrace tight and filled with unspoken promises. "You had me when you walked back in. What do I do here? There will be no nurses or doctors if anyone comes in for treatment," she said, lightly kissing Kyle's cheek slowly, holding her head against his chest.

"This place is only going to fall. There are no other people helping for a reason; everyone is trying to take care of their own families right now," Kyle said, his voice firm but tender as he followed her down the hall. He stopped at a door labeled LAB, turning the handle.

April's hand gripped his arm, her eyes wide with fear. "Kyle, no! Don't go in there." But Kyle had already seen the grisly scene within the room, stained with blood, a man's lifeless body lying on the floor.

"It's just another dead body. We've seen plenty of those today," Kyle said, trying to offer reassurance as he placed his arm around April, who was visibly shaking.

"Kyle, it was me. I had to kill him. It's why Jenny hasn't been back. Two days ago, I walked in on him trying to rape Jenny. He pushed me down, and Jenny fought back. I grabbed a pair of scissors and stabbed him in the neck. The blood went everywhere before he fell." April's voice was steady but bitter, revealing the raw pain behind her actions.

"You did what you had to. He wasn't dressed like an employee; he must be one of the people moving in," Kyle said softly, rubbing her back in a gesture of comfort and understanding.

"Those guys that came earlier, at the end of the hall, I think he was with them. I've seen them more than once, I think they're looking for him," April told Kyle, her voice trembling with fear.

"Okay, we need to get out of here. Are there any supplies we can take to help us? Or medications?" Kyle asked urgently.

"I have a box with some basics like Tylenol and Ibuprofen. Without a supply truck, everything quickly ran out or got stolen. There are some boxes of snacks, chips, jerky, beef sticks, and candy bars. They kept them for snacks; I think the vending machine guy always left extras for the nurses," April said as she led Kyle into a storage room. The dim light from the candle cast a welcome glow over the array of snacks and medical supplies.

"Grab your bag and anything else you can carry. Are you sure you want to come with me? You might not see Grundy for a while," Kyle asked, his concern evident as he gathered the medication and snacks.

"I have nothing here, Kyle. At least, maybe with you, there's a chance I might survive and have something again," April replied with a slight smile. Her eyes sparkled with a mix of hope and determination. She picked up her bag and began filling it with the supplies.

Kyle's gaze softened as he watched her. The sight of her, determined and focused, was a stark reminder of how much had changed—and how much remained unchanged between them. They had been through so much, yet here they were, drawn back together by fate and circumstance.

As April finished packing her bag, Kyle took a deep breath, strengthening himself for the challenges ahead. The connection between them was intense, a thread that had been stretched but never truly broken. He could feel the weight of their shared past and the intensity of their present feelings.

"Let's get out of here," Kyle said, his voice steady despite the turmoil of emotions he felt. They made their way back through the hospital, every step echoing their shared history and the new bond forming in the face of adversity.

CHAPTER FIFTY-ONE
"Shattered Trust"

Deanna glanced at Rocky as they sat on watchtower one, the sun beating down on them. The sky was an unbroken expanse of blue, and an unsettling silence hung in the air, broken only by the occasional rustle of squirrels bouncing in the leaves. The tranquility of the scene contrasted sharply with the unease gnawing at Rocky's gut. "I need to use one of the ATVs," she said, her voice cutting through the stillness.

Rocky turned to her, a frown creasing his forehead. "What for? Where are you going? Do you want me to come with you?"

"I just need to take a ride off the mountain, maybe walk by Uncle Tom's Pond. I've been up here for two weeks, and I have cabin fever," Deanna explained, her tone growing more insistent. She cast her eyes around the watchtower, taking in the woodwork and the view it afforded. The panoramic sight was breathtaking but offered no solace. The mountain, once a sanctuary, now felt like a cage.

Rocky felt a knot of unease tighten in his stomach. Why now? Why did she suddenly want to leave the mountain with Kyle gone and everyone on high alert? The timing seemed suspicious. "Okay, sure. I'll get the side-by-side ready for you. Just be careful. I'll take care of the girls."

He watched as Deanna descended the tower, her steps purposeful yet betraying a hint of anxiety. He couldn't shake the feeling that something was off. Still, he prepped the side-by-side, filling it with fuel. The scent of gasoline filled the air, a harsh contrast to the pine and earth that usually dominated. The heat shimmered off the ground, making the distant forest seem like a mirage. Maybe she did need a change of scenery. They all did, but it didn't sit right with him.

"Take care of the girls, and don't tell anyone I'm going off the mountain. I'll be back in a while," Deanna said, waving at Rocky before driving away, the engine's roar echoing through the trees. The side-by-side rattled and groaned as it made its way down the trail, leaving a trail of dust that hung in the air like a ghostly cloud.

Rocky returned to his post, binoculars in hand. He scanned the trail, the binoculars revealing fleeting glimpses of Deanna through the dense tree canopy. The trees seemed to close in around her, their branches deep and ominous. The farther she traveled, the more the forest seemed to swallow her up.

"Who left?" Rachel asked, emerging from the cabin with a cup of coffee, squinting against the sun. The heat was thick, and the coffee's steam seemed almost redundant against the blazing afternoon.

"That was Deanna. She's doing a security check," Rocky lied, the words tasting bitter. Rachel's gaze was warm, but the weight of his deceit was heavy. He could feel her trust in him like a physical burden.

"You're doing a fine job, Rocky. Thank you for helping us all out here. I know Kyle is depending on you more and more. That's a sign you're earning his trust," Rachel said before retreating to her favorite rocking chair on the porch, the wood creaking rhythmically under her weight. The scene was almost idyllic, but Rocky couldn't shake the feeling that something was fundamentally wrong.

Rocky muttered to himself as he looked through the binoculars again. Deanna had vanished from view. The trees stood like silent guards, hiding her from his sight. He adjusted the focus, trying to pierce through the veil of greenery, but the forest remained impassable.

"Hello, guys, I'll be back in a bit. I need to take a quick ride for some fresh air," Deanna told Herbie at the roadblock, her voice steady but her eyes betraying a hint of urgency. The roadblock was a large coal truck, a simple defense against potential intruders.

"Sure thing, Deanna. We haven't seen anyone today, but stay close and alert," Herbie replied, nodding as she drove away, the ATVs tires kicking up dust and gravel.

In the barn, Susie and Ginger were deep in conversation, their voices low and conspiratorial. The barn was dim, the air heavy with the scent of hay and something more pungent. The walls were lined with tools and supplies, Kyle's forward thinking on full display. Rachel noticed but assumed it was just sisters catching up. She continued to hum a Conway Twitty song, sipping her coffee and gazing out at the landscape. The music seemed to meld with the gentle rustling of leaves, creating an odd contrast of calm and tension.

"Who's that coming?" Miran Tate asked, hearing the distant rumble of an engine. The sound was an irregularity in the otherwise still afternoon, a jarring note in the symphony of silence.

"Another trader, ready to make a deal," Lucas said, hurrying to the counter. Business had slowed to a crawl with the fuel shortage, and any visitor was a potential lifeline. The counter was cluttered with goods and a cash register that had seen better days.

"I'm looking for Miran Tate. I don't have much time," Deanna called out as she entered the garage, her voice steady despite the tension in her shoulders. The garage smelled of oil and sweat, and the sound of the engine cooling off added a low hum to the atmosphere.

"You found him. What can I do for you, little lady?" Tate asked, eyeing her with interest. His gaze was sharp, assessing, and he leaned back in his chair, studying her with a mixture of curiosity and suspicion.

"I've come to make a deal. I want you to guarantee my family's safety, at least for me and my girls," Deanna announced, her voice unwavering despite the gravity of her words. Her hands fidgeted slightly, betraying her anxiety.

322

Tate's curiosity was piqued. "A guarantee for safety? Who are you, and what have you got to offer?"

"My name is Deanna. I can give you someone I know you want. My uncle Kyle, Kyle Blaine," she stated, unwavering. The name hung in the air like a storm cloud, the weight of it substantial.

Horrace entered at the mention of Kyle Blaine, his eyes blazing with hatred. Tate quickly placed himself between Deanna and Horrace. "You've got my interest, darling. How about you tell me a little more," he said, motioning Horrace to sit and listen.

"Where's Mommy?" Coraline asked Rocky as she approached the tower, her voice small and worried.

"She had to run off the mountain for something. She should be back anytime. Go back inside for now, watch another movie," Rocky replied, hiding his own growing worry. Deanna had been gone nearly ninety minutes. The sun's position in the sky had shifted, marking the passage of time and adding to his growing anxiety. He went to find Susie and Ginger in the barn, the smell of marijuana hitting him as he entered. The barn was thick with smoke, the air hazy and stifling. The once clean, organized space was now cluttered with discarded joints and the remnants of their indulgence.

"How many of these have you two smoked?" Rocky asked, eyeing the ashtray filled with joints.

"Have a puff, relax a little," Susie said, giggling, her eyes half-closed. Her demeanor was carefree, an ironic contrast to the situation unfolding.

"Yeah, Rocky, have a puff," Ginger echoed, clearly intoxicated, her voice sluggish. The haze of the smoke seemed to blur the seriousness of their conversation.

"You two are going to burn the barn down. Do you know where Deanna went? She left on the side-by-side over an hour ago," Rocky asked, his frustration mounting. The anger in his voice cut through the fog of smoke, making Susie and Ginger look up with surprise.

"Oh shit, I told her not to go," Susie grumbled, trying to

stand, her movements slow and unsteady. Her face was flushed, her earlier indifference replaced by concern.

"Not to go where? What the hell is going on?" Rocky demanded, his voice rising, desperation creeping in.

"Shhhhhh, not so loud, Rocky," Ginger said, struggling to focus, her eyes glassy and unfocused.

"You can't say anything about this, Rocky. It will cause all sorts of problems if it gets out," Susie said, now standing and leaning against the wooden stall. "She told me she wanted to make a deal with Tate, for all our safety. For you and the girls."

"What kind of deal, Susie?" Rocky asked, his jaw tightening, his patience wearing thin. The implications of her words hit him like a cold wave.

"She said she would tell them how to get Kyle. She would turn him in if they agreed to leave us alone. We could have the cabin here," Susie explained, her face flushing with shame, her voice barely above a whisper.

"You two knew about this and didn't say anything? Why didn't you stop her?" Rocky's voice rose with anger, his fists clenching. The betrayal felt like a physical blow.

"We love Kyle. But, this could be a good place for us all, and we would be left alone if we give him to them," Ginger slurred, her words a jumbled mess of rationalizations.

"You're right, we would have a good place here for us all. I can see what you're saying," Rocky said, looking at them both, tears starting to slide down Susie's cheeks. "We would have a place that Kyle built! While you both sat on your asses waiting for a handout, Kyle was here every day, working to build this place to protect us all. A man willing to give his life for us, and this is how you repay him."

"You're looking at it all wrong, Rocky. It's not like that," Ginger said as Susie began to sob uncontrollably, her body shaking with each sob.

"It's exactly like that. You're ungrateful, selfish people who don't deserve Kyle's protection. He's out there right now, looking to help someone, having already fought and killed defending you both. Your betrayal of him, your willingness to sacrifice him for your own comfort, is unforgivable," Rocky said, his voice breaking with raw emotion.

"You're right, Rocky," Susie sobbed, trying to reach out to him, "We made a terrible mistake. Please, don't tell anyone."

"You've already done enough damage. I need to find Deanna and make things right," Rocky said, turning and shaking his head as he walked away, his heart pounding with rage and betrayal. He couldn't help himself as he drew back and punched the wall of the barn on his way out, his soul disparaged with the betrayal he now felt. "Enemies in the yard," he muttered to himself as he exited the barn. "Now I understand what you meant by that."

As the sun beat down, Rocky lay back on the platform of tower one, placing his hands across his face. His stomach churned, and he felt like he might vomit. The weight of his new knowledge, the depth of the betrayal, pressed heavily on him. He was in complete shock. How could these people be willing to let Kyle most likely be killed, to take what he had built to help themselves? His own wife and Kyle's sisters, so dark-hearted?

The sound of an engine caught Rocky's attention. He got to his feet and looked through the binoculars, spotting Deanna hurrying up the trail. His heart shattered. What would he say to her? How would they handle this betrayal? The sight of her approaching was both a relief and a further source of anxiety. His mind raced, trying to piece together a plan while grappling with the enormity of the situation.

CHAPTER FIFTY-TWO
"Search for Stacy"

Kyle opened the truck door, allowing April to slide in on the bench seat first. The worn leather creaked under her weight, and she adjusted herself comfortably, her fingers brushing against the frayed edges of the seat. Kyle joined her and closed the door, the sound of the latch clicking sharply in the otherwise still air. Arnie, seated on the passenger's side, glanced over at April with a wide, almost nostalgic smile, though he kept silent, his eyes twinkled.

As Kyle started the engine, the truck's rumble filled the cab, and the vehicle jolted forward, leaving the hospital parking lot behind. The asphalt shimmered under the midday sun, casting fleeting reflections of the surrounding buildings. Kyle turned left, heading toward Grundy, his eyes focused on the road with a mixture of determination and curiosity.

"Is this your old truck from school?" April asked, her voice shaded with a hint of nostalgia as she glanced around the interior. The truck was a relic of a bygone era, its dashboard cluttered with old maps and knick-knacks.

"You remember this old truck, huh?" Arnie said, a snicker escaping his lips. He leaned back, reveling in the shared memory.

"Yeah, it is. I've kept it at Mom's in the garage," Kyle replied, his tone holding a note of pride.

"I'm renting a small house outside of town, going towards Big Rock. If it's not been broken into, you could stop if you don't mind," April said, her gaze shifting to the passing scenery, which seemed to blur together in a chaotic mosaic.

"Sure thing. Just show me when we get there," Kyle said,

his eyes darting between the road and April. His focus was intense, as if he feared missing any detail that might lead to a clue about Stacy's well-being.

They soon passed by the law school in town, a surprising sight in such a small community. The building's old facade, with its brick walls and weathered stone, stood in stark contrast to the surrounding rural landscape, a beacon of academia amidst simplicity. Next door, a small branch of a larger grocery store chain loomed. The once-busy parking lot, now a scene of disarray, was littered with overturned shopping carts and shattered glass. A few people wandered aimlessly among the debris, their scavenging efforts underscored by the devastation of their surroundings, their faces thin and eyes hollow with desperation.

As Kyle turned onto Route 460 East, the landscape began to shift, transitioning from the chaotic remnants of town to a more desolate, rural setting. The road was flanked by towering rock walls, their rugged surfaces a testament to the force required to carve out the new section of the road. The jagged edges of the rocks caught the fading sunlight, casting a shade across the pavement. Kyle followed Arnie's directions with precision, the truck rumbling along the uneven road until they arrived at Stacy's neighborhood.

The neighborhood was eerily quiet, a stark contrast to the bustling life it once held. The homes, once well-manicured and vibrant, now appeared as relics of a forgotten time. The few open garage doors revealed interiors that had been thoroughly ransacked, their contents strewn haphazardly across driveways and lawns, as if a tornado had passed through.

A handful of people peered from behind drawn curtains, their faces marked by a mixture of fear and guarded curiosity as the truck approached. The silence was punctuated by the distant cawing of crows and the rustle of leaves in the gentle breeze. Arnie pointed to a house in the distance, its front yard choked with overgrown grass and encroaching shrubbery. The house stood like a ghost of its former self, several windows broken and the door standing open. Kyle brought the truck to a halt, the engine's low rumble the only sound in the oppressive stillness.

"Get over here and be ready to drive, Arnie. I'm going to take a look," Kyle instructed, his voice firm. He opened the door and stepped out, the heat of the day hitting him like a wall.

"If she isn't here, I bet they are at Ryan's parents," Arnie said, his eyes scanning the surroundings with practiced vigilance.

Kyle approached the front door of Stacy's house, finding the lock shattered and the door ajar. It had clearly been kicked in, the frame splintered and cracked. He pushed the door open cautiously and stepped inside, his flashlight illuminating the debris-strewn floor. The air was thick with dust and the faint smell of decay. He spotted a note on the kitchen counter, its paper yellow and crisp. He picked it up and read aloud, "If you're looking for us, we went to our other property. You know where it is if you know us."

Hurrying back to the truck, Kyle's face was set in a grim line. "Where is their other property?" he asked Arnie urgently.

"She's talking about her husband Ryan's parents' place. They always joked about it being their 'other property'," Arnie explained, his eyes reflecting the seriousness of the situation.

"So where is it? Actually, just drive," Kyle said as he climbed into the passenger's seat, his mind racing with possibilities.

Arnie shifted the truck into gear and drove out of Stacy's neighborhood, the vehicle bumping over the uneven pavement as they rejoined Route 460. After a short distance, Arnie turned onto a side street that seemed to peter out into a gravel path. He navigated the truck carefully, the road gradually giving way to a rugged trail obscured by overgrown vegetation.

"Arnie, are you sure about this?" Kyle asked, gripping the side of the door for support as the truck jolted over the uneven terrain.

"Oh yeah, stay calm," Arnie replied, his voice steady despite the rough ride.

The gravel path descended into a narrow, winding road

that twisted through dense trees and underbrush. As they continued, the road became even more challenging, bordered by thick weeds and wild plant life. Arnie maneuvered the truck with skill, the engine growling as it tackled the inclines and turns. The trees parted to reveal a clearing where a picturesque older home stood, its grandness somewhat faded but still striking.

"This place is beautiful," Kyle said, his eyes widening at the sight. The house had tall columns on the porch that reached up to the second floor, and a large, well-kept lawn stretched out in front and on the sides of the house.

"It is. There's Ryan and Stacy's truck. We're not going any farther just yet. Ryan probably has his sights on us right now. Hand me that t-shirt in the side of the door," Arnie said, nodding towards a white shirt tucked in the truck's door compartment. He held the shirt out the driver's side door and waved it around, the fabric fluttering in the breeze.

As he stepped out of the truck, a man emerged from the side of the house, his presence initially concealed by the darkness. He lowered a rifle and waved at Arnie, signaling for them to approach.

"That's him. We're good now," Arnie said, a note of relief in his voice as he climbed back into the truck and drove up to the house.

"What's up, Arnie? How you been, buddy?" Ryan greeted them with a grin as he stepped forward, his handshake firm and welcoming. Stacy rushed from the house, enveloping Arnie in a long, tight hug.

"I'm so glad to see you, Arnie. Where's Mom? How is everyone?" Stacy asked, her voice thick with emotion as she continued to hold the embrace.

"Mom is doing great. We're all great thanks to Uncle Kyle," Arnie replied, his pride evident as Kyle stepped out of the truck.

"Uncle Kyle!" Stacy exclaimed, her eyes lighting up as she ran to hug him. "How did you all find me here? What are you doing over this way? It's gotten crazy in town, so we came here."

"Hey, Stacy. I'm glad to see you're safe. We found your note at the house. Arnie deciphered it instantly, and here we are. Ginger has been worried sick about you since this started. We told her we would find you, and I'm so glad we did," Kyle said, his voice filled with relief as he helped April out of the truck. "Stacy, this is April. She is an old friend of mine we found today at the hospital. She was trying to work the place by herself."

"Hi. It's good to meet you. I can't believe you were at the hospital. We were told it had been overtaken and the patients were either dead or had left," Stacy said, her eyes widening in surprise.

"It's in bad condition and does have many questionable people moving into it right now. It's becoming a big crack house," April said, her tone reflecting the gravity of the situation.

"Come on, let's go take a seat under the canopy," Ryan suggested, leading them towards a set of picnic tables shaded by a large canopy. The tables were set with an assortment of homemade dishes, their aromas mingling in the warm air. Kyle was impressed by the wood work of the canopy, studying it in detail, making plans to build one himself, hopefully one day.

"Where is Jackson at?" Arnie asked, his gaze searching for the small toddler.

"Ryan's parents had him downstairs. We heard the truck coming and they took him to hide. I told them it was safe and they will be out shortly," Stacy explained.

"Are you all hungry? Ryan's mom was cooking fried chicken," Stacy offered, her voice hopeful.

"How do you get fried chicken right now?" April asked, her curiosity interested as she looked around.

Kyle tapped her on the arm and pointed towards the backyard. "Do you see those chickens back there?" he asked with a grin. "There is one less than there was yesterday." His remark created snickers from the group.

"Oh no!" April exclaimed, her eyes widening in realization as she placed a hand over her mouth. "I might have been hesitant to say yes about this a few weeks ago, but right now I'm starving and willing to apologize to the other chickens." Her comment elicited laughter from the group, a welcome break from the tension.

As everyone chatted and caught up, the atmosphere lightened, despite the underlying tension of their circumstances. Stacy's eleven-month-old baby, Jackson, became the center of attention, his innocent giggles and wide-eyed curiosity providing a welcome distraction. Arnie and Kyle took turns holding him, their rough hands surprisingly gentle as they cradled the small bundle of joy. Jackson's chubby fingers grasped at their faces, his bright eyes filled with wonder as he explored the unfamiliar surroundings.

They took pictures with a cell phone and an old Polaroid camera, the whiz and click of the device punctuating their conversation. Each snapshot captured a fleeting moment of happiness, a brief respite from the harsh realities beyond the trees. Kyle carefully arranged the photos, knowing they would be a cherished gift for Ginger. He could already picture her smile, the way her eyes would light up at the sight of her grandchild, a small beacon of hope in their troubled times.

Unbeknownst to Kyle, the very person he thought of as his ally was plotting against him. Ginger, seemingly devoted and loyal, was orchestrating a web of deceit with the guidance of Susie and Deanna. Behind the scenes, she was basically planning Kyle's assassination, every move calculated and deliberate. Her outward demeanor gave no hint of the betrayal brewing within her heart.

Kyle, oblivious to the danger, focused on the present moment. He marveled at Jackson's tiny features, the softness of his skin, and the warmth of his smile. The baby's laughter was infectious, spreading a temporary joy among the group. It was a stark contrast to the cold reality that Ginger was manipulating, her betrayal looming like a dark cloud on the horizon.

As the day lengthened, Kyle felt a sense of peace, believing in the bonds of family and the strength they provided. He was unaware of the impending storm, blind to the moves his sisters and niece had been making in the background. The pictures he now held in his hands would soon become bittersweet reminders of a trust misplaced and a love betrayed.

"What about the jails, what happened with those? We are limited on our information," Kyle asked both Stacy and Ryan.

Stacy shared her harrowing experiences as a nurse at the county jail in Haysi. "All the jailors stopped coming to work right away," she began, her voice, a mix of sorrow and disbelief. "The halls echoed with an eerie silence, only broken by the occasional desperate shout from an inmate. Many of the prisoners weren't in for major crimes—petty theft, minor drug offenses. The decision was made to open the doors and let them walk. It was a chaotic scene, inmates cautiously stepping out of their cells, eyes wide with a mixture of relief and uncertainty.

But not everyone was so lucky. A few who were really bad people, in for serious crimes, were left behind. Their cells were reinforced, the heavy iron doors an unyielding barrier. They were given extra water and food, but ultimately abandoned to their fate, their cries for mercy haunting the empty corridors."

Ryan's face darkened as he recounted his own story from the prison on Keene Mountain. His voice was grim, each word weighed down by the memories of what he had witnessed. "The guards stopped coming in after the first day," he said, shaking his head slowly. "The warden received word that there would be no reinforcements. Panic set in, and the decision was made to execute all prisoners."

"What? No way!" Arnie said, his eyes wide at the thought of what Ryan just told them.

"It was a scene of unimaginable horror. Inmates were dragged from their cells and taken to the dump trailer where they were executed one by one. The sound of gunfire echoed across the prison yard, I quit counting after fifteen. Those who weren't taken to the trailer were left behind in their cells. The warden's thought process was to prevent dangerous individuals from being released back into the public," Ryan explained, moving his finger around the picnic table, drawing a blueprint of the actions.

Kyle's voice cut through the heavy silence that followed, his tone firm but supportive. "We've all had to do things we never wanted to do," he said, his eyes meeting Ryan's with a look of understanding. "Your job now is to take care of your family. That's the only important thing you need to focus on."

"Hell yeah, we have a dead body in the back of the truck now," Arnie said, raising his hands with a mock dramatic flair.

"Why is there a dead body in your truck?" Ryan asked, his brows furrowing in concern.

"He is the son of a good man who lost his life helping us. I wanted to get his body back to his family for a proper burial," Kyle explained before Arnie could make any more jokes.

"I understand. It's commendable of you to do so," Ryan said, nodding in appreciation.

"I was going to tell Stacy, since she acts like such a witch all the time, we were bringing the body for her to cast a spell and raise it from the dead," Arnie said with a laugh, slapping Ryan on the arm. "Sorry dude, you married her, you got to deal with her now."

"I'd smack the piss out of you if I hadn't missed your wisecracks so much," Stacy said, laughing as she hugged Arnie tightly.

"I hear it every day from him, Stacy. He keeps himself sharp with the cutting on people," Kyle said, joining in the laughter.

"I'm so glad to hear everyone is doing well. Tell Mom I love her and if she wants to come here, she can," Stacy said, her eyes shining with gratitude.

"You should really get a gate up or drop a couple of trees on the drive in. It's too easy right now to get a vehicle here," Kyle advised as he glanced back at the dirt road leading into the trees. "Other than that, you all just keep watch, and you should be able to make it. If for any reason you're ever flushed out, you know you're welcome to come join us."

"I'm going to miss you, sis, but we better get going. Take care of my little nephew and, like Kyle said, come to us anytime," Arnie said, hugging Stacy tightly.

Tears streamed down Stacy's face as she watched them get

back into the truck. Kyle glanced over at Arnie, seeing him wipe away a tear.

"They're in a good place, Arnie. I trust that Ryan will get them to our location if anything goes wrong," Kyle said, his voice reassuring. April, too, was visibly moved, her eyes brimming with tears as she observed Arnie's struggle to leave his sister and baby nephew behind.

As Kyle maneuvered the truck back towards the trees, the weight of the day's events settled heavily on them, a somber reminder of the harsh reality they faced.

CHAPTER FIFTY-THREE

"Let's Go Home"

"Did you notice the Pizza Hut had burned when we came by the first time?" April asked, her voice in disbelief as they passed by it again.

"I did not. I was looking ahead. The empty roadways are tripping me out," Kyle said, his eyes scanning the deserted streets.

The Pizza Hut, once a popular spot with its distinctive red roof, was now a charred skeleton. Blackened beams jutted out like the bones of some ancient creature, and the smell of smoke lingered in the air.

They soon passed by Wal-Mart, where several small businesses in the shopping center had been ravaged by fire. The windows were shattered, and black smoke stains marred the once-red brick walls. The movie theater building, perched atop a three-story parking garage, was now surrounded by heaps of garbage. People in the parking lot stopped to watch as Kyle drove by, their faces marked by a mixture of surprise and suspicion. Few vehicles were still operational, making the sight of a truck a rare occurrence.

"Is that dead bodies over there by the wall?" April asked, her voice mixed with horror as she looked across Arnie.

"It looks as though it is," Arnie said, his gaze fixed on the grim scene. Several figures lay crumpled against the brick wall, their forms barely distinguishable amidst the debris.

Kyle turned onto nearby Poe Town Road and drove up to the county public library. The building loomed ahead, its once-inviting facade now a testament to the chaos that had engulfed the town. "Ginger wanted some books to read. Let's see if I can get into the library. Arnie, come over here and sit, be ready to drive. I'll be back shortly," Kyle said, urgency in his voice as he ran up to the door. The windows were broken out, and the door hung ajar, creaking ominously as it swayed in the breeze. Kyle cautiously shined his flashlight inside, stepping over the broken glass that crunched under his foot.

Inside, the library was a ghost town. Dust floated in the air, illuminated by his flashlight. The shelves, once neatly organized, were now in disarray. Books lay scattered on the floor, their pages fluttering like wounded birds. He moved quickly to the counter, grabbing several flimsy plastic bags. He hurried to the best-seller section, stuffing the bags with as many books as he could carry. He also grabbed a selection of DVDs, filling another bag with cartoons and comedies for the girls. Before leaving, Kyle stopped at the counter, picked up a pen, and wrote a note on a piece of paper: "Took some books and movies. I will return once the fan has been wiped clean, K.Blaine."

Kyle ran back to the truck, placing the bags in the back. The smell of the dead body of Charles hit him, making him wince. He quickly closed the hatch and climbed into the passenger seat.

"Where do we go to now, Uncle Kyle?" Arnie asked as he began driving out of Grundy, following along Route 460 West.

This was a road Kyle had driven countless times, almost daily, during his younger years. The memories of this small town, the seat of Buchanan County, flooded back. It was a quiet and peaceful place, filled with wonderful, kind, and friendly neighbors.

Grundy was a town known for its parades, where people from all over the county would gather. Teenagers would cruise from the movie theater parking garage up to the McDonald's to hang out. The local town police and Buchanan County Sheriff's department-maintained order but also allowed the youngsters some freedom to socialize and have fun. This was a time before Facebook and Snapchat, when kids still engaged in face-to-face interactions.

The town was also known for its rivalries among kids from

different schools, which sometimes led to fistfights, often over girls. It hosted the annual Levisa River raft race, where anything that could float was used. Kyle fondly remembered watching the race as a kid, laughing at the guy who tied inner tubes together and used a large pair of panties as a makeshift sail, smiling and waving as he floated along. It was a great small town. That was before. This is now.

"Let's head home, Arnie. We're making good time. We can stop at April's house and then get back to the cabin. Between finding April and knowing Stacy is safe, I think that's a good run for today," Kyle said, grinning at April.

Arnie drove by the old radio station and soon approached the bank. As it came into view, they saw only the burnt remains of what once had been a bank. The outer brick walls stood, but the interior was gutted. As they passed the elementary school, Kyle wondered if the children would ever see their school again, if they would ever know the same America again.

"Kyle, this truck feels like it's pulling harder and harder to the left. I think we may have a low tire," Arnie said, firmly gripping the wheel with both hands.

"I don't want to stop beside the road. There is nowhere safe we can risk pulling off to change a tire. Can you hold on until we get to the old railroad building? We can pull around back and check the tire there, out of sight," Kyle said, watching as Arnie fought with the wheel.

They passed the turnoff to Poplar Creek Road and then the Harman bridge. Arnie slowed for the curve and turned off the road into the parking lot. The lot wrapped around the building, and they aimed to go to the backside next to the river. This would be their best chance of remaining hidden from anyone passing by.

CHAPTER FIFTY-FOUR
"Railroad Restaurant & Hotel"

Arnie rumbled over the cracked asphalt as he steered into the parking lot of the old railroad hotel. Once a lively waypoint for weary train staff and diners, the building now stood as a ghostly monument to neglect. Wood panels covered the windows and doors, their edges curling with rot. Vines crept up the exterior, turning once-pristine flower beds into tangled masses of green. Arnie slowed the truck, its engine purring as he maneuvered around a stack of old wooden pallets at the rear.

"Not much of a welcome party," Kyle muttered, peering out the window. "Let's get this tire changed and see if there's anything useful in there."

Arnie parked the truck near the building's back door, the rusty metal creaking in protest as he stopped. Kyle hopped out and moved to the rear of the truck, grimacing as he saw the damaged tire. "Not what we needed. Time for our NASCAR pit crew routine."

Kyle grabbed a spare tire from the truck bed, its rough surface gritty under his fingers. The stench of decay from the body they carried in the truck bed was overpowering, making his stomach churn. He cranked the jack as Arnie loosened the lug nuts. "You hold onto those lug nuts, Arnie. If I hear the F-dash-dash-dash word, I'm telling your mom," Kyle joked, trying to lighten the grim atmosphere.

Arnie looked puzzled. "What's the F-dash-dash-dash word? What the heck are you talking about, Uncle Kyle?" Arnie asked, confused.

"He's talking about the greatest Christmas movie ever! *The*

Christmas Story with Ralphie," April said, a look of disappointment washing over her face. Kyle assumed she was thinking about the old days.

"*The Christmas Story*, buddy. Ralphie and his Red Ryder," Kyle explained, giving a small chuckle.

April, perched in the truck's passenger seat, sighed wistfully. "Kyle and I watched that movie five times together. Those were the days."

As Kyle worked, he thought about those simpler times. The task was straightforward—remove the flat, replace it with the spare, and get moving. But the heavy feeling in the air, the sense of looming danger, made the task feel monumental.

"Hey," Arnie said, glancing at April. "You two ever think about those days?"

April's face tightened. "Sometimes. But they're just memories now."

"You wait here at the truck, I'll be back soon." Kyle said as he grabbed his body armor, placing it over his head and snapping the Velcro together. He took the Kel Tec KSG shotgun and placed the bandolier across his body, snapping the connectors into place. He tugged on the straps of his body armor plate carrier to make sure they were snug. "I'm going to see if I can get inside and check it out. If you see anyone pull in, hit the horn, and pull out. Drive across the bridge and if it's clear, wait there for me. I'll come across the river to you; the water is low, it will be easy to cross."

"I really think I should go in with you, Uncle Kyle. Let me provide backup for you," Arnie said before getting back in the truck.

"Really, Kyle? You're going in there alone?" April asked, her eyebrows scrunched.

"Just do what I said, little buddy. I know this place well. I can get in and back out quickly. April, stay in the truck with Arnie. I won't be long," Kyle said, grabbing a small pry bar from the back of the truck.

He slid a headlamp onto his head and approached the door. Kyle pushed the pry bar between the door and the frame, but before applying pressure, the door moved. He wasn't surprised that someone had already broken into the building. He withdrew his Glock and clicked on the attached light, then turned on his headlamp and pulled the door open.

Inside the hotel, the musty, disturbing interior greeted him. The once-elegant lobby was now a wreck: overturned furniture, shattered glass, and graffiti marred the walls. The air was thick with the smell of mold and decay. Kyle's footsteps echoed eerily as he moved toward the stairwell.

A pool table was flipped onto its side, likely the work of teenagers being destructive for the fun of it. An old couch was overturned, its faux leather cushions ripped apart and scattered. A stairway led from that room up to the next two floors. Kyle stepped to the stairway and looked up into the darkness, hearing the creaks and groans of the old building. Water trickled in drops, leaving a slimy trail down the concrete steps.

At the truck, Arnie kept a wide-eyed watch for trouble, glancing back and forth between his rearview mirror and the front windshield. He had a view around the building where he could see Route 460 going east into a curve.

"We got a little time. Tell me about you and Kyle. You two have some type of spark that only took about two seconds to light up," Arnie said to April.

"That was a long time ago. I should be asking you to tell me about Kyle now. What has he been up to for the last twenty years?" April asked, turning the question on him.

"My Uncle Kyle is great. He moved back here about a year ago. I didn't see much of him when I was younger, but now we do everything together, including building his cabin on the mountain," Arnie said.

"Does he have any kids?" April asked.

"Nope! He always said his job didn't allow for it. He said there wasn't enough time to have a family and travel like he had to. Mamaw always said he let the right one get away and couldn't find that happiness with anyone else," Arnie said, continuing to look ahead at the road.

"Tell me about it," April said, looking through the side window of the truck at the river. Arnie noticed she was lost in thought.

"Hey, wait a minute. Are you the right one he let get away?" Arnie asked, starting to put the pieces together.

"It must not have been me. That jerk left me standing as he went off to start his career," April said, her thoughts drifting back to old memories.

Arnie's eyes flickered nervously between the building and the road. He spotted a truck making its way around the bend, driving slow and deliberate. Three figures were visible in the truck bed before the truck disappeared around the curve.

"They see us, Arnie!" April exclaimed.

He caught a glimpse of the man quickly pointing towards them before the truck went out of sight. Arnie knew the man was most likely telling the others he had seen a truck parked behind the building.

"That's not good," Arnie said, his voice tight. "I think they saw us."

April's face went pale. "What should we do? We can't leave Kyle inside alone," she said, holding her hands over her face.

"There are reasons we must do things to stay safe. It's not only about today, but also tomorrow. That's what Kyle tells us," Arnie said to April, continuing to scan all around. Arnie's heart raced. "April, buckle up. We might have to leave in a hurry," he said, his voice a low, urgent whisper, his fingers drumming anxiously on the steering wheel.

April's eyes were wide with worry, "What about Kyle?"

"We have to trust he'll find a way out. We can't stay here if things get bad," Arnie said, his gaze darting nervously.

Back inside, Kyle peered through the door into the dark hallway. The graffiti-covered walls and broken fixtures seemed to close in on him. "This would make one hell of a haunted house," he said as he moved further inward.

He opened the door and announced himself, "If anyone is here, I'm not looking for trouble, only supplies." He wanted to make his presence known, not seeking a fight. The hallway led either to the restaurant or straight ahead.

Kyle stepped over debris, navigating through fallen ceiling tiles, pieces of furniture, boxes, and other garbage. The exercise room still held weightlifting equipment, too heavy for thieves to bother stealing. The poker table, broken and in the hallway, was most likely a casualty of teenage calamity.

Arnie, now bouncing his legs and rocking his feet up and down faster, tried to stay calm. "Stay calm and breathe," Arnie said aloud, inhaling and exhaling deeply. Moments later, the truck came back into view, creeping around to see who was at the hotel. Arnie could see three people inside the cab and three in the bed of the truck. He pressed the horn multiple times to alert Kyle, hoping his uncle heard the sound. The block walls, however, drowned out the horn, leaving Kyle unaware and vulnerable.

Arnie lost sight of the truck due to the building blocking his view. He knew they had two ways to enter the parking lot: the first entrance would lead straight in front of him, while the second would bring the truck the same way Kyle and Arnie had entered. He guessed they would take the latter, bringing the truck up behind him. Arnie turned the ignition switch, starting the engine, and waited.

"Did you hear that horn blow?" The driver of the truck asked his passengers as he stopped the truck at the kitchen's delivery entrance. Without allowing anyone to answer, he added, "The only reason to blow that horn was a warning to someone on the inside. Check it out."

Kyle continued his search, shining his flashlight around the large room. Nothing of value, just junk and more junk. Then he heard it—a faint noise, like a scuffle or a whisper. He turned, his heart pounding. "Who's there?" he called out, his voice echoing in the stillness.

The reply was a low groan, followed by the rustle of movement. Kyle's grip tightened on his Glock. He aimed it toward the source of the sound, his breath steady but his mind racing. "Show yourself!" he demanded, his voice hard.

A figure emerged from the shadows, ragged and wild-eyed. The man's clothes were tattered, his face smeared with grime. He looked desperate, dangerous. "I don't want trouble," the man said, his hands trembling but empty.

Kyle kept his aim steady. "Then don't start any. What are you doing here?"

The man glanced around nervously. "Same as you, I guess. Just trying to survive."

"Survival's a tough game these days," Kyle said, lowering his weapon slightly but keeping his guard up. "You alone?"

The man nodded. "Yeah. Just me. Name's Mike."

Kyle studied him for a moment, then nodded. "You seen anyone else around here? Anyone we should worry about?"

Mike shook his head. "No, just the ghosts. This place is crawling with them."

"Ghosts don't worry me," Kyle said, turning back to his search. "Just people."

Outside. "That's right, Blaze. Somebody is inside that building," one of the passengers said to Blaze, who was driving. "We didn't exactly bring the right crew to be facing off with anyone, especially in a building that large with no idea how many there might be."

JD, one of the passengers, was hesitant. "I don't know, man. This feels off. You sure we should go check it out?"

"This is our community, our roads, our town. We decide who takes what and where they take it from," Blaze announced emphatically, making it clear he wasn't to be questioned.

"Peanut, JD, you two get out and see if you can get through that door. I'll go around and introduce myself to the others," Blaze said with a laugh, clearly meaning 'introducing' no longer meant what it did just weeks ago. "Shoot anyone you see and take whatever they have. We didn't give anyone permission to be in this building," Blaze said, clearly the leader of this group of outlaws.

"10-4, Blaze," Peanut said as they scooted out of the truck cab.

The two men went to the door, which was an entrance into the kitchen. The lock handle had also been broken and no longer worked correctly. The men slowly pulled the door back and stepped inside. Peanut turned on the flashlight he carried while JD stood close to his side.

"Don't get away from me, Peanut. I can't see shit in here," JD, being without a flashlight, said. "We really do need some of the other guys for this. We need Twig, Alec, and Mac. Those guys are killers built for this kind of shit. I'm just a good thief."

"We can do this, JD. Stay calm," Peanut said as he shined his light in the kitchen. "This kitchen still has all the equipment in it; they didn't take any of this out. Open that door and see what's in there," Peanut said as he shined the light towards the door. JD stepped over and pressed down the lever handle to the door, pushing it inwards to open. They each entered the small room, which turned out to be a pantry. The room still held standup coolers and freezers. The doors had been left propped open to keep from building up an unpleasant odor.

"Nothing here. Let's go. We need to find whoever is here," Peanut told JD as they stepped back into the kitchen. With the kitchen being dark, JD didn't notice the stacks of aluminum steam table pans on a table in the middle of the room. He backed up, hitting the table and knocking two of the tall stacks onto the floor. The pans clanged loudly as they bounced off the floor and one another.

Kyle was in the old office room, now a wreck, confronting a possible new threat. Mike appeared to be a hobo living in the building, trying to survive himself during this chaotic time unfolding. Two desks had been turned over, and a television lay broken on the floor. More graffiti sprayed onto the walls showed teenagers had been hanging out here. "Jackie Loves Teresa" and "Benji wuz' here"—these were some of the only things Kyle could make out.

The loud sound of the pans banging in the kitchen got Kyle's attention as he spun around, holstering his glock and raising his shotgun.

"I told you, ghosts!" Mike announced hearing the pans clanging further away.

"That wasn't ghost, somebody else is here. They with you?" Kyle asked quickly, grabbing Mike by the arm holding it firmly.

"No, I swear it. I'm here alone," Mike retorted.

"Then I recommend you getting under a desk and staying quiet, I'm going to see who else is here," Kyle told Mike.

Blaze had slowly crept around to the last turn leading behind the building. He stopped with a plan for the guys in the back of the truck.

"Get out here. You guys stay until I drive around. Keep a watch on me and back me up if there is trouble," Blaze said to the three guys as he pressed the gas, moving around the building. Arnie, who had been watching, could now see the truck come around the corner and stop. He turned his head around to get a clear look. Arnie could only see one person in the truck now—the man driving.

"Shit. Shit. Shit!" Arnie said loudly as he ran options through his head of what to do. Kyle had told him to leave if there was any sign of trouble. "I trust Kyle. He says to leave, we need to leave," Arnie said to April. As he glanced down into the side mirror, he saw the truck slowly moving closer toward him. Arnie also noticed two heads peering around the corner. Arnie knew something was up and it wasn't good. He hit the horn and held it for a long blow, hoping to get Kyle's attention. Blaze stopped again, and Arnie released the horn. The door opened, and Blaze stepped out, standing behind the opened door and shouting to Arnie.

"Get out of the truck, show us your hands. We're the police," Blaze announced.

"And I'm Jesus," Arnie said, but not loud enough to be heard. Arnie knew it was time to go. He pressed the brake, pulled the shifter down to drive, and slammed the gas throttle. Arnie drove off the asphalt pavement of the parking lot and crossed a small section of dirt and weeds that led back onto the road. Blaze turned to the guys, laughing as they watched him drive away so quickly.

"He wasn't much of a partner. Now, we need to know who is in that building. We get whoever it is, and we'll find out who was in the truck and where it's going. Let's go," Blaze said as he started walking towards the same back door Kyle had used to enter the building.

Inside, Kyle had pulled the door open, leading into the restaurant dining room. It was a haunting look as nothing appeared to have been disturbed. The chairs still sat upright and pushed underneath the tables. As Kyle looked to his right, there was a jukebox that had been broken open. Someone had been looking for money in it.

Kyle was about to turn and run when he was drawn to the door leading into the kitchen. He heard voices and could see a light through the small glass in the door. Kyle could also see light now glowing through the service window. It all happened so fast—Kyle raised his KSG, gripping the shotgun firmly, his finger resting on the trigger. The door pushed open from the kitchen, and one of the men immediately yelled, seeing the light from Kyle's headlamp.

"Somebody's there. Hold it!" a voice shouted to Kyle.

CHAPTER FIFTY-FIVE
"In the Wake of Death-Back at the Scene"

In the dim light of the stairwell, Kyle held the knife tightly in his hand after slicing through Jacoby's neck. The knife was slick with blood from the fatal cut. Jacoby grasped at the large open wound, but it was too late for him, he was twenty seconds from going unconscious, and another thirty seconds from death. As quickly as his blood and loss of oxygen were gone, Jacoby's life would be as well. No amount of medical expertise would be able to alter this course, his fate would be final.

Kyle held onto him, pulling Jacoby away from the door and towards the stairs leading to the third floor above. As he laid the man down slowly, Kyle looked at him. He was hit with the sudden realization this was not a man, he was just a boy. Kyle could see he was only a kid, probably no more than fourteen, maybe fifteen years old. Kyle felt his stomach quickly knotting up and before he could stop it, vomit spewed from his mouth onto the cold concrete steps.

Kyle could handle killing someone, but a young boy was more than he had been ready for. This kid was younger than Arnie and Kyle felt his body stiffen as if he had no control over his movements. Kyle's mind was screaming for action, but his body frozen in shock. His eyes locked on Jacoby lying before him watching his life fade away.

In the East stairwell, Blaze burst through the doorway, finding JD crouched, retrieving his flashlight and pistol.

"What happened? Where is he?" Blaze demanded, urgency in his words.

"I don't know," JD replied, his voice shaky. "I slipped on these damn slick steps, and my gun went off. My ears are ringing."

"Damn it, JD! I left Jacoby alone. Get your ass up those steps and clear the second floor. I'll catch up with you," Blaze snapped, racing back into the room with the pool table. Smoke billowed through the hallway, thick from the burning debris. Blaze called out, "Jacoby, where are you boy?"

"Breathe, breathe", Kyle murmured to himself. He was struggling to snap back from the trance he felt overtake his movement. He used the sleeve of his shirt to wipe across his mouth removing the vomit that had remained around his lips, his face pale. "You're just a kid, what are you doing here?", Kyle spoke softly to the young boy's lifeless body. Two weeks ago, Kyle could have been teaching this kid survival techniques as friends, now two weeks later he had killed him as an enemy. "I'm sorry, kid. I really am."

"Jacoby, Jacoby!" Blaze said in a loud whisper, his voice echoing in the stairwell, piercing the silence. "Are you there? I'm coming up, don't shoot me boy."

Kyle was again stuck in a bad position on which way to go, feeling panicked by the situation. He carefully stepped as softly as he could across the dead boy's body, ascending to the third floor. If there were only the other two men, he knew his chances were getting better to find an escape. The only problem was how did he know for sure if only two remaining was correct, he needed a plan.

His years of working in the building as a teenager gave him a glimmer of hope, he recalled there was a ladder to the roof in the janitor's closest. As Kyle went to the third floor, he investigated the hallway with his light, needing to get to the other end. He moved quickly down the hall reaching the janitor's closest, exhaling after finding it unlocked.

The floor was wet and slippery, and he could easily see why. A bright ray of light shown into the room from the roof hatch which was fully open allowing the weather elements to fill the room. On the wall hanging on the hooks as it had been left decades earlier, was a rolled-up cable. They had once used it to hoist furniture up to the third floor when setting up the hotel. Kyle figured if it could hold a desk hopefully it could hold him.

"Jacoby! Jacoby!" Kyle heard a voice scream loudly that echoed through from the stairwell into the hallway. He knew someone had found the boy he killed.

Kyle locked the heavy metal door in hopes this would slow down anyone looking for him. He attached the hook on one end of the wire cable to the metal ladder that was anchored to the wall. He climbed up the ladder onto the roof, his eyes almost burning at the bright sunshine. The edge of the roof protruded out just enough that Kyle couldn't see straight below him where Teddy and Miller stood watch. As he was ready to toss the cable from the roof, he spotted his truck parked across the river. Arnie waved signaling him that the two men were below.

Kyle, aware of the imminent danger from those who found the boy's body, moved to the opposite side thinking it would be safer there anyhow. He prepared to slide down the wire cable which would land him on the roof of the restaurant. He only risked falling two floors instead of three if the cable didn't hold. Kyle grabbed the wire tightly and eased himself over the edge, wrapping his foot around the wire to create a brake. Kyle began to slide down telling himself, "slow is smooth, smooth is fast."

After reaching the roof of the restaurant, Kyle ran to the opposite side where the kitchen was. He sat on the edge of the roof to slide down the metal awning and onto a wall that divided the customer and employee parking areas. He lowered himself to his stomach, dropped his legs over and let himself drop to the ground, landing with a thud on the soft grass.

He was struggling desperately to breathe now, gasping for air as the weight of his body armor squeezed against his chest. A combination of the strenuous activity along with the added weight, had Kyle stumbling around the building. He wiped his eyes trying to clear the sweat that ran down his face like water from a shower. His mouth was dry, his tongue like sandpaper as he tried to create saliva.

Kyle was now doing a quick walk unable to muster the strength to run. He went around the side to the back of the building, planning to go across the shallow river to reach Arnie and April. Kyle slowly peaked around the back corner seeing the two men Arnie had signaled him about. Flipping the tube switch on the back of his KSG bullpup shotgun to the right, had the lead slugs ready to fire. It was one of the benefits Kyle liked about the shotgun, was the ability to carry and seperate two different types of rounds. Today, he carried slugs and double aught rounds.

He motioned for Arnie to target the man farthest from himself. He raised his gun taking aim at the first man which happened to be Miller. Arnie knew what he had to do right now, when Kyle fired, he would fire. Kyle was gasping for air and struggling to hold the gun up. His arms burning along with his lungs from exhaustion. Kyle wiped his face again and started to squeeze the trigger, hearing a voice call out. "Miller, you get in here and help us find this guy."

Kyle watched as Miller went inside, leaving only Teddy to guard the back of the building. As Teddy turned away from Kyle's direction, he seized the opportunity. Kyle slipped silently behind the truck Blaze had arrived in, the metal knife cold against his hands. With a practiced motion, he punctured the rear tire with his knife, the blade slicing through the rubber with a muted hiss. He then moved to the front of the vehicle and repeated the process, his heart pounding in his chest.

Breathing heavily, Kyle adjusted his vest, trying to catch his breath. His lungs felt like they were burning, but he pushed through the pain. His sole focus was ensuring Arnie and April had a chance to escape.

Arnie watched Teddy closely, his gaze fixed on the guard's movements, while April's eyes were locked on Kyle. Kyle reached the edge of the parking lot and slid down the embankment toward the river. He moved as quickly as his exhausted body would allow, each step a grueling effort. The shallow water offered little resistance, but Kyle's strength was nearly spent. He waded through the small current, the water chilling his legs and making every movement a battle.

Once across the river, Kyle began the test of climbing up the opposite embankment. His hamstrings, quads, and calves screamed in protest, each muscle burning with the strain of the unfamiliar exertion. The weight of his body armor and weapons felt like an anchor, dragging him down. He clawed at the rough terrain, grabbing onto clumps of grass and small rocks, using every bit of strength he had left to pull himself up. The effort was nearly overwhelming, but Kyle's determination to get Arnie and April to safety kept him moving forward.

The kicking of the rocks rolling down into the water caught the attention of Teddy who turned to find the disturbance across the river. He spotted Kyle climbing up from the river, assuming it was the man they were inside searching for. He turned his head scanning the whole area across the river, now noticing the truck parked between the railroad tracks and trees.

"Smile." Arnie said as he squeezed the trigger sending a round from the 6.5 Creedmoor screaming at twenty-seven hundred feet per second. Teddy took the round directly in the chest knocking him back against the wall before falling face down.

"Good shot Arnie." April said to him before looking back to Kyle's position.

"Drive April, I'll be right behind you," Arnie said removing the rifle from the hood of the truck and running along the tracks.

Kyle, completely drained and barely able to move, waved weakly to signal Arnie and April. His arms felt leaden, and his energy had dwindled to almost nothing. The adrenaline that had fueled him through the situation was long gone, leaving him with nothing but a profound exhaustion. His breaths came in ragged gasps as he lay on the ground beside the railroad tracks, his body barely able to keep itself propped up.

April, her face clear with determination, slid into the driver's seat of the vehicle. She shifted the gear to drive and stepped on the gas pedal. Dust quickly made a trail behind the truck as she moved toward Kyle, her eyes scanning the terrain ahead for any signs of trouble.

Blaze's face hardened as he exited the backdoor, barking orders, his frustration mounting. They looked at the truck across the river, before moving their eyes forward to Kyle lying next to the tracks. Shot after shot began ringing out as Kyle worked the action on his shotgun as fast as he could firing rounds of the one-ounce slugs towards the hotel.

"Inside! Get inside!" Blaze bellowed, his voice barely audible over the deafening roar of gunfire. The rounds whizzed past him with relentless intensity, forcing him to dive for cover. Kyle, his body trembling with exhaustion and adrenaline, emptied the twelve slugs he carried, his shots punctuating the chaos and providing a critical diversion.

April, determined, maneuvered the truck as close to Kyle as possible. She threw the vehicle into park and leaped out, her movements swift. She scooped up Kyle's gun, tossing it into the cab of the truck with a sense of urgency. Then, without a moment's hesitation, she wrapped his arm around her neck, supporting his weight as she helped him to his feet.

Kyle's legs were unsteady, his body ached from the exertion, but April's presence was a beacon of hope. Together, they staggered toward the truck, Kyle leaning heavily on her as she guided him to safety. His breaths came in ragged gasps, each step a battle against the overwhelming fatigue.

Blaze bellowed out a loud shout as he once again ran from the building, kneeling next to his truck, raising his rifle towards Kyle and April. With a steady hand, Arnie fired multiple rounds, sending bullets crashing through the passenger's window of Blaze's truck. The impact shattered the glass and sent a clear message as it rained down on Blaze, forcing him to take cover.

Arnie seized the moment, sprinting toward April and Kyle with a fierce determination. The roar of gunfire and the tension of the moment fueled his every stride as he reached the truck, ready to assist April in their desperate bid for escape. Climbing inside the cab of the truck, Arnie took the driver's seat and slammed the gas, speeding away.

"Let's go, follow them," Blaze commanded.

"We got two flat tires over here Blaze, we ain't going nowhere." Miller said looking at the deflated tires.

Blaze jumped around the truck, seeing the flattened tires for himself. "Damn it!"

"Keep driving Arnie. This goes back to 460 about a half mile down. It's straight home then." Kyle said visibly exhausted.

CHAPTER FIFTY-SIX
"Blaze Vows Vengeance"

"Who was that guy?" Blaze angrily asked.

"I've never seen that truck before. I don't know who it was," JD replied.

"Roy! It's Blaze. Come back," Blaze said over the CB radio in his truck.

"This is Roy. Go ahead, Boss," a voice responded.

"There will be a camouflage-painted truck coming your way soon. Follow it. I want to know where it goes," Blaze instructed.

"10-4, Blaze. I'll get someone on it. How far do you want it followed? Do you want us to take the truck?" Roy asked.

"Do not engage with them. They will stop somewhere. Follow it until they do, then report back to me. Send someone to the old railroad hotel; I need two tires replaced," Blaze said.

Blaze dropped heavily onto the worn sidewalk, his back resting against the rough block wall of the building. The evening air was thick and stifling, carrying the faint scent of smoke and decay. He reached into his pocket, pulling out a crumpled pack of cigarettes. With a flick of his lighter, he ignited the tip, the flame briefly illuminating the lines of fatigue etched into his face. He took a deep draw, the smoke filling his lungs with a familiar burn that momentarily distracted him from the chaos around him.

As he exhaled, Blaze tilted his head back, his eyes tracing the few clouds visible in the sky. The waves of smoke curled upward, dissipating into the blue and white above. He savored the moment of stillness, a stark contrast to the turmoil within him.

"Go get Jacoby," Blaze ordered, his voice gravelly and cold. "He's dead on the second floor, west end stairway. Wrap him in some sheets and bring him to the truck." He punctuated his command with another long drag on his cigarette.

The others exchanged uneasy glances, their faces pale and tense. Without a word, they turned and headed back into the building, their footsteps echoing in the silence. They moved quickly but quietly, the weight of Blaze's simmering anger hanging heavily over them. None dared to speak, knowing that a single misplaced word could provoke a violent outburst from their volatile leader.

Blaze watched them go, his expression unreadable. He continued to draw deeply on his cigarette, each drag a brief respite from the storm of emotions raging inside him. The smoke swirled around him, a fleeting curtain that couldn't obscure the harsh reality of their situation.

Arnie followed the railroad tracks, the truck bumping along the uneven terrain until they reached a crossing that led back onto Route 460. Kyle leaned his head against the door, his eyes closed as he tried to calm his racing heart and steady his breathing. April, sensing his distress, gently placed her hand on his shoulder and began to massage it in slow, soothing circles. The tension in the truck was clear, a silent acknowledgment of the danger they were in.

Arnie drove on for a few miles, the tires humming against the asphalt. Suddenly, he noticed another car pulling onto the road behind them. It was a sleek, newer model black Camaro, its presence immediately setting off alarm bells in Arnie's mind.

"Someone's following us. Are you awake, Kyle?" Arnie asked, glancing in the rearview mirror.

Kyle raised his head, his eyes opening slowly, looking over at Arnie. The weight of his recent actions, the face of the young man he had killed, hung on him like a heavy shroud. He turned his attention to the side mirror, where he could see the black Camaro trailing them at a distance.

"Speed up a little. Let's see if they do the same," Kyle instructed, his voice steady despite the turmoil inside him.

Arnie pressed down on the gas pedal, the truck accelerating

from forty-five to nearly sixty miles per hour. The Camaro mirrored their speed, maintaining the same distance behind them.

April, her nerves frayed by the tension, tried to lighten the mood. "I think I was safer at the hospital with the crazies there," she said, smacking her knees and shaking her head in disbelief.

Kyle's eyes remained fixed on the mirror. "Slow down and let's see if they pass us now," he told Arnie.

Arnie eased off the gas, the truck's speed dropping to twenty miles per hour. The Camaro matched their deceleration, its driver clearly intent on keeping pace.

"I am renting a house on Shooting Star Road. Pull over when we get there and see what the car does," April said.

"Yeah, that sounds like a plan. Let's see if they follow us across the creek," Kyle added.

Arnie turned off Route 460 onto the narrow Old Rock Lick Road, driving a short distance to their next destination. He slowed the truck, making the turn across the small bridge leading to Shooting Star Road, the Camaro didn't make the turn. April guided them to her house, and Arnie stopped on the street in front of her home. It was evident the house had been broken into as the front door was fully open.

"I was afraid someone would break into my home. We can continue; no need to go inside now," April said.

"We're going inside. You can at least get a bag of clothes and any personal items you want," Kyle said, opening his door and stepping out. He removed his vest, the shirt underneath soaked in sweat. As Kyle peeled off the wet shirt, Arnie placed his hand in front of April's eyes.

"Don't be checking him out; we're in a time of misery," Arnie chuckled, noticing her watching Kyle remove the shirt.

"Oh, hush, Arnie. The misery we are facing is probably more reason for me to check him out," April said, sliding out of the truck.

"Whoever was in that car may have been planning to rob us," Arnie said.

"Either way, let's just get in here, get you some things, and be on our way," Kyle said.

Kyle raised the seat forward, grabbing a dry shirt from behind it, slipping it over his head. The feeling of fresh, dry cloth was a welcome reward to his skin. He carried the KSG with him and led April to the house. After Kyle went in first and cleared the house, April followed. The house had been ransacked, and Kyle expected her to have a small breakdown seeing it. Surprisingly, she showed no emotion as she went to a closet, pulled out two suitcases, and began filling them.

"I'm sorry you have to see your home like this," Kyle said.

"It's okay, Kyle. It was never a home, just a place to sleep," April said, zipping the suitcase closed.

"Let's move if you're ready. If you need a minute, take it. I'll get your bags into the truck," Kyle said, carrying the suitcases out and loading them into the back of the truck. He paused momentarily as he looked at the body bag containing Charles's. Kyle had almost forgotten they were carrying the body after what he had recently been through. He only wanted to be home now, sitting on his rocker, drinking a cup of coffee. He pictured his mother, Rachel, sitting there watching the birds, she was an amazing woman, so filled with love.

"Alright boys, let's roll out," April said, sliding into the cab of the truck.

"That's a big 10-4," Arnie said, dropping the truck into gear and proceeding onward. He drove less than a mile before they passed the black Camaro again. He looked into his side mirror, seeing the Camaro stop, making a U-turn in the road, smoke bellowing up from the tires as they spun rapidly.

"They just turned. They are following us, no doubt about it," Arnie said.

"I bet they thought we lived back there. Just drive, Arnie," Kyle said.

Arnie proceeded to follow Old Rock Lick Road, his eyes flicking nervously between the winding path ahead and the Camaro trailing behind them. The tension in the truck was heavy once again, each bump and jolt a reminder of the precariousness of their situation. As they neared the top of the mountain, the air grew thinner and the road more treacherous, but Arnie maintained a steady pace, determined to keep his passengers safe.

"Stop at the peak," Kyle instructed, his voice firm despite his exhaustion.

Arnie complied, bringing the truck to a halt right on the mountain's peak. The Camaro also came to a stop, maintaining a distance of about fifty yards. The sun was dipping below the horizon, it's shade a canopy across the rugged landscape. Kyle opened the door and stepped out, the cooler mountain air bringing chills to his fragile, dehydrated skin. With a determined look on his face, he grabbed his AR-15, the weight of the weapon both comforting and sobering.

He aimed it at the Camaro, his heart pounding in his chest. The car's engine revved three or four times, a deep growl that seemed to echo the tension between the two vehicles. Despite the show of defiance, the Camaro remained stationary. Kyle narrowed his eyes, taking a deep breath to steady his aim.

He fired a warning shot, the crack of the gun echoing through the mountains. The bullet struck a road sign near the car, sending a metallic clang reverberating through the air. He waited ten seconds, the silence heavy and thick, then fired again, this time hitting the left headlight of the Camaro. The glass shattered, the pieces scattering like ice.

"What?" Kyle screamed, his voice raw with frustration. "What do you want?" He shouted again, the words torn from his throat.

The car remained, its engine idling ominously. Kyle's patience snapped. "Enough of this," he muttered, firing two more rounds in quick succession. One bullet hit the bumper, sending a shower of sparks flying. The other pierced the middle of the windshield, leaving a gaping hole.

The Camaro's engine roared to life as the driver hastily threw the car into reverse. The tires spun wildly, kicking up gravel and dirt as the car executed a sharp turn and sped away, disappearing into the trees down the curvy road.

Kyle stood there for a moment, his breath coming in heavy gasps, the rifle still clenched in his hands. He watched until the Camaro vanished from sight, then lowered his weapon and turned back to the truck.

"Arnie, try to get us back home now," Kyle said wearily as he climbed back into the passenger seat. His body ached all over, every muscle protesting the movement. The adrenaline was fading, leaving behind only exhaustion and a deep-seated weariness.

Arnie nodded. He put the truck into gear and began the descent down the mountain, the road twisting and turning beneath them. All they wanted was to get home, to find some semblance of safety and rest.

Arnie took his time getting them back, not wanting to sling Kyle around on the curvy roads. They drove a few miles, eventually passing the burnt remains of Fred's Gas and Go and, technically, the actual burnt remains of Fred.

"Kyle and I used to get movies and pizza there when we were younger," April said, looking at the burnt debris scattered on the ground.

"That's back when you still rented DVDs," Arnie said, snickering. "That was the old days," Arnie added, trying to cheer April up with a joke.

"That was before DVDs, Arnie. We rented VHS tapes," April said, smacking his shoulder for making jokes about her age.

Arnie drove to the roadblock and stopped to speak with Blackout and Scott, who were currently standing guard.

"Everything been good today?" Arnie asked.

"Been quiet so far. Hope it stays that way. Were you able to find Charles?" Scott asked.

"We did, but it wasn't good. Charles was killed at the hospital a few days ago. This is April. She works at the hospital and helped us recover him. We have his body in the back, and we're taking it to his house," Kyle said.

"Charles too! That's a dang shame, man. Thank you for

getting him back. Do you care if we take him from here? I'd like to be the one to return him to his family," Scott asked Kyle. "I'll tell them you went and got him."

"This isn't about credit, Scott. Let me help you get him out," Kyle said, helping Scott and Blackout load the body of Charles into Scott's truck.

"You okay, Kyle? You look like you have been through hell and back," Scott said, seeing Kyle's exhaustion.

"The main thing is I made it back," Kyle said.

"Joel is on his way here now. As soon as he arrives, I will take Charles home," Scott said. "Deanna took her a ride earlier, said she needed a break."

"Where did she go?" Kyle asked, confusion on his face as he looked at Scott for an answer. "Anyone with her?"

"She was alone. I offered to send someone with her, she said she was fine, Kyle, I would have gone myself," Scott replied, nervous that Kyle might get upset about them letting her go alone.

"It's fine, Scott. I wish they wouldn't do things like that, but I understand. I just want them safe," Kyle responded. "Thanks again, we're going to get on home."

At the home of Blaze, JD, Miller, and two more of Blaze's crew worked tirelessly under the oppressive heat, shovels biting into the hard earth as they dug a grave on the hill across from the house. The small family cemetery, with its weathered headstones and simple markers, contained mostly family members of Blaze who had been laid to rest over the years. Each shovelful of dirt removed felt like a sting as it was preparing for one of their fallen.

Blaze sat on his porch in a battered wooden chair, the weight of recent events pressing heavily on his shoulders. He watched the men take turns digging, their movements steady and graceful. In his hand, he cradled a bottle of Wild Turkey bourbon, taking slow, deliberate sips. The fiery liquid was a small comfort against the backdrop of his wife's anguished cries that drifted through the open windows of the house. She had just learned of Jacoby's fate, her sobs a haunting counterpoint to the thud of shovels striking dirt.

The sound of an approaching engine broke the heavy silence. Blaze's eyes flicked to the driveway, where the black Camaro rolled to a stop. Two men emerged from the car, their faces clearly showing their concern for the upcoming conversation. They walked with purpose towards the porch, where Blaze remained seated, his gaze never wavering from the cemetery. Roy, alerted by the noise, stepped out from a small outbuilding he used as a radio room, and joined them on the porch.

"Where did they go?" Blaze asked, his voice low and even, not breaking his eye contact with JD, who was digging across the road.

The first man shifted uncomfortably, glancing at the grave being dug before responding. "We lost them at Big Rock Mountain. They started shooting at us. You can see the car... the headlight, windshield, and bumper are all hit."

Blaze's grip tightened slightly around the neck of the bourbon bottle, but he said nothing, waiting for the man to continue.

The man took a deep breath. "They stopped at the top, and after the shots were fired, we had to back off. We caught up again on the Hurley side, but they had a coal truck blocking the road. Locals told us only residents were allowed through and to move along."

Blaze took another sip of his bourbon, the alcohol burning a path down his throat. He finally tore his gaze from the cemetery and looked at the man, his eyes cold and hard. "Ricky, Ricky, Ricky. Are you telling me you turned chicken shit and ran? Is that what you're telling me?"

Ricky swallowed hard, shaking his head. "No sir. We retreated from the shooting to avoid getting killed. We tried to get back in, but they were prepared."

Blaze sat in silence for a moment, the only sound the quiet digging and his wife's distant sobs. He handed the bottle to Ricky, who took a hesitant drink before passing it to Roy.

Taking a large drink from the bottle, and choking out

several coughs, Roy looked at Blaze before speaking. "Blaze, I know this is a tough time, but I got an important message for you over the radio."

Blaze turned his head, looking at Roy questions evident in his eyes. "Spit it out, Roy. What's the message?"

"Officer Langston of the Sheriff's department wants to meet with you. He says not to be concerned; he isn't after you. They want our help with a matter, involving a guy in Hurley," Roy said.

"Be nice to have the Sheriff's department on our side if there was an actual department remaining. This Langston, he has no authority anymore. But, set it up, we'll hear them out," Blaze said calmly, looking back to the hillside.

"You see that graveyard over there, Ricky?" Blaze said, his voice soft but menacing. "That's where I'm about to bury my fourteen-year-old son."

Ricky's face paled. "I'm sorry about that. Jacoby was a good kid."

Blaze's eyes filled with fury. "This isn't over. It's not even close. We're going to have a proper funeral for my boy in a couple of days. Then we're going to Hurley. I'll find that truck and everyone in it. And I'll kill them all. Everyone connected to them."

The men fell silent, the weight of Blaze's words settling over them like a shroud. Blaze took the bottle back from Roy, taking a long, final swig before returning his gaze to the cemetery, his face hardened by grief and vengeance.

CHAPTER FIFTY-SEVEN

"Celebratory Dinner"

Rocky pulled Deanna aside before everyone arrived back at the cabin. "We need to talk about your plans with Miran Tate and the others. I can't keep this from Kyle," he said, his voice low but firm. "What exactly did you agree to with Tate? We' need to tell Kyle and get ahead of whatever is coming."

Deanna looked at him, a mix of guilt and defiance in her eyes. "We'll see about that," she said, "this is my family here, I don't recommend you saying anything to Kyle. Besides, maybe he won't even make it back, then this all goes away," she added walking away, leaving Rocky with a heavy heart.

"Is someone coming after us tonight? My girls are here," Rocky asked, visibly frustrated.

"No, Rocky. We're fine tonight, we'll talk about it later," she retorted, her expression blank.

"Deanna, what are you saying? Arnie is with Kyle, do you want him to make it back?" Rocky asked, his body trembling at what Deanna was saying to him.

"This place would be perfect for us, at least a smaller group of us," Deanna said, her eyes void of any recognizable feelings. She turned away holding her hand before Rocky could say anything else.

Rocky walked step after step around the property, guilt flooding him as he knew Deanna was a conniving and manipulative person. He never thought she would be willing to partake in something this insane, this horrific.

The day had continued into the late afternoon, Rocky torn with emotions, the very sight right now of Ginger, Susie and

Deanna made his blood boil and heart pound. He took his place on the watchtower, trying to figure out what his next move would be, surely if he told Kyle, they would be exiled from the mountain. "Kyle wouldn't do that, he'd probably still let them all live here," Rocky mumbled to himself. This would be a test of his morality, his maturity and his manhood.

"Here they come! They're back!" Rocky shouted as he spotted Arnie and Kyle coming up the trail through his binoculars.

Everyone gathered near the front of the cabin, anxiously waiting for Arnie and Kyle's return. Although most were happy to see them, some were disappointed he made it back. Rocky could tell this by the look on Deanna's face as she dropped her gaze from his, refusing to make eye contact. This would have been the answer they needed to their plan, as dark as it was, for Kyle not to make it back alive. The sound of the ATV engine grew closer, and as it approached the gate, the excitement grew. Coraline waved frantically, her teeth showing white through the dirt on her face.

"Mommy, is that Kyle's old girlfriend April with them?" Ginger asked, her eyes widening at the sight of the third person.

They stopped the ATV and slowly climbed off. Rachel's facial expression almost blank, as she gazed at April as if she was from a different planet. Susie, and Ginger stood still, their expressions unreadable, their smiles non-existent. Both Susie and Ginger, wondered if Rocky would say anything, although Deanna had assured them, he was too afraid of her to do so.

"Is something wrong?" Kyle asked, noticing their looks.

"Is that April?" Rachel said, walking over to her. April nodded, and Rachel hugged her tightly. "I don't know where or how, but I'm so glad to see you again, sweetheart."

Ginger and Susie followed, hugging April as Kyle watched.

Rocky grabbed Kyle tightly, holding him in a tight embrace, pulling Arnie in next. Ginger hugged Arnie tightly, rubbing his hair with her hand.

"We have a lot to fill you in on. Stacy and the baby are safe and doing great. We'll explain more later. Right now, can someone show April inside so she can shower and clean up? Arnie and I will use the porta shower at the bunkhouse. We've had a wild day and just want to wash the stink off," Kyle said.

"Yeah, you should do that, Uncle Kyle. You really do stink!" Coraline exclaimed, holding her nose.

"What about Charles? Did you find him?" Rocky asked, his face falling as he saw their expressions.

"We found him, but not alive. We brought his body back. Scott took him home," Kyle said.

Silence fell as they absorbed the news. It was hard to digest, feeling sorrow for Charles and Snaggle's family, yet relief for Kyle and Arnie's return.

"I'm going to fix a dinner so we can celebrate tonight. Let's get everyone cleaned up, including you, dirty girl," Rachel said, squeezing Coraline's cheek. "I'm going to use some of Kyle's canned meats, so let's hope he sealed them properly." She went inside to get started.

"Deanna, let's walk a moment," Kyle said as he put his arm around her and pulled her away.

Rocky looked at Susie and Ginger, his feelings a mixture on what Deanna had done and now he wondered what Kyle wanted to talk to her about. He couldn't help but wonder if Kyle knew something.

"I understand you took a ride today," Kyle said as they walked.

She looked at him quickly, "who said that?" Kyle could see a look of fear wash over her face.

"It doesn't matter who told me. I understand if you need to get off the mountain, to have a moment for yourself," Kyle said as they walked. "I wish you would let someone go with you or let me scout it out first. I want you safe, and right now safety isn't the norm."

"I was fine," she said, stopping in their tracks as she wondered what he knew exactly. "I needed fresh air is all."

They turned, walking back to the cabin. "Just please stay aware and be cautious, I will give my life to protect you all," Kyle said to her.

Deanna looked at him and smiled, "that's good to know, Uncle Kyle."

Rocky placed a fold-up table next to the larger dining table while Susie and Ginger helped Rachel in the kitchen. They prepared a meal with New York strip steaks that Kyle had canned, served with rice, macaroni and cheese, green beans, and corn. It was an amazing spread given the country's turmoil.

Uncle Tom arrived, after being at Willie's, listening to the radio waves. He smiled at the sight of the food.

"I'm just in time," Uncle Tom said.

"Yeah you are. Thanks to Kyle looking out for us way ahead of this while we didn't do shit, we have food to eat," Rocky said, his agitation clearly present to everyone. Kyle patted his back and laughed a slight chuckle, feeling Rocky's tension.

"No worries, Rocky," Kyle said chuckling. "We all have a part to play."

"Come on in, it's hot and ready," Rachel said to Tom.

"Kyle, may I get a word with you outside first?" Uncle Tom asked.

"Sure. What's up, Uncle Tom?" Kyle said, stepping onto the porch.

"Thank you for getting Charles back, even though he didn't survive, it will mean a lot to his family. I owe you an apology, Kyle. I took my anger and pain out on you, and that was wrong. You're the reason we're thriving. The reason we have a hot meal inside. I just want to say I'm sorry," Uncle Tom said.

"It's okay, Uncle Tom. I understand your pain. It's water under the bridge. Really, please don't think another second on it," Kyle said, patting him on the back. "Now, let's get inside and get us a bite."

Everyone piled their plates high with food, their stomachs begging for it. Arnie and Rocky couldn't wait, using their fingers to pick up pieces of steak.

"Have some manners, Arnie bug," Rocky said, trying to show a giggle, fighting back his unhappiness with Deanna.

"You both need to have some manners; we have a guest,"

Clara Beth said, pointing to April, who smiled and tossed a piece of steak into her mouth. Arnie high-fived her, and April felt happier than she had in a long time.

"Let's say grace. Will you do it, Kyle?" Rachel asked.

"If you would like to bow your heads, please do. If not, allow us a moment. Dear Lord, we come to you with heavy hearts this evening. Be with the families of those we have lost, whether good or bad, their families need you. Bless this food to our bodies and those who prepared it. We're all walking in darkness, and we need your light and guidance. Forgive us for our sins and walk by our side. Amen," Kyle said.

"Amen," Rachel said as she smiled at Kyle.

"Okay, I can't wait any longer. Please tell me about Stacy and Jackson," Ginger said before taking her first bite.

Kyle powered on his phone and handed it to Ginger along with some polaroid photos. She was joyous as she looked at pictures of Stacy, Jackson, and Arnie together.

"Thanks, Kyle, for these. It means the world to me. Jackson looks so much bigger in just a couple of weeks," Ginger said.

"Yeah, thank you Kyle, you risked your life to get those pictures, not many people would have done that," Rocky said, his eyes cutting like a laser into Ginger.

Kyle and Arnie explained where they had found Stacy living, a good place for now. Kyle had invited them to join if they ever needed to. The property had room to grow a garden, hunt, and fish. It was secluded and could be well-protected.

"I knowingly ate the freshest chicken I've ever had," April said, slapping her hands to her face.

"She was too hungry to pass it up," Arnie said.

They discussed the deteriorating situation at the hospital. April explained the people trying to move in, and Arnie described the morgue. Kyle told them about his quick trip inside the nursing home and the damage they had witnessed.

"Uncle Kyle saw a ghost in the morgue," Arnie said.

"You saw a ghost?" Susie said, laughing. "Did it say boo?" She clapped her hands, her laughter contagious. She laughed until her eyes met with Rocky, who met her with a cold stare. He knew Susie was probably the least likely of the three to go against Kyle, but he also knew she was willing to and that's all that mattered.

"I don't know what I saw. It was a crazy situation. I'm just glad I'm back here with all of you," Kyle said. "Let's build a bonfire, roast marshmallows, and make s'mores."

"I'm thankful you made it back and didn't become a ghost yourself," Rocky said, his laser focus now bouncing between Deanna and Susie.

As the meal continued, Rocky's discomfort grew. He could see Ginger and Susie putting on a fake disguise with Kyle, acting overly sweet and helpful. It made him sick to his stomach knowing what they had been planning with Deanna.

Unable to stand it any longer, Rocky excused himself and walked outside. He leaned against the porch railing, taking deep breaths to calm his nerves. He respected Kyle and knew he had to tell him the truth soon. The weight of the secret was too much to bear alone.

Inside, the laughter and conversation continued, oblivious to the storm brewing just outside the door. Kyle excused himself, feeling the need to talk with Rocky as everyone was finishing up their meals.

"I'll start stacking wood for the fire," Arnie said.

"Come on, April, I'll show you my rabbits," Clara Beth said, taking April by the hand.

"Really!" Coraline said, rolling her eyes. "It's always those damn rabbits." She trotted out the front door, shaking her head.

Everyone looked shocked before Rachel snickered loudly, and soon everyone joined in the laughter.

"You feeling okay, big guy?" Kyle asked Rocky as he joined him on the cabin porch. "Let's take a walk."

"I'm sorry, Kyle. I'm wound up right now, been a lot going on," Rocky said, wanting to open up about what he now knew.

"Okay, buddy. I understand. If you ever need to talk though, I'm here for you," Kyle said as they turned, walking back to the cabin.

CHAPTER FIFTY-EIGHT
"Beneath the Surface"

Rocky and Arnie had the bonfire burning big and bright, its crackling warmth highlighting faces around the fire. Kyle had gathered tree logs to make seats, placing them neatly around the fire pit. The relaxed atmosphere was a welcome reprieve from the tension they'd been feeling since the attack.

Rachel had set up a serving tray with chocolate bars, marshmallows, and graham crackers, preparing for s'mores. Uncle Tom had used his knife to fashion sticks for roasting marshmallows. He gave them a few slices with his knife to remove the outer bark, leaving a pointed end to stab the marshmallows with. Ginger and Susie were seated next to each other, taking shots from a bottle of Kyle's 1800 Silver tequila, shaking salt on their palms and licking it with each shot.

"Wow, who would have ever thought to have extra tequila on hand? In case the world ever crashed so we would have something of comfort," Rocky expressed, still struggling to hold his raging emotions from spewing between his lips.

Kyle patted Rocky on the back, "easy boy," isn't that what you tell the horses, Kyle said laughing at Rocky. Kyle knew Rocky was upset, but he wasn't pushing him for answers. Kyle and April took a moment to themselves, walking over to watch tower two and climbing up to the platform. They sat on the edge, letting their feet dangle over the side as they watched the sun setting over the mountain.

"What do you think of my little sanctuary here?" Kyle asked April.

"It's beautiful, Kyle. If there hadn't been an attack, this

would still be an amazing place to live. You've done really well here," April said, patting his hand that was placed near hers. "It's all wonderful, except for those damn rabbits," she laughed. Kyle looked at her, unsure how to respond. "That's what Coraline told me earlier," she added with a chuckle.

"Yeah, she isn't too fond of those rabbits, and it's been made known to everyone," Kyle said, laughing along with April. "I'll fix you a room tomorrow so you have your own place to sleep and put your clothes and things. It may be the couch for tonight if that's okay. Arnie, Joel, and I sleep in that bunkhouse there, Rocky and Deanna have that one. I had the third one almost completed, but we can finish it up tomorrow for you." Kyle pointed around at the various structures.

"I need a good lock on it, I don't want you getting any ideas and trying to sneak over," April said, laughing but with a hint of seriousness. She knew the old spark of young love was still there, buried beneath the years.

"I can't be doing that; I don't need mom giving me the birds and bees speech again," Kyle chuckled before changing the subject to something more serious. "I want to ask you about what happened with the guy at the hospital. How are you dealing with it? If it's okay for me to ask? If not, don't answer."

"It's really weird, honestly. I took a person's life. I killed someone. Yet, I know if I hadn't, there would have been two people killed—Jenny and I. I know I'm not being judged by anyone, the police, you know. I think that makes it easier, maybe," April said, looking down over the edge of the mountain. They sat in silence for a moment. "What about you, Kyle? Have you had to kill anyone? We haven't discussed what happened today inside that building, so I don't really know," April said, her eyes filled with tenderness, not judgment.

"I won't lie to you; I have killed some. I'm not proud of it," Kyle said.

"Some? How many?" April asked gently. "You can tell me; I think it will help me with what I had to do."

"The first one happened in Kansas, twenty-three months

ago. I had been in a bar after work, and there was a girl at the bar ordering. She accidentally bumped into me, no big deal. I told her it was fine. She rejoined her friends at a pool table, and one of them, clearly her boyfriend from the look he gave me, seemed to question her speaking to me." Kyle took a deep breath, looking straight ahead.

"It's okay if you don't want to talk about it," April said, rubbing his arm.

"You were the one I told my secrets to. I haven't told anyone else the details about this. We had a little trouble inside the bar, but I thought it was over with. It was raining that night; I wasn't in a hurry, waiting for the rain to stop. I listened to the music for a while and cleaned up my email. As I was walking across the parking lot, her boyfriend ran up to me. It was still raining hard. He pushed me, and I took him to the ground. I told him to go home; I didn't want trouble. I turned to go to my car, and he tackled me from behind," Kyle said, recalling the night he took his first life.

"Did you shoot him?" April asked, holding Kyle's hand tightly.

"His girlfriend was screaming. I got back to my feet and punched him, again trying to walk away. He charged me, trying to tackle me. I grabbed him around his waist, pulled him up, and slammed him down on the asphalt. His head hit first, fracturing his skull and breaking his neck. The police were called; they held me briefly. I told my boss, who was a friend, and soon made the decision to move back home," Kyle said, looking at April, waiting for her reaction.

"It sounds like you defended yourself. I think that's all you can do," April said, her voice reassuring. Kyle felt a sense of relief at finally sharing his burden with his old friend, though he hadn't given all the details. They might discuss it more another day.

"After the attack, I shot a man in Hurley the first day. He had attacked my sister Ginger and killed a good man. The next time I killed one, maybe two, at the bottom of this mountain in a shootout. One today. I'm more concerned about Arnie; he has killed two now," Kyle said. "That's my count. I'd like for it to stop, but I'm not sure it's going to yet. Are you ready to go back to the fire, maybe roast a marshmallow?" he asked, watching as April's eyes sparkled in the moonlight.

"I've missed you so much," April said before awkwardly turning her head away. "I didn't mean for that to come out. I'm sorry, Kyle."

"Don't be sorry. I've missed you, April. You probably had a lot to do with me staying single. Come on, let's go get a marshmallow," Kyle said, standing and taking April's hand to help her down the ladder. He knew he could sit with her all night and talk, but there were important matters to address with the family.

Kyle didn't want to dampen the mood but needed to discuss the events of the day. "I know it's been a great evening for us, and thanks to everyone for preparing food and creating the fire. I think we need to talk about some things before Uncle Tom leaves tonight," Kyle said, taking a seat on one of the stumps by the fire.

"What did you do, Rocky?" Deanna blurted out.

"Easy Deanna, Rocky seems to have had a rough day, he only dropped his marshmallow," Kyle said, unaware of what she was actually snapping at Rocky over. Realizing this, Deanna pushed out a fake laugh.

"I agree with Kyle; we need to discuss some things. I also got some news today that everyone needs to know. It's best we get it out in the open now," Uncle Tom said, looking around at everyone gathered. "Go ahead, Kyle. You go first."

Kyle proceeded to explain what had happened at the hotel, struggling to detail the young man he had killed. He also mentioned the black Camaro that had followed them up Big Rock Mountain. Joel spoke up, interrupting Kyle.

"That black Camaro came to the roadblock today. Scott told me it had two guys in it. They asked about who was in the camo truck and wanted to get past the roadblock, but Scott wouldn't let them," Joel said. "Scott also mentioned wanting to come up with a name for the roadblock, but we can figure that out later."

"Let's honor the fallen. Maybe call it checkpoint Charles or Snaggle's stop," Kyle offered up, heads nodding in return.

"There's more everyone needs to know," Uncle Tom added. "While at Willie's earlier this evening, we heard some interesting information. Miran Tate is requesting volunteers for his goon squad, calling it the community outreach team. He wants people to come to his barter store and will offer payment to anyone who volunteers." Uncle Tom explained, everyone looking at him with growing concern.

"I'm worried about Tate and what he might try. I don't think they'll just leave us alone," Kyle said. "He is a taker, and he's going to take everything he can from everyone he can."

"I agree with Kyle. We need to create a plan for dealing with Tate. As for the people you ran into at the old railroad hotel, I think they might be a group called Blaze's Angels. They've been terrorizing folks from the Kentucky state line to Grundy," Uncle Tom said.

"That's exactly who it was. I met the main man, Blaze himself. I'm not positive, but it might have been his son that I killed," Kyle said, noticing the look of despair on everyone's faces.

"They were using multiple radio frequencies asking about a camouflage truck. That's what I wanted to tell you earlier," Uncle Tom added.

On Lynn Camp, where Blaze lived, he had gathered his group of Angels. He slammed his fist down on the table, commanding attention.

"I want to know who was in that truck. I want to know who killed my boy. That is our only goal and mission right now. I'll allow my family time to mourn over the next few days. I have a meeting tomorrow with a cop from Hurley. I want you all actively searching during that time for this man. I'll reward anyone who finds him. I say to you all now, this fight is far from over!" Blaze declared, his gaze strong and determined.

At Miran Tate's garage, Langston had assembled a small group of volunteers to hear Tate's announcement.

"To each of you here this evening, I want to thank you for

showing up and doing your part with the community outreach team. We have a common enemy; his name is Kyle Blaine. He is armed and dangerous and should not be taken lightly," Miran Tate was at his best when motivating for a bad deed, and he was clearly on top of his game today. "We have new intel now, we know of his location and have someone on the inside to help us." He continued as he looked over the faces in the small crowd, seeing the uneasiness from many. "Under my authority and the declaration of martial law, you have permission to shoot on sight. A reward will be offered for bringing me the head of Kyle Blaine. We will be sending our community outreach team, led by Officer Langston, to track down and eliminate this target. He thinks he can get away with his recklessness and vigilantism, but he is sorely mistaken. I tell you now, this fight is far from over."

Kyle's family discussed the dire news and the information from Joel and Uncle Tom. They knew that this was shaping up to be a bigger fight than they could have anticipated, and the stakes were high. Despite the gravity of their situation, Kyle told them they would face this danger together.

"I would like for us to enjoy tonight. Let's enjoy each other's company and welcome April to the camp," Rachel said, taking a glass from Susie and tossing back a shot of tequila.

"I agree, Maw. It's time to be thankful tonight. We can worry about tomorrow when it comes," Arnie said, reaching for the shot glass before being turned down by Rachel. "Ah hell with it, go ahead, Arnie, have a shot," Rachel said.

"Agree. We can put our worries off until tomorrow. But when tomorrow comes, this isn't going to be easy, and it's only just beginning. We can do this, but we've got to believe in one another. I will give my life for each of you, you are my family, and nothing is more important than that," Kyle said, raising his glass in a toast. "This fight is far from over."

"Enemies in the yard," Rocky muttered low as he looked at the dirt, not making eye contact with anyone.

The family gathered around the fire, the warmth of the flames offering a momentary comfort against the encroaching

374

darkness. They laughed, shared stories, and savored the simple pleasures of s'mores and each other's company. The weight of the night's revelations was momentarily set aside as they embraced a sense of normalcy.

As the evening wore on, Rocky, visibly agitated by the earlier conversation and the tension it had stirred, excused himself from the gathering. He walked towards the barn, unable to fully mask his displeasure. His frustration was evident in his brisk stride and the way he kicked at the dirt beneath his feet. The weight of their situation was beginning to press heavily upon him, and he needed a moment alone to process everything.

Meanwhile, Ginger and Susie continued their charade of cheerfulness, keeping up appearances as they interacted with Kyle and the others. They laughed a bit too loudly and shared more tequila than was likely good for them, all while maintaining a face of normalcy. Their actions were designed to placate Kyle and the rest of the group, masking their own underlying anxieties and ambitions.

The night wore on, the crackling of the fire and the soft hum of conversation providing a temporary balm for their troubled minds. As the stars sparkled overhead, each member of the group silently contemplated the challenges ahead, finding solace in their unity and the strength they drew from each other.

When the time came to retire for the night, the family members headed to their respective sleeping quarters, each carrying the weight of the day's events and the uncertainty of the future. Kyle's thoughts lingered on the discussions with April and the looming threats from both Miran Tate and Blaze's Angels. But for now, they allowed themselves the small comfort of a night spent together, hoping for better days ahead and the strength to face whatever challenges awaited them.

"Kyle, we need to talk," Rocky said as he placed his arm around Kyle, leading them off into the darkness of the night.

THE END – UNTIL NEXT TIME

EPILOGUE

The mountainside was quiet now, but the air was thick with the promise of impending storms. Kyle Blaine stood alone at the edge of his homestead, looking out over the rugged landscape that had become both his sanctuary and battleground. The fires of conflict had left their mark, and the horizon seemed to hold a restless energy, as if echoing the struggles yet to come.

As the last remnants of daylight faded, Kyle's thoughts turned to the coming fight. Supervisor Miran Tate and Blaze Stiltner loomed large in his mind, their threats forming long shadows over the lives of those he cared about. The betrayal of Deanna, Susie, and Ginger was about to shake the foundation of trust within his community, and Kyle knew that the path ahead would be fraught with peril. He had to be ready, not only to face external threats but to address the fractures within his own ranks.

The sanctuary he had built was more than a refuge; it was now a symbol of hope and resistance. But as he looked over the faces of those who had stood by him, he knew that every one of them would become a target in the days to come. The fight for survival was no longer just about protecting their home; it was about uniting a fractured community and fortifying their defenses against a relentless adversary.

Far from the mountain, in Scott County, Virginia, Kyle's brother, Spencer Blaine was busy building his own homestead in Duffield. His efforts to provide safety for his family were not without challenges. The underhanded crooks and deceitful relatives trying to infiltrate his sanctuary posed a constant threat. Spencer's determination to safeguard his loved ones mirrored Kyle's own resolve, and the distance between them did little to diminish their shared struggle.

Sawyer Blaine, the eldest brother, faced his own formidable journey. With six hundred miles of treacherous terrain ahead, he was determined to reunite with Kyle and Spencer and secure a future for his family. The road was fraught with obstacles, from hostile encounters to the harsh realities of a world in upheaval. But Sawyer's determination was unwavering, driven by the hope of a new beginning for those he loved.

As Kyle took one last look at the tranquil yet ominous landscape, he knew the coming days would test the limits of their endurance. The fight was far from over, and the stakes were higher than ever. Yet, amidst the uncertainty and danger, there was a glimmer of hope, a belief that, together, they could weather the storms ahead.

The night grew darker, and the mountainside fell into silence. Kyle turned and walked back to his home, ready to face the challenges of tomorrow. For now, they would take solace in the strength of their unity and the promise of a new dawn.

The fight for survival was just beginning, and as long as they stood together, there was a chance for victory. The worries of conflict might loom large, but hope and determination will have to light their way through the darkness.

This story will continue in book two, "Sanctuary of Strength" as part of the "Enemies In The Yard" series.